Praise for Nickolas Butler

"In this deeply felt debut, Nickolas Butler paints a place and its people with such love that you'll find yourself falling for them, too. This is a novel about home, and home is how the book feels. With all the pull and power of the word, it brings us face-to-face with the most important things: how hard it is to love well, to stay loyal, to act right, to know what that means. It is Butler's great achievement that this utterly American story—one that sings of the country without sentimentality or cynicism, but with the sweet sound of true sight—helps make it all a little more clear."   —JOSH WEIL,
AWARD-WINNING AUTHOR OF *THE NEW VALLEY* AND *THE GREAT GLASS SEA*

"*Shotgun Lovesongs* is an unswervingly bighearted and compelling novel about an indie rocker made good and his best friends back home in Wisconsin, all of them navigating their way through different iterations of the American Dream, trying to make authentic lives and find meaningful love. Nickolas Butler conducts a soaring, meditative chorus of voices in his first novel. And it's absolutely beautiful."   —DEAN BAKOPOULOS, AUTHOR OF THE
NEW YORK TIMES NOTABLE BOOK *PLEASE DON'T COME BACK
FROM THE MOON* AND *MY AMERICAN UNHAPPINESS*

"Listen to Nickolas Butler and his *Shotgun Lovesongs*, listen to the unforgettable characters and their chorus of voices—as they sing about longing, about betrayal, about friendship and marriage, about the green explosion of summer and the white music of winter, about the gravity of home—and you will be moved to laughter and tears, plugged in to a melody that brilliantly shares the story of all our lives."   —BENJAMIN PERCY,
PUSHCART PRIZE–WINNING AUTHOR OF *RED MOON* AND *THE WILDING*

"*Shotgun Lovesongs* is a welcome new treasure. Nickolas Butler manages to shake off the cynicism of his generation to deliver a beautifully written, heartfelt novel about young men in the Midwest grappling with the slipperiest bits of life. Butler has the gift of making the everyday seem new—from the odd way fame silently separates old friends, to the disheartening foibles of a new marriage. This is a talented, thoughtful writer who throws his characters against the singular Wisconsin backdrop and coaxes them to live and breathe. Read *Shotgun Lovesongs* with caution—these guys will stay with you for a while."   —KATIE CROUCH, *NEW YORK TIMES* BESTSELLING
AUTHOR OF *GIRLS IN TRUCKS*

"Instead of stringing together superlatives, may I just say that *Shotgun Lovesongs* is as true as an honest day's work, as serious as a busted heart, as welcoming as a warm home fire burning. In these pages you can hear the lonesome whip-poor-will, see the blood on the tracks, sense the mystery of 'arboretic truth,' and witness best friends come together in times of love and betrayal. With *Shotgun Lovesongs*, Nickolas Butler has written a Mid-western masterpiece and has done for the modest splendor of verdant farm-lands what Larry McMurtry did for the brutal beauty of small-town Texas."
—AMBER DERMONT, AUTHOR OF THE *NEW YORK TIMES* BESTSELLER *THE STARBOARD SEA* AND *DAMAGE CONTROL: STORIES*

"Nick's literary focus . . . explorations of the human quest for meaning and value . . . is a much-needed addition to contemporary fiction in that it ex-plores beyond the conventional repositories of 'self'—job security, family bonds, for example—and reintroduces us to the settled world of nature, where we can explore into both new and ancient meanings of the term."
—JAMES ALAN MCPHERSON, PULITZER PRIZE–WINNING AUTHOR OF *ELBOW ROOM*

"Nickolas Butler ripped my heart out with rare honesty and good, old-fashioned, unapologetic love. A book that makes you want to call old friends. A writer who makes you feel more human than you thought possi-ble."
—MATTHEW QUICK, *NEW YORK TIMES* BESTSELLING AUTHOR OF *THE SILVER LININGS PLAYBOOK*

"In fresh, gorgeously wrought prose, Butler weaves an intricate, irresistible tale of friendships old, new, lost and found, of love and betrayal, of forgive-ness, of growing up, and, most of all, of what it means to be 'home.' Hoo-ray for this warm, wise, bighearted book."
—EMILY JEANNE MILLER, AUTHOR OF *BRAND NEW HUMAN BEING*

"What a cracking book. Full of heart, full of compassion, full of characters who have you rooting for them from the very first page. Butler's sense of place is so strong that, reading *Shotgun Lovesongs*, I became a temporary resi-dent of small-town Wisconsin—and once I'd finished it, I wanted to go right back there."
—SHELLEY HARRIS, AUTHOR OF *JUBILEE*, SHORT-LISTED FOR THE 2012 COMMONWEALTH BOOK PRIZE

SHOTGUN LOVESONGS

NICKOLAS BUTLER

THOMAS DUNNE BOOKS ST. MARTIN'S PRESS NEW YORK

This is a work of fiction. All of the characters, organizations, and events portrayed in this novel are either products of the author's imagination or are used fictitiously.

THOMAS DUNNE BOOKS.
An imprint of St. Martin's Press.

SHOTGUN LOVESONGS. Copyright © 2014 by Nickolas Butler. All rights reserved. Printed in the United States of America. For information, address St. Martin's Press, 175 Fifth Avenue, New York, N.Y. 10010.

www.thomasdunnebooks.com
www.stmartins.com

Designed by Steven Seighman

Library of Congress Cataloging-in-Publication Data

Butler, Nickolas.
    Shotgun lovesongs : a novel / Nickolas Butler.
        p. cm.
    ISBN 978-1-250-03981-1 (hardcover)
    ISBN 978-1-4668-4079-9 (e-book)
    1. Brothers—Fiction.   2. Homecoming—Fiction.   3. Sibling rivalry—Fiction.   4. Families—Fiction.   5. Change (Psychology)—Fiction.   6. Maturation (Psychology)—Fiction.   7. Wisconsin—Fiction.   8. Domestic fiction.   9. Psychological fiction.   I. Title.
    PS3602.U876S56 2014
    813'.6—dc23

                                                    2013031435

St. Martin's Press books may be purchased for educational, business, or promotional use. For information on bulk purchases, please contact Macmillan Corporate and Premium Sales Department at 1-800-221-7945, extension 5442, or write specialmarkets@macmillan.com.

First Edition: March 2014

10 9 8 7 6 5 4 3 2 1

For Regina & Henry & Mom & Dad

For Swan, who hears sunsets

And for Levon Helm (1940–2012)

But, heave ahead, boy, I'd rather be killed by you than
kept alive by any other man.

—HERMAN MELVILLE, *MOBY-DICK*

SHOTGUN
LOVESONGS

———

WE INVITED HIM TO ALL of our weddings; he was famous. We addressed the invitations to his record company's skyscraper in New York City so that the gaudy, gilded envelopes could be forwarded to him on tour—in Beirut, Helsinki, Tokyo. Places beyond our ken or our limited means. He sent back presents in battered cardboard boxes festooned with foreign stamps—birthday gifts of fine scarves or perfume for our wives, small delicate toys or trinkets upon the births of our children: rattles from Johannesburg, wooden nesting dolls from Moscow, little silk booties from Taipei. He would call us sometimes, the connection scratchy and echoing, a chorus of young women giggling in the background, his voice never sounding as happy as we expected it to.

Months would pass before we saw his face again, and then, he would arrive home, bearded and haggard, his eyes tired but happily relieved. We could tell that Lee was glad to see us, to be back in our company. We always gave him time to recover before our lives resumed together, we knew he needed time to dry out and regain his balance. We let him sleep and sleep. Our wives brought him casseroles and lasagnas, bowls of salad and freshly baked pies.

He liked to ride a tractor around his sprawling property. We assumed he liked feeling the hot daylight, the sun and fresh air on his pale face. The slow speed of that old John Deere, so reliable and patient. The earth rolling backward beneath him. There were no crops on his land of course, but he rode the tractor through the fallow fields of prairie grasses and wildflowers, a cigarette between his lips, or a joint. He was always smiling on that tractor, his hair all flyaway and light blond and in the sunlight it was like the fluff of a seeding dandelion.

He had taken another name for the stage but we never called him by that name. We called him Leland, or just plain Lee, because that was his name. He lived in an old schoolhouse away from things, away from our town, Little Wing, and maybe five miles out into the countryside. The name on his mailbox read: L SUTTON. He had built a recording studio in the small, ancient gymnasium, padding the walls with foam and thick carpeting. There were platinum records up on the walls. Photographs of him with famous actresses and actors, politicians, chefs, writers. His gravel driveway was long and potted with holes, but even this was not enough to deter some of the young women who sought him out. They came from around the world. They were always beautiful.

Lee's success had not surprised us. He had simply never given up on his music. While the rest of us were in college or the army or stuck on our family farms, he had holed up in a derelict chicken coop and played his battered guitar in the all-around silence of deepest winter. He sang in an eerie falsetto, and sometimes around the campfire it would make you weep in the unreliable shadows thrown by those orange-yellow flames and white-black smoke. He was the best among us.

He wrote songs about our place on earth: the everywhere fields of corn, the third-growth forests, the humpbacked hills and grooved-out draws. The knife-sharp cold, the too-short days, the snow, the snow, the snow. His songs were our anthems—they were our bullhorns and microphones and jukebox poems. We adored him; our wives adored him. We knew all the words to the songs and sometimes we were in the songs.

Kip was going to be married in October inside a barn he'd renovated for the occasion. The barn stood on a farm of horses, the land there delineated by barbed-wire fences. The barn was adjacent to a small country cemetery where it was entirely possible to count every lichen-encrusted tombstone and know how many departed were lying in repose under that thick sod. A census, so to speak. Everyone was invited to the wedding. Lee had even cut short the leg of an Australian tour in order to attend, though to all of us, Kip and Lee seemed the least close among our friends. Kip, as far as I knew, didn't even own any of Lee's albums, and whenever we saw Kip driving around town it was inevitably with a Bluetooth lodged in his ear, his mouth working as if he were still out on the floor of the Mercantile Exchange.

Kip had just returned to Wisconsin after about nine years of trading commodities in Chicago. It was as if the world had just gotten small again. For years, decades, our whole lives, really— we'd listened to the farm reports in our trucks on the AM radio. Sometimes you'd even hear Kip's voice during those broadcasts as he was interviewed from his office down in Chicago, that familiar self-assured baritone narrating fluctuations in numbers that dictated whether or not we could afford orthodontia for our children, winter vacations, or new boots, telling us things we didn't exactly understand and yet already knew. Our own futures were sown into those reports of milk and corn prices, wheat and soy. Hog-bellies and cattle. Far from our farms and mills, Kip had made good, manipulating the fruits of our labor. We respected him just the same. He was fiercely intelligent, for one thing, his eyes burned in their sockets as he listened intently to us complain about seed salesmen, pesticides, fertilizer pricing, our machines, the fickle weather. He kept a farmer's almanac in his back pocket, understood our obsession with rain. Had he not gone away, he might have been a prodigious farmer himself. The almanac, he once told me, was almost entirely obsolete, but he liked to carry it around. "Nostalgia," he explained.

After he returned, Kip bought the boarded-up feed mill downtown. The tallest structure in town, its six-story grain silos had always loomed over us, casting long shadows like a sundial for our days. Very early in our childhoods it had been a bustling place where corn was taken to be held for passing trains, where farmers came to buy their fuel in bulk, their seed, other supplies, but by the late eighties it had fallen into disrepair, the owner having tried to sell in a time when no one was buying. It was only a few months before the high-schoolers began throwing stones through the windows, decorating the grain silos with graffiti. Most of our lives it was just a dark citadel beside a set of railroad tracks that had grown rusty and overgrown with milkweed, ragweed, fireweed. The floors had been thick with pigeon shit and bat guano, and there was a lake of standing water in the old stone basement. In the silos, rats and mice ran rampant, eating the leftover grain— sometimes we broke inside to shoot them with .22s, the small-caliber bullets occasionally ricocheting against the towering walls of the silos. We used flashlights to find their beady little eyes and once, Ronny stole one of his mother's signal flares from the trunk of her car, dropping it down into the silo, where it glowed hot pink against the sulfurous darkness, as we shot away.

Within ten months Kip had restored most of the mill. He paid local craftsmen to do the work, overseeing every detail; he beat everyone to the site each morning and was not above wielding a hammer or going to his knees, as needed, to smooth out the grout, or what have you. We guessed at the kind of money he must have thrown at the building: hundreds of thousands for sure; maybe millions.

At the post office or the IGA, he talked excitedly about his plans. "All that space," he'd say. "Think about all that space. We could do *anything* with that space. Offices. Light industry. Restaurants, pubs, cafés. I want a coffee shop in there, I know that much." We tried our best to dream along with him. As young children, we had briefly known the mill as a place where our mothers bought us overalls, thick socks, and galoshes. It had been a place that smelled of dog food and corn dust and new leather and the halitosis and the cheap cologne of old men. But those memories were further away.

"You think people will want to have dinner inside the old mill?" we asked him.

"Think outside the box, man," he crooned. "That's the kind of thinking that's *killed* this town. Think big."

Near the new electronic cash register was the original till. Kip had saved that, too. He liked to lean against the old machine, his elbows on its polished surface while one of his employees rang up customers at the newer register. He had mounted four flat-screen televisions near the registers where it was easy to monitor the distant stock markets, Doppler radar, and real-time politics, talking to his customers out the sides of his mouth, eyes still trained up on the news. Sometimes, he never even looked at their faces. But he had resurrected the mill. Old men came there to park their rusted trucks in the gravel lot and drink wan coffee as they leaned against their still warm vehicles, engines ticking down, and they talked and spat brown juices into the gravel rock and dust. They liked the new action that had accumulated around the mill. The delivery trucks, sales representatives, construction crews. They liked talking to us, to young farmers—to me and the Giroux twins, who were often there, poking fun at Kip as he stared at all those brand-new plasma television screens, doing his best to ignore us.

Lee had actually written a song about the old mill before its revival. That was the mill we remembered, the one, I guess, that was real to us.

Our friend Ronny Taylor was an alcoholic. The drinking had made a bad detour of his life. Once, he had fallen down drunk onto the curb outside the VFW on Main Street and banged his head hard, broken some of his teeth. He'd been belligerent and loud that night, hitting on other people's girlfriends and wives, spilling his drinks, and twice he'd been seen peeing into the alley behind the bar, his dick out in the breeze while he whistled "Raindrops Keep Fallin' on My Head." Sheriff Bartman had no choice and picked him up for public intoxication, though Bartman had no quarrel with Ronny and simply wanted the man to dry out somewhere safe, to not jump behind the wheel of some pickup truck only to kiss an oak tree at seventy miles an hour later in the evening. But of course the damage had already been done. All that night and into the next morning as Ronny lay cooped up in jail for public intoxication, his brain was bleeding from the inside. By the time the sheriff took him to the hospital in Eau Claire for emergency surgery, it was too late. Damage had been done that could not be undone. No one ever said as much, but we wondered if all that alcohol had thinned his blood, worsened the bleeding. Ronny was never the same after that, but some slowed-down version of himself. More happy perhaps, but also less aware, and if you were a stranger meeting him for the first time, you might just think he was a little *slow,* but then again, maybe you would think he was normal. Either way, you might never have guessed about the young man that existed before in that same body. His sentences just didn't come as quickly and frequently he repeated himself. But it didn't mean that he was dumb, or handicapped, though sometimes, I wonder if we treated him that way.

Ronny dried out in the hospital over the course of several months, often restrained in his bed, and we came to the hospital to hold his hand. His grip was ferocious, his veins seemed everywhere ready to jump right out through his sweaty flesh. His eyes were scared in a way I had only seen in horses. We wiped his forehead and did our best to hold him down to the earth.

Our wives and children came to visit him too and he liked that. It forced him to mellow. Our children brought crayons and paper to the hospital and drew crude portraits of him, the colors always happy and beside his head a glowing sun or a leafed-out tree. Sometimes after the children left we would find him clutching their art and bawling, other times, holding them tenderly, studying them and touching their work like sacred artifacts. He saved those pictures and later hung them in his apartment.

After a period of time he came out of the tunnel and we took care of him as best we could because he was ours and he had no other family; both his parents had passed away when we were in our midtwenties—carbon monoxide poisoning at their cabin up on Spider Lake, near Birchwood. Ronny was Little Wing's orphan.

He had been a professional rodeo. He was tender with horses, brutal with cattle. He knew ropes and even before the accident he'd suffered any number of vicious injuries and insults to his body. There were times when he came over to our house for dinner that my children would ask him to list off his broken bones. That inventory took some time.

"Let's see," he'd say, pulling off his tired cowboy boots. "Well. I had all ten toes broken, I know that." Next he'd pull off his holey socks. What toenails he still had were yellowed and the dirty milky color of quartz; they seemed to grow in defiance of his flesh. "Some of these toes were broken twice, I think. An angry brahma is going to come down wherever they want to come down, see, and sometimes that'll be on you." Ronny would pick up our son, Alex, and set him on his back on the living-room floor and then pretend to be a bull, crashing down gently on the little boy's body, tickling his ribs, armpits, and toes. "In Kalispell they wanted to take both pinkie toes, but I escaped the hospital before they could put me under. Had a girl there who I called and she was waiting outside with the engine running. . . .

"This scar here," he said, indicating his pale right ankle, "a bull named Ticonderoga come down on it and snapped my leg in two."

My kids thought this was the best game in the world—seeing how many garments they could get Ronny Taylor to shed, how many broken bones he could remember, how many nasty scars their little fingers could trace.

But the drunken fall had ended his rodeo life, and we were sad for that. He had dropped out of high school to rodeo; he had no trade and no skills.

Lee paid for his medical expenses, his apartment, his food and clothing. We weren't supposed to know any of that, but we had grown up with Rhonda Blake, who worked in one of the Eau Claire hospital's medical records departments, and she told Eddy Moffitt one night at the VFW. She had been shaking her head and smiling kind of winsomely and Eddy went over to her, bought her a drink, and asked what was going on.

"You know, I could get fired for saying something," Rhonda said, "but the thing is, something like this. People ought to know.

I never heard of a good deed like this. Christ, I could lose my job, but truth is, it'd be worth it."

And then she told Eddy that Ronny hadn't had insurance. That the bills had been well over a hundred thousand dollars.

"One day," she said, "we get a delivery from New York City. An envelope from some record company to Ronny's attention. And sure enough, a goddamn check for a hundred and twenty-three thousand dollars."

She drank her beer fast, her eyes wet.

"It was just so sweet," she said, "I couldn't keep it to myself."

Eddy told us all this story one night after a high school football game. (Us versus Osseo.) None of us had children old enough to be in high school yet, but when you live in a town as small as Little Wing, Wisconsin, you go out to the high school football and basketball games. It is, after all, something to do, cheap family entertainment. We all stood underneath the bleachers, some of us sharing a pouch of Red Man chewing tobacco, others passing a bag of sunflower seeds, listening to Eddy as the crowd thundered its support right above us, boots stomping the wooden bleachers, the rickety metal scaffolding shaking loose rust. From overhead, aluminum cans and crumpled-up hot dog wrappers rained down. We crossed our arms, spat, tried to imagine what a check for a hundred thousand dollars even looked like.

Lee was already our hero, but this only deepened our love for him, grew his legend. We all went out the next day and bought ten more of his albums, each of us, even though we had duplicates at our homes. And that money we spent was precious too because so many of us were just scraping by; it could've been plugged into savings or used for groceries. Still. We mailed them to relatives and distant friends, donated them to libraries and nursing homes.

Ronny never saw a bill; Lee's lawyers took care of all the logistics. Ronny would be taken care of forever. Ronny did not seem to know that he had a patron in life, or, maybe he did, I don't know. All I know is that Lee never talked about it, and neither did Ronny. Then again, it was only right. There were countless posters of Lee in Ronny's apartment, and they had been there well before the accident and surgery. Most had gone a little faded with sunlight, greasy with kitchen smoke. They had adorned those shabby walls *long* before Lee became famous. Ronny had always loved him the most.

The invitations to Kip's wedding were heavy with paper and ribbon and glitter. We carried them from our mailboxes and vehicles into our houses carefully, reverently, as if they held priceless, exquisite news. We vaguely knew the woman he was marrying. Felicia was from Chicago and now worked as a consultant from their new house just outside town. Exactly what or with whom she consulted, we didn't really understand, though Eddy claimed that it had something to do with pharmaceuticals. She had come out to the VFW a few times with Kip, always beautiful, her makeup and hair and nails all perfect. We remembered her for her high heels, which she wore all through the winter, her toenails a sharp shiny red. She was plenty nice, but there was something in her manner that seemed to indicate to us that our town was just a temporary place for her, a kind of layover, and that we were layovers too. Layovers to later be flown over one day and waved to. Flyover friends.

We scanned the invitation, surprised to see that Lee would be playing a song during the ceremony. He had not played songs at any of our weddings, and though we had all wanted him to, none of us had even thought to ask him for that kind of favor. We hadn't really thought of him attending as a performer, just as our friend.

Not long after the invitations arrived at our houses, Lee came home from Australia, as run-down and misspent as we'd ever seen him. We let him be a few days, like we always did, and then my wife, Beth, invited him over to our farm for dinner and a bonfire. He always seemed to like playing with our children and the fact that we didn't have cable television, that in fact our *only* television was an ancient model inherited from my parents that looked more like a gigantic piece of wooden furniture than something that might actually connect us to the outside world. We owned a newish record player though—I collect old vinyl—and he always blushed as he passed it and noticed one of his LPs underneath the needle. Our kids knew all the words to his songs.

The kids squealed that night as they saw the headlights of Lee's old truck come down our driveway toward the house. They ran in circles and galloped, singing out all his trademark lines with gusto.

"All right, all right, all right!" Beth said, laughing. "Enough. Now you're gonna give Uncle Lee some room. He's tired, all right? He just got home from Australia. So don't pester him too much." Shooing them away from the front door, she checked her reflection in the mirror, pursed her lips, and ran her fingers quickly through her hair.

He came to the door carrying a bouquet of carnations that were obviously bought in a hurry from the IGA. Beth took the flowers and they hugged. He had grown skinny over the years and his hairline was quickly receding, though he let the strands grow long. He had a beard and his forearms were scattered with tattoos.

"Hey buddy," he said, grinning at me. "Good to be home. Missed you a ton."

Lee always gave good hugs. I felt his rib cage against my own, his long arms around me. The smell of tobacco in his beard and in his hair.

"We missed you too," I said. Then the children attacked him and he fell to the floor in mock defeat. Beth and I went to the kitchen and brought the meal out to our old dining-room table, where there were candles already lit. Beth went to the turntable and flipped his record, placed the needle in the wide black groove at the edge.

We heard Lee groan from the entryway as he stumbled toward us, dragging Eleanore and Alex, his arms underneath their armpits, and shaking his head. "Let's listen to something else, huh?" he said. "I'm so friggin' tired of myself."

We watched him eat, wolfing down the food; it made us happy to feed him. We drank wine and listened to jazz and outside the windows the autumn leaves were loud and dry on their branches. Snow was not inconceivable.

"Heard you're playing a song at Kip's wedding," I said, after some time had passed.

Lee leaned back in his chair and exhaled. "Yeah," he said, "I guess I am. Got a text from him one day out of the blue. I was so surprised, I didn't give my reply much thought. Maybe I should've."

"You okay with that?" Beth asked. "Singing, I mean. For Kip of all people?"

He shrugged. "You know, I like Kip just fine, but it's not like we're close. He's more like an acquaintance at this point than a friend. But I came back, you know, to see you all and—I don't know—to support him. Old time's sake and all. He's done some good things. The mill, for one. I think he's a good thing for this town. Anyway, I'd rather be here than the outback."

"Oh," Beth said, putting her chin in her hand and smiling,

"your life's not so bad." She traced something on the surface of the table with her other hand.

"No," he said. "My life is good. Very good. But I get lonely too. For people I can trust. People who don't want anything from me. It, it changes you after a while, you know? And I don't *want* it to change me. I want to be able to come back here and live here and just be who I am. With you guys." He exhaled deeply and took a long sip of wine.

We followed his lead, raising our wineglasses to him, and they made a sound like dull chimes. Then there was a silence. Just the children's feet swinging beneath the table and the wind in the desiccated corn stalks and tree limbs outside, and Lee smiled again and poured himself another glass of wine and we could see that his teeth were already stained purple and that he was happy.

"I wish I had your lives," he said at last. "You know?"

I kissed Beth's hand, then took it in my own, looked at her. She smiled at me, blushing, then looked at the floor.

Lee rose from the table then, pressed his knuckles into the small of his back, and stretched like a cat, before collecting our plates and walking them to the kitchen sink. Beth followed him, wineglasses clutched in her long fingers, and I watched for a moment as they stood close beside each other, cleaning, him passing her wet dishes that she dried with a towel. His hands soap-sudsy, then hers too, both of them swaying back and forth just a little with the jazz. It made me feel good, to have everyone together, to have him back. I took a roll of newspaper and some matches and went out into the darkness to light a bonfire.

The wind carried cold and the stars were all out, the blue-white throw of the Milky Way grand overhead. I went to the woodpile and carried a load of logs to our fire-ring in the backyard, then broke up some kindling and lit a match, blowing carefully against the tender new flames. I have always loved bonfires.

Lee came out of the house at some point, and I sensed him behind me.

"Want a joint?" he asked.

I looked around, though we had no neighbors for hundreds and hundreds of yards. "The kids in bed?" I asked, rubbing my hands for warmth, blowing into them, the smell of alcohol still there, faintly.

"Beth's putting them down now," he said, grinning. We were silent a moment. "I needed tonight, man," he said finally. "Needed to be with you guys. Just to, you know, have a little room to breathe. Eat some good food. I can't tell you."

There were rolling papers in his hands and he passed me a plastic bag, heavy and pungent even through the plastic. He pinched the buds into the paper and licked it along its edges. He always made great paper planes.

"Wanna just share?" I asked.

"Why not."

So we stood that way, our faces red and orange before the fire with two different fragrances of smoke swirling around us, and overhead the heavens very slowly spinning and strange beautiful lights arcing down to earth every so often.

Lee started laughing at one point, shaking his head. I touched the flannel of his jacket and said, "What is it? *What?*"

"I'm dating someone."

"Yeah? You're *always* dating someone."

"Not like this," he said. He looked at me and raised his eyebrows. The smoke was big in our lungs, sticky and good. We passed the joint between us.

"So, who is she? Come on now."

I choked on the smoke when he told me, coughed into the

night before beating a fist against my chest. Lee was dating a movie star who appeared regularly on the glossy pages of at least three different magazines lying around our house. She was famously elegant, unfathomably beautiful, undeniably talented.

He nodded his head at me, still smiling.

"And what's she doing with a bum like you?"

"A guy's entitled to get lucky every now and again," he said, shrugging his shoulders, though I could see perfectly clearly that he was in love with her.

"I'm bringing her to Kip's wedding," he said, a moment later. "I can't wait for you guys to meet her."

"Jesus, Lee, I'm—*shit*, I'm just really happy for you," I said, though there was something in my chest that snagged like jealousy. "I'm so happy for you," I repeated, staring into the fire, past the flames to where the coals were throbbing, the palest, brightest orange. I wondered what it would be like to touch her body, to be with a woman that beautiful. Then I shook my head, shook away those thoughts and was back alongside Lee, happy and proud of him.

Strange, I thought to myself right then, how his life was like my own and yet not at all like it, though we came from the same small place on earth. And why? How had our paths diverged, why were they still even connected? Why was he then in my backyard, on my farm, the sound of almost two hundred cows, faintly in the background, mooing and lowing? How had he come back, this famous man, this person whose name everyone knew, whose voice was recognizable to millions in a way that made it impossible for him to be a stranger in so many places?

It was difficult for me to look up at the night sky and not think of Lee and his fame. All over the world at that very moment there were people no doubt listening to his music. I watched him take a final drag on the joint before flicking it into the fire. He was incandescent.

Ronny frequently stayed over at the old schoolhouse when Lee wasn't on tour. They played music together, Ronny on the drums, banging away, Lee smiling appreciatively at his damaged friend. They rode on Lee's tractor together under the sun. Lee made Ronny breakfast, lunch, and dinner. The two of them would sit on Lee's huge porch, just being quiet. They watched the bats swooping in the night against a backdrop of stars. They listened to the owls. Watched deer grazing out in the fields.

Lee was careful about Ronny's sobriety. They would sit together in their Adirondack chairs with mugs of coffee or hot chocolate, and that was good and enough. When he was with Ronny, Lee was clean, or mostly clean. And if they went out to the VFW in the evening to watch a Packers game or to eat a hamburger or share a paper boat full of cheese curds, Lee kept Ronny close, ordering his friend Coca-Colas and paying rapt and sincere attention to his friend's sometimes convoluted observations and conversation. Prior to Ronny's accident, none of us had fully understood the alcoholism that had almost killed him, but it seemed that alcohol had become his closest companion while traveling for the rodeo. After an event was over, sprawled out in some motel bathtub icing his purple-bruised body, he would grow drunk on cheap beer or rotgut vodka. Drinking became his lover and his lullaby, his needle and his pillow.

Lee had had an entire bull killed and taxidermied and then mounted to a platform on four sturdy tires. The two friends would roll the dead bull into one of Lee's fields and then spend the afternoon taking passes beside it on Lee's tractor, a lasso in Ronny's hand, expertly twirling over his smiling face and then thrown out into the field, where it never failed to snag the impassive creature's two shining horns.

"All his muscles still remember," Lee would say, shaking his head in sadness. Then, "I ought to buy him a horse."

The bachelor party was a mess. Kip had rented a stretch limousine and bought us all matching Polo shirts to wear for the day. We were to spend the day golfing. Thirty-six holes. He had rented out the entire course and the clubhouse. There was a rumor of strippers. But Kip had not invited Ronny, and Lee was irate. I wasn't surprised. Kip had a way of moving too fast, of talking too fast, of barely listening, and he'd always been that way; he and Ronny had never quite meshed and maybe none of us ever really meshed with Kip. But certainly not Ronny, who would just stare at him, even when we were young, and say things like, "Now Kip, who gives two shits about advanced placement history? I mean, really. There's a party at the quarry this weekend. That's what I'm focused on. Focused on getting laid." When I imagined the party we were invited to, I pictured his colleagues from back in Chicago: suit-and-tie men, martini men, expense-account men who'd gone to good universities and drove nice cars. These men would own their own sets of new golf clubs and spiked golf shoes. Their hands would be office-soft. Perhaps Kip had not invited Ronny to protect him, or because he was too embarrassed. But I also knew that none of those excuses would fly with Lee, whose love for Ronny was almost righteous.

Ronny had marked the date of the wedding on a calendar that hung from a magnetic hook attached to the side of his refrigerator, and in the preceding months, he asked Lee and me regularly when the bachelor party would be.

"*Got* to have a bachelor party," Ronny would say. "You just got to. It's the last hurrah. Right? The last hooray."

It made me sad to think that Ronny himself might never be married.

Lee and I went to Ronny's apartment on the day of the bachelor party.

"Did you get an invitation?" Lee said, looking anxiously through the mass of mail piled up on Ronny's kitchen table, mostly junk: coupons, political propaganda, credit card offers; no bills were ever posted to Ronny's apartment.

"Nope," Ronny said, "probably just lost in the mail. I know he wants me there."

"Oh, no doubt, bud," said Lee, seething with anger, "no doubt. Hang on there, buddy, okay? I got to make a phone call real quick." He eyed me seriously and I knew to watch Ronny, to keep him entertained. I turned on the television and flipped the channels until we found a nature program about a herd of Montana buffalo.

"You can use my phone!" Ronny yelled, but Lee was already down the stairs and outside. I watched him from the window as he paced the sidewalk and shouted into his mobile. He looked like a man who needed something to kick.

A few moments later Lee came back up the stairs, his face red. "Hey buddy, look, no problem, all right!" he said, reentering the apartment. "I just talked to Kip and he explained everything to me. Your invitation, turns out, just now came back to him in the mail. He had the wrong address or something, I guess."

Ronny was watching the television, buffalo grazing on an endless expanse of prairie. "But I don't understand," he said. "Why didn't he just bring the invitation over himself? I wave to him every day when I walk by the mill." Ronny shook his head at the illogic of it and chuckled good-naturedly.

Lee exhaled. "I don't know, buddy. It's a good question." His fists were clenched. He looked outside. It was a beautiful October day. The sun bright and clear, the autumn leaves a cool inferno across the land. In the air: the smell of overripe apples, manure.

Not long after that, a limousine pulled up outside Ronny's apartment and blared its horn six times. Lee looked at me and I saw then, noticed for the first time, that he was a powerful man, that he could get things accomplished with a single telephone call. I saw that he was used to getting his way, he was not accustomed to disappointment.

Ronny turned from the television, his face bright with excitement. "Party time," he said, grinning, and he gave us hard, loud high-fives. My palm hurt.

We nodded. "Party time," we said with as much enthusiasm as we could muster.

We all went downstairs to the idling limousine. It was packed with most of our better friends as well as a few strange faces, among them a photographer, a young woman with two different cameras slung around her neck. She seemed to be capturing just about any moment of even the slightest interest with her elaborate Nikon, paying particular attention to everyone's hands, where glasses of champagne, bottles of beer, and highballs of whiskey sloshed extravagantly.

"Yeah!" Ronny shouted, taking all of this in. "Yeah! Yeah! *Yeah!* Party tiiiiime!" The tight little crowd cheered reflexively.

We ducked into the limousine after Ronny and settled in as the stretch turned off Main and reoriented itself like a giant compass needle toward the golf course. The vehicle was loud with music that I didn't recognize, and Lee leaned in close to me. "Don't let Ronny out of your sight. Don't lose sight of him," he said. "Do you understand me?" I nodded, realizing that the limousine and the party had been a bad idea, that it was all a very bad idea, and now we were swept up into it; Lee had demanded that Ronny be invited, but now he saw the party as being a great danger to his friend. Lee sat rigidly, his fists clenched, jaw set.

"Get him something to drink," Lee growled at me through the racket. "No beer, though, no booze."

I reached for a can of Coca-Cola and popped the top for Ronny, who slugged at the aluminum can. "Yeah!" he said, coming up for air and wiping his mouth with his forearm. "Yeah!"

"Hey, hey, hey!" Kip called out now. "Hey!" He rapped a Swiss Army knife against his champagne flute. "I need to make an announcement, all right? Announcement time!" He reminded me of a Scoutmaster who could not control his troop. "Can everybody please shut the fuck up? Hey!"

"Speeeeech!" the mob called out. "Speech! Speech!" The group was mostly comprised of our friends, but in that moment, I felt that it was just me and Lee, with Ronny beside us. The photographer aimed her camera at us, at Lee, and the flash went off momentarily with light, blinding us. Perhaps not surprisingly, she seemed to only be interested in taking photos of Lee, and I could already imagine her cropping Ronny and me out of the image. I wondered if this was what fame was—a lot of strangers with cameras and then the subsequent blindness of some unexpected portrait. I thought about a middle school history class in which we were taught that some Native Americans thought that having their photograph taken was tantamount to their souls being stolen.

"Can't tell you guys how much it means to me that you're all here today," Kip said, "helping me celebrate my big day tomorrow. I'm overcome, guys, I really am," though he did not look overcome. His reddish brown hair was thick and long and greased up away from his tight calm face and the closely trimmed beard that followed his strong jawline, his smile utterly controlled and almost ironic. "Me and Felicia," he said, "we're so happy you've all welcomed us back into the community the way you have. With open arms. And that you're excited too, about the mill. You know? It means the world to us. And *tomorrow*"—and here he paused with all the phony gravitas and dramatic flair of a seasoned corporate toastmaster—"we're all going out to that big old barn to see a great wedding and to *par-ty heart-ty*."

He was not finished with his soliloquy, but Ronny yelled, "Party time!" and pumped his fists in the close boozy air. Some of the group laughed a little uncertainly, but Lee threw an arm around his friend and whispered intently into his ear. I watched Lee's lips move, though I could not hear his words. *You stick close to me, buddy*, I imagined him saying. *We'll party hearty together, okay? You and me.*

Nodding indulgently at Ronny, Kip moved on. "So listen," he said, "I got you all a little present, okay? Some shirts. It's not much, but hey—it's something, right? I want you to put them on now. Because today, we're like a team. A team of friends. You know? I want you to have fun. I want you to forget about everything else today, all right? Okay. So that's it. I've said what I had to say. Now, let's go have some *fun*."

He reached into a black plastic garbage bag and pulled out a multitude of red Polo shirts all specially embroidered across the left breast with two crossing golf clubs and the date. Kip began passing them around. He even knocked on the Plexiglas window of the limousine and passed a shirt up to the driver. Then he passed one to the photographer. It appeared to be at least one, perhaps two sizes too small for her, and I averted my eyes as she gamely removed her button-down shirt to don the confining garment. Some of the assembled cheered at the frustratingly brief exposure of her stomach and bra. And then Kip tossed a shirt to each of his assembled friends. To everyone, that is, except Ronny Taylor, whose face drooped, almost imperceptibly, his hands empty and waiting. Lee noticed it immediately and handed his Polo shirt to Ronny.

"Here you go, buddy," he said. "Kip must've just forgot about getting me one."

But when Ronny looked back at his friend, his face was sad with knowing. Ronny paused a moment before he pulled off the shirt he was wearing, and we saw then the scars of his rodeo days, the meat grossly missing from an area near his shoulder, the crudely sewn stitches of some arena paramedic or small-town ER. His stomach, still admirably flat, was corrugated with muscle, and a tattoo over his heart in blurred blue lettering read CORVUS—Lee's stage name—along with a roughshod image of a crow perched atop a telephone wire. The tattoo, already almost ten years old, had been there before Lee was even famous, when we were all little more than kids.

"I still can't believe you ever did that," Lee said now, reaching out to touch his friend's tattoo. He shook his head and smiled.

"I believed in you," Ronny said with all the earnestness in the world. "I still do. You're my friend."

All eyes in the limousine were on them. Outside the long automobile, the world continued to move on—traffic slowly blurring by, the occasional tractor, an old farmer walking along the gravel shoulder, perhaps toward the bank or library downtown—but inside, life was a diorama of open mouths, unblinking eyes, and held breaths. Then Kip broke in. "You, Lee. Where's your shirt?"

"I didn't *get* one," Lee said. He had a hand on Ronny's knee. His voice was stern. "But don't worry about it, chief. It really doesn't matter."

"But," Kip began, and even as his eyes fell on what had to be Lee's shirt, *right there,* on Ronny's back, we could all hear in the falter of his voice that he wouldn't push Lee any further. That even though everyone in the limousine was equally uniformed except Lee, who sat heavily against the limousine's glossy leather upholstery in his omnipresent flannel shirt and torn blue jeans, Kip would not now challenge him. Kip rapped his knuckles against the glass of the limousine driver's partition and we began to move faster still, the volume of that bass-heavy music increasing even as the giant vehicle picked up speed.

We were farmers, most of us, not golfers. But it was a good day and the course unfolded before us spectacularly, the links verdant and shimmering, the sky overhead unfettered by so much as a single cloud. Kip had rented carts, and we were divided into pairs. Eddy Moffitt and I were to share a cart, and I noticed that Kip had paired himself with Lee. The photographer was quick to snap several shots of the two men standing near each other, clubs in hand. Ronny stood off to the side, examining the sheet of pairings, a finger scrolling down the page, but never finding his name. I watched him scratch his head and then, leaning in close to Eddy's ear, I said, "Listen, Eddy, I'm going to partner up with Ronny, that okay?"

Eddy was a good guy, everyone's insurance salesman, and he understood immediately. "Hey Ronny!" he called out. "Ronny! Yo, you're over here with Hank." Then Eddy slapped me kindheartedly on the back with a big thick hand and pulled my head in close to him, whispering, "I don't know what Kipper's pulling here, but it's some real bullshit. Anyways, you guys have fun. I'll just head over to the clubhouse. See if those strippers have shown yet." He patted my back again with the slab of his hand. Eddy had farmed for many years before a tractor accident had sent his farm into bankruptcy. He'd hadn't had any insurance, had never been able to afford it, and the hospital bills had ruined him.

I shook Ronny's hand and we found a cart with two sets of bags attached to the back, and then drove off to the first tee. Sitting in a rack just above the clubs was a cooler of beer. I saw Ronny's eyes go right to it, the ice within jiggling against all that cold aluminum with every bump of the cart. I braked and got out to remove the cooler. The Giroux twins were holding down their own cart, and as they moved to pass us, I handed the cooler to Cameron, who gave us a surprised salute as his brother Cordell stomped his foot on the accelerator, no doubt for a fast getaway before we could change our minds. Ronny seemed to deflate just a bit and I saw him lick his chapped lips as he watched our other friends drink in the warm sunlight, their throats working the beer down, lips wet, the air suddenly perfumed with the sweet aroma of cheap American beer. It was the smell of our childhood: the smell of silos and of barns and of harvest-time fields. Beer was our tonic, and I understood Ronny's torment. His brain wasn't so damaged that he couldn't recall the dim lights of our favorite bars and the boom of our favorite jukeboxes. The nights we had spent parked in the countryside, laying in the bed of an ancient pickup truck, emptying dozens of cans of beer and throwing the empties out into the ditches, into those infinite fields of corn. The drunken lovemaking that ensued: the touch of fingers, the weight of breasts, the caress of legs, the struggles with stubborn zippers, the yanking down of too-tight blue jeans. All our best memories were fueled by beer, and I saw then just how sorely Ronny missed his favorite vice; that somewhere in the broken circuitry of his brain there was still an unquenchable thirst. Part of me wanted to help him, but of course I could not and never would. And maybe we could have offered him a beer every now and then, but no one wanted to take that chance, and *what for?* What good could *possibly* come from it?

We golfed for hours, our faces sunburned, our lips growing dry and cracked. Carts came by with cheeseburgers and hot dogs and bottles of water and Cokes, but it did not matter; the golf exhausted us. The sun arced over our heads and began its descent in the west. We were brutal golfers, Ronny and I. But every now and again, we might light into a shot and send the little ball sailing over the countryside toward some small banner over a minor cup in the earth. We laughed together and I could see all of a sudden why Lee was such good friends with Ronny. Of course, they were both bachelors, natural grown playmates, no children or wives to encumber their fun, and maybe that was why I hadn't called Ronny more, invited him to go grouse hunting with me, or take a trip to the implement dealer to price out equipment. I don't know. He was kind and sincere and gentle. All afternoon we rode together over the links, taking our swings and encouraging each other, and he asked me the best questions: about Beth and the kids, my farm and tractors. He was not interested in our scant income or our used vehicles or our paltry investments. His concerns were real. I invited him to come to dinner at our house.

"Thank you," he said. Then, "What can I bring?"

"Just bring yourself, Ronny. Just yourself."

Thirty-six holes of golf later, our palms riddled with blisters, we turned back toward the clubhouse, though Ronny seemed content to simply drive around, looking at the different holes—all the berms, sand traps, ponds, long narrow fairways. We were not the first ones to come back. Most of the bachelor party was already there, drunk and on a slide to either camaraderie or savage belligerence. Standing atop the bar were two female dancers, nude, their bodies shining with what appeared to be spilled champagne. I watched Ronny's face break into a sunburned smile. I smiled, too.

"Party time!" he announced loudly, at which the entire bachelor party turned to him and roared their agreement. In that moment, Ronny had become their mascot. Someone grabbed him from me and pushed him toward the bar and dancers, where he stood, mouth agape, staring up at their hard, tanned bodies. They were attractive in that more and more familiar way, unapologetically enhanced, the scars of plastic surgery darkening the skin just beneath their breasts, their gaze out over all of us at once energized and stupendously bored. I realized that to them, Ronny must look normal, even handsome. Before his accident he had been our homecoming king, dated the best looking girls in our town. Even now, his body was rodeo lean, his face brutally handsome and carved. He looked at the dancers and I could see he was remembering some previous time in his life, some western town where perhaps he'd fallen in love a night or two. Motel magic in Butte, or Billings, or Bozeman. There were times when it was too easy to forget that Ronny was still a virile man.

So I retreated to the margins of the party, watching Ronny from a distance as he stared up at the dancing women, his fingers occasionally reaching out for their toned calves, their painted toenails, supple ankles.

It was dusk before Kip and Lee finally entered the clubhouse, faces badly burned, hair crazily windblown, both of them scowling at each other. They went to either ends of the bar, ignoring the naked women dancing above them, and I saw them both order what looked to be whiskey. As soon as they'd tossed back their glasses, they ordered seconds. Their eyes were angry. Finally, after ordering a third glass, Lee left the bar and slumped into a chair beside me.

"Fucker made me play *every fucking hole*," he said. "All thirty-six. Fuckin' death march." The ice cubes in his glass sloshed as if in gasoline. "He throttled me! Every hole. And not by a stroke or two. I mean, by like, six, seven strokes. Every hole. No mulligans, no nothing. Made me count everything. Laughed his ass off at me the whole time. Fucker." Lee eyed Kip at the bar.

"Lee," I said, "relax. Everybody's got to be friends by tomorrow."

My eyes were still trained on Ronny up at the bar. He was holding a single dollar bill in the air, like a torch. One of the women accepted the bill between her breasts, and I could see him sigh with something like ecstasy. The wedding party had moved away from the bar, and they were watching him too. Feeding him singles.

"Fuck him," said Lee. "Seriously! Fuck *him*. I get paid ten thousand dollars sometimes just to *show up* at a place and play one goddamn song. Fucker treats me like that. Shit."

He was quiet then, and I was too, his words hanging in the air like smoke that could not be wafted away. I had never heard him say anything like that before, had never heard him talk about money before. He clenched and unclenched his hands in his lap and then reached up to smooth the hair on his scalp.

"Sorry, man," he said. "That was shitty. It's his big day. Who cares if he beats the shit out of me golfing? I never golf. Goddamn yuppie nature walk."

We sat that way awhile, and there was nothing for me to say. It had been a difficult year for me on the farm, with low milk prices coupled against exorbitant diesel and fertilizer prices. I'd also just had to replace my combine and pay for Eleanore's tonsillectomy. We were at a point with our dairy herd where the general feeling was *grow or die*. Either we invested more in the farm and took on more cows, or else it was time to think about getting out. Beth and I were mortgaged to the hilt and there was no room to save for the kids' educations, our investments having tanked along with everyone else's. Beth had just brought home information about food stamps and state health care. I hadn't been sleeping well at night, and didn't know what I'd do if the farm failed. Until that moment I hadn't had any concept of how much Lee made, though we had wondered, sure. But I understood that his income was like his travels—inconceivable to me. Now, the starkness, the reality of it all made me very sad.

I had considered asking Lee for a loan in the past, when things had been especially rough; Beth had even encouraged me to do so. But I never had.

"Look, Lee," I began, and he looked over at me, his pupils still small and angry. But I could not continue.

"Come on," he said, "let's get Ronny and get out of here. I have to pick up Chloe at the airport tomorrow morning early. We oughta get out of here before something happens."

But Kip had come over in that very moment and was now hovering over us, the photographer just over his shoulder, balanced on her toes, snapping photographs in the half-light of the clubhouse. Kip held a bottle of Johnny Walker Blue in his hand, his lips shiny with alcohol.

"So where's your uniform anyway?" he barked down at Lee, something between a smile and a sneer on his face. He gave Lee's arm a gentle jab. "Huh?"

Lee shook his head. "You forgot mine, remember?"

"No, I didn't," Kip said. "You gave it away's what happened."

Lee shrugged and looked at Kip, and I saw then that something had shifted—that they were no longer friends, or even friendly, just two men who didn't like each other, two men who shared nothing anymore, beyond a common geography. Any intersection in their lives now, and moving forward, would be like mere coincidence.

"So, when do I get to meet her?" Kip bellowed over the blaring music. Behind him, the dancers had moved off the bar, grinding their tawny hips against Ronny.

Lee stared at Kip. "*Get to*? What the fuck, Kip. What, you want her fuckin' *autograph*?"

Kip absorbed Lee's words for a moment, and smiled, then turned back to leer at the dancers. "The driver will take you back, if you like, boys. I certainly don't want you ruining your voice yelling at me." He took a pull off the bottle and walked back to the rest of the group, though by then, I recognized few of their faces. Gone were the Girouxs. Gone was Eddy.

We rose, collected a somewhat resistant Ronny, and left the place, ear drums pounding, the smell of strange perfume in our hair, noses throbbing with sunburn. Ronny slumped back against the soft leather seats and looked up into the night sky through the open moonroof. There was a smile on his face and two scraps of paper lodged in the pocket of his Wranglers: both dancers' numbers scrawled out with their names—*Lucy* and *Brandi*—and embellished with red lipstick Os where their lips had kissed the paper good night.

"Not my first time at the rodeo, boys," he kept saying. "Nope. Not my first time at the rodeo."

Lee put his arm around Ronny and they looked up at the stars in the sky. I smiled at the two of them, closed my eyes, and let the driver take me back home to my bed and my wife and my children.

I can recall that next morning with perfect clarity. The chaos of our house, Beth's parents downstairs with the kids and the television loud with cartoons. Beth was in the shower, taking a little longer than usual. A radio on in some room broadcasting an early football game. I stood in the mirror and knotted my tie. It had been my father's actually, and the silk was frayed in places, the design already dated. I did not like my face in the mirror that morning, my nose red from the prior day's sun, a razor burn beneath my jaw, the first sagging signs of a double chin. I sucked in my gut as I buttoned my pants. I needed a new suit probably, but there was no money for new suits. I knotted the tie over and over again, but each time the silk just ended up looking flimsy, too narrow. In the mirror my hairline looked almost cowardly, creeping away from my eyebrows, and I was suddenly nervous about meeting Chloe. Beth and I had been invited to brunch at Lee's place before driving out to Kip's hobby farm. Lee had picked her up from the airport in Minneapolis early that morning. We were supposed to collect Ronny en route.

Beth changed her ensemble five times that morning, switching out her shoes, her necklaces, her earrings. I understood. Had I owned more than one suit, I would have done the same thing. As it was, I just sat in a battered old chair in our bedroom and watched her. She was beautiful to me. I could see that she had shaved her legs, supple and taut above the easy grip of her heels. She mussed her hair and pursed her lips at the mirror.

"What do you think?" she said finally, turning to me.

I stood and went to her, understanding right then that we were already growing older, that we would grow old together.

"I think you're beautiful," I said. I kissed her.

"Hey—watch the lipstick," she said, swatting me away playfully before pulling me in close again. She set her chin on my shoulder and we slow danced that way, there in our bedroom, the worn carpeting beneath our best scuffed shoes. "I love you," she said, "even if you're not a rock star."

"I love you," I said, "even though you're not a movie star."

We kissed again and held hands as we walked downstairs, our

garments good enough. The kids came up to us, hugged us good-bye. Beth's father shook my hand, and I noticed for the first time in that instant that the skin of his left ring finger had begun to overcome his wedding band. The ring had become part of him, in the way that a fence-tree gradually absorbs the barbed wire wrapped around its bark. I felt happier then—less, I don't know, anxious. I knew that we would make it together, Beth and I, no mattered what happened to the farm or anything else.

The town was abuzz. The local B&Bs and motels were full, the VFW and the other scattered townie bars jumping. Even the Coffee Cup Café was busy, with patrons banging the screened door shut as they walked out of the restaurant carrying Styrofoam cups of coffee. Main Street was bustling with strange vehicles adorned with out-of-state plates. Eddy had heard the guest list totaled over five hundred. An entire truck full of kegs had been driven up from Milwaukee, with a separate truck carrying hard booze. The caterers were not local; they'd come all the way from Minneapolis. I suppose Kip didn't want to take any chances; only the best would do.

The day was a golden kind of gray, the gauze of clouds in the sky occasionally obscuring the bright coin of the sun. It was a good day for a jacket.

Ronny sat on the curb out in front of his apartment, his hair wet and combed back. A scrap of red tissue clung to his chin from where he'd cut himself shaving. He waved happily at us as we approached, unself-conscious in a tight polyester suit, a white shirt, and bolo tie. His old cowboy boots had clearly been shined up with polish.

"Looking good, Ronny Taylor!" Beth said, sliding over toward me on the bench seat of our pickup truck while Ronny took her spot near the window. She kissed his cheek, and he blushed as she proceeded to rub the lipstick off his newly smooth skin.

"Thanks, Beth," he said, shyly.

We listened to the radio the whole way there: local sports scores, the weather, a story about a cougar sighting not far from town. The truck hugged the back roads smoothly and we rode toward Lee's place silently, nervously, happily. Chloe was a major actress, well known and loved. Between film projects she worked on Broadway. She had won a Golden Globe for playing a poet whose name eluded us all.

They were out on Lee's front porch as we bounced down his driveway toward them, their shoes off, feet propped up on the railing and they waved to us cheerfully as soon as we came into view. Even at fifty yards, we could see the steam rising off their coffee mugs and the smoke meandering off of what I assumed to be two smoldering joints in Lee's favorite ashtray. There was a big herd of deer out in Lee's pasture and he pointed to them as we approached the schoolhouse.

"They've been there all morning!" Chloe cried out, smiling at us, her hand shading her eyes from a patch of sunlight that careened through a hole in the clouds.

"Sweet," Ronnie said cheerfully. "I loves me some venison." Beth punched him gently in the ribs and we laughed together as the truck came to a stop before the schoolhouse.

Other than Lee, I'd never met anyone famous before, and like I said, even though we *knew* he was famous, we didn't really think about it that way. But meeting Chloe . . . it blew my mind. Her hair smelled of vanilla and I remember the feel of her skeleton, her fine bones in my hands as she embraced me. Her strawberry blond hair was lustrous and thick and her eyes were wide open and slightly pink from the weed. She held my biceps loosely in her hands and studied my face, appreciatively I hoped, until I broke my gaze and looked down at my old shoes.

"Lee says you're his best friend," she said, still holding onto me. "It is an honor to meet you, Hank."

"I thought *I* was your best friend," Ronny protested, genuine hurt in his eyes.

Lee touched him. "You are, Ronny. Just don't tell Hank."

"I love your movies," I said to Chloe. "You're my favorite Juliet."

She blushed politely, flexing the arch of one of her beautiful feet. Her sole, I could see, was dirty, and I wanted very much to hold her feet in my hands and massage them.

Beth hit me gently in the arm and broke my reverie. "I thought *I* was your favorite Juliet," she said. We all laughed and then Beth and Chloe hugged each other. Lee went into the house and came back out with an orange plastic prescription cylinder. Inside were two more joints. He passed them to me and Beth.

"We forgot to make brunch. So this'll have to do. You want a Coke?" he said to Ronny, but Ronny was just staring at Chloe, couldn't take his eyes off her, couldn't stop smiling.

It was a good morning. We sat together on the porch into the early afternoon, slouched out in our best clothing, our shoes kicked off. We watched the deer and smoked dope and the day slowly warmed, the sun burning the wispy clouds away. Chloe asked us about our kids, and from my wallet and from Beth's purse we produced several dog-eared, well-faded photographs, the kids all much younger in the photos than they were by now.

"Sorry," we apologized, "we need to get some new ones. They're so much bigger." Almost all my friends owned fancy new cell phones, but Beth and I didn't. We got by on our old flip phones, whose cameras were too pixelated to take a decent picture.

Eleanore and Alex knew enough to tease us about them, calling them "antiques." But sitting there, pointing at those old photos, telling Chloe how old Alex was in that photograph, or how this was a photograph of our last family trip up to the harbor in Duluth, I was filled with pride and a sense of our own mortality, as if we were somehow older than Lee and Chloe in that moment, though it was of course untrue. But our lives were unfathomably different.

"They're the best kids," Lee said. "I love those kids. So good."

"They love *him*," Beth said, smiling at Lee. And in that pause in the conversation I understood that what Beth must have wanted to say aloud was: *He would make a fantastic father. He should be a father.*

Ronny had gone into the house for more ice cubes and came out saying, "It's one o'clock, you know. . . . Weren't we supposed to be there at one-thirty?"

It was a startlingly clear moment for Ronny, and we stared at him for a beat as we processed his question. Then, without a word, Beth and Chloe jumped up and slipped into their heels. We all ran toward the truck, scattering the deer out in the fields. We were going to be late for the wedding, and we were stoned.

Beth drove with Chloe riding shotgun while Ronny, Lee, and I sat in the bed of the truck, clutching onto whatever we could. We smiled at one another, our hair wild in the wind, the air tearing fresh and good into our nostrils. We pounded the ancient metal of the racing pickup truck with the palms of our hands, and we were happy and alive and on our way to a wedding. I suppose in that moment, we'd forgotten whose wedding it was we were racing toward.

"*Go! Go! Go!*" we yelled over the rushing air. Ronny was thrilled with the speed of the vehicle and giggled uncontrollably. Chloe and Beth glanced at each other and began laughing too. The barn was still forty-five minutes away; then again, the truck was doing eighty.

Lee and I settled back against the front of the truck's box, our backs against the window of the cab, and we watched the world behind us retreat away: the colors of autumn punctuating the unchanging green of the balsams and white pines, the almost perfectly reliable yellow and white paint of the road lines spooling out for miles beneath us. Farms with red and white barns. Cows and horses and sheep, and every now and again a slowgoing Amish buggy. Once, Ronny stood up in the bed of the truck and Lee and I reached for his belt loops, reached to pull him back down, but up he stood, against that great rush of wind, his arms out for a while in an iron cross, his eyes closed, hair blowing. And sitting there, watching him with a mixture of concern and admiration, you could still see the old Ronny—all that balance and strength and wild energy.

We arrived only a few moments late, the fields around the barn jammed with vehicles and wedding-goers still making their way clumsily toward the barn in high heels and probably rented, too-tight patent leather shoes. Old people clutched onto their younger kin. The horses looked on, chewing. We leapt out of the truck, all of us out of breath and smiling. Chloe and Beth looked youthful and resplendent, Chloe's dress a marvel of the finest materials and delicately sequined. She whisked hair from her eyes and deftly brushed some makeup over her face. She and Beth shared a tube of lipstick, touching up each other's lips with their little fingers because there was no mirror and no time for a mirror. Lee matted down his hair with a palm full of spit. I did the same and adjusted my tie. Ronny just grinned away happily. And then we joined the throng, glad to be entering all together. Then, suddenly Lee stopped. His face had gone white.

We stopped too, and looked at him.

"Shit," he said, in something like disbelief. "Shit, shit, shit. *Fuck.*"

"Your guitar," I said. He nodded his head and then shook it.

"Guess you'll just have to go a cappella," Chloe said cheerfully, taking his elbow. "No big deal, right?"

I nudged Lee. "It's all right, buddy," I said. "Give Kipper something to sweat about."

We headed toward the barn again, outside of which we noticed a mob of what looked like photographers intermingled with the wedding attendees. Suddenly they seemed to be moving toward us, holding their cameras above their heads as they picked up speed, some of them even running now.

"He couldn't have *hired* all of those people," Beth said as we walked toward them.

It was Chloe who understood first. "It's okay," she said. "Seriously, it's okay. I think I even recognize some of these jokers. Maybe we can talk to them, you know? Give them what they want, real quicklike. Get it over with, right?" Then she leaned into Lee's arm and we could see that his face had grown red, that he was furious. Chloe placed her delicate hands on his jaw, and it seemed that she was trying to make him look at her, that she was trying to calm him.

And then the paparazzi were upon them, nearly knocking Ronny down as they surged right past him like a stampede. They shouted Chloe's name, shouted Lee's name, his stage name. They instructed Chloe and "Corvus" to pose, to hold each other. They moved in close to the couple. One of them even reached out to adjust the fringe of Chloe's dress. Lee kicked at the man, but

Chloe held his hand tightly, and we watched as her face changed, hardened even, I couldn't help thinking. Her lips now became bulbous, her eyes cool and inviting as river stones. She thrust a leg forward, heels braced confidently in the mud. She knew what she looked like.

Lee pulled roughly away from her and stalked toward the barn. I went with him, Ronny behind us. Lee found Kip at the door of the barn, where he was busy greeting guests. He was just checking his watch when Lee grabbed him by the shoulder and pushed him away from the crowd, around a corner. He took Kip by the black of his necktie and brought their faces close together.

"What the fuck, man?" he said. "What the *fuck*?"

Kip shrugged, smiled, removed Lee's hand from his tie and smoothed it back. "Hey, all publicity's good publicity, right?" he said. "Look, you're famous. Your girlfriend's famous. I don't know, I thought you'd be used to this kind of thing." He smirked. "Doesn't seem so bad to me. Besides," he said with obvious satisfaction, "it was you that invited her."

"Not here, man!" Lee growled. "Not here. Never *here*! This is my home, all right? This is my *home*." He was fuming, close to tears. He paced the area in front of Kip, fists clenched up white.

"One more thing," Lee said, his voice suddenly controlled again. He was in Kip's face again, the veins on his forehead pulsing. I had never seen him so angry. Ronny put a hand on his shoulder and pulled him gently away. "I'll sing one song. And then we are *done*. You hear? Forever. Don't ever call me again. You understand?"

"It's okay," Ronny said. "It's okay, buddy."

We went into the barn then, found our seats. The space was

full of people: some in the hayloft, most on the vast refinished wooden-planked floor, with some of the spillover even down in the stone basement, where the skeletons of ancient stanchions were still bolted into the floor. Still more people mingled and wandered outside, peering in through the doors. Votive candles hung down from the rafters, and gauzy fabric from the door frames.

Light filtered inside through chinks in the barn's siding as a booming sound system now broadcast Pachelbel's Canon in D Major, and from the back of the barn Kip's bride walked forward in her white dress, one arm hooked tight inside her father's right elbow. She was luminous. Her father's wrinkled cheeks were wet with tears. They moved slowly forward through the attendees, toward Kip and the pastor, and as I watched their approach I wondered whether the slow pace of a wedding march was for the benefit of a bride on her most beautiful day, or for the aging father preparing to give her away. Flashbulbs popped, some still trained upon Lee and Chloe.

Midway through the ceremony, the pastor motioned to Lee, who rose quietly from his chair and walked to the front of the barn. I watched him shake Kip's hand firmly and then kiss the bride on her cheek, before whispering something in her ear that made her smile in a way I'd never seen before. You'd never have known he was furious with Kip. He was that graceful. Then he went to the microphone. All of the cameras were upon him. He straightened his wrinkled suit and smoothed his hair.

"I forgot my guitar," he said sheepishly.

The grateful crowd laughed and it was good, some of the ceremony's tension released and several in attendance even clapped and whistled. Lee shrugged, raised his empty hands in the air and made a face as if to say, *What the hell.*

"So, listen," he said, "I thought we'd just sing together. A sing-along. I thought maybe we could hold hands, you know, and sing together. I think most of you know the words to this one, but if you don't, I do. I'll lead you. So don't be afraid, okay? Don't *ever* be afraid to sing."

I gripped Beth's hand on one side and Ronny's hand on the other. We looked up the aisle at our friend as he began singing. We sang with him. We all knew the words.

Wise men say only fools rush in,
but I can't help falling in love with you.

We were a town then, all together, a band of friends and strangers all clad in our Sunday best, and we were touching, holding hands, and singing, our voices shooting straight up into the rafters and moving the flames of the candles, our voices enough to reverberate off the rusted tin roof and echoing out into the fields where the horses must have been lifting their heavy heads and pricking up their tall ears to wonder what that new strange sound was. I felt Ronny's hand in mine, his well-calloused skin, and I squeezed it and I felt sad for him, and at the same time happy to be beside him, happy that he was there. Just then I remembered holding his hand in the hospital all those years before, and I felt my throat thicken. And I felt my wife's soft hand too, and touched with my thumb her veins and her nails, and inside my heart was a great well of love that I knew was not just overflowing but infinite. Before us stood our friend, his voice intermingling with ours, and I winked at him and he winked back at me.

The song ended, but I did not let go of the hands of those two people I loved, and throughout the barn I could tell others had done likewise, clinging to their friends and family and the travelers who had come to witness this wedding inside a barn. Lee stepped away from the microphone, nodded once at Kip, and then kissed Felicia once more and sat down. Chloe kissed him softly on the temple and they looked to be in love.

Kip turned to his new wife and kissed her, and we all stood and applauded. Bags of rice were quickly circulated as the newlyweds strode down the center aisle and out of the barn, and we all threw our white confetti at them, rice clinging to the bride's veil, her hair, her well-tanned cleavage. We went outside then, into the fresh air, and there was a reception line. I noticed that Chloe and Lee had ducked away to an outside corner of the barn, near the foundation of an old stone silo, where they stood smoking cigarettes and looking elegant almost despite themselves. Beth and I greeted Kip and Felicia, who could not have been more gracious on this day that was hers.

Dinner was served on vast, long tables that had been erected out in a nearby field. We drank wine and chatted, ate pheasant and gnocchi and greens and fresh, warm bread. There were toasts, silverware chiming against glasses; at several points the bride and groom stood and kissed deeply, eliciting yet more applause and catcalls. Everyone was happy. Even Lee seemed pleased, and Ronny high-fived him repeatedly, singing: "Dar-ling so it goes, some things are meant to be-ee-ee!"

The gloaming had set in as we leaned back in our folding chairs, overfull and sipping more wine than we needed. Waiters cleared the dirty plates and set out cups and saucers for coffee. Their arms moved swiftly over our shoulders as they decorated the tables with fresh plates of cake, new spoons, little pitchers of cream, small bowls of sugar. There was cake frosting smeared across Ronny's face. Beth removed the icing with a fingernail and licked it off playfully. Lee produced a pack of cigarettes and shook some loose. He lighted three cigarettes in his mouth, then passed one to Chloe, and one to Beth. My wife took the cigarette, smiling, and inhaled deeply. She held the smoke for a long time in her lungs and then breathed out, a jet of gray smoke departing her lips. I leaned back and considered her.

"You don't smoke cigarettes," I said, my brow wrinkled more than I might have liked.

She shrugged and smiled at Chloe. "It's a good night for a cigarette." They touched wineglasses and laughed. Ronny and I accepted cigarettes, too, and we all smoked, watching the stars poke through the darkening blue wool of night.

A strange whooping sound came over the trees and fields then, at first almost imperceptible, but then more persistent. *Whoop-whoop-whoop-whoop-whoop.* We turned in our chairs to scan the fields. The horses were restless, whinnying, their teeth huge and white in the gathering dark. Suddenly, a helicopter came into view over the treetops, bending great boughs and upsetting every leaf, it seemed, within a mile of us. The grasses of the fields danced madly. The helicopter had a spotlight and it scanned the partygoers, many of whom had now raised their middle fingers. Finally, the light settled on Lee and Chloe. We saw a man lean out of the chopper with a camera. Lee tossed his cloth napkin onto the table and strode off toward the barn.

"I'm sorry, you guys," Chloe said loudly and to everyone, "I'm just so *sorry*." And we saw that she meant it.

The helicopter hovered over our table for some time and the tablecloth snapped like a sail where it was not weighted down by silverware or ceramic plates, the fabric flapping loose over our knees. Ronny rose from his chair now and stood up on the table, his cowboy boots sharp and gleaming on the white cloth. He was wearing a belt buckle from a rodeo he'd won in Missoula.

"LEAVE MY FRIEND ALONE!" Ronny screamed. "LEAVE HIM THE FUCK ALONE!" He was crying. We pulled him down.

The helicopter hovered another few moments before finally circling the barn once and absconding. Evening was now draped dark over the barn, little candles burning everywhere and in places, lanterns too. Some had been blown out by the aircraft, and the wedding-goers went around with lighters and matches, gamely relighting as many wicks as they could. We heard Sinatra playing from the barn and took our drinks in with us. Ronny was still upset.

We found them in the basement, sitting in a corner, Chloe on Lee's lap, running her fingers through his thinning hair. He looked older, just then. I handed Lee a brown bottle of beer, and he took it from me, tipped his head back, and sipped. But he would not look at us. We stood there awhile, in silence, our arms crossed.

"It's not your fault," Beth said to him finally. "We know you didn't want this."

"I don't want this," he said vaguely. A moment passed as we waited for him to finish. Then, "Maybe I need some air," he finally said.

We followed him outside, into the pasture, and Chloe and Beth removed their heels as we continued. I loosened my tie. We went to the horses, their eyeballs still big and wild. Ronny was talking to them up ahead of us, his voice low and soothing. And then he was singing to them, his voice like a ragged lullaby, and we stopped to watch him. He sang: "Shall I stay, would it be a sin, if I can't help, falling in love with you. . . ."

He touched the horse in front of him then, his gnarled rodeo hands soft on the velvet of the horse's muzzle, the muscles of its great breast. His mouth was near the horse's ear, he was singing to it. We sat in the grass, watching him, listening to his sweet warble.

Lee moved to New York not long after the wedding, and we saw him less and less. The packages still came, and sometimes letters, but the time between his visits became greater and greater. Grass began to sprout in his driveway. In time our children stopped asking about him. But we still listened to his albums, and my daughter even began to play the guitar. She had taped a photo from *Rolling Stone* to the wall near her bed. In the photo, Lee is on stage somewhere in the world, a spotlight shining brightly on his sweaty face, his eyes closed in concentration, his mouth nearly wrapped sideways around the microphone. In his arms, the very guitar he had once forgotten to bring to a wedding.

It was hardest for Ronny, but we tried our best to fill the void Lee had left. I drove Ronny to his doctor appointments and to the grocery store. We cooked for him, and there were nights that he watched our children. He was very tender with them. They sat in his lap and on the arms of chairs as he read Dr. Seuss to them. Frequently they corrected his pronunciation. Sometimes they read books to him.

One Saturday afternoon I walked the long walk down our gravel driveway to the mailbox. Spring had come, and the ditches were full of meltwater, the fields and trees timidly green. I had just finished changing the oil on one of the older tractors. Plowing and planting would begin soon. I reached into the mailbox and there was a thick envelope from Lee's address in New York

City. The paper was expensive and our address and names had been written in calligraphy. I opened it.

He was getting married to Chloe. Inside were four airplane tickets and a hand-tooled note:

> *Henry, I miss you like hell. Come out and see us.*
> *Make sure Ronny gets his invitation.*
> *And tell him to bring a date.*
> *Love, your best friend, Lee*

THE DAY AFTER KIP'S WEDDING they came down the driveway like tourists on safari, big cameras aimed out the windows of rented Jeeps, gawking behind expensive sunglasses. The first one actually got up to my house before I noticed, before I grabbed a shotgun and came out onto the porch in my boxers. They didn't know that the gun was unloaded, that I'd run out of shells months earlier. It's a beautiful gun, my Ithaca. A pump-action with ornate scrolling and nice bluing to the steel. I bought it as a gift to myself after *Shotgun Lovesongs* first went platinum. It seemed fitting enough.

"Get the *hell* out of here!" I screamed, pumping nothing into the chamber. "Go on! Go before I call the police!" In truth, I knew it would take the police a half-hour or more to get to my place—part of the beauty of the Ithaca. They retreated, sending gravel flying into the air and kicking up a plume of dust. I watched their heads bounce against the ceiling of the Jeep as they raced back up the driveway to the road. Two more trespassers came down the road that morning until finally I'd had enough and towed Ronny's taxidermied bull to the mouth of the driveway, where I left it with a cardboard sign draped around its neck that read: NO TRESPASSERS! THIS MEANS YOU!

Chloe found it all somewhat amusing, in the way that I now know she finds so much in life amusing. Nothing ever seemed to upset her. Those weeks at my house, that time after Kip's wedding, they were some of the happier days of my life. Chloe, walking barefoot around the house in one of my old flannel shirts. Or the two of us, building a fire beside the creek at night so that after we finished skinny-dipping, we could warm ourselves against the autumn chill. Sometimes we'd go to Henry and Beth's house and cook for them in their kitchen, and standing at the stove I'd watch Chloe on the floor, playing checkers or jacks with the kids. But most of the time I wanted her to myself. Wanted to show her my world, make her fall in love with Wisconsin.

Cell phone reception is spotty at my house, so I've always insisted on a house phone, which is mounted to the kitchen wall. My Internet connection is also hit-or-miss, oftentimes only a minor upgrade over dial-up. Chloe would insist that we drive or walk to the tallest nearby hill, where we'd stay for an hour or so while she checked her email or talked to her agent back in New York and I'd sit beside her, combing her hair with my fingers or warming one of her hands in my own.

Some nights we would get bored and drive to the VFW and sit at the bar and shake dice in an old leather cup or just watch a football game on the television, and on those evenings it was not uncommon for a young woman or a middle-aged man to tap on Chloe's shoulder with a single finger and then produce a magazine for her to sign or even just a cardboard coaster from the bar. But no one ever asked for my autograph anymore and that was exactly the way I wanted it to be. What was more surprising were the evenings when no one said a word to us, when the bar was dead, when we sat on our stools with perhaps one or two geezers and simply played cribbage or euchre and drank Manhattans or brandy old-fashioneds, and in those times I felt that maybe we could actually stay in Little Wing, that Chloe might come to love Wisconsin.

One night we were driving back to my house, and as she sat close to me on the bench seat and we held hands, I said, "Do you think . . . do you think you could ever see yourself living here, with me?"

She snuggled closer against me, into my right shoulder. I could smell brandy on her breath and I knew that she was closing her eyes to fall asleep.

"Chloe?"

"It's so quiet here."

"But isn't it nice? No one bothers us, we're just like normal people. We have normal friends here . . ."

"Oh, Lee," she said. "Let's be quiet now, can we?"

"No, come on. We should talk about this." Behind everything I was thinking, *I want to marry you.*

"I don't know, baby. I haven't wanted to be normal in a long time. I like my life. I like New York. Everything is in New York. Everybody wants to be in New York."

I couldn't say, *I don't want to be in New York.*

"Besides," she yawned, "think about it: we're busy people. You tour. I'm on location. New York just makes sense. It's easy to fly out of. The media is all there. Projects are there. People like you and me, Lee, we don't live in small towns." She kissed the palm of my hand. "You know?"

When I had nowhere else to go, I came back here. When I had nothing, I came back here. I came back here and made something out of nothing. I could live here on next to nothing; there is nothing to spend money on, no one to impress. No one here cares about anything other than your work ethic and your kindness and your *competence*. I came back here and I found my voice, like something that had fallen out of my pocket, like a souvenir long forgotten. And every time I come back here I am surrounded by people who love me, who care for me, who protect me like a tent of warmth. *Here*, I can hear things, the world throbs differently, silence thrums like a chord strummed eons ago, music in the aspen trees and in the firs and burr oaks and even in the fields of drying corn.

How do you explain that to someone? How do you explain that to someone you love? What if they don't understand?

THIRTEEN, FOURTEEN YEARS AGO, we used to go up there with a backpack full of pilfered beer, maybe a joint or two or three. I never smoked, but they did—Lee and Henry and Ronny. We were always up there, especially during summer, when there was nothing else to do. The feed mill was closed then, derelict, and it always seemed to be on the brink of being razed, but then someone would put up a big stink, hold a town meeting, maybe even throw a fundraiser—a pig roast, a bake sale, raffle off a new Ford pickup—and the mill's sentence would be stayed. The taxes would get paid and there would be rumors of some out-of-town messiah come to save the day, some corporation come to breathe new life into those old beams and bricks and stones. Other buildings, beautiful buildings, were demolished: the old depot, the original post office, even an old opera house; a four-story hotel that in later years became first a flophouse for migrant workers, bikers, Vietnam vets, then later, something like a nursing home. The building so old it lacked an elevator shaft. The most feeble of the building's occupants were always lodged on that first floor. On soft spring evenings, crisp autumn afternoons, many of them sitting on the elevated front porch, an architectural remnant of the

American Old West, the frontier. They rolled wheelchairs out there or sat on the porch swings, rocking, watching the sporadic traffic on Main Street. On the Fourth of July, those geezers clutched small American flags in their trembling hands, waved them at the morning parade, and in the weeks and months that followed, still waved them at pedestrians, at funeral processions, the after-church crowd rushing home for Sunday football, until the red, white, and blue fabric faded and frayed at the edges.

My grandpa lived there for two years before he died. We used to visit him on Friday evenings in the old hotel's tall-ceilinged dining room. The room was dimly lit, and what light did enter the space seemed to pass mostly through ancient, warped windows, the glass thicker at the bottom of the pane than at the top. I imagined another time when candles and kerosene threw a different kind of golden light onto linen tabletops. We ate poached cod, mashed potatoes, peas, dinner rolls. My grandpa picked fish bones from his dry mouth and set them on the rim of his plate. It always took him a long time to remove the bones from his mouth, as if he had swallowed a hook himself. There was a bar in there too and rumors that once upon a time, *way way back*, the hotel had been a brothel. Sometimes you would see an old man or an old woman at the bar, peering around for a bartender, saying in a sad, confused voice, "All I want is a taste, just a little taste." But the bar had been bereft of bottles since the flophouse evolved into a nursing home.

The old hotel finally came down in 1988, when I was nine years old. By then, Grandpa was gone, buried in the cemetery just outside of town along the Little Wing River where it is dammed up, where the water grows green with algae in the summertime and thick with ice in winter. We call that stretch of the river Lake Wing, and in summertime occasionally we'd go out there on water skis, though the "lake" was hardly more than a pond, and our circuits were confined to tight nauseating circles behind a small-ish outboard motor better used behind a sixteen-foot aluminum fishing boat, the water so silty and thick with lily pads and algae you could almost walk on it with a pair of snowshoes.

No demolitions expert was needed. A sweep of the building was made to ensure no senior citizens had holed themselves up in a broom closet or stairwell; then, when the hotel was confirmed to be totally and finally vacant, the biggest excavating machine I'd ever seen rolled right down Main Street, its steel-fanged bucket held at the ready. The volunteer fire department kept a steady stream of water aimed at the hotel as the excavator began gnashing at the old bricks and wood. Families came out for the demolition, laid blankets on the sidewalk, packed picnics. It was a Saturday in October, the air dry and cool. My mother handed us cold fried-chicken sandwiches wrapped in paper toweling. We drank warm apple cider from a thermos, ate potato salad, baby carrots, pickles. Dad was a volunteer firefighter, and that was the first and only time we'd ever see him in action. In his uniform, underneath his fluorescent yellow helmet, he looked so official, so heroic, so brave.

Mom elbowed us gently. "Isn't your father handsome?"

Along the sidewalks, the hotel's former inhabitants looked on, chewing their tongues like jerky, looking defeated, depleted. I don't know where they went after the building came down, though I suspect many ended up in Eau Claire, just north of Little Wing. It made me sad to think of them, most of them likely to be separated into different institutions, like elementary school children whose parents all suddenly decided to take jobs in new cities or neighborhoods, and the kids, shuffled someplace new without a say in the world.

When the old hotel was finally gone there was nothing but a new hole along Main Street, a gap between the pharmacy and hardware store where only a pile of rubble lay. We pushed a red wheelbarrow down Main Street and spent afternoons collecting the leftover bricks, though, at that age, we could only fill the barrow up halfway before it became too much to push. Then we brought the bricks back to my father, who paid us a dime for each one we scrounged. He built an outdoor fireplace with those bricks, a little grotto of fire we congregated around in warmer months, a place where we could toast marshmallows or roast hot dogs.

Sometimes we took girls up to the top of the feed mill, but mostly, it was just us. Just the four of us: Lee, Ronny, Henry, and me. Nights, it was better than any telescope, better than the planetariums we visited with our middle school or high school teachers. Because on top of those old wood and cement grain silos, we found narrow places to lie on our backs and stare at the stars, to drink beer, to talk big, to dream. Our town, Little Wing, down there, not much to see and always shrinking, not even a stoplight blinking against the night, and everyone, all of us, putting it down, talking about leaving, going somewhere, going anywhere but here. The sense that staying in town meant we were failures, meant we were yokels—who the hell knows what we thought back then on those nights.

Henry and I, we preferred mornings. Dawns, sunrises. It's funny—but I suppose he was already becoming a farmer back then, getting up early, helping his dad with the family dairy operation, working on old engines, listening to all the retired or bankrupt farmers after church. And it wasn't many mornings, but there were a handful, when we'd climb up those steel rebar stairs all the way up to the top of those grain silos and wait there, the air cool and blue, our breaths just barely visible. Maybe a thermos of coffee between us, or a stolen bottle of brandy or blackberry schnapps from our parents' liquor cabinets. And there must have been a morning or two when we didn't bring anything, just hugged our knees, blew hot air into our hands, waited for the sun to come, the day to begin warming. At the time I didn't think much of it, but I suppose looking back, it was mostly me who called Henry, mostly me doing the inviting. We didn't talk much on those mornings. Just sat and looked out, as if we were waiting for a ship.

I've never been to the Grand Canyon, to Yosemite or Yellowstone, to any of the places you hear people talking about—spectacular places, I mean. But, even without having been to the Grand Canyon, I imagine a sunrise there has to be something bordering on a religious experience, all that ancient red, orange, and yellow rock lighting up in their striated layers, all those majestic deep purple shadows.

I wish you could see a sunrise from the top of those grain silos, our own prairie skyscraper. I wish you could see how green everything is in the spring, how yellow the corn's tassels even a few months later, how blue the morning shadows are, and creeks winding their own slow paths, the land rolling and rolling on and on, studded here and there with proud red barns, white farmhouses, pale gravel roads. The sun emerging in the east so pink and orange, so big. In the ditches and valleys, fog collecting like slow vaporous rivers, waiting to be burned away.

I really can't remember who I was back then, that teenage version of myself, what I was thinking. I guess, like everyone else, I was restless. Maybe I was lonely. Maybe being up there, at the top of those grain silos, maybe I thought I could see something, my future, some spot on the horizon where I'd land, some future version of myself, some girl I hadn't met yet, my future wife. I don't know. But it felt good I guess. Maybe it even felt like something *artistic*, something *thoughtful*, the kind of thing that our old high school art teacher, Mr. Killebrew, would never guess we had in us.

Lee and Ronny preferred sunsets, moonrises. Some west-bound freight train roaring through the night below, never stopping, its cyclopic light to cut the night, its whistle the loudest thing in the world, and high on top of those towers, feeling wobbly-kneed, as if the train might shake the building to the ground. Those two: always high, always singing "Idiot Wind" or "Meet Me in the Morning," hurling their beer bottles out into the night, out at the passing trains, listening for a *crash*, listening for police sirens that never came, the voice of authority telling us to "Get down goddamn it!" But no—the entire town always too mild, too asleep, dozing in front of blue-faced televisions as Johnny Carson charmed everyone into a satisfied snore.

But sunsets. That was how I first understood that Lee was different from us, that he was maybe even destined to be famous. Because in the ten or twenty minutes before the sun was totally extinguished in the west, he always demanded our complete silence. And I don't know why, but we listened, we acquiesced. And we'd sit there, sipping our dads' beer, looking out on that chameleon sky, and we'd listen to Lee. Listen to him hold court.

"You hear that?" he'd say, not so much asking as telling. "You hear that tone, that note? I swear to god, that color over there, that pink color. When that pink color starts to really blush, it's like this note, I can't describe it, this sweet high note. And you hear that, that orange? Not that marmalade orange, but the peach one? You hear that? Oh, man! I can't wait for the blues! The blues and the purples! And then that last long, low black note—that reverberating bass note that says, 'Go on now, good night. Good night, America, good night.'"

I never knew what he was talking about, but I tried. I *tried* to listen, tried to hear that sunset music he was talking about. But I couldn't. I just couldn't hear it. Those guys, they listened to music *all the time.* I'd come over to Henry's parents' house—this is back in elementary school, middle school—and those three would be down in the basement, listening to Henry's dad's old records, anything they could get their hands on. And then Lee joined a record club after seeing an ad in the back of a magazine: *Ten albums for only a penny!* A penny!

Even in elementary school, in middle school, Lee was the first person I knew who owned a Walkman, and he carried it everywhere—out to the playground during recess or walking home from school. He even tried to sneak it into church, and tried to listen to it while we watched all those educational film strips at school, even during lunch. He listened attentively to all the cassettes—and later CDs—that older kids gave him, like contraband. Gangster rap and metal and early grunge. Public Enemy and N.W.A giving way to Anthrax and Metallica and then Nirvana, Stone Temple Pilots, and Soundgarden. He wore nothing but flannel for years and years. Flannel and torn blue jeans, Chuck Taylors covered in cryptic little poems and epitaphs.

Up on top of the feed mill, the sunset almost entirely washed away now by a sea of black and blue. "I didn't hear it," I'd admit to them. "I didn't hear it at all."

They'd laugh at me. Laugh and laugh. And Lee would say, "You're not listening. Look, I know you're *trying* to hear, but you're not listening, man."

A few times he tried to make me listen to this album *Kind of Blue,* but that didn't help at all, because much as I tried, I just couldn't find anything to listen to—there weren't even any words to grab on to, nothing at all, just these spaces of lonely trumpet and mellow piano notes, but so many spaces of *almost nothing at all.*

Felicia used to ask me after we were married, "Why did you want to come back here? What is it? We had everything we ever needed or could have wanted in Chicago. Why come back? What for?"

I don't know that I ever found the right way to answer that, but I suppose it all comes back to those nights and mornings, those guys. Feeling like we were apart from everything we'd ever known and maybe better than the place that made us. And yet, at the same time, in love with it all. In love with being small-town kings, standing up on those bankrupt towers, looking out over our futures, looking for something—maybe happiness, maybe love, maybe fame.

And when I found some of those things along a Gold Coast, along a Miracle Mile, inside a Loop, the only thing I could think to do was to come back home, out of exile, to show those boys—now men—*Look. Look what I did. Look at who I am now. Look at me.*

That's why I came back. Except that now I'm the only one going back up there. I'm the only one climbing to the top of those silos. Looking at sunrises that just make me wish that I was back in bed with Felicia. Or back in Chicago, waiting for the taxis to begin waking the city up.

ATOP THOSE BULLS, I never thought about anything except hanging on. My life was lived in eight-second chunks, and most of the time, a lot shorter than that. I miss it. These days, I don't know what to do and sometimes it feels like no one will let me do anything. Truth is, I don't want to drink because I want to get drunk, but, maybe, if I had a drink, I could *bend* things, you know? Like how the world looks? Or even time? My life now, it stretches out before me like a highway to nowhere. One of those prairie highways where you can be driving eighty, ninety, a hundred miles per hour and the only way you can tell you're flying is the sound of the engine burning and the way the gas needle starts to lean toward that big old *E* quicker and quicker. But there ain't anything to measure yourself or your speed against. No trees, no buildings—if you're lucky, you got a string of telephone wires, but most of the time, nothing.

Most days I wake up and do a hundred pushups just *because*. Because *what the fuck*. Because on the teevee is the same old shit. Old news recycled into new news and all the same old problems all over again and I'm supposed to care, or get worked up. Here's what I've *gleaned*: more and more people, less and less planet, and everything keeps getting hotter and hotter. That about sums it up, far as I'm concerned.

People like to tune the teevee to something they think I'd like, usually a documentary about nature. Or the West. Or horses. Makes me feel like I'm at a nursing home or something, some well-meaning nurse coming into my life telling me what kind of teevee to watch like I can't use a remote control myself. I think they do that because they don't know what to say to me anymore, because they're sad for me, or because they think I'm sad. And most of the time, guess what? I ain't. I ain't sad. I'm just bored stiff. I'm so goddamned bored that watching a documentary about *The Wild Horses of Colorado* gets me to thinking about one thing: if I was a wild horse, I'd bolt right off and just keep on running.

I want to break out of here so bad and I don't even know where I want to go. Maybe Anyplace, I guess. I know they think I can't take care of myself, but I sure as hell can. I'm not a smart man—I know that—but I ain't dumb. And the way things are, it's like I'm in a cage. People forget, I think, that I've ridden more bulls and more horses than I can count, that I've gotten in barfights from here to Boise and all the way down to Baton Rouge, that before my accident, I used to walk into a bar, *any bar*, and go up to a girl and there was a damn good chance I was going to make her my *friend* for the night. Easy as pie.

I am a *man*. I'm a goddamned *person*. And I'm restless as hell.

I've tried running away. I try about three times a year. Mostly in the summer. I'll wake up early as I can, pack a bag, buy some food from the gas station, and just start walking west. I suppose I could steal a car, but that's not what I want. I'm not a criminal. I just want to disappear. At least I did before I met Lucy.

This place has some crazy kind of gravity. I know that's a funny word to use, a big-sounding word, but I've thought about it.

It must have some kind of power otherwise Lee wouldn't have never come back—but he did. And Kip and Felicia. Not to even mention all them people who never left to begin with, people like Henry and Beth and Eddy and the Giroux twins. Hell, they didn't make it as far afield as even I did when I was a rodeo. And, you know, it's crazy, but it was on those mornings when I left town, trying to run away, I felt it most. That pull.

Walking on the gravel shoulder of County Y or X, old Highway 93 or Missell Road and enjoying the walk: the red-winged blackbirds and startled deer and the morning fog, and on those mornings I'd walk with sneakers instead of cowboy boots and I liked that, those shoes like two clouds beneath my feet, carrying me along.

One time, about two years ago, I figured I made it about twenty miles out of town. I knew I was getting closer to the Mississippi because the land changed on me, went all rolling, all sandstone draws and deep cool forests, and I didn't make such good time in that country and the towns get fewer and fewer in between and I suppose it was about suppertime and who should pass me but Eddy Moffitt, heading back toward Little Wing. I heard him brake his Ford Taurus and then pull a U-turn and he came back behind me and at first I kept walking but then I stopped and sat down in the gravel and just listened to the insects in the trees and the sound of his engine until Eddy shut off the car, stepped out, and came over to me. He was wearing what he always wears in summertime: a short-sleeve dress shirt, a tie, and khakis.

"Ronny," he said, scratching his head, "you lost?"

"No," I said, spitting.

"Well, what are you doing out here?"

"I don't know," I said, "I just started walking."

He patted his belly. "Hmm. Look, can I maybe buy you a cup of coffee and some dinner? I'm famished and you must be too."

I think he knew what I was up to. Eddy's like that. He's pretty perceptive, sensitive—not all the time, but more than most people. I knew he wouldn't let me be. So without saying anything I dusted off the seat of my pants, picked up my bag, and climbed into his car. What I wanted to do was start punching things—not Eddy—but *goddamn* it, I would have liked to punch out a window or a headlight or some damn thing.

Eddy put his hand on my shoulder. "Come on, let's get something to eat."

We ate at the last diner left in Little Wing, a place called the Coffee Cup, with a rotating carousel of pies and walls stained brown with cigarette smoke and grill smoke and white-and-red checkered tablecloths that stick to your hands and forearms like flypaper. I don't ever eat there if I can help it because the food runs through me like my guts were a sieve. But Eddy opened the door for me and led me toward the back of the restaurant, where a line of five stools sit below a beat-up counter and dishes full of pink and blue and white packets of sweetener and sugar and little plastic cups of cream and glass bottles of ketchup, the grill directly ahead and the owner, Howard, back there, nodding at us as if he were exhausted with work, though we were only two of four customers in the whole place.

"Hey Ronny, hey Eddy," he called, waving at us with his spatula. "Waitress'll be right with you."

We both knew, of course, that by *waitress*, Howard meant his wife, Mary, who I could see perfectly well, standing behind Howard at the far back of the building, blowing cigarette smoke out a tiny little dirty window.

"The Coffee Cup exists," Eddy said, with a funny look on his face, "because of Midwestern guilt and Sunday after-church breakfast. In all my travels, only in the Midwest would someone spend their money in a place they hate simply because they feel bad for the proprietors. Also I suppose, because they know your name."

"And, it don't hurt to be the only spot in town," I added.

Eddy raised an eyebrow at me. "No, it sure don't. It sure don't."

By and by, Mary came around with a pot of burnt-smelling coffee and filled our mugs. Eddy ordered their roast beef with gravy and mashed potatoes.

"Howard!" Mary hollered toward the grill. "Roast beef?" Her voice made me jump. The café was quiet as a Monday morning church.

He shook his head.

"All out," she said. "Dinner rush," she said, eyeballing the ancient pressed-tin ceiling.

"How about the fried walleye?" Eddy asked.

She shook her head.

"Cheeseburger?"

"We can do that," she said, and nodded. "Ronny sweetheart, you want anything?"

I didn't, but I ordered a slice of banana cream pie anyway, because Eddy was paying, and because I like Eddy, and besides, I didn't want to go back to my apartment, even if the restaurant smelled funny. Sometimes, you just want to be with another person, and even though Eddy had lassoed me back to Little Wing I knew it was only because he cared.

Mary moved off, toward the front of the café facing Main Street, where nothing stirred—no traffic, no evening strollers. She sat down at an empty table where a half-finished game of solitaire lay out and gazed through the window for a moment before standing, walking back toward the grill, and tossing our order at Howard, who clipped the paper above the grill and began to fry Eddy's burger. The dining room filled with the smell of greasy meat.

"So," Eddy said, "you just out for a walk today? Long ways from Little Wing." He sipped his coffee, organized the sugar and sweeteners by color, stacked and restacked the little packages of jam and marmalade according to flavor.

I nodded, shrugged my shoulders. "I ain't got a car."

"You know anyone in town would give you a ride if you asked. All you got to do is ask. Hell, I know Henry or Lee, even me or Kipper, we'd drive you down to Chicago if that's where you wanted to go." He spit into a paper napkin and wiped at the counter. Muttered, "Filthy."

I looked at the pinwheels spinning in my coffee where I added creamer after creamer.

"I know."

"You bored, is that it? You want a job?"

I looked up at Eddy. Beyond us, at the grill, Howard was whistling a song I recognized from my childhood, something my grandpa used to whistle while we sat in the back of his car— "Magic Moments"—Perry Como, I think.

"I get it," Eddy continued. "I do. They all treat you with kid gloves. And you, you're bored to death. Right? You want to contribute. Let me think about it. Somebody must need some help. We'll find something."

He patted me on the back just as Howard strode up to us, holding two plates. "Who's got the pie?"

I raised my hand.

Setting our plates down on the counter Howard sighed, "Slow as hell in here tonight."

Outside, night had fallen and I could just hear the sound of the jukebox at the VFW spilling out into the street. Someone was playing Bob Seger. In the days and weeks that followed, I'd see Eddy around town, he'd wave at me from his car, or heading out of church with his family, but he never did call me about any work, and after a while, everything slipped back to the way it was, and I began to want to leave again, to run away from this little old town.

Our children stood on the front stoop with their grandparents, waving us good-bye, and there did not seem to be a trace of sadness on their faces. In fact, they smiled as we pulled away, and before we were even out of sight, they turned to go back inside our house, tugging at my parents' old hands. It is a strange feeling when your children show no signs of missing you, and I must admit that in that moment, I wondered if going to New York City was the right thing, or whether perhaps we would have been more gracious simply sending our regards and a gift.

"He sent us the airline tickets," Henry had argued one night in bed. "What's our excuse? Our social calendar is too full? Besides, who else is going to take Ronny?"

"I don't know," I said, "his date maybe? He's not helpless, Henry."

"Come on," Henry cooed.

I sighed in resignation. And it was true that I had never been to New York City and that I was excited to go. To see Central Park and Broadway and the Empire State Building and all the other places and things that no doubt were invisible to natives of the city. It is odd to think that such a thing as a skyscraper could ever become invisible to someone; I don't know that it ever would for me. I know that sounds naïve, but there are buildings I always notice in town, no matter what. Kip's mill, for example. Or the Lutheran church where Henry and I were married. Or the silo between our farm and town where people spray-paint their most important announcements:

BORN! WILLIAM CHRISTOPHER BURKE 6/1/11
8 LBS 9 OZ

Or:

I LOVE TINA

Or:

CLASS OF 1998 FOREVER!

I look at that silo every day on the off chance that its graffiti might have been refreshed overnight. My world is full of landmarks that I have come to love: an ancient burr oak in the middle of our alfalfa field, a glacial erratic in front of the high school, even the truckstop on the edge of town with its towering pole and oversized American flag. I always know when someone has died just by looking at that flag; I knew immediately, for instance, that the Swenson boy would never come back from Afghanistan.

Kip drove us all the way to the Minneapolis–St. Paul airport in his black Escalade. Henry was up front with him and I sat in the backseat with Ronny and his date, a woman named Lucinda.

"But you can call me Lucy," she had said to me brightly as we shook hands there outside of our house, watching Henry and Kip wedge our luggage into the rear of the gleaming SUV. The

65

bangles circled up and down her arm were too numerous to count.

"Lucy," I repeated, studying her face.

In that Friday morning light, I suppose I would not have known her to be a stripper, had Henry not warned me beforehand. She was certainly attractive, her body working all the right curves and undulations, and I'd be lying if I said that I did not peek for a moment at her unmoving chest and deep cleavage. I knew it was no miracle bra—I had tried many after the kids and nothing, no invention yet devised can defeat the powers of time, gravity, and motherhood. Still, I could see that she was excited for the weekend and I wanted to be excited too. I thought, *It'll be good to have another girl along for the ride.* Always, it seemed, I was the only girl, the only woman, amongst a pack of Henry's bachelor buddies, with the exception of Kip, though his wife, Felicia, seemed to be away almost as much as Lee.

After his wedding, we had all ignored Kip for several months, which is difficult to do in such a small town. We did not return his telephone calls, we did not visit the mill, we did not invite him over for dinners or bonfires. On Main Street we did not pause to make conversation with either him or Felicia; instead, we waved briskly. Winter in Wisconsin is the ideal time to avoid someone because our garments grow ever larger, ever thicker, and we go about the frozen world insulated beneath knit caps and mittens, our feet clad in mukluks or boots. How many times after that wedding did I wave to Kip with a mittened hand, when beneath the crocheted wool only my middle finger waved? If Felicia or Kip had pulled me aside and asked why I hadn't said hello to them at the post office I was well prepared to blame my winter cap, my earmuffs, a highly contagious case of strep throat.

But by mid-March Felicia had had it. She blew up one day in the grocery market: threw a gallon of milk onto the floor and

66

accused us all of being backwater hillbillies. I suppose for someone from the outside it is understandable to mistake loyalty for ignorance. Why wouldn't we want to sell out our best friends for a few pieces of silver? Still, in that moment I did respect her anger. Everyone in our town is so polite. Sometimes a little anger is entertaining, even invigorating. I wasn't in the store the day she lost her temper. But word traveled fast through our little network. Wives starting calling wives who called their husbands who called their friends.

Apparently, Felicia had rushed into the store for a few quick items and somewhere in dairy she had said hello to a face who ignored her. And that was it.

"What I heard," Eddy would report, "is that she played it cool for a while. But then as she was turning to go to the register, she just spiked that gallon of milk down on the floor and went off with a whole wheelbarrow full of f-bombs and other choice words and—this is from Dickie, who was working at the register that day—he said the best part was watching her step right through the slick of milk in her black high heels like it was a springtime puddle or something. He said that before she left, she grabbed a big ole honeycrisp apple off the shelf and walked right out without even paying for it."

Henry is a good man, and forgiving, and so it was one night not long after her breakdown he invited them over for dinner. They knocked on our door sheepishly, impeccably dressed. I remember they wore matching red cashmere scarves, elegantly knotted, and they stood there, waiting to come in and carrying two bottles of wine, the labels of which I knew not to be stocked at the local liquor store.

Our house was a mess that night, I remember. I had been busy all day: buying groceries, volunteering at the library, and driving a great-aunt of mine to her doctor's appointment, and Henry had been sequestered in the pole-building, working on a tractor that would soon roll through our fields tilling the earth. Spring is a nervous time for him, I know. He is eager to get back out into the fields, to make a go of things. So I didn't bother him that afternoon while I prepared and cooked chicken marsala in our cramped and overheated kitchen. I did not hassle him to come in and pick up all the toys and magazines and candy wrappers that decorated our living-room floor. When Kip and Felicia arrived, our house looked like a grenade had just exploded inside the living room. The dining-room table had not yet been set.

"I love your house!" Felicia said graciously, and a little too exuberantly. Though, to her credit, I appreciated the enthusiastic effort.

"Uh, maybe I'll just go find Hank," Kip said, before retreating back out the front door.

I yelled up to the kids to come down and greet Felicia, but my plea was met with stony silence. I could imagine them up there: Eleanore surfing on Henry's computer while Alex leafed through pages of books he could not yet read, or both of them playing in their "fort": a collection of duct-taped-together cardboard boxes that formed a matrix of listing rectangular tunnels.

"Oh," Felicia said, "never mind me. Let me give you a hand with things."

And that is how it came to be that Felicia and I were drunk an hour before dinner was supposed to be served.

I had returned to the chicken and was frantically washing dishes and there she was: one of the bottles already uncorked, a smile on her face, asking, "Where are your glasses?"

I paused with the knowledge that our good stemware was probably dusty in a cupboard I was too short to access without a chair.

"Well, I think . . ."

"All I need is a juice glass," she said. "Or a jelly jar, maybe?"

I leaned against the counter, crossed my arms, and looked at her, with a smile of my own.

"I have to tell you," she said, "I'm ready to tie one on tonight."

"All right, then," I said. "Let's light this candle."

These men, these men who have known one another their entire lives. These men who were all born in the same hospital, delivered by the same obstetrician. These men who grew up together, who ate the same food, sang in the same choirs, dated the same girls, breathed the same air. They move around one another with their own language, their own set of invisible signals, like wild animals. And sometimes, it is enough for them just to be in one another's company, walking through the forest, or staring at a television, or flipping steaks on a grill. I've seen them do it. Entire days spent splitting cords of wood with maybe a dozen words shared between them. Were it not for the smiles permanently etched into their faces, you would think they were bored with each other, or that some unspeakable hatred raged between them. I peered out the window toward the pole-building. I could see Henry's footpaths through the snow, the brown stains in the snow where he dumped coffee out of his mug on the way back to the house. I imagined him out there now, joined by Kip, inspecting some motor, some transmission. Maybe Kip holding a funnel while Henry poured motor oil. Maybe Henry saying, "Kip, can you grab me a three-sixteenth and maybe a quarter." And maybe Kip, eager as ever: "You know, Hank, I got a guy who could probably get you a good deal on a new John Deere." And maybe Hank, ignoring the question, well aware we couldn't afford a new tractor: "You sure you're all right in here with those clothes on? I could get you a pair of work bibs or something?" Then Kip: "No. It's all right. Hey, did you see the Girouxs bought the Everetts' land? Give those two a couple a years and they're going to own everything!" And Henry, focused entirely on the machine before him: "Is that right . . ."

I am not a jealous woman. I know that I'm desirable and intelligent and strong and sexy. So most of the time, I roll my eyes at Henry and his friends. And truth be told, Henry is, as I have said, a good man. He isn't out all hours like the Giroux twins, chasing tail and winking at barmaids. He works too hard for that kind of shenanigans. But early on in our marriage, it seemed that he shared an intimacy with those guys—with Lee, with Ronny, with the Girouxs, even with Eddy or Kip—that was enviable. And I wanted that familiarity, that ability to run together, to move together without ever talking. That kind of stillness.

The bottle of Oregon pinot noir was empty, our glasses full, sloshing as we gestured wildly in the kitchen. Felicia had put a Van Morrison record on the player. She sat perched on a chair, her knees up, her long elegant feet pointed out in either direction.

"I mean," Felicia said, "how can I compete with the history they have? How can I?"

"You're not in competition," I said. "You're part of it all now."

"Come on," Felicia snapped back, "that's bullshit! You've all been giving us the cold shoulder. I'm not an idiot."

It was true, of course, and I could not meet her eyes right then, because I knew there was a good chance they'd be misty. I took a deep sip of wine, choosing my words carefully.

"The thing is . . ." I said calmly, flatly.

I tell my children: when you're caught in a lie, or when you do something wrong, just *stop*. Don't make excuses. Don't keep talking. Don't try to explain yourself. Just own up to what you've done wrong. When you do that, things inevitably work out better. You *look* and *feel* better. More likely than not, you also catch the other person off guard.

"I'm sorry, Felicia," I said. "I'm sorry that these last few months have been pretty rough for you. Henry and I . . . we definitely could have been better friends to you and Kip. And I'm sorry. That's my fault."

"I just don't *understand*. What did we do wrong? Was it the paparazzi? Because, I mean, that was *not* my idea! And can I tell you something, because it's eating me alive and I need to tell someone: Kip spent too much damn money on that fucking mill, and now we're in over our heads. If it wasn't for my job, we'd be sunk. *He* called those magazines and tabloids because they paid him some kind of finder's fee, which he dumped back into the mill," she said. "The whole thing: moving here, the mill, the big wedding, that fucking Cadillac monstrosity out there—all of it's a big goddamned mess!"

I heard the back door open, and the scuff of size-twelve Red Wing boot treads on the rug.

"They're back," I whispered.

"Let him hear me," Felicia brayed, "what the shit." She took a sip of wine, then nearly spit it out for the giggle suddenly overtaking her. "What bitches we are, huh?" she said. I loved her impishness right then, the fact that her lipstick was no longer perfect, that the kohl outlining her big brown eyes was now smeared.

"Hey Beth," Henry said. "Uh, can I give you a hand with dinner?"

There is nothing low rent or undignified about the word *pasta*. It's a noble word, a noble food. On television, I see celebrity chefs churning out their own freshly made pasta, talking about the food culture of Italy, and how pasta is this soothing culinary balm that nurtures and restores the Italian people. These chefs dress up their pasta in a million different ways: with fresh herbs, with fresh seafood, with garden-grown tomatoes. It's all so wholesome, so easy, so elemental and picturesque.

And yet, when I tell another mother at a PTA meeting, or a church function, that I was tired the night before and the only meal I could prepare for my children was macaroni and cheese, I can see the disappointment and judgment registering on their faces. Never mind that macaroni *is* pasta.

The kids had finally emerged from their rooms, rubbing their bellies like hungry refugees and opening the refrigerator to stare blankly, helplessly into its milky light.

"Mom," they whined, "we're starving."

It was by now half past eight, and their mother was on her way to Drunktown.

"Mac and cheese?" I asked.

They nodded enthusiastically.

"Do me a favor then, and set the table for us, huh?" I asked. "And go find Kip and Felicia. Introduce yourselves." They went off toward the china cabinet. It is a wonder how *trainable* children can be. It doesn't matter that they ignore fifty percent of the requests I make of them. What matters, what thrills me, are those moments when I watch them dutifully arranging plates and silverware on the dining-room table like two well-mannered little domestics.

I set a pot of water on the stove, sprinkled a handful of salt over it, and cranked the heat.

Just then I felt Henry slip his cold, dry hand around my waist and he whispered into my ear, "Everything okay?" I peered over his shoulder to the dining room, where Kip and Felicia stood beside the record player, and I could see they were quietly arguing. Her finger was pointing into his stomach like a revolver. I thought, *These are real people. Look at them: they're arguing right here in our house, just like real people do.*

"Your hands are cold," I said, shivering. "I love you. But get those mitts off me."

I kissed Henry on his chin, his whiskers cool and sharp. He smelled of fresh air and diesel and old hay.

"Besides, you probably oughta go rescue Kip," I said. "Why don't you two go into town and grab us some beer and wine. I might have dinner ready by ten."

"We'll have to rush," Henry said. "The liquor store closes at nine."

"Then rush," I said.

I watched Henry walk toward Kip and Felicia, and then the two men were gone, out the front door, the dull roar of the truck's engine against the winter night, then the sound of snow tires crunching down the snowy driveway, and for a moment, their headlights illuminating our family-room window and the couch where the kids sat, watching television.

"Well," Felicia said, "we still have another bottle of wine to drink, don't we?"

In bed that night, weary and wine drunk, I listened to Henry's breathing slow into sleep. I was tired, but wired too, that strange fatigue that comes after the exhilaration of hosting a dinner—the blend of caffeine and alcohol coursing through my bloodstream. Lee calls this "a sideways buzz," when you can't tell if you're floating up or drifting down. I tapped Henry on the shoulder to awaken him.

"Kip's losing his ass on the mill," I said at last, my shoulders cold where they peeked out from underneath the covers. I rubbed my feet against Henry's.

"What?" he said, rubbing his eyes.

"Felicia said that Kip's losing his ass on the mill. That they'd be in deep trouble without her job."

"Jesus," Henry murmured. "Yeah. He did seem a little distracted tonight."

"They're not so bad, you know," I said. "Those two. I feel bad. I feel bad we haven't had them over before."

"Well, I'm still pissed about that paparazzi bullshit. Bush league, if you ask me."

I decided not to tell Henry about the finder's fees. I wanted things to heal, I wanted the town to start growing again, and the truth was, as much as Lee had made us feel good about who we were and where we were from, we needed people like Kip— people with a different kind of vision. It was thrilling to lie there in bed and imagine some future version of our town where I could visit a boutique and buy a dress that didn't look like a shower curtain, a dress I might wear in Minneapolis maybe, should Henry ever surprise me with a night out on the town.

"Well," Henry said, "it's a tough time for a lot of people. Kip can be a real asshole, but I don't wish anything bad for them. He's still one of us." Then, "We're still friends."

What Henry neglected to say then, and what of course I knew too, was that times were tough for *us*. I knew Henry thought about picking up side jobs. I'd even thought about getting a job at the IGA or the hardware store downtown; there were jobs in Eau Claire, too, though I loathed the idea of having a commute.

I kept thinking about that night, as we drove toward the terminal, airplanes lined up in the heavens to land on runways I could not yet see. The traffic surprised me, as it always does. So many different cars, and taxis. When we were kids, there was a single taxi in our town. It was actually a station wagon, with an orange light on top, like those used by rural mail route carriers, or land surveyors. The taxi was driven by an older woman, Miss Puckett, who always seemed surprisingly busy, given that hardly fifteen hundred people live in our town. She made her living shuttling the elderly to their medical appointments, drunks home from the VFW. In winter, her services were in greater demand from those senior citizens fearful of sidewalk ice and broken hips. She took people to the airport too, as Kip was doing for us now, and I suppose if she were still in town, we would have paid her to drive us. I remember her great fleshy arms and the angle at which she sat in the driver's seat, almost in full recline, her dull, reddish hair always sweaty looking, and a pair of outdated glasses on her big, bulbous nose. She was a sweet lady.

One of my friends from those school days, Heather Bryce, had always taken the taxi home from school in the afternoon. She was a latchkey kid, and her parents must have contracted with Miss Puckett to ferry her home after school each day. There were days I went to Heather's house after school, and how excited I would be, climbing into the backseat with Heather, our backpacks full of books and folders, and how difficult it was to swing those long, heavy station wagon doors shut. In the far back of the automobile was a series of jumper seats, and sometimes we would crawl back there and watch the road unfurl behind us as Miss Puckett listened to the Grateful Dead on dozens of cassette tapes, which I later realized were bootlegged. From the rearview mirror hung a purple dancing bear and her cab always smelled of incense. The passenger seat beside her strewn with empty Fritos bags. It took me years to connect all the dots.

I don't remember Miss Puckett ever dying, but it seems strange to imagine her in another town or city, where she would have been required to purchase an official medallion and meter. We didn't notice her absence right away, because by the time she had disappeared, I had my own driver's license and so did all my friends, and those were the nights and weekends of driving through the countryside with a cooler full of Bartles & Jaymes, or a bottle of SoCo and a twelve pack of Coca-Cola.

We were stopped in traffic. I haven't been to too many big cities— just Minneapolis, St. Paul, Milwaukee, Chicago, and Denver. But one thing about Minnesota traffic is that no one honks. It can be eerie, at times, sitting in traffic like that in perfect quiet, like the whole world has been muted, or the pall that fills a car as you approach a terrible highway accident. I was happy for the quiet that morning, happy to be reminded of Miss Puckett, because in all other ways, I was not really looking forward to Lee's wedding, and that filled me with a low-grade sadness. Beside me, Ronny and Lucy whispered sweet nothings to each other, their foreheads touching, while up in the front seat, Henry and Kip talked with their hands, murmured about baseball, corn futures, taxes.

I had been in love with Lee once, I think, and I suppose that many women in our town and now all around the world could say the same thing. The difference is, I *think* he may have been in love with me too, though time has muddied things so that all I have now are memories from ten years ago or more, before Henry and I were even married, before the kids arrived, when I was younger and the margins of my world seemed more flexible and indistinct. When it seemed that there was a chance I might not live in the same place on earth all the years of my life.

Thinking about him, about Lee, about myself, and that time in my life, when I was younger, I feel a blush blossom up from my chest and across my face. The truth is, I don't think too much about it, and I try not to think about Lee that way either. But sometimes I do. Everything back then was up in the air and blurry and if you asked me who I was going to marry, I'm sure I would have told you Henry, because I am a practical woman, and because Henry is so *good*. But I think I could have seen then another path, a much different path, in which I was married to Lee, and I still sometimes imagine what that would have felt like: traveling the world and being treated differently than normal people, standing on a red carpet with the cameras aimed at me, rather than standing at a grocery store, looking at a glossy photograph of Lee with another woman on his elbow.

And what bed would we lie in? And would we make babies together? And would he write songs about me? And would women in town treat me differently, whisper behind their cupped hands and smile at me stiffly when I paid for groceries with fifty-dollar bills? Or would everything be the same? Would Lee and I come over to Henry's house and have dinner with him and his wife, their children buzzing all around us, and would I look at Henry and detect some infinite sadness, an emptiness that was my absence in his life?

The Escalade began rolling forward again and soon we were parked outside the terminal, the air hot and full of exhaust, the faint smell of final cigarettes and the snap of cinnamon gum. Henry collected our luggage from the back and shook hands with Kip. Ronny and Lucy stood on the curb, shifting their weight from leg to leg. They were dressed a little garishly, as if headed to Branson or Gatlinburg, or some other two-bit destination. I gave Kip a hug and he handed me a small package, small enough to fit inside my purse and wrapped in thick, brown paper.

"Would you please give this to Lee?" Kip asked me. His face was serious, etched with an emotion I had never seen before in him and I might have called remorse or resignation. "Tell him we're happy for him, okay? Tell him congratulations. Will you do that for us please?"

"All right, campers," Henry said, clapping his hands together, "let's get moving."

"New York City," Ronny said. "New York City."

Minneapolis is the nearest *big* airport to our town, though as I have said, we are from Wisconsin, and though the two states embrace each other along the Mississippi and the St. Croix, all the way up to Lake Superior and all the way down to Iowa and Illinois, I still *feel* that they are separate, unique places. And flying up and over Minneapolis and its skyscrapers and then over St. Paul's older, more humble skyline, it felt as if I could draw a very detailed map of the landscape that grew in scope beneath me. The tapestries of fields, the ridgetop and valley bottom forests, the creeks glinting silver and blue, the teardrop ponds, the innumerable lakes, the yellow gravel roads and the blacktop lanes and highways. Then, directly below us, our town.

"Wave to the kids," I said to Henry.

"You think that's Little Wing?"

"Sure, look—there're the railroad tracks, and the mill. The pond, the golf course. No seriously, look—you can tell because of the quarry, look at that water."

"It's almost turquoise," Henry said, and nodded, "like the Caribbean. I still don't think that's Little Wing."

I turned to him. "Why not?"

"That golf course only had nine holes, I think. Ours has got eighteen."

"What? No, that one had eighteen." I turned back to the window, but by then we were already over another city, a city that was much bigger than our town. Maybe Eau Claire. "I was sure that was Little Wing."

"Wake me up when we get over Lake Michigan," Henry said, closing his eyes.

Suddenly, Ronny was in the aisle.

"Hey Ronny," I said.

"Yeah, hey—Lucy was wondering if you would trade seats with me so you could go back and talk about something."

"Ronny, *something*?"

"I dunno, dresses or something. Shoes. She's worried about her shoes."

I nodded, collected my purse, and slid past Henry, who patted me gently on the butt. I was more than a little nervous about my own dress, but I wasn't sure that Lucy would have been my first choice as fashion consultant. I moved into the aisle and Ronny jammed past me, jarring Henry. He threw himself into my seat, and peered out the window. I heard him ask Henry, "Did we pass Little Wing yet?"

I paused a moment in the aisle to allow a flight attendant to slide past me.

"Beth thought she saw it," Henry mumbled. "Ronny, get some sleep."

"Can't sleep on planes," Ronny said, "never could."

"Did you fly a lot when you were doing the rodeo?" Henry asked.

"Never," Ronny said. "We always drove ourselves. Or went Greyhound."

Henry looked up at me and shook his head.

Lucy was waving me back, the bangles on her arms sounding like a tambourine. I smiled at her, folded into Ronny's seat, and then felt a moment of uncertainty, that I had nothing to say to this woman, this *stripper*, whose body my husband had surely seen at Kip's bachelor party. I placed my hands in my lap and felt uncomfortably proper.

"Leland must be a real nice guy to fly us all out there like this," she said, turning her body toward me.

I nodded. "Well, you know, he adores Ronny."

"He's so famous! I didn't even know who he was, but then Ronny was showing me all his scrapbooks and I mean, shit—Lee has been in *Rolling Stone* and *Spin* and even *People*."

I was miffed not to be sitting next to Henry and I admit to being a little pissy with Lucy. "It's true," I said, "even *People*."

"Okay, so, tell me about what you're wearing," Lucy said, undeterred.

I had been jogging every day since the afternoon Henry returned from the mailbox with Lee's invitation. And I had been jogging *hard*. It was spring then, and desperate for the sun, desperate for fresh air, I would get the kids sent off to school, clean up the kitchen, and then hit the back roads jogging as the day warmed, the air still cool and damp.

I wanted my body to be lean for the wedding; I did not want to be standing in some posh New York City hotel lobby looking frumpy and pale, like some backwater wallflower. So mornings when the vernal ditches sluiced noisily with meltwater and over the unplanted fields terrestrial fog hung in the air, like so many surprised ghosts, I went running, the gravel beneath my sneakers soft and a little unsteady. The first morning, the most important thing to me was *not to stop*, so I ran all the way into town. Five miles. By the time I reached Little Wing, my feet were riddled with so many blisters I was forced to call Henry and have him pick me up from the library.

But it became easier after that, more fluid. Leaving Henry to his cows and machines and fields, I would run down the driveway and out onto County Road X, waving at slowly passing pickup trucks and tractors. One day, I decided to run out to Kip and Felicia's place. It was seven miles, but the morning was young, the temperature perfectly mild, and so I found a sustainable pace and grooved there, aware of my breathing, the bounce of my body.

As I jogged up their driveway, Felicia waved to me from their wall of south-facing floor-to-ceiling windows. I had hoped to surprise her, to discover her not in fact working, but perhaps loafing around the floor plan of their sprawling, immaculate house. Or maybe watching soaps or some inane game shows. If I was real lucky, she might even be sprawled out on their couch, eating a bowl of Fruity Pebbles while she guffawed at the cartoons, colored cereal lodged between her teeth. I had wanted to catch her in disarray, hair piled atop her head as if a squirrel's nest, in her pajamas and glasses, last night's facial mask still caked to her cheeks, chin, and forehead. But no—even from their driveway I could see she was put together in slim yoga pants and a sleeveless shirt, her hair looking as if she'd just been to the salon that morning. In one hand she held a coffee mug, and I could see that she was speaking into a cordless telephone with the other. She motioned me inside, as if I had wandered into her office without an appointment. Which was actually exactly what I had done.

Twenty feet from their front door I broke my pace and began stretching my aching legs. I was pleased not to be out of breath, that the running was already changing me. One of the things I liked best about being pregnant was that my body offered me surprises; that I could somehow contain this little secret, and then deliver it out into the world, and endure such pain, my very bones yielding and bending, my body immediately capable of feeding a new person; immediately! I could see then, in those moments after a long run, that exercise could take on that same unexpected hue—that I could surprise myself and run ten miles without much discomfort.

"How about a bottle of cold water," Felicia said, holding their glass door open. "Come on in here and take those shoes off. Sit down and relax."

"Water sounds divine," I said. "Busy morning?"

"Not really. That was just Kip calling. With all the spring rain and melting, they've got water in the basement of the mill and he's spending *more* money, installing sump pumps and a new drainage system." She shook her head. "I *get* what he's trying to do. I *get* his vision for the place. But, Beth, I gotta level with you. The place is a goddamn money pit."

"Maybe it won't always be," I offered.

"You're too kind. Anyway . . . let's talk about something else, okay? Please."

"Well," I said, all of a sudden uncertain, "I do have a question for you."

"Shoot."

"I need a killer dress."

"Black or red?"

"Hmm. Maybe black."

"Come with me," she said, moving off toward their bedroom. I followed, gingerly at first, and then with unabashed curiosity. I had been in their house before, once. It had been a welcoming party, their first summer in town, and though Kip had guided groups through the house, calling attention to lumber salvaged from long-since-demolished Chicago department stores and industrial fixtures scavenged from defunct Milwaukee breweries, I could not remember entering their bedroom.

It was stark, modern, white. A vase of daffodils stood on each bedside table. The bed was perfectly made, and dozens of throw pillows festooned it near the headboard. The space seemed too big, too empty for my taste, but then I remembered my own bedroom, *our* bedroom back home. The walls practically bowed with family pictures, threadbare chairs in the corners, paperback mysteries stacked three-deep on Henry's nightstand alongside the old clock radio, romance novels and Kleenex on mine. Clothing everywhere and every surface covered: parental consent forms from school, children's books, perfume bottles, cologne bottles, shoehorns, and lotions. Not *even* for an instant was I envious of Felicia's life, which then appeared before me as so fashionably barren. Ours was a *home*. A nest. A place well lived in, and loved. Maybe it's a good thing, from time to time, to spy on other people's lives. For me, anyway, it has the effect of making my own life feel like a well-loved thing.

"Here," Felicia said at last, emerging from a cavernous walk-in closet. "Try this." She held a dress up against me. I was aware then of my own perspiration, and inched backward. She stepped toward me, following me. "Don't be silly—come on."

"Felicia, I can't."

"Please. Try it on. Look, if you hate it, I'm just going to take it to Saint Vinnie's."

I did as she said. And it was perfect, the dress. We chatted the remaining hours of the morning away, and then, graciously, she offered me a ride home. On the drive, gazing out the window of her Land Rover, I thought about the fact that she and Kip had not been invited to Lee's wedding, and though it made perfect sense, it also seemed unfair to her, this woman who had done nothing wrong to Lee or Chloe, and who had been nothing but decent to me. Better to me, truth be told, than I had been to her. For all of our Middlewestern *niceness*, I realized that we, that I, could be every bit as cold as our longest season.

Slipping Felicia's dress on in front of the mirror back home, I stood on my tiptoes, and imagined what shoes I'd wear. The dress was silk, but felt more like a part of my own body—as if some dark paint had been applied to every curve, every muscle, every bone of my being, rendering me no longer nude, no longer a figure even, but an invitation.

"I don't know how to describe it," I told Lucy, "it's almost *too* sexy, without actually being too sexy. It makes me feel younger. I don't know. That probably doesn't make any sense." I felt embarrassed, opening up to her, this almost-stranger, about my body, about what I thought was sexy or not.

Lucy put her hand on my forearm and looked at me meaningfully. "Girl," she said, "I *hope* to Jesus there's no such a thing as 'too sexy,' 'cause I intend to let it all hang out."

I smiled. Over her shoulder, I could see Lake Michigan, its millions and millions of scalloped waves shimmering like blue and silver sequins.

LaGuardia was stifling hot, and the cab ride into the city as different from Minneapolis as imaginable—the traffic dense, erratic, competitive. I held Henry's hand the whole way, and not out of affection. I felt as if I had just boarded a malfunctioning rollercoaster or a rocket. Ronny naturally took shotgun, intrigued by the Sikh driver's orange turban and walrus beard, and frequently turned to face us through the glass partition, grinning wildly.

The hotel lobby was cool, the carpeting thick and inviting beneath my swollen feet. I tried not to gawk at the lobby's grand furnishings, or the other guests streaming past us in their chic sunglasses and unwrinkled linens and silks. Although some, I noticed, were not suave enough to leash their own stares when Ronny waltzed into the lobby, *holy cowing* the scene entire, his cowboy boots announcing him like a drumroll.

At check-in, the concierge informed us that our rooms were already paid for, courtesy of a Mr. Leland Sutton.

"Goddamn it, Lee!" Henry hissed, though I suspected he was just as relieved as I was, given that the rooms would have cost us upward of five hundred dollars or more a night, money that we just didn't have.

"He also left you this," said the concierge, handing us an envelope. The paper carried Lee's sloppy left-handed chicken scratchings. Henry opened it.

> *Dinner tonight at Chloe's. A car will pick you up at seven.*
> *Enjoy the city.*
> *Love, Lee*

"Hey Ronny," Henry said, "you two lovebirds gonna be all right? Beth and I might just take a nap."

Ronny's arm was around Lucy's waist. The smile that formed over his face broke slowly, exposing all of his teeth, and making his eyes shine. He nodded at us, as if privy to some secret of ours, something juicy and incriminating.

"Oh, *we'll* be all right," Ronny said suggestively. "We was just about to head up to our room to take a *nap* too, right, Luce?"

He slapped her ass playfully, right there in the lobby of that five-star hotel. I glanced quickly at the concierge, whose look of amused disdain might have been worth the cost of the trip alone, had we to pay it. Ronny nudged the gas-station sunglasses off the crown of his head and down onto the crooked perch of his nose. He showed his magnetic room key to us like a golden ticket, and said, "Sometimes I even nap with my boots on."

I do not relish leaving home, leaving my children, leaving the familiarity of my bed, my coffee maker, my slippers. But I do love hotels.

Up in the room I kicked off my shoes and immediately went to the window. Below us were the HVAC units of a lower building and off to the side were the skeletal fire escapes. Above: taller skyscrapers, clots of pigeons racing through the sky, and a single sheet of newspaper, somehow blown hundreds of feet up off the hot pavement below. The din of car horns, though muffled by the triple-glazed windows before me, was incessant, like a hidden alarm or a telephone ringing off the hook in some vast warehouse. I called my parents, eager to verify that our children were still, indeed, alive.

"We're doing fine," my dad said. "Haven't eaten anything but pancakes, chocolate chips, and maple syrup since you left."

"The kids are doing okay?"

"Kids?" Dad asked, calling out away from the phone. "You okay?"

I heard no response from the muted background.

"They're okay," he said. "We were thinking about maybe driving into Eau Claire, go see a movie at the mall or something."

"They'd love that."

"How's New York? Your mom and I haven't been there since before you were born. Still just a bunch of hookers and porno theaters?"

"Oh, Dad, I don't think it's been that way for a while now." Sitting on the edge of the bed, I ran my hand over the duvet, appraised the new television, the framed art prints on the wall. In the bathroom, Henry was trimming his nose hairs with little scissors, his shirt off, studying himself in the mirror. I watched as he ran his hands over the gray hair above his ears. He frowned at himself.

"Well all right, pumpkin," Dad said. "Enjoy yourselves, okay? And if you don't hear from us, everyone's probably alive and well."

"Probably?"

"All right then," he said, cheerfully, and hung up.

"I love you," I told the dial tone.

Henry came out of the bathroom, a length of floss wrapped around two fingers. He sawed at his teeth and gums, as if with a bow. "Wanna go for a walk?" he asked.

I thought about Ronny and Lucy in their room, and for a moment, I have to say that it did turn me on, the notion of a cowboy and this stripper, fucking with abandon in a New York City hotel room, cowboy boots and heels still on, their anonymous bed frame rattling almost apart. They seemed well matched that way, though I can't say that I had ever given much thought to who Ronny might end up with, because if I was honest, I would have told you that I doubted he would have found someone. I put my hands over my eyes and shook my head, trying to disrupt the image I had formed of them.

"Yeah," I said, "I *would* like to stretch my legs, I think."

"You going to wear sneakers?" Henry asked.

"It's either that or the heels I brought for the wedding."

He nodded. "I know. I'm in the same boat. But I don't want to look like a goofball. This is a pretty high-class joint."

"Well," I said, "we can look stupid together." Then I motioned him toward the bed. "But maybe we oughta take care of something first."

We rode the elevator down to the lobby, in our sneakers, holding hands, feeling as if we had accomplished something, which was true. It isn't very romantic, but after you've been married almost ten years, an afternoon fuck can feel like you've gotten away with a minor crime, an act as thrilling and banal as shoplifting. And with the kids, that element of our marriage had become at once more satisfying and a great deal less frequent. As partners, as lovers, we've become better attuned to each other, to each other's bodies. We know what things to whisper, to scream, to beg for. But it isn't as if we're making love every night. Sometimes, a week goes by, or two. Especially in the fall, during harvest, when Henry comes back into the house late at night, corn dust and loose loam caked all over his body and in his nose, every fiber of his hair dirty, his eyes red and tired.

We stood on the sidewalk, the city sweeping past us, and glancing over at Henry, I could see sweat beading on his forehead. He gripped my hand tighter.

"So much to see, huh?" he said, laughing uncomfortably. I watched him check his old wristwatch, the crystal long since broken. "Well?" he asked.

"Let's go to the park," I said.

He nodded. "Sounds good."

With several hours before we needed to be at Chloe's house, we strolled north along Madison Avenue, our hands growing sweaty, and as we passed by giant flagship stores and chic little boutiques, there was the desire to go in and look at the dresses, suits, shoes, books, scarves—all those things we could not and would never find in Little Wing. And yet, standing before the shop windows in our sneakers and shorts, sweating, Henry in his battered Milwaukee Brewers cap, there was also the notion that perhaps we were better off pounding the pavement, stopping at food carts and shaved ice carts, rubbernecking the people and buildings. We had only a general idea where the park was and where we had come from, and were terrified and too embarrassed to ask for directions. So we wandered.

In the park, Henry removed his shirt and we sat on it, watching the joggers and jugglers, the young families and dog people throwing frisbees.

"I'm going to take a nap," I told Henry, my head in his lap. I threw an arm over my eyes to shade out the light.

"Do you want my hat?"

"No," I said. "That thing reeks. You need to wash it."

"Naw," Henry said, "I could never wash it. That'd be sacrilege."

While the rest of us doggedly plowed our way through college or two-year technical schools, Lee was forming short-lived bands, traveling the Midwest and the mid-Atlantic, playing bars, fraternity parties, and talent competitions. Word came back to us every so often that he was picking up momentum, that some record label or another was interested in signing him, that a celebrity had seen him play in Chicago, or Boston, and dispensed some champagne-and-caviar advice, but it never seemed to pan out and every year was another year Lee grew older, and the notion of his musical success seemed less and less likely.

His friends, Henry included, understood. They were defensive of him, of his dream. In crowded dorm rooms and in smoky off-campus apartments smelling of spilled beer and stale bong water, they played his demo tapes to strangers, people we hadn't grown up with, people whose parents didn't clip out every positive newspaper article, every wishy-washy concert review ever published about Lee.

"He's going to be famous," they'd say. "You hear that? You hear what he just did there?" I can still see Henry, going over to the stereo and rewinding a few bars of music, turning the volume up, and then hitting Play. "There." He'd point at the speakers.

"And there again. Do you hear that? You're not supposed to play the guitar that way. You take guitar lessons or go to Juilliard or some shit, they'll beat that right out of you. But the thing is, that's *Wisconsin*. That's *winter*, right there."

After college, Henry and I split up for a while. This is a polite way of saying that we wanted to have sex with different people, though our timing never seemed to be quite in sync back then. When I loved him, he was interested in Tara Monroe or Rachel Howe. *Whores*, I thought at the time. Likewise, when he was in love with me, when he wanted me back, there were months when I thought I might prefer Cooper Carlson or Bradley Aberle. Or Leland.

Lee had just broken up with his band, a group of guys who weren't from Little Wing, but from the nearby town of Thorp. They had grown tight together, even toured in Germany, France, and England. They were close to honing, calibrating a sound of their own, something new, something that at first I didn't like or couldn't appreciate. It didn't sound like Lee's music, or at least not anything I recognized as Lee's music. It was cold, lonesome, and discordant. The best I can describe it is the way sound travels in winter, when everything is cold and still. How, at first, there is no sound. You can't imagine anything living or moving around. And then, after you tune your ears, after you wait, you begin to hear the crows in the treetops, the barely perceptible sound of their flight, their wings on the crystalline air. And then more: a far-off chainsaw, a motor idling, ice forming, creek water burbling past that ice, icicles dripping, birdsong. Layer all those tiny noises beneath Lee's sad, sad falsetto, and you had an anthem for our place on earth.

He was depressed, living in a rented room, in a huge farmhouse outside town. No one had seen him; he wasn't coming into town, he wasn't drinking at the VFW. He was living like a coyote, out on the margins. And I wasn't talking to Henry, so I heard none of the intimate reports I normally would. But then a letter came to my parents' house, addressed to me, though I'd moved to Wabasha, Minnesota, after graduation.

"I could hardly read the envelope," my mom said. "It looks like a kid addressed it."

"You didn't open it, did you?" I asked nervously.

"Should I have?"

"No," I said. "I'll be home next week. Please put it in my old room."

That next week, I drove home in my old Pontiac, the heater close to dying. I had to drive wearing my parka, mittens, and hat, a layer of long underwear beneath my clothing, just in case, and on the coldest evenings I frequently had to stop the car and scrape the windshield because the defroster was so useless. I was working two jobs in Wabasha: answering the telephone at a hair salon and in the evenings, waitressing at a fried chicken and beer bar. My hair always stank of fried chicken grease, even though the stylists gave me all their free samples of designer shampoo and conditioner.

"Honey," they would say, "most of us buy expensive perfume to get the right guy. You're the only one we've ever met who is trying to catch the dudes going around smelling like a bucket of extra-crispy wings."

I don't remember that time of my life, that so-called freedom, as being particularly happy. I was living in a studio apartment, eating for free at the bar at night, neck-deep in credit card debt, and working around a salon full of female egos all day long.

"Hey, Fried Chicken," they'd joke, "how's that college education treating you now?"

Or,

"Who majors in English? Couldn't you speak English *before* college?"

If I met men, it was at the bar. Men working the railroad, married men, many-times divorced men, sad men, old men. Most of the time, they treated me with respect. Some I got to know pretty well, what drinks they favored, what sports teams they wanted to follow on the corner televisions, whether they'd had a good day, or a bad one. Some nights, though, I was treated a little more shabbily. My ass would get pinched, some guy with a wedding band would leave me his telephone number on a receipt, or a hotel key and a condom beside it. But that didn't happen too often.

All just to say: I was happy to be returning to Little Wing for a weekend of my mom's cooking, for free laundry, a respite from the bar. And an envelope from Lee waiting for me. Keyed up to open his letter, and excited to be out of Wabasha, I drove the Pontiac recklessly, slipping on black ice, swerving away from raccoons and wayward deer. After pulling into my parents' humble one-lane driveway, I waited inside the car a moment, collecting myself. I could see my mom's face peeking around the drapes, then again from the front door, where she stood, waving at me, her slippers pointed out into the chill of the night. I pulled a laundry basket from the car, my toiletry bag atop it, and walked up the front path toward her.

"Hey Mom," I said.

"So good to *see* you," she said, hugging me, though my arms were full and I could not return the embrace.

"Mom, let me put this stuff in the wash real quick while I'm thinking about it."

"Oh, you let me do that. Go find your father. I think he's in the living room."

I shut the door, happy to be inside that familiar house, its smells and drafts and sounds so much the fabric of my life. I removed my shoes, rubbed my feet against the thick brown hallway carpeting. Mom had clearly spent hours getting the house in order for my arrival. I could see the lines of the vacuum sweeper in the carpeting, could see that all of the candles burning in the dining room were new and tall, that from the oven gasped rich food smells. Casserole, I knew, of course. Hamburger, corn, onion, ketchup, and cheese casserole.

"Hey Dad," I said.

He sat in his chair, reading the *Eau Claire Leader-Telegram*. The television was muted, but I knew that Dad liked to look up from his paper occasionally to monitor the world, now and then turning the sound up to listen to the weather report, or sports scores. The rest of it depressed him to tears, he said, that's why he would never move away from Wisconsin.

"Hey pumpkin," he said, rising from his chair to kiss me. I hugged him fiercely. "You smell good," he said. "What is that? Like some kind of expensive lavender shampoo? Burdock? What is that?"

I looked at him. "You have to be kidding me, right?"

"No, you should tell me what it is, so I can get a bottle for your mother."

"Seriously. You're fucking with me, Dad."

He held up his hands in surrender. "I'm not screwing with you. I like the way you smell. See if I compliment *you* again."

I slumped into a chair. "God, I love this house."

He looked over the V of his newspaper and then settled his eyes on me. "You all right, kid? You look a little tired. How's Henry? You guys still incommunicado?"

"Dad."

"What? I'm not allowed to ask?"

"I'm just not in the mood."

"Well, I don't know what you birds call it these days, but I wouldn't experiment too long. I think you might regret losing him."

He smiled at me, turned the pages of his paper, and then held them up again, like a blind between us. "Dads know these things."

I sighed heavily. Mom appeared from the basement, where I could hear the washer, the water sloshing, the air already heavier and filled with the smell of soap. "Hot dish?" she asked.

After dinner I indulged them, revealing only the highlights of my recent employment history while also motioning toward brighter prospects on the horizon. Possibly graduate school in Minneapolis or Madison. Maybe a paralegal program in Milwaukee. It felt like a job interview, like my mom was actually interrogating me for a newly open position as her adult daughter. She smiled at me, took my hand, told me how proud they were. I kissed them both good night and went up the stairs to my room. Moments before I had feigned sleepiness, but now my body felt electric. The letter was sitting on my bed, Lee's handwriting one rectangular smear of graphite. I lay on the bed, ripped open the envelope, and read.

He hadn't talked to anyone since coming back. He felt like a failure for the band's dissolution. He didn't know what he was doing. He didn't know about the new music he was making. He was lonely. He was considering giving it up and applying for college. He was thinking about a normal job. He was thinking about moving away. A telephone number was scrawled beside *PS* at the very bottom of the page, as if an afterthought.

I folded the letter and slipped it back into the envelope. I went to the bathroom, showered, and stared at myself through a smudged porthole of clean glass in the otherwise foggy mirror.

I was, he was, we were all in that peculiar rut of our midtwenties, when just enough of our friends or classmates had found some measure of success, so that it taunted those of us who hadn't. Kip was down in Chicago and already he was living in a huge condo in the John Hancock building and had season Cubs tickets and a vintage Mustang that he drove along Lake Shore Drive and Michigan Avenue, the ragtop pulled back so that the quartz obelisks of the city's skyscrapers swam above him. Eddy and Henry had gone down for a weekend and come back with tales of Brooks Brothers suits, five-hundred-dollar steak dinners, and Northwestern coeds who looked like runway models, ballerinas, or the heirs of a social stratum many castes above our own. Kip, I was told, served a martini to a young woman using her high-heeled shoe as a flute.

I dressed quickly, dried my hair, stuffed Lee's letter in my pocket, and readied myself to find him. In the kitchen, I dialed the telephone number, holding my breath while I listened to the rings. I could hear my parents moving clumsily around the floor above me, like livestock.

"Hello?"

"Lee?"

"Beth? That you?"

"Yes," I exhaled. "I got your letter. Want a visitor?" I noticed my fingers playing with the cord, winding it around my wrist and knuckles, until the fingers turned white.

"Yeah, come on over. Can you find it okay?"

"I'll find it," I said.

Mom caught me at the door, struggling to put on my winter boots.

"I thought you were tired," she said, crossing her arms. "It's almost ten o' clock."

"I know, Mom," I said. "I just have to go check on something."

She raised her eyebrows at me. "When should we send out the search parties?"

I stood and reached for the doorknob. "I'll be home for breakfast." I gave her a peck on the cheek.

"You need to take a shower to *go check on something*? And *perfume*?"

"Mom."

"Watch those roads."

I didn't know what I was doing, except that I was curious, that I was also lonely, that I wasn't constrained by anyone or any relationship, and driving in my rusty Pontiac in subzero temperatures, one headlight out, I couldn't feel the cold. Cold, my dad always told me, is all psychological, all in your head. I could hear him: "People in Florida think that sixty degrees, fifty degrees is cold. The key is good socks and a good breakfast. But more than that, the key is being happy. And more than that, the biggest key is working hard."

I ground my heel into the accelerator and drove through the night, out into the country. Lee had sketched me a map, indicating my parents' house with an asterisk, or maybe a star, his own address with an *X*.

The night was bright with starlight and the searchlight of a nearly pregnant moon. I pulled onto the gravel driveway and a dog began barking. It sounded like the loudest noise in the world. I parked the Pontiac beneath an ancient oak tree and checked my reflection in the mirror. I could hear the dog's claws against the ice and gravel, coming toward me. Too excited to be frightened, I stepped out into the night.

It was one of those giant old yellow-cream brick farmhouses surrounded by winter fields of stubble corn and snow. It can be difficult to find the front door of such houses, when in every direction the house faces fields and the infinitely straight grid of county roads. Those old American four-squares are inevitably wrapped in deep porches and always without a doorbell or mailbox. I noticed a few windows going from dark to light above me, and curtains being pulled aside at the bottom corners. Eventually, I found what I took to be the front door and knocked.

Lee answered, and I breathed a deep sigh, smiling at him. He smiled back as he motioned me in. "Shush," he scolded the dog. "Come in or stay out," he whispered to it. The dog wagged its tail and slipped into the house.

"Yours?" I asked.

"Naw," he said, giving me a hug, "It's Joaquin's. He lives upstairs too. So you got my letter?"

I almost patted my back pocket, but instead nodded, unsure what else to say. "Show me where you live."

An old woman padded out of the kitchen in a pink muumuu, her long white hair a cape behind her trailing down just above the backs of her knees. She wore tortoiseshell glasses and clutched a cup of what smelled like chamomile tea. She smiled at us.

"I made a bed up for you," she said.

"Mrs. Cather," Lee said gently, "this is my sister, Beth. Beth, Bea Cather."

I looked at him, confused at first, and then catching on. "Pleasure," I said, extending my hand. He nodded and winked at me, gamely.

She set her tea down on a coffee table littered with *National Geographics* and took my hand in both of hers, and they were trembling, birdlike little hands, blue-veined, warm, and dry. She looked at my red-cheeked face with watery eyes. "Your brother plays beautiful music," she said. "He's the finest guitar player I've ever heard."

"Oh, Bea," Lee said, laughing, "come on, now, don't embarrass me."

"No," Bea said, pointing a finger at him, "he's too modest. Was he always that way? So humble, I mean?"

"Always," I said, nodding theatrically. "Nothing is ever enough with Lee."

"Well, I suppose maybe that's a good thing," Bea said.

"Nothing more unattractive than a blowhard. My first husband was like that. He could spend all day telling you that his farts didn't stink. Gets to the point where you just tune it out."

"Yes ma'am," I said.

"Well," she said, "Leland said you might be tired from your traveling, so I made up a bed for you. It's in the room next to mine. I didn't want you upstairs, near all the boys. Those Mexican men, I tell you. Hard workers, all of them. And fine accordion players. But they all fancy themselves Casanovas too. If I was twenty years younger. Anyway. It is a *pleasure* to meet you. That brother of yours is an angel."

"Thank you," I said.

"Good night, Bea," Lee said.

"Good night, darling," she called, mug back in hand, her slippers scuffling along the old wooden floor.

"Casanovas?" I asked.

"Uh, yea. Bea rents out the whole top floor to farm workers. So I share a bathroom with them—Joaquin, Ernesto, and Garcia. And they *do* like the ladies. It's true."

"Show me your room," I said, hooking my arm in his elbow. We walked up the creaking staircase, past dozens of pictures of Bea's family, her earlier past in black-and-white and sepia, then, with the passage of years, becoming more and more colorful, first in muted Polaroid hues and then the bold Technicolor shots of grandchildren, or perhaps great-grandchildren.

"Sister, huh?" I asked.

Lee blushed. "Well, I just didn't want Bea asking too many questions."

"But you *presumed* that I would sleep over."

We stopped at the top of the stairs. Suddenly, he looked sad. "I'm sorry. I just . . . I just don't know what the fuck is happening right now, and I heard that you and Henry were, you know, broken up. Look, I'm sorry. I'm really sorry."

"No," I said, "it's okay. Listen, it's just good to see your face." And then, I reached out to touch him, his chin and beard. Beneath the whiskers his face was gaunt, his cheekbones rising like two beautiful dunes of bone. "You're not eating," I said. I'd never touched him before like that. It was thrilling.

"Bea is trying to fatten me up."

I let my fingers touch his lips. "Good."

"Beth?"

I kissed him, gently, and he kissed back. The frequency of my world suddenly seemed to fuzz, my face so warm that I felt I was melting. Lee is tall, and so I had to rise up on my tiptoes, and I liked that feeling, of being next to a taller man.

"Come on," he said, "I don't want you to fall down the stairs."

"Right."

He led me down a central hallway and toward one of the bedrooms, where I could hear laughter, muffled voices, soft radio. "These clowns," said Lee. "Every night."

He opened the door of the bedroom a crack, and laying on the floor were what I supposed to be his three male housemates, sprawled around a Risk board, a clock radio beside the bed playing Top 40 hits. The smell of beer was in the room and I could see several open bags of chips, a few tins of nuts. They waved sheepishly up at me. At least two of them had teeth adorned with gold caps.

"Left to right," Lee said, "it goes Garcia, Joaquin, and Ernesto. Say *hola*, gentlemen."

"Hello," they said.

"Hey, did you let Fernando in?" asked Joaquin.

"Yeah, he came in with Beth. Pretty cold out there."

"You two want to play?" asked Ernesto. "We just started."

"Naw," Lee said, "I want to show her around."

"Right," Joaquin said, smiling a little too broadly. "Show her around."

Lee rolled his eyes at me and shut the door. "Every night. If it's not Monopoly, it's Risk. Or Axis & Allies. They like war games."

His room was spare, and I remember feeling a great sadness for him, as I looked at the little square of a space: a mattress on the floor, a red plastic milk crate holding some books, a lamp, a guitar, a card table, and a folding chair.

"Jesus, Lee. If you need some furniture, you could have called my parents. Or talked to Henry or the Girouxs or Eddy. Anyone. You're living like a monk in here."

He nodded. "I know. That's the plan. Let me show you something else."

We went back down the stairs, stepping gingerly. "Bea's a light sleeper," he whispered.

At the door we slipped on our boots, hats, and mittens. We helped each other into our parkas. Fernando the dog watched us from the top of the stairs, sniffing the air, but he declined to follow us out into the cold. We began walking away from the house, toward a barn and a collection of smaller, ramshackle buildings. A sodium-nitrate light hummed blue in the sky.

"Hold on," I said, and tugging his arm I pulled him close to me and we kissed again in the cold.

When our lips separated, he leaned his forehead down and rested it on mine. I looked up at his eyes but they were closed.

"Beth," he said, "I don't know."

"I don't know that we have to."

"I don't know what I want right now. I wouldn't be good to you. And Henry is my friend." I could see that he was wincing and I imagined him, replaying our kisses, his letter, in his head. "I mean, I really care about you. I don't know."

"What?" I said. "What *is* it?"

He looked up at the sky and I saw him exhale deeply. "Come on," he said, "I want to show you this thing."

We walked past the barn, past a pole-building filled with anti-quated threshers and discing machines, chains swaying gently with what little breeze blew and maybe just the tumbling of the earth through the heavens. He led me into a long, low building, and I recognized it as a chicken coop. As we entered, he flicked a switch on the wall and a single exposed bulb hanging from the ceiling slowly brightened. Inside the narrow space was a small piano, a set of drums, a guitar, and a few other instruments. Everything looked secondhand, like instruments left behind a century or more before by some ragtag gypsy troupe. He had tacked some old carpeting to the walls, littered the floor with hay.

"My workshop," he said, spreading his arms.

"Lee," I said, "it's so cold in here."

"Aha!" he said. "I have this!" In one corner of the coop was an old woodstove. Lee knelt down in the hay and began breaking kindling, feeding it into the stove along with a few balls of rolled-up newspaper, and then tossed in a lit match. In moments, the coop filled with the delicious smell of woodsmoke, and the faint popping of an infant fire.

"That sound, right there," he said. "Those little snaps. I'm laying down a track where the fabric behind everything is that sound. A loop of fire." He grinned sheepishly. "But who knows? Maybe I've kind of gone off the rails."

"How are you recording everything?" I asked.

"Pretty basic—just a computer and a mic," he said. "It's a lot easier these days. Guerrilla recording."

What I wanted to do was sit beside him on a bale of hay and

kiss, to be warm together, maybe to let things go and unfurl as they might. But I didn't, and I didn't talk about the kisses we'd just shared, or why he sent me the letter in the first place, or what he was trying to say, but apparently couldn't. I just sat close to the stove and we talked, occasionally stopping so that he could sing me a few bars of something he was working on. Finally, he glanced up with a somber look on his face.

"I didn't want to come back a failure," he said. "You know? I just don't know what to do except to keep trying. I'm not any good at anything else."

I think I'm like most people in the world, which is to say, untalented. I can't sing, can't dance, can't paint, can't run fast, can't write poetry. And sitting there, listening to him, as I would for years into the future when he came to visit Henry and me at our house and sat at our dining-room table, I wondered, *What is it like for him? What does he see? Where does all this music come from?*

We let the fire burn down, extinguished the light, and moved back into the night. Inside the house, he hugged me, kissed me on the cheek, and said, "I'm glad you came out here tonight."

"Me too," I said, though in that instant, I was confused, more confused than I had been before showing up at Bea Cather's old farmhouse. I had no idea where we stood, Lee and I, to say nothing of what I would tell Henry, *if* I could tell Henry.

"Good night," he said, and then I watched him climb the stairs, his shoulders hunched over, as if he were an old bachelor farmer, retiring for the night.

I crept through the darkened house, touching the walls as I navigated toward the bedroom Bea had prepared for me. I climbed into the bed fully dressed, afraid to disrobe, afraid to fall asleep, excited by the notion that somewhere overhead, Lee was lying on his own mattress, perhaps thinking of me. I lay that way a long time, hours maybe, I had no way of knowing, until finally I got up, and retraced my steps to the front door. I stood on the welcome mat, my boots lying on an old woven rug, and just as I reached down to pick them up, I heard a creak at the top of the stairs. I looked up.

It was Lee, in a pair of black polka-dotted boxer shorts, his pale chest bare, his long arms marked with tattoos, his thin hair standing in a thousand different directions. He looked at me with a sad smile on his face. I climbed the stairs and took his hand.

I left that morning, before dawn, driving slow, watching for the sunrise, taking the roads with care. Just beyond a narrow bridge over a nameless creek, I stopped the car and left it to idle. I watched the sun come up purple and orange and pink.

At my parents' house, I stole in quietly, removed my boots, and crawled into bed.

We rode through the skyscraper canyons in a Mercedes-Benz with a cool leather interior and smoked windows that kept the din of the city snugly at bay. Twice, I found myself opening and closing them, just to study the contrast between the world outside us and the one we experienced inside. We rolled through the city, the driver indicating points of interest in a tone at once bored and kind. I held a pale blue shawl over my shoulders. Henry held his own hands, played with his wedding band. In the front seat, Ronny gazed, openmouthed. Lucy blew on freshly painted purple fingernails. There was tension in the air that I can only describe as similar to that which descends over a pregame stadium, or the seats of an elementary school pageant just before the child-players walk onto the stage. Lucy had seen something on the television about the wedding tomorrow.

"They said on the television that everyone in town who's anyone's gonna be there," she told us in the lobby.

"Wonder where we fit in?" Henry said with half-hearted irony.

"Where is the ceremony?" I asked. Lee's invitations had been so vague, with just that note and the plane tickets.

"All I know is that we're supposed to show up at some mansion tomorrow night at five. Lee didn't say anything other than that."

"Is Chloe religious?" I asked.

"No idea," Henry replied.

"So, no church?" I continued.

"Kip and Felicia weren't married in a church," he countered.

"I suppose not."

The driver stopped on a brick-paved street bereft of trees and opened our doors. Henry tried to slip him a tip, but the man waved it off.

"My pleasure," the driver said. "You guys were a hoot. Now, just head up inside there. Take the freight elevator up to the fourth floor. And I'll be waiting down here whenever you're ready to go. No hurry."

He waved us good-bye and then leaned against the hood of the car. We watched him fiddle with an expensive cell phone while lighting a cigarette.

We were quiet in the elevator. Lucy and I straightened our men's collars, arranging their hair for them, and then quickly applied our own lipstick. I wore a light peach cocktail dress that I'd had for years, a dress that I loved in the summer, when my skin was tanned brown. In winter, when my skin is so starved for the sun, that color would make me look like a ghost, but now, after months of jogging and gardening and watching the kids' soccer games, it made even my moles and freckles look decorative. I felt confident.

Ronny yanked open the elevator doors with an ancient leather strap. A deejay spun records in one corner, breezy, fun music, and the party thrummed with conversation, some in attendance already swaying with the beat. The air smelled of lime juice and alcohol, expensive perfume and seafood. A hundred and fifty people must have been there already, shoulder to shoulder.

"Wait," Lucy said, "you guys go ahead. I have to ask Beth something." Lucy waited for the guys to step out of the elevator and then pressed the G button and slammed the elevator door down.

"So, um, here's the thing," Lucy said. "I thought I wanted to come to this thing—you know, to meet Ronny's friends, and honestly, it's been great getting to know you and Henry, and the hotel room is fabulous and Ronny's fabulous, but I have to tell you."

"Tell me *what?*"

The elevator reached the ground floor. Two well-dressed couples started to enter the elevator, and Lucy pulled me out quickly, our high heels loud on the steel floor of the car. The partygoers now standing in the elevator regarded us quizzically. I thought I recognized one of the women from my mom's favorite soap opera. We moved out onto the brick sidewalk.

"You know what I am," Lucy said. "I mean, you know how I met Ronny. What the *hell* am I doing here? What am I going to tell these people when they ask, 'So, what do you do for a living?'" She had intoned a haughty, upper-crust delivery, and it made me smile. "I'm a fucking stripper, okay? I dropped out of college after one semester. Occasionally, I may like to do a little blow. You know?" She was silent for a moment. "I feel like these people are going to look right through me."

I understood, though; until that moment I hadn't considered that it might not be enough for any of us, just to be Leland's friends. That perhaps, people in attendance might well judge us not just by our inexpensive clothing and shoes, but our jobs and income as well. Since Henry and I had been married, I had worked only infrequently, more often than not staying at home with the kids. The last job even worth putting on my resume was probably the receptionist gig at that hair salon in Wabasha.

"Got any cigarettes?" I asked.

"*Hell* yes," she said.

She passed me a cigarette, lighted it for me, then sparked up her own.

"You know who we are?" I asked. "Tonight, I'm going to be either a chef or a restaurant owner. I haven't decided. And I think you should be a . . ." I appraised Lucy a moment while I drew on one of her Misty 120's. "I think you should be a photographer. Or, even better yet, maybe a painter."

She smiled. "What do I photograph? Or, you know, paint?"

"Nudes."

"I do have some expertise in that department," she said.

I gave her my elbow. "Let's go for a walk. I don't think they'll miss us."

We laughed as we clattered loudly down the sidewalk, two unlikely girlfriends in sudden solidarity. Our heels did battle with the cobbles and bricks, mainly losing, and even before we returned to the party my feet hurt.

Chloe had lost weight, I noticed, her arms too thin, the veins of her feet oddly bright and blue. She greeted us warmly, complimented Lucy immediately on her dress and nail polish. I could see that Lucy was smitten, that some of her inhibitions were quickly melting away. She held her champagne flute casually, keeping Ronny tight at her side.

She had found him immediately when we finally entered the party, at a table of hors d'oeuvres, tossing grapes into his mouth. I wondered what the room thought of him, of them, but I also knew that Ronny couldn't have cared less. He grinned broadly as we approached him, took a big swig of his Coke, one hand perched on his big belt buckle.

"They put a lime in my Coke," he said, leaning into me confidentially. "I kind of like it."

"Very cosmopolitan of you, Ronny Taylor." I made a mental note to stick close to him, to watch the waiters circulating through the flat with their trays of easy cocktails.

"Where's Leland?" I asked Chloe.

"Oh, he's out on the deck, I think. He's been looking for you guys. I think Henry is with him," Chloe said, giving my arm a little squeeze, before excusing herself to chat with other guests.

Sprinkled throughout the long, lofty space were faces I recognized from magazines and television: actors mostly, but also musicians—musicians whose work I knew my daughter, Eleanore, had begun listening to in the privacy of her still-pink bedroom, and I knew then in a different way than I ever had before how important Chloe and Lee were, that these sorts of people had come out to pay their respects to them, to be *seen* with them.

They were indeed out on the deck, Henry drinking a mojito, Lee nursing what looked like a cranberry juice. He smiled broadly when he saw us approach. His eyes were tired looking, but he looked fit in a trimly cut suit, his face tan and shaved, hair cut short.

"Hey, Beth," he said, hugging me.

"Lee," I said, "congratulations. That fiancée of yours looks exquisite."

"Thanks—and, really, thanks for coming out, guys," he said.

"It would have been nice to get hitched in Wisco, but Chloe's people are from out here, and you know . . ." He cocked his head in resignation.

"Why the hell are you apologizing to us?" Henry said. "Gives us an excuse to abandon the kids for a few days. See the city."

Lee set his drink down quickly. "Oh man! I wanted them to come too, but we decided to have a no-kids wedding, you know. No crying babies in the back, no early night for the parents. I guess tomorrow night's going to be the real deal."

"So where's the church?" I asked.

He shook his head. "No church. We're just having a friend of Chloe's do the vows. He's actually studied religion at Yale. Really neat guy. Then a dinner and dance."

There is a certain charm to the wham-bam-thank-you-ma'am wedding ceremony. Excluding great-aunts, mothers, and grand-mothers, no one flies cross-country for a stuffy ceremony. No one buys an elaborate wedding gift to hear some hackneyed homily about the Institution of Marriage, or some second-rate vocalist's screeched-out solo. Somebody's barely literate cousin butchering Bible verses or a Neruda poem. People come to see their family and friends, to get drunk, to kick off their heels and mimic a de-ranged chicken. To hear a brother give a long-winded and mostly inappropriate best man's speech. To watch the bridesmaid weep through her own cavalcade of saccharine teenage memories and inside jokes. I'm no different.

But here's the thing, the older I get, the more *I do* care about the ceremony. Because the reason you invite anyone to your wed-ding in the first place is because you want your friends and family to share in the ritual. If the ceremony wasn't worth anything, ev-eryone would just have parties and exchange rings, no problem. I was nervous as hell the day Henry and I got married. I was afraid of tripping down the aisle on my train, of fainting during the service, of botching the vows, of crying, of looking like a bad kisser, or worse, looking like *too experienced* a kisser. I was terrified. And as the pastor stated the vows for me to recite, I thought about the words, each of them, weighed them out like something precious. I knew, when I said them, that I meant it. That even in that moment of recitation, even as the words came tumbling out of my mouth, I could foresee the challenges that would surely come down the line over the course of our marriage. I knew it was unlikely we would ever have much money. That Henry would always work more than I'd like him to. That we would probably never move away from Wisconsin, ever, not even to *try out* a city like Minneapolis, Chicago, or even Duluth. That marrying Henry was tantamount to marrying his family's three hundred acres of corn and soybeans and alfalfa and cows. But it felt good to say those words, those vows. And I remember how happy I was, staring into his face, focusing on him.

Standing there now outside that stuffy loft on the breezy deck, beside Lee, the menthol taste of a cigarette still in my mouth, the refreshing coldness of the champagne against my fingers and palm, I remembered too how I'd thought of Lee during my vows—if only for a split second—thought about that night in the old farmhouse, how it might have been the only time I'd ever truly betrayed Henry. Because I could never tell him. Henry and I have been married almost ten years, and if I've harbored any secrets from him, they've been innocent ones: money I've spent shopping, money I've squirreled away for the kids' college educations, the lump I found one morning that turned out to be benign, the hope I have that we can vacation more once the kids are grown and gone to college. I wondered if Lee would think of me as he said his vows to Chloe, or if he ever thought of me at all in that way.

"Well," he said, "I got to keep mingling." He shook Henry's hand and moved into the room of strangers.

The evening passed pleasantly. None of the anxieties we'd carried into the party seemed to matter much. A few new faces introduced themselves to us, people from Lee's record label. They asked us questions about Little Wing, about the mill, about what Lee was like as a boy. My heart nearly stopped when one woman asked me, "So, did you ever date him?" I know I paused overly long, tilting my head, before simply saying, "Oh, no. We're just friends. Always just really good friends."

She waved a hand in the air, frivolously, innocently. "I just thought, you know, it seems like such a small town. Maybe everybody's sleeping with everyone."

Henry must have been half-listening to our conversation because he came up behind me just then, an arm around my waist, and said, "Let's hope not." He kissed me, and I smelled alcohol on his lips.

Around midnight we crawled back into our car and rode back through the still-alive streets. In the hotel room, champagne drunk, I fell asleep quickly in the big soft bed, and I don't think a million taxis blaring their horns could have stopped me from dreaming.

We slept until almost noon, the sound of the maid's knuckles on our door. *"Room service!"*

Henry impressed me by howling in a low, deep voice, "GO AWAY!" It was enough apparently to back the maid away from our room, the retreat of her cart audible as it wobbled down the hallway away from us. Satisfied, he lay on his stomach, and I draped an arm over his back.

"We haven't slept this long in years," I said.

"My body feels like wet cement," he said.

"Hungover?" I asked.

"That too," he said, "but mostly, I'm just so relaxed. Every-thing feels heavy. Loose."

"Maybe we should get away more," I suggested. "We could just do some little vacations. Weekend trips. Leave the kids with Mom and Dad. Go to California. Vegas."

He sighed, like a little boy. "I love our home," he said, almost wounded. "Everything we need's right there. And what about the herd? What about the milking? We can't afford to *pay* someone. Not right now anyway."

"It's just—you just said how relaxed you were. I worry about you. You know? I want us to travel, to do things together. To see the world. Don't you ever get bored of just the same old stuff? Don't you ever want to get out of Little Wing? Even just a weekend?"

He turned his head away from me, cleared his throat. "I don't know," he said. "Do you?"

"Maybe," I said.

I thought of our children. Of weekend mornings.

"But it's okay," I said, "to take a break every now and again, don't you think? Things look better sometimes after you go away for a little while."

I lay on my back, thought briefly about the notion of making another baby, rested my hand on my belly button.

Henry sat up slowly, put his feet on the floor, rested his head in his hands. "Lord," he said. "Champagne bubbles. It's like they're all popping in my skull right now." I watched him rise to his feet, scratch his stomach, pad toward the bathroom. I climbed out of bed too, opened the blinds, stood in the midday sunlight, naked, for about a minute's time, scanning every window I could see for an observer, but no one was watching. I pulled the blinds shut and walked into the bathroom. Henry was sitting slumped on the toilet, head propped against his fists.

"Let's find some coffee," I said.

In high school, our art teacher was named Roger Killebrew. How he came to live in Little Wing, none of us could say, but he'd been there forever, had even in fact taught my mother. He was a dapper man, with dark brown hair that was clearly dyed. He wore well-tailored tweed suits, fine leather shoes, and cologne that could not have been purchased from the local pharmacy or variety store.

I think of Mr. Killebrew quite often actually, but most often when I find myself in a city. So I wasn't entirely surprised that, as Henry and I walked the streets of New York in search of a café, I thought of our eleventh grade painting class. We were studying modern American abstract painting—Killebrew had prepared a slideshow, and some of the boys in our class were snickering at the Rothkos and Pollocks.

"Boys!" Killebrew barked. "Anything particularly wise to add to the discussion?"

I don't remember what exactly was said, but Henry, a seventeen-year-old version of Henry, said something along the lines of, "Only in a big city would anyone be dumb enough to spend a lot of money on junk like that." Other boys in the class were whispering, as they always did, about Killebrew's wardrobe, his gesticulations, the way his wrists worked, his high-toned voice, his cologne, his sleepy eye, his loud small-town bachelor status.

But what I do remember is Ronny suddenly announcing, "Painting is gay." The classroom exploded in laughter, boys high-fiving Ronny as if he'd just scored a winning touchdown and spiked the football defiantly.

Mr. Killebrew extinguished the slide projector, circled the room to turn on the lights, and then returned to the front of the class, where he leaned against the chalkboard, not saying a thing, just staring, his hands resting in the chalk trays behind him. He waited for us. He might have waited one minute or five minutes, I don't know. But I remember really *loving* Mr. Killebrew right at that moment, because he wasn't like any other man that I knew. Every year, he hosted an art-club trip to Chicago. He had friends down there, some in hotel management, others who owned res-taurants, or cafés. So, for a weekend, we were treated to the best of the city: We slept in a posh hotel, ate in a different restaurant every meal, and for two days we explored the Art Institute, posed for pictures in front of those great green lions. Our world was largely flat, but Roger Killebrew made sure that our horizons ran at least as far south as Chicago.

When the classroom was finally quiet, he said, "First of all, I want you to think of the city as a collection of people. That's easy, right? You think of Minneapolis or Chicago or Milwaukee, you think of hundreds of thousands of people. Millions of people. That's what you think of right away. Maybe you think of sky-scrapers too, I don't know. But *I* think of people. The next thing you should think about is ideas. Think of each of those millions of people as a set of ideas. Like, *That woman is a ballerina, she thinks about ballet.* Or, *That man is an architect, he thinks about buildings.* If you begin thinking about it that way, a city is the greatest place in the world. It's millions of people, brushing up against one another, exchanging ideas, all the time, at every hour of the day."

"But we don't live in a city," Cameron Giroux had said. "We live here."

"And this is a good place," Killebrew said. "I love this town. But don't be so quick to disparage the city. Good people live in the city, too. And they're not all painters and sculptors. Think about your favorite baseball and football players. Without cities, you think those athletes would have jobs? You think there'd be any stadiums or fans?"

"I don't get it," Ronny said. "I thought we were talking about paintings."

Killebrew had walked toward Ronny's desk. He liked Ronny, despite his obtuseness. "We were," Killebrew said.

Inside a café off Sixty-whateverth Street, sipping coffee, lost in the city, eating croissants, I said to Henry, "Let's go to the art museum, huh? We have time."

"Really?" he asked. "The whole city and you want to go look at paintings? They've got paintings in Minneapolis." He held his forehead, wincing every time the bell over the door jingled to signal a new or departing customer. Outside, horns blared, sirens wailed, policemen whistled and windmilled their arms. "Christ," Henry said, "how do you survive a hangover in this city?" He closed his eyes, chewed at his croissant.

I touched his hand. "It'll be quiet in the art museum," I whispered. "I promise."

He opened one eye to look at me, smiled.

The wedding was held in a mansion that looked more like a medieval fortress, though all the flowers and decorations did something to soften and brighten the sharp, dark edges of the grand, red-bricked castle. Security guards manned the doors and we were asked to show identification. Inside, the building felt like a jewelry box, the air close and dark, and likely to shimmer and dazzle.

We moved around dutifully, like figurines on a track, Ronny and Lucy close by our sides, their mouths agape, their eyes wide open. Movie stars brushed past us like warm, slow comets. Faces we recognized from grocery market tabloids, *right there*, looking impossibly skinny, shiny, beautiful. Henry held Kip and Felicia's gift close to his chest, like a football, as a gauntlet of forcefully helpful arms and hands ushered us toward a ballroom where our designated chairs awaited us at our designated table. We took our seats like nominees at an award show in which it was very unlikely our names would be called.

"Jesus," Ronny said, "we ain't in Wisconsin anymore."

"I've never seen nothing like this," said Lucy. "Even in Vegas." She looked at me knowingly. "And I *have* seen some shit in Vegas."

After all the tables had been seated, after the room had buzzed in anticipation for half an hour or more, after we had drunk two glasses of champagne, and after the already advantageous lighting of the room dimmed into what seemed golden starlight, they entered the grand space, Lee and Chloe, and everyone rose, as you might for the arrival of the president or the royalty of some faraway land. I glanced over to gauge Henry's reaction, and like many of the attendees, he was clapping, his eyes trained on Chloe, I suppose—her off-white dress, so slim and so gauzy, revealing nearly her entire back, her shoulder blades, her long, yoga-strong arms. She and Lee moved toward a stage at the front of the room, two hundred feet or so from where we stood watching.

An officiant greeted them on the stage. He was young and handsome, in a white nondenominational robe, with a tuxedo beneath. His face seemed familiar to me, and for several minutes I ignored the man's words, focusing all of my brain power on where I had seen this man before, until I realized that he had played Romeo opposite Chloe's Juliet. Now Lee and Chloe held hands, a microphone between them.

Maybe it's because I'm a mother, because I'm used to children lying to me, or *trying* to lie to me. Maybe it's because of spending my whole life around Henry and his friends and listening to their lame excuses for returning to our house late, their pant cuffs caked in mud, brandy on their breaths, the bed of our truck suddenly loud with empty aluminum cans. I don't know. But I watched Chloe closely. I watched her eyes, her shoulders, her feet. She seemed skittish, too cute. They giggled throughout their vows, which is something I distrust. A little laughter, okay. But constant giggling, no. This is an oath. This is a promise.

I wanted very badly to share with Henry what I was thinking, but I kept it to myself. *I don't think they'll make it. I give them a year, two, tops,* I thought. It didn't seem right to speak it aloud somehow, no matter how right I might've been.

When the vows where finished, they kissed, and I must say, it was a convincing kiss, long and passionate, arms draped everywhere. The wedding party loved it, began banging away at their glasses with what appeared to be genuine silverware. But I must confess that the whole time they were embracing, all I could think was: *She does this for a living. She is an actress.*

Lucy leaned into me and said, "He looks like a pretty good kisser."

I blushed, unable to respond.

"Well," she said, "I'm just sayin'."

We shared a table with Chloe's college friends from NYU and, situated in the very middle of that grand room, it felt like we were the hub of a great wheel, our heads turning to gawk at celebrities as they passed by us, their actual hands on the backs of our chairs. It was a good night, truly. Once I allowed myself to sink back into the pomp of the evening, to simply enjoy the excellent wine and champagne, the dinner, and the company, time began to race by, and it was enough simply to sit beside Henry, to watch Ronny and Lucy together, to feel happily lost.

Late in the evening, Lee and Chloe came to our table to shake our hands, and accept our congratulations. Lee beamed out straight love, his eyes glossy with happiness. I watched how he touched her, directed her about the room, his hand in the small of her back. He was sweet with her. I wondered if she knew yet, if she would ever know, how lucky she was to possess him as a husband. If she understood how talented and kind and tough he was as a man. It made me self-conscious, made me dip my face into my purse to rifle around for lipstick, breath mints, anything, *anything*, to take my eyes off them, to center myself back in the present, to be there, beside Henry. Good Henry, decent Henry. Henry, father of my children. Henry, back-breaking farmer and carpenter, autumnal hunter and vernal fisherman. Henry, who, only hours earlier, had patiently walked with me through the endless and labyrinthine Met, badly hungover, pausing in front of the paintings and Egyptian artifacts and aboriginal art to read their placards. Henry, who had surprised me, standing before a Warhol, saying, "I don't know, maybe we should save some money. Buy a nice painting. Something we could pass on. We don't really have much to pass on to the kids. Nothing worth keeping." He seemed to be really appraising the painting, really scrutinizing it.

I decided to test him. "What do you mean?" I whispered. "Like a hunting scene or something? Like ducks or eagles or something?" I hoped not. I sincerely hoped not.

"No," he said, "I don't know. Maybe we could head into

Minneapolis. Visit a gallery. I think I just want something very green. Something to look at during winter."

I thought to myself, *Here is a sweet, sweet man.*

Lee and Chloe were still on the other side of the table, attending to Chloe's people, shaking hands and offering their cheeks for kisses—a practice totally foreign to us Midwesterners. By and by we stood and waited, our hands in our pockets or crossed over our stomachs, until it was our turn to hug the bride and groom, to tell them how beautiful they looked, how happy, how magical a night this was.

"I almost forgot," said Henry, "Kip and Felicia send their regards." He handed Lee the box.

"Should I open it here?" Lee asked, frowning.

"Why not?" said Chloe. "As long as we don't forget it."

"Yeah," said Ronny, "open it, man."

"We can leave it with your driver," I offered, "or even take it back to Wisconsin, if you want."

Lee nodded. "All right."

It was a small black-and-white picture of the mill, elegantly framed. In the picture, our town looked different, both more primitive and more civilized than it did now, with two- and three-story brick buildings on Main leading to the mill. With horses and carriages, with men in wool three-piece suits and women in long dresses. Every building in the photograph looking as if it might and should stand forever, though most, we knew, had been demolished in the seventies and eighties, if they'd made it that long at all.

"God," he said, "look at that. Home." Chloe stood beside her new husband, at a sudden loss for what to say, simply staring at the photograph with a look I recognized: *Not on my walls.* He passed it around to us. Ronny was the one who found the inscription on the back of the image in a strong, careful cursive: *To Chloe*

& Leland: In big cities and small towns we wish you the best of love and luck. Your friends—Felicia & Kip Cunningham.

"Well," Chloe said, recovering. "That was a thoughtful thing to do. They certainly didn't *have* to do that."

"I really think they're trying, you know? To be, I don't know, better people," I offered at last, careful to avoid bringing up Kip's wedding day or the bachelor party, but defensive of Felicia, my new friend, a woman I knew to be so graceful, and kind, and thoughtful.

The photograph had returned to Lee's hands. He studied it with an odd look on his face. "You wonder," he said, quiet enough that he might have been speaking to himself. "You really just have to wonder about people."

"Why don't we take that home for you?" I offered. "We'll wrap it back up in its box, and next time you come through town it'll be at our place, waiting for you." I assumed that after the wedding, after their honeymoon, after things settled down, that Lee and Chloe would return to Wisconsin, that we'd start up again, that eventually, everything would slip back into its rightful place the way it had been before Kip's wedding. But I watched as Chloe wound her arm around Lee's now, and his expression shifted and darkened.

"That's okay," he said. "I'll take it home with us tonight. We've found a place here, but the walls are still pretty bare." He looked at Henry. "Be sure to thank Kip for me, though. This is really something."

Then Lee hugged us all one more time, as if we were going away for a long, long time. I felt his rib cage against my chest, remembered how skinny he was that winter, at Bea Cather's farmhouse out on the range and, kissing his cheek, I said into his ear, "Take care of yourself."

I don't know why I suddenly felt so sad, but I did, I really did. New York City felt as far away from Wisconsin as I could imagine.

When he waved to us and moved to another table, smiling, laughing at their jokes, I thought, *Maybe we weigh him down. Maybe he needs to let us go.*

I looked down at my dress, Felicia's beautiful dress, at my body, hardened from all the miles I had pounded out on the roads near our house, and that was the only place I wanted to be—back home. The kids, crawling into our bed on a Sunday morning—or not, just Henry and me, watching the new white-yellow sunlight set the lace curtains on fire, the black fields beyond, studded in green and growing greener every day; mourning doves on the telephone wires and perched atop our silo, cooing; and all those men, all of Henry's friends, stopping by our house unannounced, throwing our children in the air effortlessly, crowding around our kitchen table for coffee and pie. I thought of the Giroux twins, standing around Henry, almost like a football huddle, talking about seed or tractors, talking about rain or erosion, talking loud and sure, like two men who'd never left town and never would. Two kings sharing a kingdom. It is true that I smiled then, thinking of them. Thinking of pot-bellied Eddy Moffit lumbering down Main, grinning kindly at passing cars, tapping them on their slow-moving trunks, hiking his pants up only to have them drift down again, beneath the great, fleshy porch of his belly. Eddy, in our church, reading out that week's scripture, doing so with a rich, generous baritone, the kind of voice you imagine as a child, reading you bedtime stories. Eddy, looking out over the church, out over reading glasses like two half-moons. Easing his Bible shut and saying, "Here ends the reading." Or Ronny. Ronny roaming Little Wing's streets, falling asleep in the warmth of the public library, a newspaper spread out before him, and *What do you suppose he was reading?* Or volunteering at the high school as a varsity football coach, bracing tackling dummies for collisions, the town kids protecting Ronny, treating him the way you might a revered uncle, a damaged angel.

Ronny, lonely on a Tuesday night, wandering into the VFW, where the bartenders know to serve him only Coca-Cola, to place bowls of popcorn before him, to switch the big television up top to rodeo coverage on ESPN, or nature documentaries of the American West on PBS.

"Come on," I said to Henry. "I'm tired. Let's go."

He looked at me, pulling back to survey my face. "You sure?" he asked. "The night's young. You want to dance? We haven't even had cake yet."

"I'm sure, let's go. Come on, let's get a cab."

I kissed Ronny on the cheek, so happy that he was there, there with a woman, just like any other man, and to anyone else in the room, no different. Lucy sat in his lap, her long legs crossed, off the ground.

"Go on," she said, "I think we'll hang on here for a while." She shooed us away with a hand. "Don't worry—I'll watch this one."

Outside the mansion, we found our driver, rolling dice against a curb with three other chauffeurs, dollar bills stacked on the pavement, music pumping from the back of a parked limousine. We told him to wait for Ronny and Lucy, that we were going for a walk. He seemed unconcerned, and waved us good-bye, hunched over the curb and rattling the dice in a big noisy fist.

We did walk for a while, watched the NYC police, leaning against their squad cars, the street vendors, lit by greasy light-bulbs, slinging food into waxed sheets of paper, into paper boats. Watched diners through the huge windows of fashionable restaurants, bouncers with folded arms outside clubs with no windows, and young people: the cocktail-dress girls on the prowl, the throwback hipsters in secondhand shoes and skinny jeans with suspenders and ironic facial hair, the seersucker-bow-tie boys with deck shoes and Ray-Ban sunglasses at ten o'clock at night.

I moved off the curb, hailed a taxi, the easiest thing in the world for a woman in a tight-fitting evening dress to do. Two fingers in the night air, as if I were testing the temperature, one leg out, at a thirty-degree angle, the other straight up to my shifted hip. Henry behind me, like a boy seduced. A yellow shark crossed three lanes of traffic with an almost unsettling swiftness and pulled right up to us, suddenly at our service.

I passed the cabbie a hundred-dollar bill, a gift from my parents before we'd left. My father had handed it to me saying something like, *Have fun, okay? Don't worry about anything. You two kids have some fun.*

"Just drive us around," I said, "I don't know. Show us whatever you think a tourist should see. We're staying at the Waldorf. So whenever we run out of money, just drop us off there."

He took the money wordlessly, eyeballed us in his mirror, and eased the cab away from the curb, soon settling into a speed that seemed just about right for touring. I leaned into Henry, rested my head on his chest, felt his heartbeat.

"You okay?" he asked, kissing the top of my head. "You seem a little out of sorts."

"I'm fine," I said. "I think I'm just ready to be home. To see the kids."

Skyscrapers flashed by, all of them invisible to me just then, all of them the same.

"Maybe we can come back here," Henry offered. "I don't know. Next spring? Come out and visit them. Make it a yearly thing. You could go shopping. I'd like to see a baseball game here." He looked down at me, his chin compressing itself, the type of angle you only see on the face of a person you love—his nose hairs, the crow's feet about his eyes, his hairline, gently receding. I pulled his face down to me, and we kissed.

I didn't answer him, just closed my eyes, felt the road beneath us, traffic lights flashing, flooding over my face, Henry's hands in my hair.

I don't know how much time passed before the cabbie pulled the car to a stop, said in a deadpan voice, "The Brooklyn Bridge," as if we had requested this destination as part of our tour. "Go on," he said, "take a look. I'll be right here."

We stepped out of the cab, the air suddenly warmer, wetter around us, and above, hulking over everything, this great gray bridge of granite and steel, the lights of cars traveling both toward us and away, the gentle lapping of the black river water, a tugboat's horn, faint laughter.

"Mr. Killebrew used to tell us that he thought the world's best cities all had one thing in common," I said, looking at Henry. "Do you remember that?"

Henry nodded. "I do," he said. "He really liked bridges, didn't he?"

"You remember?"

Henry said, "I was afraid to admit it then, but I really liked him, you know? He tried to get me to go to college for painting, you believe that?"

I could actually feel my jaw drop, my mouth hanging wide open. It's a funny thing, being married to someone for so long, being someone's best friend for so long. Because on those few occasions when they surprise you, it feels like the biggest thing in the world, like a crack in the sky, like the moon, suddenly rising over the horizon twenty times bigger than the last time you looked.

"I had—I never knew," I stuttered. "What did you paint?"

He kicked at an upturned street-brick. "I liked to paint the mill. Tractors. Creeks. I don't know. I think Killebrew was just being nice."

We watched the traffic on the bridge, stood against each other, quietly.

"Come on," Henry said after a while. "Maybe he'll take us to another one."

We rode the city, holding hands, sometimes stealing little kisses, other times as composed as perfect strangers next to each other, staring out our separate windows.

"Can I tell you something?" I finally said, breaking the silence.

"What is it?"

"I don't think they're going to make it. Lee and Chloe, I mean."

Henry studied me, exhaled deeply, looked out at the city. "Why not?"

"I don't know. I just have a feeling."

"I feel like he's not coming back," Henry said. "Like he's gone already."

"I'm sorry."

"I suppose you get to a point where you can't be, you know, stymied anymore. Where you need to find a bigger place. I mean—is he really supposed to stay in Little Wing? I don't know."

"I'm sorry, Henry."

"We've been friends since we were eight years old."

"I know."

"And now it's like, I don't know, it doesn't *feel* like him anymore."

"I'm not sure I like her," I said.

We stopped at an intersection bathed in red. An old man pushed a three-wheeled shopping cart loaded with what looked to be everything he owned in the world. I watched him struggle to push the cart up a curb. The light turned green.

"I miss winter," Henry said.

"I miss fall," I said.

I pulled the U-Haul to the side of Uecker Road, to the mouth of my driveway where the gravel scatters itself out onto the asphalt like a runaway game of marbles. My mail had been forwarded on to New York the last few months, but still, circulars and a few envelopes littered the dirt and weeds around the mailbox. I stooped over, collected the soggy paper into a sodden bundle. The mail was everywhere, and many of the letters were hand-tooled—*fan letters*. I can recognize the handwriting of a heartbroken thirteen-year-old girl from across the room: pink ink, that big bubble alphabet, exclamation marks galore. Or the handwriting of a down-on-his-luck twenty-something Midwestern meatpacker or pipefitter: bold angry block lettering, yellow legal paper, misspelled words crossed out everywhere. Some of the letters had blown all the way into the ditch. My legs were tired from the drive, but ambling down into the ditch, into the cattails, it was a pleasure to feel my spinal cord unbow. My Red Wings became soaked, my socks sopping. I had no idea how long ago those letters had been delivered, how long they'd sat in the ditch, their ink bleeding out, but I couldn't leave them there like that, strewn around like so much garbage—like I didn't care. Because I do care. I was happy to find them there. Especially just then, arriving back home. It was as good as someone hanging a giant WELCOME HOME banner across the driveway. Though, of course, no one did know that I was coming home. Anyway, I knew I'd have something to read, someone to write to if the loneliness was too much.

After I was satisfied that all the wayward mail had been collected, I set the wet stack on the bench seat of the truck, then walked toward the thick steel chain that hangs across the entrance of my driveway. Just six months before, I'd dug two holes, setting the posts into the stony ground on either side of the driveway, and then poured cement around the posts, and when the cement set, I hung the chain, padlocked the works, and caught a flight from Minneapolis to New York. I'd never done anything like that before, never fenced myself or my house off from the outside world, never felt the need for it, even with the occasional trespassing journalist, autograph hound, or groupie. I remember thinking that the chain was something *new*, some kind of *sign*, that I was becoming less attached to Little Wing, to Wisconsin. It had scared me. But that was in the spring, before my wedding, back when I was still officially single. And now I was single again, I guessed, though technically, *legally*, we were only separated. We were getting a divorce, Chloe and I. The wedding ring was still on my finger, but it had begun to feel more ridiculous each day I wore it. The whole drive from New York back home I hung that left arm out the driver's-side window, letting the night cool contract my skin and always with the idea that I might lose it somewhere along the way. But it hung on, still noosing my finger tight. Sort of a souvenir of love, I thought, spinning it around and around.

I slid a key into the silver padlock and it sprang open with a jerk. *Maybe I'll mail the ring to a fan*, I thought. *Wouldn't that be something?* I set the chain down in a shiny pile off to the side, returned to the U-Haul, fired up the ignition, and pulled the cumbersome truck off the road in a cloud of black and blue exhaust. It labored down my long, long driveway, almost begrudgingly, and I rubbed its dashboard affectionately; it had gotten me home, after all. Overhead a canopy of autumnal maples formed a tunnel of fire—oranges, reds, yellows, a few greens still. I rolled the window all the way down, rested my elbow on the door, though it was fairly cool outside, and breathed the air in.

Home.

The dirt and gravel potholes were filled with rainwater and I intentionally aimed the U-Haul's wheels for each one. I've always liked to hear that splash, liked to feel the coils under my seat bounce and groan as I inched closer to home and the meadow, the trees I've planted and the creek beyond.

I relaxed, felt my shoulders loosen, my eyes widen. I hadn't felt that way in months. Hadn't felt *healthy.*

Home.

The woods opened out now into the meadow, where I could see in the early-morning light that the summer grasses and raspberry bushes had gone yellow-brown in patches. And then, *look:* a dozen or more deer, their ears suddenly pricked up at attention, their white tails semaphores of caution. What could they have been thinking, as they watched the approach of that big, boxy, unfamiliar truck? Did they recognize me? I watched their very skin and musculature ripple and tremble with excitement and fear. I waved to them, waved goofily, waved like I knew I was alone, yelled out the window, "Hey, deer! I'm back! Lee's back!" And that sent them scattering away.

I need to get a salt block out there, I thought. *I'm going to need some company.*

I parked the U-Haul in front of the driveway and went up to

the front door, fumbling with my keys, and opened the place up, leaving the door yawning open so I could carry in a few loads. Stretching, groaning, scratching my head, all I wanted was a shower, to brush my teeth, to drink a cold glass of water. *The water tastes better here, tastes like something—like iron,* I thought. *Or maybe it's the absence of things. The absence of chlorine, of sulfur, of being recycled a thousand times over.* Outside, the deer had begun drifting back toward the shadows of the trees near the hem of the pasture. There was so much to do and at the same time, nothing to do at all. God, to just make myself a pot of coffee, to spark up a cigarette on the porch, to find out if the old tractor would turn over. I'm sure I stood in my entryway a full five minutes, just walking in circles, just happy as hell to be home.

Home.

The air inside the house smelled stale. Dead flies lay scattered on the window sills and the floors beneath. A layer of dust over everything: the furniture, my books, on the television screen. At the kitchen sink I turned on the tap but the pipes just coughed hoarsely, like they had an announcement they weren't entirely sure they wanted to make. I remembered I'd shut off the water, had of course never thought that I'd be back this soon. And yet, there I was. Down in the basement, I turned the water back on, heard the kitchen tap sputter then rasp out water, at first haltingly, and then coming in an easy flow. All around the house I could hear the pipes saying *ooohhh* and *aaahhh,* as if they were happy to have me back. I climbed the stairs slowly, the muscles in my back and butt still sore and tight. The refrigerator hummed out a drone and I peered in, looking for a beer. There was one! A Leinenkugel's! I drank lustily, like a man who'd just wandered out of the desert.

Pacing the house I turned the dial of the thermostat, waited to hear the groan of the furnace, that good basement fire—then shut the furnace off again. I rolled open windows, switched on the radio, opened the refrigerator again to see if any more beer or food had magically materialized. Then closed the door. Opened it again—still nothing.

Standing over the bathroom toilet, peeing, I held the beer up to my lips with my free hand—the breakfast of champions. Taped to the bathroom mirror was a photograph of Chloe from Kip's wedding. It was a perfect picture of her. One of the paparazzi, a friend of hers from New York who worked at one of the grocery store rags, had taken it and then sent her a nice copy along with a note, apologizing for the ambush. He'd sent along a few other good shots of the two of us but I'd left all those in New York. She could keep them if she wanted; I wondered if she would.

Souvenirs. Mementos. Keepsakes.

I flushed, went to the bathtub. The showerhead spat at first, but then gushed out hot water enough to steam the mirrors and warm the room—apparently I'd left the hot-water heater on, a happy mistake. I stripped, threw my clothes into a ball, stepped into the water—and then stepped out again, still dripping, to snag the brown bottle of beer, before returning to the shower. I leaned gratefully against that wall of tiles, swallowing down the cool of the beer in water so hot it reddened my pale skin. I closed my eyes, breathed deeply, slipped all the way down into the tub, and fell asleep in there, hot water still raining down all over me.

Home.

I don't know how long I slept, but it couldn't have been too-too long because I woke up with an empty bottle of Leinie's between my legs and cold water coming down. If Chloe could have seen me: a goddamned shivering prune laying one-beer drunk on the bathroom floor, licking his wounds. Anyway, there was shit to do. Namely to return the U-Haul truck. Also: beer. I knew I needed beer. Cases of beer. And food. I wanted a freezer full of pizza and fish sticks. A refrigerator full of bratwurst, steaks, and pork chops.

Standing before my bathroom mirror, I surveyed the goods: a waif, an NYC hipster waif. *Well fuck that.* It was time to get ready for winter. Time to put on a few pounds. Time to split some wood. A towel wrapped around me, I went out of the bathroom and into my bedroom, put on some of *my* clothes—an old green chamois-cloth shirt and a pair of Carhartts, some nice thick wool socks. Then, pulling on an old mesh Brewers cap, I went out into the living room.

And there, standing four-legged and yellow-furred in the middle of my living room, was a coyote—the front door still wide open behind it. I froze. The coyote lifted his head, appraised me, lifted one white-socked paw to scratch the air between us.

I couldn't tell you how long we remained that way, sniffing each other out, but at last I had the presence of mind to say sharply, "Go on now, shoo." I had been afraid my voice wouldn't work.

And he did, turning slowly, like a scolded dog, and went right back out the front door in what turned into a jaunty lope, before breaking into an outright run in the strip of lawn that separates my house from the driveway, before entering the meadow, where I saw his white-yellow back occasionally popping up over the tall grasses and wildflowers. My hand shook as I shut the front door. Then, I actually locked the door—something I rarely do, but I did. I sat down, I sat down, I sat down. I stared at my hands. I felt alive, every fiber of me vibrating, every atom energized, my blood rushing.

I live here, I have chosen to live here, because life seems *real* to me here. Authentic, genuine—I don't know, *viable.* I suppose maybe everyone feels this way—but maybe not. I don't know. What did Chloe think about New York? It's true—that city throbs, every day, all day, time fusing like a weld: late night and early morning, dawn and noon, lazy afternoons and late nights and early mornings all over again and people never leave that island, they live seventy, eighty, ninety years in one small apartment. They're in love with the very idea of being marooned.

But I was never in love with New York, or any other city for that matter. None of the cities I ever toured in. Here, life unfurls with the seasons. Here, time unspools itself slowly, moments divvied out like some truly decadent dessert that we savor—weddings, births, graduations, grand openings, funerals. Mostly, things stay the same. There is Henry in his fields, waving his ball cap at me from atop his tractor. There is Ronny, on Main Street, kicking a stone with his cowboy boots, both hands in his pockets. There is Beth, sitting with the kids outside the Dairy Queen, wiping ice cream off their faces with a wet paper napkin. There is Kip, standing outside the mill on his cell phone, waving his hands like some eccentric conductor who has lost his orchestra. There is Eddy, outside the post office, his white short-sleeve dress shirt tucked in tight against his grand belly as if his gut were a great gust of wind billowing out a spinnaker, buying a red plastic poppy from an old Vietnam vet.

And in the fields as it is in the forests: the springtime prairie fires and tire fires and shit-spreaders slowly spraying the fields with rich, rich manure. Sandhill cranes and whooping cranes in the sky big as B-52s and all the other myriad birds come back home like returned mail, making the night sky loud as any good homecoming party. And then summer comes, the green coming in such profusions that you think maybe winter never even happened at all, never will come again. Long days, languid days and the VFW Post #88, all neon brewery signs, all open windows and screen doors and sweet, smoky darkness. And Kip's mill, throwing long shadows over the whole town. Pigeons and mourning doves cooing there in the cool dewy dawns, bursting off to seed blue skies with the first early-morning traffic, as the farmers arrive to sip their scalded, gas-station coffee, come to eat stale doughnuts, come to bitch politics, taxes, the price of commodities, and everything in between. Late-night softball games at rural diamonds behind crossroads taverns where the sodium-nitrate lights bring in billions of bugs and moths, and wives and mothers and aunts sit in stands checking their cell phones and filing their fingernails, pretending to look on with even a halfway interest in the proceedings. And in the backyards clothes pinned to lines snap in the cooling-down breezes that signal autumn's arrival, that elegant season, that season of scarves and jackets, that season of harvest and open night windows and the best season for sleep. When in the fields everything waits to be sown, the pale yellow corn, dry as paper, and then the soil turned over once again and left to rest until next year. The October air filled with corn dust enough to make each sunset a postcard, with colors like a benign nuclear explosion. And then snow. Snow to cover the world, to cover us. Our world left to sleep and rest and heal underneath those white winter blankets. The forests that in October threw hallucinogenic confetti at the world now withdrawn, bereft, composed, and suddenly much thinner, looking like old people who know their time has just about come. Winter: make like the bears and stay in bed, hibernating, growing paler, reading Russian novels and playing chess through the mail with distant relatives and exiled high school friends. Winter: strap on a pair of skates like two knives and carve a frozen pond with your footsteps, slap a frozen puck with a long hockey stick, then stand still, catching your breath, sweating out there in subzero temperatures. Winter.

Leave your front door open here and a coyote strolls in. But it could've been a bear. Once, Henry and I got stoned down by the creek. And as we passed a joint back and forth, an eagle landed in the boughs of a huge cottonwood just across from us. And we saw him and we were happy for his company. Then a crow landed on a huge rock in the middle of the creek and you might have thought it was his pulpit. And we were happy to see him, too. Finally, a seagull, blown about as far off course from any saltwater sea as could be, set down on the peak of a tall white pine. Three such different birds, and they formed a kind of quorum, evenly spaced along the water before us. We waited, watched, said nothing as they began *talking* to one another. First the eagle gave his high whistling sound, then the crow's gruff caw, then the garish squawk of the gull. Back and forth they went, never leaving their perches, never interrupting one another, each in turn—*How could it have been anything other than a conversation?* We watched, listened, and I could not tell you how much time passed before finally, the gull rose up off the white pine, made three lazy pirouettes in the air, and then skimmed the surface of the river with one wingtip before disappearing over the trees. Like a ribbon-dancer, showing off.

The wolves, the bears, the phantom elk and bobcat and cougars. The geese in their uniform squadrons and the ducks and wild loons. But the deer remain my favorite. That pasture that I watch, their families moving through like nomads or refugees or better natives—I'll never know. I have fallen asleep in their bedding-down places, the places in the pasture where they have laid the grass down flat, warmed it with their bodies and fallen asleep dreaming of, *dreaming of what?* Other Wisconsinites, I know, think of them almost as vermin, a pestilence, some kind of creature that is nothing but an inconvenience, a species that daily commits mass suicide by walking into oncoming traffic, a creature that harms crops, that ruins gardens, whose population has grown to the point of infestation. But I've never believed any of that. *We're* the reason there are so many deer. It's not their fault. Maybe there are too many of us: too many people driving cars, eating too much corn, building too many houses, crowding out the wolves and coyotes. I love deer.

Leave your door open in the big city and you'll wake up with no furniture and no clothing. Leave your door open here and a coyote comes in looking for a handout.

This is my home. This is the place that first believed in me. That still believes in me. This is the place that birthed the songs on that first album.

I called Henry. Beth answered.

"Hey Beth," I said.

"Lee?" she asked. "Leland? That you? Everything okay?"

"Um, yeah, Beth. Things are good, real good."

I was embarrassed. Embarrassed to be hardly thirty years old and getting a divorce. Henry and Beth have been together forever, it seems. I've never seen them fight. They don't even seem to bicker. That great house of theirs, their great kids. Everybody always outside playing or working on something. I'll drive by their farm and they're all on their front lawn sitting at a picnic table, eating dinner, passing platters of I-don't-know-what, natural as can be. Or Henry in the fields, in his pole-shed, in the milking parlor, out beside his herd: delivering calves, administering shots, his hands cleaning their teats—rubbing rust-colored iodine onto that pale pink skin. The Browns live life so easily, it seems. For years now I've been envious of Henry. Married to a beautiful woman, doing exactly what he wants to be doing. Out there, under the sun, connected to everything. If he'd let me, I'd invest in their operation. I'd sink everything I had in their farm. I'd quit music to learn from him, turn my place into a little organic farm. I'd grow carrots. Acres and acres of carrots. Pull them out of the earth, big and orange and sweet as candy. Run a big hose out there into the field and wash off my long, sweet organic carrots and eat about two dozen a day.

But just then, on the phone with Beth, still faintly buzzed from that single beer and the drive west, everything in my life felt discombobulated and frankly, depressing. I hadn't been able to stay married for even a year. I couldn't make her love me. And to make matters worse, I'd abandoned my hometown and all my best friends to act like a big shot in New York.

"Where *are* you?"

Also, my whole life, I've been at least halfway in love with Beth. I've never admitted that to anyone. In fact, until that moment, on the telephone with her, I don't know that I'd ever admitted it even to myself. But it's true. Or I think it's true. I can't easily tell anymore, can't tell you the difference between love and loneliness, homesickness and weakness. What the hell do *I* know about love?

"I'm over at my place."

"It sounds so quiet though," she said. "All I remember from New York is horns and sirens and bass. How's Chloe?"

"She's great. She's filming something in Prague right now, actually." A total fabrication. I had no idea where she was. I had a suspicion she harbored a fetish for musicians and was chasing her next husband. Even before we started falling apart she'd started talking about some rapper from Cleveland, listening to his music incessantly, making *me* listen to it. The day before I left I got a phone call from an industry friend saying, "You in Cleveland? Because I just saw Chloe backstage. . . ."

"Is Henry there?"

"Hey, you okay?"

"I'm fine, Beth."

"Lee, I'm confused. Are you in New York or Little Wing?"

"I'm here."

"Here *there,* or here *here?*"

Deep breath. "Here *here.*"

"Lee," she said gently, "are you guys okay?"

My kitchen is toward the back of the house. The windows there look out on the creek below, a descending ridge covered in sumac and red pines that I planted when I first bought the place. Down there, the creek runs gray and blue reflecting the sky and its surface is decorated in red, orange, and yellow leaves that float along like star-shaped badges. I love my kitchen.

I sat at the breakfast bar, on a stool, the telephone to my ear. *Why haven't I made coffee yet?* My head pounded, blood surging through my ears and eyelids.

"We're getting a divorce."

I heard her breathing change. The phone shuffled between her hands. *Did you ever love me? Could I make you love me?*

"I'm so sorry to hear that," she said. "We liked Chloe."

"Well, turns out she didn't like *me* that much, I guess."

"Can you come over for dinner? Now that you're back. You'll have to come over. We need to have you over. For dinner."

With Beth, I suspected I could have spent one hundred years in bed. Kissing her nipples. *I still remember the shape and color of your nipples. Would we have had children together? What would their names be? Who would they look like?*

"Um. So is Henry around?"

"Yeah, let me find him." A pause.

Is the telephone cradled in her neck? In her hand? Down on the counter?

"I love you," I whispered.

136

Nothing. Not even static. Not the dry rub of skin.

I whispered again, "I love you." *You're throwing yourself off a fucking cliff now. What the hell are you doing? Don't fuck up their lives too.*

And then the sound of Henry clearing his throat before picking up the phone. I imagined a red handkerchief in his hands, wiping away black motor oil and grease. Perhaps Beth standing behind him, filling a chipped coffee mug and placing it in his hands.

"Lee? That you? Long time no hear."

Henry's voice—the voice of an old friend—like finding a wall to orient you in some strange, dark hotel room. The world is still out there. Henry is still out there. Real as a fencepost.

"Hey buddy, good to hear your voice."

"You all right? Beth said you were back in Little Wing. Where's Juliet? Where's my favorite Juliet?"

Henry is handsome enough to be an actor. I doubt he knows that, or would even care, but it's true. I've met and known a lot of actors by now, and most of them are five and a half feet tall with a look in their eye hovering somewhere between vacant and crazy. They're all handsome, but they're about as genuine as plastic. The first time you meet Henry you think, *Here is a capable man*. His hands are big and dry and they come for *your* hands like warm mittens. He's not quite as tall as I am, maybe about six foot—but he's broad as an ox, with friendly deep brown eyes. And his skin, no matter the season, is a couple shades darker than a Ritz cracker. At Kip's wedding, Chloe pulled me aside and said, "If I wasn't already so in love with you, I'd be scheming a way to steal your friend away from that wife and farm of his." Then she licked my earlobe. I'll say this, there were warning signs that we weren't going to make it, me and Chloe, but she was a pretty decent lover.

"Tell you what," I said, "meet me at the U-Haul lot in Eau Claire and I'll give you the whole story."

"Wait a minute, you're already unloaded?"

"No," I said, "but I didn't bring back much either. Won't take me long."

"Hey Lee?"

"Yeah?"

"You sure you're okay?"

"Meet me in two hours."

This whole *mythology* started to grow around those first ten tracks. Where I'd recorded them, how I'd recorded them, the heartbreak, the drugs, the alcohol. Most of it isn't true. Those first ten tracks, that album, *Shotgun Lovesongs*, it just sort of came out of me. I was tired, I guess. Tired of failing, tired of moving around the country, the globe, touring. Moving from city to city where no one knew who we were, who I was. Singing to people in Germany and France and Belgium, wondering, *Do these people even understand a goddamn word I'm singing?* And when the last band broke up (as they always did), coming home, feeling like the biggest failure in the world. Thinking about jobs—about real jobs. About giving up.

Music is a crazy thing to do. It doesn't make any sense. Most musicians are just barely scraping by, trying to find gigs here and there, more than happy to play a wedding or a bar mitzvah. Most musicians have no insurance, very little income, and not much of plan as to how they're going to break on through. But I understand them; they're obsessed, in love with music, in love with playing music alongside other people, with making an audience happy, with receiving that applause adulation that comes at the end of a good night, like a whole town suddenly deciding to adopt you, and anyone in that audience willing to host you for a night, feed you, lend you fresh clothing and give you money for a cab or bus ride home.

When I was kid, lying in bed, I'd hear these *riffs*, these *words*, and then I could *see* them, layering on top of one another, and I saw the way they were supposed to fit and gel. I suppose back then, most of the things I was hearing in my head were echoes of Bob Dylan or Neil Young, permutations of *their* work. But even then I was learning, building my own sound, my own style. I still don't sleep well at night because I'm afraid if I don't get out of bed and write shit down, it will vaporize and I'll never get it again. I'd rather stay up until dawn writing down a bunch of nonsense that never works than find myself well rested but unable to piece back together something that, who knows, might have been good. Most of the drawers in my house are filled with scraps of paper on which I've written incoherent ramblings, tiny poems or images that I wanted to plug in to some future song. Beside my bed is a yellow legal pad so covered in ink it looks like a box of pens must have exploded there.

Now, here I was. Back in Little Wing. And getting a divorce. I still didn't entirely understand. The wedding had been beautiful, the honeymoon lovely (St. Bart's, where I ate lobster every day and befriended a cabinet maker named Jimmy who's going to come up here someday to redo this whole kitchen), and then we were back in New York, out at dinner one night, and Chloe just sort of looks up from her cell phone and she's another person I've never met.

"I'm not sure this is working out," she said. She often resorted to clichés, a hitch in her vernacular I credited to too many poorly written scripts.

"Not sure *what's* working out?" I said, ready to fucking throw my napkin at her face, depending on what she said next. Never have I chewed food the way I chewed my food in that moment.

Afraid to throw up, afraid of my jaws clenching so tight I'd break something. I knew what was coming. I hadn't *seen* it coming, but once she'd said what she said, I knew exactly what was coming.

"Or maybe not," she said, nonchalantly, pushing a single leaf of lettuce around her plate. Her fork made a high sharp noise on the porcelain of the plate, like a nail dragged across old steel. "I've never *been* married before, you know?"

She said *been* the way I knew she delivered a line. A certain affectation, a certain stress, making a throwaway word mean everything in the world. Making *been* sound like a prison sentence, a crime, a war-torn country, a past life. I knew that in two weeks she was bound for Vancouver, a movie shoot. We'd planned on renting a condo there. I was excited to try writing music in a new place. Not Wisconsin, not New York, but someplace altogether different.

"We have been married," I said, swallowing, "four fucking months."

I knew people in Little Wing who had been married *half a century.*

"It *feels* like forever," she said, examining the illuminated screen of her cell. "You know?"

"No," I said, "I don't. I'm totally fucking confused."

I knew then that she was going to break my heart.

"Look," she said, "I think I'm going to crash at Jenna's house tonight. Let's have coffee tomorrow?"

I leaned across the table, whispered, "Chloe, we are married. We don't sleep in separate beds. We don't sleep at other peoples' places." I took her hand in mine. I took her hand with more pressure than *gently.* I took her hand a little less firmly than if she were dangling off the side of a building. *"Chloe?"*

She looked at me. Looked at my hair, my shaggy beard, my long ears, the tattoos, my skin. I know *that* look. I know my body.

I'm not a movie star; I don't look like Ronny or Henry—big Midwestern guys, all brawn and gallant rodeo sunlight and black-loam hands. I've slept with more women than I care to remember, but I know *that* look.

A woman will think she can fall in love with you because you can write a song, because you can touch some raw emotional nerve that most people don't even bother thinking about. Because you can write a fucking lovesong. Because you're famous. And for one night: you're golden. I've been golden all over the world. Been golden with women whose names would make you blush, they're so beautiful and so famous for it. Been golden with two, three, four women at *once*. All of their mouths on me, their tongues. But I also can't tell you the number of mornings when those women were gone before I even woke up, before I'd finished my morning shower. Suddenly, after they've consumed you, after they've peeled away all your armor and your privacy, they see you're just an average guy. An average white guy from a small town in Wisconsin.

"You ever been to Wisconsin?" I'd ask them. "It's the most beautiful place in the world. Great lakes, big forests, rolling hills, the Mississippi."

"Is that near Montana?" they'd ask. "Because it sounds like Montana."

"No," I'd say, "it's north of Chicago."

A surprising number of them can't find Chicago on an atlas of America, even if you tell them it's in Illinois, or on a Great Lake.

Two weeks after that dinner, I was reading about rumors of my own divorce in the papers, avoiding the outside world. New York isn't, wasn't ever my town. I never felt comfortable there. The speed of things, the lights, the fashion, the money. And after the separation I liked the city even less. I could never go anywhere without a troupe of photographers following me, pestering me, asking me personal questions that I didn't have the answers to. "What happened? Where did Chloe go? Where is she living? Hey! Yo Corvus!" The upshot of the marriage dying early was that I didn't have to sell a house, didn't have to move much. I rented a U-Haul truck, pulled in front of our building, and ended up taking a couch, a leather chair, a new television, my books, guitars, and the picture Kip and Felicia had given "us" for the wedding. I paid a bum fifty bucks to help me carry the heavy stuff; I would have called a friend, but I really didn't have any in New York. All of *our* friends were actually Chloe's friends. I left three thousand dollars in cash on the kitchen counter and a note telling her to call my attorney in Little Wing if she wanted to talk to me. The number I scribbled down was Eddy Moffitt's. He might not have been a lawyer exactly, but I knew he'd handle the situation with aplomb and good humor. I also doubted very much that Chloe would remember Eddy, though I'm sure I had introduced them on more than one occasion.

When I emerged from the building for the last time, I stood on the sidewalk and smoked a cigarette, took a last look at the city. The doorman left his post, stood beside me, and then said, like he'd never seen me before, "Sir, I'd appreciate it if you could smoke over there." He pointed with a white-gloved finger to an alley full of dripping Dumpsters, thick brown puddles, and wet newspaper.

"Hey, Tino. It's me," I said. "It's Lee. Chloe's *husband*. Remember?"

He folded his arms over his chest, frowned at me.

I stubbed out my cigarette in front of her building, spat in the street, said, "Hey Tino. The Yankees *suck*."

I admired the covert way in which he managed to grab his crotch and flip me the bird, right there in his navy blue velveteen doorman's uniform, and all with the grace and arrogance of a true, blue-collar New Yorker.

People ask me about the title of that first album and I've told dozens of different magazines dozens of different stories, trying to make my lie original each time. I've told people it's an homage to Guns N' Roses. I've told people that's it about a suicide that happened, three towns over, each time changing the number of towns over or the cardinal direction in which that journalist ought to head. I've told people that it's about being heartbroken—and that might be the closest thing to the truth. They ask me about the songs, about my process, and I can honestly say that I've never been rude to any of my fans—to the press, maybe, but not to my fans. I feel pretty goddamned lucky to have made it—to be a musician, professionally. But it isn't necessarily comfortable for me to talk about that album, because the fact is, I was in a pretty dark place when I put it together.

Because what happened was this: after those first few bands didn't pan out, after we'd disbanded and gone our separate ways, I came back home to Wisconsin, licking my wounds, my tail between my legs, waving a white flag—all that shit. I was as embarrassed back then as I was now, after the divorce. The only difference between then and now was that now I had money. I didn't have to worry about who was going to sell my next record.

I had returned to Wisconsin on Halloween. It was a perfect Midwestern day that buoyed my spirits: fast-moving clouds traveling over a blue, blue sky, and cool, fresh air that smelled of rain and the western prairies. I whipped through Chicago along Lakeshore Drive, great whitecaps crashing against the concrete shore, towers of industry hulking up and over me to the west, clouds breaking against those buildings only to reunite beyond them. I remember thinking about Kip, up there somewhere, or perhaps deeper in that city, in the Loop, on the floor of the exchange, shouting imaginary numbers, flinging pink paper in the air, and flashing hand signals like a third base coach. The truth was, I had no idea what his job was like. But I knew then that he was *making it,* making a name for himself. All along the Gold Coast, I stared out my window and thought to myself, *Fuck you, Kipper.* Though, Kip had never wronged me in any way. I had no legitimate reason to resent his success. I continued north and west, through endless suburbs and tollbooths, until I reached the flatlands of northern Illinois, where the earth looks as smooth and dull as if the planet were a giant cube sailing through outer space, nothing to break the monotony but a huge automobile factory, a few road-side "oases," and an endless series of heavy-duty electrical poles and wires, carrying energy away from the Dakotas and Canada and into the metropolis of Chicago.

My parents divorced after I graduated high school. It was a quiet separation, I suppose. As far as I know, there was no infidelity, no drugs, no gambling, no problems with booze. None of the normal reasons. I don't think of my parents as particularly interesting people, but apparently, ever since my birth they'd been growing away from each other. I heard my father once, in the garage, say to my uncle Jerry on the cordless telephone, "We just don't have anything left to say to one another. We don't like the same things. I just don't see what the point is anymore. Nobody's happy." So while I was touring the back-roads bars and bingo halls of the Midwest, while my bands and I drove the American coasts or toured western Europe, my parents sold my childhood home and went their own ways, Dad taking a job as a warehouse manager in Arizona, Mom moving back to her hometown in northern Minnesota, along the Canadian border, where she found work as a secretary and Sunday school coordinator in the church where they'd been married.

"I don't need much anymore," she explained to me. "I bought a small house up there with a lot of space for gardens. It'll be good to see so many familiar faces." I imagined her licking the envelopes of church mailings and restocking brightly colored construction paper.

And Dad: "I wanted to try living someplace warm for a while. Enough of this shoveling snow bullshit. Someplace warm. I got an apartment in a complex. Across the street there's a cantina where I go for dinner every night. I drink Coronas and eat tacos, except they taste way better than your mom's tacos in those hard shells. You should come down. Pretty Mexican girls. We'll sit by the pool, drink beer together. Drive in the desert looking at cacti."

And so they left me homeless, Little Wing being the only place I really *knew*, despite trotting the globe. Little Wing, where all my friends were. Where I could always score a Friday or Saturday night gig at the VFW if I wanted to try out new material. Hell, I could even play covers all night long. And even if Henry wasn't there then, I knew he *would* be in the future—I knew he'd come back. And Ronny. Out on the rodeo circuit—out in who knows where—Butte or Bozeman or Billings, Las Vegas or Laramie or Las Cruces. I had a hunch Ronny would come back someday too.

Because Ronny was Little Wing's first celebrity. I still remember the night he appeared up on the television set at the VFW one Friday night. The bar was packed, the whole town there. Ronny was slated to ride a bull named Texas Tornado, a black ten-gallon Stetson pulled tight to his head, everything about Ronny tight. His forearms bulging almost grotesquely in the paddock as the bull surged impatiently beneath him. His face so chiseled, so focused. His Wrangler blue jeans practically sewn directly onto his thighs they were so tight and a big silver buckle over his crotch, like a welterweight title belt, like a proclamation saying "World's Biggest Dick."

When that paddock door burst open into the brown dirt arena there in Amarillo, Texas, we all gasped. And then cheered. God, did we cheer—the whole town against that bull—all of us hollering, spilling beer, jumping up and down and pressing up against one another, and Ronny—*that cool son of a bitch*—hanging on for all he was worth, one hand high in the air, as if pleading for applause, the other like a lanyard attached fast to the bull. Silver spurs shining, black hat bounced off, V-shaped hooves kicking into the air, bull-snot flying. Eight seconds to glory, and when a rescuing horse came to take him off that bull we shook that bar to its very timbers. God, was I proud. And Ronny, scooping that Stetson off the dirt and then bowing to the crowd like a real, bona fide cowboy, an American matador, before scaling a fence beside the paddock to wait for his scores.

He won that rodeo. A five-thousand-dollar purse and a new shiny buckle and everyone in Little Wing thinking, *Shit, Ronny Taylor is a rich man! Ronny is a goddamned TV celebrity!*

I wanted what he had, I guess. I wanted to come back to Little Wing and have the girls from our high school, girls like Beth, come up to me at the VFW and stick their tongue in my ear, tell me how beautiful and rare I was, how they wanted to have my babies, how they wanted me to tie them to a bed frame in the motel between Little Wing and Eau Claire, that eight-room motel where we went as kids sometimes to smoke marijuana, where sometimes two guys and two girls would take two beds and two bottles of Jack and sometimes in that room the math became a little fuzzy, and a loyalty to one bed or one lover became blurry at best and sometimes it was three of us and sometimes it was all four, on a bed or on the floor, sixteen limbs intertwined and in the morning, too many people for one small motel room and not hardly enough towels.

So I drove through southern Wisconsin, past Madison, past the Dells, and farther north, the aspen trees so yellow that when a shaft of sunlight hit them it actually looked like a *sound,* like a high-pitched musical note so pure it was hard to keep my eyes open—the sound of some divine sword splitting the air. And the maples, their reds as bold as the hearts we colored back in elementary school, those paper hearts we crayoned the hell out of to give to our mothers. I drove faster. Embarrassed that I was coming back with nothing in my hands, to show for myself, embarrassed that I wasn't a superstar, but so happy to be home.

Stopping at the IGA to pick up a celebratory sixer, I saw a handwritten note in an unsteady cursive advertising a room in a farmhouse outside of town at the ridiculously low rate of a hundred dollars a month. There was a telephone number and a county road address. I had about four thousand dollars cash saved up from our gigs and from odd jobs I'd worked on certain tours. I knew that if things ever got dire I could also sell my car, a dilapidated powder blue AMC Gremlin. I dialed the number and arranged to meet with the "landlord," an obviously elderly woman named Bea Cather.

She seemed to like me immediately, though maybe she was just lonely for visitors. She invited me in for lunch—tuna sandwiches, stale potato chips, homemade pickles, whole milk. We sat at her kitchen table looking out at an expansive backyard that led out toward endless acres of corn. Birdhouses and feeders spaced about every ten feet. Yard tchotchkes, garden gnomes, and purple-blue reflecting balls littering the space out there.

"I could mow that yard for you," I offered.

"Oh, that's sweet of you, but Joaquin's already got that taken care of."

"Joaquin?"

"One of my other tenants."

I heard footsteps above us, the faint sound of a radio.

"How many other tenants live here?"

"Right now, three. Four, if you include me. And the dog."

"This is going to sound kind of funny," I said, "but . . . I don't have any furniture."

"Don't worry, dear, the room I have's already furnished. There isn't much up there, but it should suffice."

"Oh, and I'd like to pay you ahead of time. Six months. Is that okay?"

I pulled out a wad of cash and counted out six one-hundred-dollar bills, laid them on the table.

Bea raised a white eyebrow, looked at me over her reading glasses. "You aren't one of those meth cookers, are you? I don't need any drug dealers around here."

"No, ma'am," I said, "I'm a musician."

The best thing about touring, about music festivals, about new cities, is meeting other musicians. I'm at a place in my life right now where I can pick up a phone and call my label or my agent and get pretty much anyone's number. I have Bob Dylan's number written on a receipt taped to the wall of my studio. It just says "Bob," and some numbers. Not that I've ever actually called it. I'm sort of afraid to. First of all, I'm afraid that he won't know who I am, but also a little embarrassed that I *care* that he does know who I am. So for now, it's enough that it's there, that I *could* call him if I wanted to. For me, it's about as close as a person gets to having a hotline to God. Maybe I should call him someday though. He grew up around here. Minnesota is right next door.

But the point is, when you're around so many musicians it can be great—new ideas, new sounds always bombarding you. Every day you can collaborate if you want to, bang crazy ideas off of people who won't think they're crazy. If you're lucky, your sound gets more and more complex until you're weaving this tapestry out of fabrics you don't even remember owning, buying.

But when I lived in that farmhouse, it was just me—no other musicians. I lived with people, but they mostly left me alone to work. The day after I arrived in Wisconsin, the day after I paid Bea that six hundred dollars cash, I awoke at noon to heavy rain hitting the tin roof of that old house. It was November first. I hadn't unpacked my clothes, and the truth was, I didn't really have any cold-weather clothes, hadn't needed any in months, living on the road such as I had. So I opened the little closet. Wire hangers and a threadbare pink robe, the initials "BEC" embroidered in blue on the left breast. I put on the robe. My shoulders stretched the old fabric and my knees were well exposed. I threw on a pair of blue jeans, some socks, a long-sleeve shirt, and wrapped myself again in the robe, tying its pink sash tightly around my waist. I padded down the stairs.

Three Mexican men were sitting at the kitchen table, eating from a cast-iron pan of huevos rancheros, tortillas in their thick brown hands. I must have startled them, because all of their Spanish chatter stopped abruptly. They all just stopped eating and stared at me with tough, black eyes.

Then Bea's voice, loud and brittle, from the wraparound porch outside: "It's okay, boys. He lives with us now." They resumed chewing.

I stood there, my hands in the pockets of the pink robe, studying the linoleum floor, then the magnets on Bea's refrigerator, then a collection of porcelain chickens perched on a shelf over the doorway.

"Sit down," one of them said. "I'm Joaquin. That's Ernesto. And that's Garcia. Come on, *sit*. Tortillas?"

And so I ate with them, silently, listening to them speak in Spanish, and I felt their dark, dark eyes upon me, studying me, their new roommate, dressed in an old woman's clothing. The food was delicious. As depressed as I was those first few months, I must've gained fifteen pounds on Joaquin's cooking. The beans and tortillas and menudo and rice.

"Excuse me," I said, standing up when I'd finished. "Thanks for breakfast."

"Almuerzo," said Garcia. "Lunch." He shook his head.

I walked out onto the porch, pulled the robe tightly around my stomach. The rain was knocking the leaves off the trees, all those beautiful colors that had lit and adorned the sky yesterday now mostly on the ground—and the sky as gray as graphite. My breath steamed out before me. Bea sat rocking in a chair, holding a cup of tea in her hand. She didn't look at me.

"I couldn't live here alone," she said. "I couldn't stand the quiet of this house all by myself."

I nodded. It was hard to tell how old she was. Maybe seventy. Or maybe ninety. Her voice warbled when she spoke, and yet the tone was confident, definite, precise.

"It doesn't even look like the same place," I said. "All that color. Gone."

"What's your music like?" she asked.

I looked at the sky, the unbroken cloudscape hanging low, dropping gray etchings of rain over the black farmland, the bleached tan stalks of leftover corn.

"I don't know," I said. "Winter, maybe."

She nodded. "It's coming."

———

Those first few days I walked Bea's property. I walked out to the road, walked along the gravel shoulder. Walked through the waiting fields; let myself feel lonely. I wanted to scout my new world.

Not far from the farmhouse was an old chicken coop. The coop faced south, light filtering into the low narrow space inside through a series of grimy little windows about eight feet up, not far from the uninsulated ceiling. The floor was dirt, and chicken shit coated some of the walls like a white-and-black fresco. The air smelled of urea, rotten straw, and cold wet air.

This will do.

I cleaned the coop up as best I could. Raked out abandoned bird nests and dead mice. Swept the walls and ceilings free of cobwebs. Cleaned the windows with newspaper and vinegar water. Between the old walls and new plywood I nailed up, I stuffed fresh straw. Bought five rectangular bales of hay to sit on, and to set my computer on. Electricity had once run to the coop to light a single naked bulb hanging from the center of the ceiling. Light is good for laying chickens, it warms the coop and staves off broodiness. Joaquin helped me rewire the coop and then he found me a four-by-ten piece of remnant carpeting that we laid down over the dirt floor. I bought an old woodstove at an auction in Eleva and set it in the corner. Joaquin cut a hole in the ceiling, ran a chimney, insulated the flue.

I had a studio.

The snow came early. Before Thanksgiving. I remember standing in my bedroom, looking out at a mid-November blizzard so fierce I could see no part of Bea's red barn. The Mexicans were already at work (they woke early every day, worked late, milking cows, mucking out stalls), and so I went downstairs and made coffee. Bea sat in the parlor, reading a *National Geographic*.

"You've been here two weeks," she said somewhat sternly, "and I haven't heard you so much as play the radio."

"Well," I stammered, "I've, you know, been setting up the studio . . . getting settled and whatnot."

"All right," she said, "it's just that I thought you were a musician."

Maybe I needed a little talking-to, because I began waking up early too, as soon as I heard the Mexicans rising. I ate breakfast with them. Made them coffee. We sat together in the early-morning darkness and ate, wordlessly. They left without good-byes, piling into one old truck, and pulling out, the headlights sweeping across the porch and the front of the house, the taillights red and sleepy as they disappeared onto the road. Three men, one bench seat. Garcia, there in the middle, rubbing the sleep from his eyes, finishing the last of his tortillas slathered in butter and maple syrup.

I washed and dried their dishes. Cleaned up the kitchen. Filled a thermos with coffee and got myself ready for the cold. Long underwear, thick socks, Red Wing boots, flannel, a good jacket, wool cap.

Ninety-nine paces to the coop. That was my commute. Time enough to finish half a mug of coffee if I didn't have to watch my footing for ice, mud, or deep snow. Inside I had stacked dry firewood—oak—and within an old plastic milk crate were sheaths of newspaper, pine cones, and other kindling. That was my favorite time, making a fire, starting my day, my belly still full and warm, coffee already made, my fingers and toes cold but growing warmer. Sometimes I sat for an hour or more, hunched over the stove, just warming my palms. Bea gave me an old shortwave radio and I plugged that in, listening to whatever I could find: French lovesongs from Quebec, zydeco from New Orleans, bluegrass from Appalachia, even gospel from one of the local Bible-thumper stations.

Then I'd start scratching out songs, ideas, poems. About anything I was lonesome for, which, at the time, turned out to be just about everything. I hadn't told anyone I was there, not even Henry or Ronny. Eddy was in town, I knew that, and the Girouxs. But I hadn't seen anyone. I never went into town, which was a scant five miles away. Bea liked to drive into Little Wing every day, so if I needed groceries I just gave her a list and some money. If I wanted beer or booze, I slipped Joaquin some cash and he brought me whatever I wanted. Also, Garcia could always score weed.

The music sounded a lot like that coop: a cold place hungry for heat. Songs started slow, then thawed and began to flow. If the woodstove popped midtrack, midrecording, then so be it. If the wind was howling down hard from the Dakotas, from Alberta and Saskatchewan, and rattling the loose windowpanes, so be it. Reminded me of old jazz recordings—John Coltrane captured asking for a cigarette, Miles Davis murmuring to a producer, or those live tracks from the Village Vanguard—glasses tinkling, ice cubes calving, high heels clicking down stairs from Greenwich up above.

Musicians I meet on tour, especially the young ones, younger than me, they ask, "How do we get where you are? How do we take that next step?" I never know what to say exactly. I think most of the time I probably tell them to just keep on keeping on. Stay after it. But if I was drunk, if I was really spilling my guts, I'd say this:

Sing like you've got no audience, sing like you don't know what a critic is, sing about your hometown, sing about your prom, sing about deer, sing about the seasons, sing about your mother, sing about chainsaws, sing about the thaw, sing about the rivers, sing about forests, sing about the prairies. But whatever you do, start singing early in the morning, if only just to keep warm. And if you happen to live in a warm beautiful place . . .

Move to Wisconsin. Buy a woodstove, and spend a week splitting wood. It worked for me.

I walked the envelope down Bea's gravel driveway, every step more difficult than the last, the mailbox and county road like some terrible black hole sucking that letter out into the world, toward Beth. I stood at the mailbox for several minutes before finally sticking the envelope in the box and closing the door behind it. A moment later I opened it again, put the letter in my pocket. And then I swore at myself, and put the letter back in. Then I took it back out. I looked both ways down the road, for motorists, bystanders, witnesses. Of course there were none. Possibly Bea herself, standing at the porch window, spying at me through her bird-watching binoculars, thinking, *Fool musician*. Finally, I put the letter in the box, walked down the road about twenty paces, and sat myself down, flicking gravel with my fingers. It was a warmish day for January and a friendly fog hung over the bauchy patches of snow.

By and by, the rural route mail carrier came along in an old minivan, the steering wheel on the right side of his vehicle. We never got much mail, but I'd taken on the responsibility of walking to the mailbox to retrieve whatever might have come. Mostly bills. Coupons. A circular advertising used cars, real estate. No one knew where I was, so I never expected anything. Sometimes a letter came from Mexico and I enjoyed touching those foreign stamps, holding the envelope up to my nose to see if I could smell anything exotic, but no. The mailman finished plugging our box and then closed the door. He eased his minivan beside me.

"That letter in there," he said, "you address that?"

I nodded.

"I know Beth," the mailman said, "sweet girl." He eyeballed me suspiciously. "Do I know you?"

"Probably not," I lied, "I'm just passing through."

If there's ever a drawback to living in a small town it's that you can't ever disappear from your neighbors. They know where to find you. And more often than not, they do find you. Because they need you, or your tools, or your truck. See, we depend on one another. I recognized the mailman, if only dimly. Though I hadn't lived in Little Wing for years, his face was familiar. He drank at the VFW early in the evening, preferred a cocktail called a rusty nail, and sometimes played cribbage at the bar with another rural route carrier.

"You *do* know this is her parents' address, right?" he asked. "Not hers."

I nodded, stood, wiped the wet gravel off the seat of my pants. "Well, thanks again," I said.

"Next time," he said, "use a pen. I can hardly read this."

I just wanted to be close to her, I think. I wanted to be in a woman's company. I wanted to lie in bed with a woman and smell a woman's hair and touch a woman's stomach, and more than anything I wanted to talk to someone. Was the letter I wrote to Beth honest? I think it was. I think it was utterly sincere, though all these years later, maybe it's hard to say, really. We slept together, that much is undeniable, and I refuse to regret that, exactly, and I'll remember that night the rest of my life. By now, I've slept with hundreds of women. Maybe more than a thousand. I've probably had more lovers than Little Wing has residents. But that night, with Beth, it's the one I remember. It's the one that confuses me, that makes my heart ache, that speeds my blood.

What kind of friend am I? To have slept with my best friend's wife? Sure, they weren't married at the time—they weren't even together at the time—but still. I've kept a secret all these years. And I imagine Beth has, too. Does that mean we're ashamed of what we've done? Or does it just mean we want it all to ourselves, like an inexplicable dream, a dream you wake from and want to deliciously return to, a dream that you could dwell in for ages, as your body grew older, as your bed grew more exhausted, as the ones you love faded and died on the margins of your reality.

The morning after we slept together, Beth was gone before dawn. I could hear the Mexicans in the kitchen, breaking eggs, frying tortillas in lard, beans bubbling away in a pot. Bea shuffling around in her slippers, whistling "Don't Sit Under the Apple Tree." The radio murmured in a corner beside the toaster, smoking slightly from a largish crumb of Bea's banana bread.

"*Buenas,*" I said to no one in particular, to all of them in general. I was happy to see that coffee had already been made and I poured myself a cup and blew away its steam.

"*Buenas,*" said my housemates, while Bea eyed me up and down as if I were nothing more than a bum.

"Your sister, huh," she said.

Garcia snickered, forked eggs into his mouth, then choking, coughed, sipped orange juice and sat upright, recovering.

"She could have joined us for breakfast, you know," Bea said, "*your sister.* She was certainly welcome."

"She had an early flight to catch," I said.

"Did someone get up in the middle of the night?" Joaquin asked. "I thought I heard someone at the front door."

"You know," I said, "I think maybe I'm just going to take my breakfast and coffee and head out to the studio today."

I scooped some eggs and beans into a bowl and laid three tortillas over it to trap the heat, then carried my food and cup of coffee and went outside. No jacket, no long underwear. Inside the studio I kicked the door shut, set the food down on top of the woodstove, started a fire, and that day, I finished *Shotgun Lovesongs*. I worked nonstop. When I needed to, I stepped outside, out of view of the farmhouse and Bea's binoculars, and pissed into a snowbank. When I was hungry, I ran inside for more tortillas, more coffee. It was a Sunday, the Mexicans' sole day off, so they lounged and loafed in the living room, watching college basketball, professional wrestling, a documentary on humpback whales. In the kitchen, menudo steamed the windows. Somehow, everyone seemed to understand what was happening, what I was doing—when I entered the house they simply nodded at me. They kept brewing pots of coffee. When I came in after dusk, an apple pie was waiting on the counter, the kitchen smelling of cinnamon and nutmeg.

The reason they're called *shotgun* weddings is that the father of the bride is holding a shotgun to the groom's back. Something has happened. A pregnancy, a popped cherry, a bankruptcy, a war broke out. Whatever it was that happened, though, that wedding is going to happen, and happen quick. No planning. Probably straightaway to the courthouse and maybe a nice reception sans alcohol in the basement of the bride's church. No honeymoon, no aluminum cans dragging behind a limousine.

That's how I thought about *Shotgun Lovesongs*. It felt like I was holding a shotgun to my own back. I felt this pressure, this incredible pressure to *do it*, to finish, to prove to Little Wing, to Beth, to Kip, to Ronny, to Henry, that I wasn't a failure. That I could do it, I could do something beautiful and different and noteworthy and I could do it quick and dirty in an ancient chicken coop with just my shitty little personal computer and a woodstove to keep me from freezing to death.

That album, that album that cost me basically six hundred dollars to produce, it sold one point six million copies. It's *still* selling. It sells more every week than the week before that. And the lovesongs. They were all written for Beth.

I drove the U-Haul into Little Wing, past the quarry, past the golf course, over the railroad tracks, and over a no-name creek. There was the mill, Kip's mill. Trucks assembled outside, even a rumbling train accepting a freight of corn. The air seemed to idle, yellow corn dust rising up into the heavens. Men dangled from hanging platforms off the side of the mill's tallest tower; painters. Up high, the mill was going from battered gray to a honeyed cream color. Against the blue sky, it looked like small-time prosperity, though closer to the ground, beneath the painters, the mill remained a building that had suffered too many long winters. I drove on, Eau Claire still twenty-odd miles away.

Henry was waiting for me, in the U-Haul parking lot, leaning against his truck. We greeted each other with a big, hearty bear hug, smiled at each other.

"You look like shit," Henry said.

"It's good to be home."

"What do you have to do?"

"Give them the keys and then let's skedaddle. I wanna go grocery shopping, get some beer."

On the way back to Little Wing after stocking up on groceries, we rode in an excited silence, the particles of air between us electrified and happy, though neither one of us knew exactly what to say.

"So," Henry said, and I knew it was his way of asking about my divorce.

"I don't know. I don't *know* what happened. Nothing dramatic. We just—shit, we had no business getting married. You know? You and Beth. You guys got it figured it out. I don't know. I really have no idea how you even do it."

We were silent a moment, focused on the road.

"So, now what?"

I shrugged, looked out my window: a valley full of rusty tractors and junked pickups, ridgelines delineated with rock walls and ancient oak trees connected by strands of barbed wire. "I guess I'm here. I guess I'm divorced. Excuse me. *Getting* divorced. Separated. We're separated."

"Well, me and Beth feel awful for you guys. We liked Chloe. *I* liked Chloe."

"A lot of men do, apparently."

"Lee."

"No, apparently it's true."

"I don't know. I don't know what to say."

We rode on in silence. Over there: a herd of cows in a line, all walking daintily toward a red barn. And there, far off on the horizon: a hot air balloon, yellow as a New Mexico license plate.

"Feel like getting drunk?" I asked.

Henry turned to me, then nodded his head slowly, as if he

needed a little time to consider this question. "I think I do feel like getting drunk. Yes. Now that you mention it. Yes. Though, you sure that's what you need?"

"It couldn't hurt."

We stopped at a liquor store and I bought so many cases of beer, so many cases of wine and booze, that the old man who owned the store lent us a dolly to better transport it all out to the truck. Back and forth we went, Henry holding the door open for me while I shuttled in and out, loading the alcohol into the bed of Henry's truck.

"You think that ought to be enough?" I asked at the cash register, winking at Henry.

"I don't know," Henry said. "Maybe not."

I shrugged. "Sell us another three cases of Leinenkugels."

The old man blinked big behind his thick glasses before adding this onto our tally. The receipt tape on the cash register grew longer and longer, like a tiny scroll.

"You throwing a party?" the old man asked, peering up at me.

"A welcome back party," I said, smiling, and placed ten one-hundred-dollar bills on the counter.

Back at my place, we unloaded the booze and groceries. There is an old General Electric refrigerator in the garage and we filled it entirely with beer. Then we restocked the kitchen until the pantries brimmed with cereal, crackers, potato chips, olive oil, pasta, spaghetti sauce.

"I oughta call Beth and check in," Henry said. "Mind if I use your phone?"

I waved a hand. "Invite her over. Tell her to bring the kids."

"You sure?"

I shrugged, let my shoulders fall. Looking out the window I suddenly felt like a very old truck whose odometer has lost track of its miles. I was overtaken by the desire to get drunk and stay drunk, but I dreaded the next day or the next, the notion of being alone, of thinking about Henry and his family. Of Henry and Beth in bed. Them touching, kissing. Them just being together. Her reading him the newspaper. Him painting her toenails.

"Why not?" I said.

"All right, I'll see what she says. I can't remember. Maybe one of the kids has practice. I can never keep it straight in my head."

"Kids," I said. "Kids." I wondered what it was like, to be a parent, to be responsible for another human being.

Henry was punching in numbers on my house telephone, and he looked over at me. "You okay, buddy?" he said gently. "We don't need to get lit, if you don't want to. We could just make some coffee, take a walk. I don't know, make a fire or something. Make sure your truck is running okay. Mess around with the tractor."

I stood in front of the sink, arms braced straight out in front of me. Outside the window and down below the house was the coyote, standing at the edge of the treeline, where the sumac stops because of the thick shade. I was crying, quietly—I couldn't help myself, it just broke. I hunched over the sink, my shoulders heaving, my heart breaking in a way it never had in New York, and I could feel my lungs burn for oxygen—I had forgotten to breathe—and by the time I opened my mouth I was sobbing. All that I could do was sob. And I was so embarrassed, so sad. I was getting divorced. We had fallen apart.

Henry set the phone down quietly on its cradle. I heard him there behind me, right behind me, but he did not touch me and I wanted him to, though I understood why he did not, why one grown man does not touch another, even if it is the right thing to do.

"What the fuck," I said, "you know? What the fuck. She

fucking left me." I pulled at the hair on my head, pulled at my big, red ears. My whole face hot and dripping. I hung my head in the sink and just let it go, just let everything flow out of me and down, into the porcelain, down the drain. It sort of echoed there, my blubbering, and that half-sobered me up. I didn't want Henry seeing me that way, didn't want anyone to see me that way. I ran the tap, felt cold water on my face, ran water onto my hands and soaked my neck, my eyes, my nose. Coming up for air, I breathed deeply, wiped my face with the dry of my forearm, tears and snot glistening over my tattoos. The first time I took a shower after getting a tattoo, I was worried the ink would bleed right out of me. But by now, they're just faded things, like old graffiti. "Sorry about that. I don't know what's wrong with me."

"Maybe that's a no on the kids," Henry said.

I laughed, wiped my nose. Still, I couldn't look at Henry. I looked again out the window and the coyote seemed to be looking back up at me. A crow flew over the ridge, black and shiny.

"I'll make some coffee," Henry said.

"Henry, can I ask you for a favor?"

"Anything," Henry said. I must have looked so frail, so sad.

"Don't leave me alone, all right?"

Then Henry did hug me and I began crying again, but he squeezed me so hard he might as well have been trying to break my ribs, and it was clear he wasn't going to let me go until I stopped crying. I understood then what kind of father he was, what kind of husband and man he was. I understood that he was stronger than me, better than me.

We sat beside the creek, passing a joint, watching the water carry leaves toward the Mississippi. I hadn't gotten high in weeks and just then, I got stoned quickly, words flowing out of my mouth like musical notes that I could see and touch—the letters of those words out there in front of me like an alphabet banner floating away.

"I'm so embarrassed," I said. "I'm sorry, man. Sorry you had to see that back there. I don't know. I'm just so sad. I'm sad and I'm confused and I don't know what's happening. I'm one of those people you read about at the grocery store. You know? Christ. We weren't even married for a year. Who can't stay married a year?"

"Nobody cares," Henry said. "Nobody *will* care. Just give it a couple months—you'll see. We're just glad you're back."

"But you know what I mean, right? You see it. God. The *fuck* was I thinking?"

Henry didn't say anything, just tossed sticks into the river and watched them drift away.

"You talked to Ronny lately?"

"No. He okay?"

Henry smiled wryly, nodded. "Better than okay, I'd say. He's getting hitched."

"Oh, that. Yeah, he called me a ways back. I'm supposed to be the best man."

"So you heard then."

"What?"

"That they're pregnant. You know, that Lucy's pregnant—the one who came to your wedding."

"What? You're fucking with me."

"I swear."

"Lucy. The one who came to the wedding. She's pregnant? They're pregnant?"

"Yep."

"Is this really happening, or am I just, like, totally stoned?"

"She's pregnant."

"No."

"Yup."

"No."

"Technically speaking," Henry said, "depending on when your divorce is finalized, she'll have been pregnant longer than you were married."

I looked at Henry, ready to take a swing at him, and then, I burst into laughter. And he joined in, and now we were riding it for all it was worth, our laughter loud enough to startle a grouse from the long grasses not twenty feet away.

"You should call him," Henry said. "He wanted to tell you personally. You being the best man and all."

"I don't know what kind of best man I've been, tell you that. I feel like I've been a real shit-heel this whole last year. I don't know what got into me."

Henry continued throwing sticks into the creek, looking away from me. "I thought you were going to leave us for good."

"No, I'd never have done that," I lied. Then I said, "Henry, I got something I have to tell you."

Henry's eyes were on the creek, the joint burnt down to a roach between his lips. The sun was down in the west, the day's light almost all gone. It had grown cold and we pulled our jackets tight, blew into our hands.

"Yeah?" He passed the joint back to me.

I peered back at the house—the telephone poles and telephone wires linking my house to the world, the birds sitting on those wires like notes on a single lone unending line of music.

"Well, it's kind of a compliment, I guess." *Everything inside me is so blurry, so sad.*

"Everybody likes compliments."

It won't be a secret if you say something. . . . "I might be in love with Beth." I took a hit. *Too late.*

Henry was silent. I waited for him to say something. But he didn't. He just sat, ripping long blades of dead grass from the earth, his jaw strangely set.

I wanted him to understand what I was trying to say. "I don't know, Hank, but I think I'm in love with Beth. I think I've been in love with her actually a pretty long time." *She's so beautiful. . . .*

Henry was quiet for a long time, and stoned as I was, I couldn't discern how time was moving, if he had been quiet for a matter of seconds, or minutes, or hours.

"I know we've been getting high together," Henry finally said, "but I'm going to give you a chance. If you're really fucked up and these things are just coming out of you and you can't control it, then now might be the time to just say, 'I'm sorry, Henry, I don't know what came over me.' Otherwise, man—I don't know—we're going to have problems."

You don't know what you're saying. "I think she might love me too."

"Lee, shut the fuck up."

"I'm sorry, but I just got to say it."

"Why? *Why* do you have to say it?"

"Because it's true. We slept together." *Stop talking.*

Henry stood, took two steps toward me, and lowered his face down beside my own. I stared out at the creek, could see his fist raised over my head, could feel his hot breath near me, could smell the tang of marijuana all over him.

"Who *the fuck* are you?"

"I'm sorry, man." *This was a mistake.*

"Stay the fuck away from us, you hear?"

"Henry." *Why did you say anything?*

"We're done. All right? And don't let me see you around, either. We're done."

I did not watch him go away, did not watch him walk up the ridge, toward my house, did not see him pick up a stone and pitch it hard, straight through my kitchen window. Did not see him fire up his old truck and go peeling away from my house, kicking gravel thirty yards behind the snow tires he'd just put on.

But I heard it. The glass breaking, the rage of that V-8 engine, the flying dirt and stones. And then the woods and meadow and sky were suddenly very quiet. Everything seemed to be watching me, waiting for me to move. And yet I sat, there in the dark, scared to do anything but breathe.

MY FATHER DIDN'T HAVE ANY friends. He didn't play in any soft-ball leagues and he wasn't a member of any civic organizations. He shook hands with other dads at church, and I can remember that now, his short-sleeve dress shirts in summer and his navy blue wool suitcoats in winter. I can see him, holding a hymnal in his hands so that we could both read the words, his finger scrolling beneath the musical notes that neither of us could read, understanding only the rises and falls of the music; his baritone and my soprano mingling in somber, self-conscious monotones. I can smell his cologne and feel his hand on the back of my neck. I can remember all that. But I don't remember that he had any friends.

He was a farmer, too, though back then, he and my mother milked about fifty Guernseys and Jerseys—a fairly sizable herd for that time. I've more than doubled the herd and right now, it's all that I can do to keep up, even with Beth's help. But it's fair to say that he worked harder than I do and I remember that, too, him out in the milking parlor, hands buried beneath a cow's udders—this was before all the new machinery that I have now, though Dad began installing his own machinery in my teens. I remember his hairy forearms, and how in the late mornings, they

would be covered in motor oil and axle grease from the old tractors that he was perennially fixing. And mornings in our kitchen,
sipping coffee and eating a plate of scrambled eggs. At lunch:
standing over the sink, eating a salami, onion, and mustard sand-
wich, as he looked out over the fields or toward the barn, the herd
out there, lazing and grazing. A look in his eyes that could have
been pure contentment just as easily as it could have been the
shock of seeing a ghost, the sure knowledge of being haunted.

Evenings we ate early, my mother leading us in the same
nightly supper prayer, and afterward, I carried our dishes to the
sink as Dad retired to his favorite chair to watch the nightly news,
always shaking his head. "I don't even know why I watch," he
would say sadly.

He died, three years ago. I'm happy to say that he met our
kids, that he had time to play with them, to hold them in the hospital after they were just born. I know he was proud of them, of
Beth, of me. I think I can say that he was happy, coming over to
our house with Mom, surveying my new equipment, nodding his
head as I talked about improved crop yields or greater milk pro-
duction.

But he didn't have any friends. The telephone rarely rang for
him. And I don't think he desired friends either. I don't think he
was lonely. When I think about my dad, what impresses me is
how dedicated he was to his farm, to my mother, to us kids. *We*
were his life; *we* were his friends. When he sat down to watch a
football game on Sunday, when he cracked a can of Walter's Beer
or balanced a plate of cheese and crackers on his chest and
cheered on the Green Bay Packers, it was me who sat with him,
who cheered with him. When he had high-fives to give, it was my
little hand that he sought. When he felt like dancing, like singing,
it was my mother who he grabbed to clumsily waltz or polka with
in our kitchen. When he talked politics, it was with me, or my

sister, pointing a steady and patient finger at us, saying, "I don't care about left or right. It's all nonsense. All I ask of you is this: Be kind. Be decent. And don't be greedy."

My whole life, thirty-three years, and it feels like I've never been *without* friends. They've always been around, always been there. And maybe my life, our lives, have been richer for it. Ronny babysitting the kids, or, hell, the days when Lee would come over for dinner and play guitar for my daughter, showing her chords, placing her little fingers in the right places. My dad never had that. As kids, *we* didn't have that.

But I wonder now whether the reason my dad didn't have friends, the reason he didn't care to socialize, is that to be close to another man, to invite another man into your house, is to shake the dice. Because when it comes to men and women, to sex, maybe you can't trust anyone, maybe everyone is an animal. You think you know someone, but you can never really *know* someone. You can't monitor every shift in their eyes, every time your wife bends down to pick up a dropped spoon or stretches to unload the dishwasher. When I think now of all the times Lee visited us, it feels like my home was trespassed, that I was violated, lied to.

No, the safest thing is to become an island. To make your house a citadel against all the garbage and ugliness in the world. How else can you be sure of anything?

After Lee's wedding I began painting again for the first time since high school. I can't explain it, maybe it was walking around those museums or just talking to Beth, but I couldn't help myself. In the back of my tool shed I hid an easel and a plastic shopping bag full of oil paints in their tubes, and a collection of brushes. After taking the kids to school, I'd go out to the shed and I painted in the dim light of that building. Other times I would carry all my supplies elsewhere in a backpack. Out, way out, away from any of the roads and far enough out that Beth would never think to follow me. Tucking a little folding easel beneath my jacket and wearing knee-high black Wellingtons, I trudged over the resting fall and winter fields. I'm sure there must have been mornings when Beth watched me from the kitchen window, asking herself, *Where is he going? What the hell is he doing?* Maybe she thought I was out there hunting arrowheads, or killing varmints with my .22 rifle. Maybe she just thought I wanted to be alone—which was true. Later in the afternoon, she never seemed to notice me at the kitchen sink, washing paint from my hands, or sitting at the dining-room table with a pocketknife, cleaning dried paint from underneath my fingernails.

I brought a little camping chair, and on the far side of a glacial ridge I sat and painted the creek that runs through our fields. I painted the cottonwoods and dead elms and poplars that line the creek like inverted buttresses. But mostly my paintings tended to be all sky—wide swaths of bruised purples and blues, foreboding whites and grays. I suppose I painted the sky because I'm not good enough to paint the things of the earth convincingly. When I finished a canvas, I built a bonfire so that I could incinerate the painting immediately. I'd throw the still-wet canvas on the fire along with our household garbage, old tires, or whatever other junk the farm produced. I hated most of my paintings and I was reluctant to tell anyone about my little hobby. So far, I'd painted only two pieces that I thought were decent enough to drive down to the St. Vincent's store off Main Street, where I donated them both, telling Arnold the general manager that they had belonged to a great-uncle of mine who had recently passed away.

In the weeks that followed, I'd stop in at the St. Vincent's store on my trips to Main Street for postage stamps or groceries, gasoline or toilet paper, to check on my paintings. Arnold had hung them on a beige wall over a hideously upholstered second-hand couch, and in a way, they seemed naturally gaudy together, two paintings and a piece of furniture so ugly they were inevitably destined for someone's fishing or hunting cabin, but certainly not anyone's *home*. I had told myself that if either of the paintings sat there over a year, I would come back to the store, buy them, and incinerate them too.

But then, one day, one of the paintings was gone.

I found Arnold at the register, where I paid for a Duke Ellington LP in decent condition.

"Hey, Arnold, who bought one of those paintings that I brought in? You remember?"

He made change, dropped it into the cup of my hand, shrugged his shoulders. "Must have sold over the weekend. I was gone, snowmobiling up near Hurley don't you know. You'd have to ask Brenda. She was manning the tills. You want me to leave a note?"

"No," I said, "that's okay." I left the store, looking at the blank place on the wall where one of my paintings had hung. I wondered who had been foolish enough to buy it.

The only friendship that ever mattered to my dad was my mom's. They were best friends. You could see it, how much they cared for each other. How the love was there, how the love had changed, evolved into something different than what it was before we arrived, or even after we left the house, but was nevertheless still there, inside of them, inside the house they shared.

When I think about that, I think, *This is your fault. You didn't know your own wife, your own best friend. If she felt she could have trusted you, you would have known this about her years ago. It wouldn't have been this sudden tectonic secret, this bomb dropped on your heart.*

We think the world is steady, rolling through space beneath our feet, day and night, rain and sunlight. And then, one day, you just fall off the planet and drift away, into outer space, and everything you thought was true, all the laws that bound your life before, all the rules and norms that kept things in place, that kept *you* in place, they're gone. And nothing makes sense anymore. Gravity is gone. Love is gone.

One afternoon in February, months after Lee's little revelation, I drove into Eau Claire, drove to a bar that I used to frequent back in college. I sat at the bar, ordered a whiskey neat, determined that if a woman were to sit down next to me and smile at me, and if we were to start talking, and she were newly divorced or even separated . . . or if she were in town on business . . .

I sat at the bar all afternoon and into the early evening, drinking slow enough that I never quite got drunk, just tired. I sat and drank and stared up at a television screen watching hockey highlights, basketball highlights, football highlights. A few women did come up to the bar, but they sat together in little groups, talking to each other, laughing into their martinis, daiquiris, and light beers. They didn't seem to notice me, even when I occasionally rose to walk toward the back of the bar where the bathrooms were. And standing there, over the sink, washing my hands, I looked into the mirror. I just stared at myself. I said out loud, "Now what the hell are you going to do, bub? Huh?"

Returning to my bar stool I remained invisible, and after paying my tab I went out into the gray evening cold and thought, *What a strange place to try and find love.* In the parking lot, my truck looked at me like a disgusted old friend who had waited there all along, so patiently. I drove home, took off my boots, and went into the basement, where I rummaged through my Craftsman tools, not sure what I wanted to fix or why, until Beth yelled down the stairs, "Henry, dinner's on."

But I didn't say anything. I wasn't hungry.

Outside, the day was white as heaven, and entering the bar, I had to pause just inside the door to let my pupils adjust to that box of darkness. There wasn't any music playing, but above the bar was an ancient television mounted to the ceiling where Alex Trebek stood browbeating three nerds in turtlenecks: *Jeopardy*. The female bartender, oblivious to my entrance, was mumbling out answers in the form of questions. I peered deeply into the bowels of the VFW and thought I saw a hand back there, long fingers, waving. Felicia. I moved past a row of illegal slot machines, past the battered pool tables, past a collection of pool-cues standing in a corner, and then past the jukebox so old it seemed almost senile, repeating the same songs like so many shell-shocked war stories. Felicia was sitting alone in a booth, a pitcher of beer in the middle of the table near two glasses.

"Thanks for coming," Felicia said. "I really didn't know who else to call." She poured beer into the glasses, offered a half-hearted toast, and then took a little sip. And then a bigger one.

I set my purse down inside the booth, removed my coat, and settled in. The beer was cold and the first taste didn't set well with me, I would have rather drunk a coffee or tea, even hot chocolate, anything but cold, wheaty beer, but this was the VFW, and *no one* orders *tea* at the VFW. Across the table, Felicia was taking another long pull from her glass, a little foam collecting in the very fine invisible hairs above her lip. The foam only there for a second before she ran the back of her hand across the lip, like a little girl wiping away her runny nose.

"Kip and I are separating," she said, and the statement just hung there a moment, ugly, awkward, and unbelievable. She shrugged, and then began crying, covering her face.

My first reaction was to collapse into the wall on my right, the one graffitied over with the names of Little Wing residents who drank there. *Is everyone getting a divorce?* I thought. *Has the whole world lost its freaking mind?* But I moved out of the booth momentarily and slid in beside Felicia, pushed the beer away from us, and handed her a Kleenex. I was unsure whether or not to touch her back in comfort, but then decided to, rubbing her shoulder blades and neck much as I might rub my own children's bodies. Felicia blew her nose, loudly. It sounded like a foghorn on a soupy Lake Michigan day. The bartender looked up for a moment as if she had forgotten she had any patrons at all, then resumed her focus on *Jeopardy*.

"He doesn't want kids," Felicia said, "doesn't now, never did. I don't know what I was thinking. I have no fucking idea what I was thinking. Marrying him. Coming here." She looked up, held her palms out in surrender. "No offense, it's not your fault. But I'm just—I'm fucking *pissed*. Ever since I came to this place, my whole life has just been one big shit-show."

I shrugged. "Don't worry—none taken." I reached for my glass, the one without lipstick, and took a long drink. The beer was warming; it tasted better now, smoother. I glanced at the bar. "Hold on, okay? I'll be back in a flash." I slid out of the booth and moved back toward the sound of Trebek's voice.

I leaned against the bar. The bartender sat on a stool, her thick arms crossed, and said at the television, "Who is Bart Starr?"

"Excuse me," I said, "I'd like to order a few shots."

The bartender held up a finger. "Who is Vince Lombardi?"

"Ma'am?" I said.

"Hold your horses, sweetheart. Today, they actually got a category I know something about." She bounced a finger against her lower lip, then erupted in a triumphant smile. "Who is Brett Favre!"

"Ma'am."

She turned from the television and said, "If there's anything I know about, it's the Green Bay Packers. Now. What can I getcha?"

"Two buttery nipples."

The bartender, a woman who looked like she'd ridden a hundred thousand miles' worth of back roads on the saddle of a Harley-Davidson, looked at me with two squinty eyes and said, "Darlin', did I just hear you right?" She leaned warily against the back rail, against a rack of potato chips that made a noise suggesting that the contents had just been pretty well pulverized. Also behind her: cheese doodles, pork rinds, and bags of peanuts. And the monster jars: one of pickled eggs. Another of pickled pigs' feet. The jars were dusty, as if they hadn't been touched in decades, and it wasn't hard to see why. She recrossed her arms, pursed her lips, and cocked her head at me. "Care to tell me how the hell I'm supposed to make one of those things?"

"Half butterscotch schnapps, then a little Irish crème, and a little Midori, I *think*." It was a shot I'd always favored in college, and later on, at that fried-chicken bar where I worked as a waitress. I looked outside. It was a little past noon on a Monday. The kids were at school, Henry at home. When I left home he was reclined on the couch, reading a book about Lewis and Clark. *Henry can take care of the kids*, I thought. Already, the light outside seemed to be waning. The winter solstice had been three weeks before, so that the daylight was actually elongating with each new day; but still, it felt like Siberia, like we lived in some suicidal Lapland backwater. "Hell, make it three. You ought to have one, too. My treat." I reached across the bar and extended my hand. "Beth."

The bartender stepped forward, accepted my hand. "Joyce." She set three shot glasses down the bar. "I know who you are, by the way, Ms. Brown. You're Henry's wife, right? You might not come in here much, and I might not get *out* of here much, but that don't mean I don't know what's happening in the world. I know just about everyone—or who they are anyway."

"Pleased to meet you, Joyce." I suddenly remembered with a trace of embarrassment that Joyce had worked in our elementary school, cooking the food that had once nourished me and now, for all I knew, nourished my children. She had grown old, cigarette smoke and alcohol leaving her skin gray, her fingers yellow. She looked ragged.

"Now, what'd you say was in these"—and Joyce paused a moment, peering at me with a half-grin—"buttery nipples?'"

"Butterscotch schnapps, Irish crème, and Midori. Or, I think you can also use cinnamon schnapps. I can't remember." I hadn't had one in years but all of a sudden, there it was, the perfect elixir for this deeply discouraging afternoon.

Joyce nodded, and began grabbing bottles, pouring each in turn. "Well, what I propose in an instance such as this is that we do a little taste test. How 'bout that? You buy this round, I'll buy the next. Dial in our recipe, so to speak. We're still confused, why, your friend back there, I bet she'd welcome another round." Setting the three shot glasses on a cork-bottomed tray, Joyce moved out from behind the bar. "Here, lemme take these back to you. Hate to drop such a thing as a buttery nipple on our nice floor here."

I glanced at my winter boots. Beneath them: a detritus-field of peanut shells, spent matches, empty matchbooks, pennies, dried gum. I followed Joyce back to Felicia, who was hastily wiping her face of tears. Joyce tenderly set the shots on the table. "To a new year," she said. "'Cause the last one sure as shit wasn't anything to brag about." Felicia barked out a surprise laugh, her sudden smile so reassuring. "Cheers," we all said, touching glasses, which were immediately emptied.

"What *was* that?" Felicia asked.

Joyce nodded her head. "Not too bad," she said. "Not too bad at all."

"Buttery nipples," I said, smiling broadly. "Buttery nipples."

For a moment, I regretted buying the shots. Felicia had asked me there, after all, to *talk*, not to drink. But then, the shots weren't really for Felicia. They were for me. Felicia and I had become friends. Which is a cowardly way of saying that Felicia *is* my friend. She really is. She isn't *one of us*—not exactly—but that isn't *her* fault, and I came to realize that if I continued to ignore her, I'd be the one losing out. Having her there in town, having someone to call, having someone to jog with—these were pleasures I'd never had before she and Kip moved to town. And here's the thing: she's a sweet lady. It's not her fault that she's incredibly put together, that she's intelligent and driven, and beautiful. Maybe in a bigger city I could afford to hate her. But not here. Not in Little Wing. I'd certainly rather be friends with Felicia than the she-vampires out on the edge of town in their trailers, cooking meth or huffing gas or doing whatever the hell it is they do out there. Felicia is interesting and kind and generous, and she's never been anything but genuine to me.

And now this. Another divorce. Before Henry and I were married, our church made us go through premarriage counseling. We took compatibility tests, talked about money and children. The marriage counselor was surprised to learn that we'd known each other since childhood.

"That's pretty unusual," she said, "you know, these days."

The fact is, half of all marriages end in divorce. But it's not like, when you walk up to the front of the church the pastor or priest asks you, *What'll it be? Heads or tails?* Lee and Chloe and now Kip and Felicia. And, of course, ever since Lee lost his mind and began spilling his guts about what happened *almost ten years ago*, Henry was as pissed with me as I could ever remember. Taken all together, it was almost more than I had it in me to process. And so for a long time after finishing our shots we just sat there quietly, Felicia and I, in the half-dark of the old cinder-block VFW post.

I couldn't blame Henry. As secrets go, it was a bad one. That day when Lee came back to Little Wing, Henry was supposed to bring him over for dinner, but when I looked out the front door at Henry's truck he was just sitting there behind the wheel, the engine idling, this look in his eyes like all the light normally stored there had suddenly failed. Maybe I should have intuited what the matter was, but I didn't. I hollered at the kids to set the table and they did, excited to be near Lee, to see him again. I threw on a sweater and went outside to check on Henry. He didn't notice me until I was right beside his window; I actually tapped on the glass and he turned his head, looked at me. There were tears in his eyes.

"What is it?" I said.

He looked away from me.

"Roll down your window. Is everything okay? Is *Lee* okay?"

But he wouldn't roll down the window. He just sat there. His hands on the wheel, like a little boy pretending to drive a truck.

I circled the truck and got in, sliding over the bench seat next to him. He wouldn't look at me. And so I grabbed his face and turned it toward me.

"Don't. *Fucking*. Touch me," he snapped. "Don't *touch* me."

I moved away from him. Henry never spoke like that to me. He never so much as raises his voice. Never.

He shook his head, the way I've seen him shake his head when a bill comes in the mail and I know he's thinking, *Where the hell did this come from? What the hell am I supposed to do with this?*

"Henry, come on. Come on inside. The kids."

"Let me be, all right? Damnit. Will you please *just go away?*"

"Baby, tell me what's wrong. What can I do? What can I do to make it better?"

He turned on the radio. Turned the volume way up. Old-timey country, voices that sounded like hyenas, banshees, sirens. I went back inside the house.

The kids asked where Uncle Lee was and I told them he'd gotten sick, that we'd all see him soon, though I knew then not what Lee had told Henry, but that *something* had come between them. We ate in silence—the kids and I—and when bedtime came they asked me, "Is Daddy still out in the truck? Can we go out to the truck too?" And I said, "No, your daddy's just thinking." "Is he listening to music out there?" they asked. And I said, "Yes, I suppose he is. Now get upstairs and brush your teeth."

I watched him from the front door for an hour, but he never moved, just kept the truck idling, the country music flowing out loud enough for me to identify Patsy Cline's voice and then some newer stuff too. At ten o'clock I went up the stairs and crawled into bed; I'd left the dishes to soak, and a lasagna out on the table for Henry, if he wanted to eat.

Sometime after midnight I heard the front door open and close and then the sound of Henry taking off his boots. The sound of him in the bathroom, peeing, washing his hands. I imagined him looking at himself in the mirror, washing his face, touching a day's worth of whiskers. He never did come to bed, though; I waited and waited, until the red digital clock beside our bed read 1:01, at which point I must have fallen asleep.

I woke up again at four in the morning and reached out for him in our bed, but he wasn't there. I went downstairs, quietly, as quietly as I have ever descended those stairs, and there he was, lying on the couch, in his clothes, a quilt wrapped around his body, his head on some smallish throw pillows. He started, as I sat down beside him, and turned to look at me, his eyes bleary and tired-looking. I touched his forehead, brushed the hair there. I had witnessed in slow motion, this man, my husband, as he grew older, as the years whitened his temples, wore away at his hairline, made his bones creak.

"Come to bed," I said gently. "Come on."

He looked at me, like a stranger. "All these years," he said, "you two have this secret. All those nights he came over to our house. My friend. Played with my kids, ate my food." And then he looked away from me and turned his head too.

I began crying. It felt like he'd punched me in the gut, all my wind gone. I wasn't heartbroken for myself. I was heartbroken for Henry—this decent, decent man, this good man—my husband.

"Henry, Henry, I'm so sorry, baby."

"You fucked him," he said. "There it is." He didn't bother whispering. He just said the words out loud, as if he didn't care if our children heard, as if to make abundantly clear that the dishonor was my own.

"Henry—"

"What else is there to say? You know? And Christ, now the fucker's convinced he's *in love* with you. He told me. One minute, we're about to come over here for dinner, and the next minute, he's saying, 'I think I might be in love with Beth.' Fuck. We live in a town of a thousand people, Beth. How long before people start talking, huh? How long before I'm walking around town with people whispering about us? *Jesus!*"

He pushed his legs out away from the couch, and they brushed against me roughly, not a kick exactly, but close enough that it was clear Henry did not have the same regard for my body, in that moment. He placed his feet on the ground, lowered his head between his knees, ran his hands through his hair. "I can't fucking sleep," he said. "*Every time* I close my eyes, *every time*, I start to imagine you and . . ." He stood up, exhaled so loudly I thought he might wake the kids, and then said, "I'm going for a drive."

"It's four in the morning," I protested. "Come to bed. Please. Please just come up to bed."

I watched him lace up his boots, watched his arms find the sleeves of his jacket, watched the keys in his hand as they loudly jingled.

"Fuck you," he said. "You know? I love you, but *fuck you*."

Then he slammed the door and started the truck, the headlights suddenly so bright in our front window that I had to turn away and shield my face. And then he was gone, down the driveway and out onto the road.

"I've asked him probably a thousand times," Felicia said, "why it was that he wanted so badly to come back, and, you know, he could never tell me. He'd start talking about the mill, or his friends, and I *tried* to understand. I thought I understood. Wanting to come back home, to be surrounded by people you know. I get it. And he's never told me in so many words, but I really have to wonder if Kip *ever* fit in here. I mean, even back when you guys were all kids. And I'm not asking you to tell me either. Because I think I already know."

I took another shot, then a sip of beer. Outside, the day had almost totally yielded over to evening blue. Two hours ago I'd called Henry, told him to pick up the kids. It was easier now, between us. Some of the ice had thawed from his voice. He had even begun touching me again, allowing himself to be touched. We were making love again, although, sometimes I recognized that the way he fucked me wasn't all love either. There was anger there, too. I understood. That there was probably a part of him that might like to slap me, to shake me, but that he never would, never could. Henry, gentle man. So tender with our children. There were times *I wanted* him to explode—to call me names, to throw a plate, to break a window. But he wouldn't, not ever. And yet I thought that if he ever did, if he ever so much as pushed me, we might be more *even* again. So most nights he just simmered away on low, faced away from me in bed, and I knew, of course, that his eyes were wide open, watching the snow that fell beyond the frost-laced window of our bedroom. I knew that he was thinking about spring, about being back in the fields, about his tractors, about work, about being away from me. He'd begun to spend more time in the milking parlor, and the kids said that sometimes they found him in there, talking to the cows. *Maybe spring will help*, I thought.

"I've always wanted a baby," Felicia continued. "I wanted a house full of babies." She smiled at me, almost condescendingly. "I bet that surprises you, doesn't it?"

I looked at my own hands, at the scarred tabletop, at the bubbles of my beer, rising slowly and dying. I knew I could not meet Felicia's eyes without displaying the very disbelief she'd anticipated. I glanced up. "No. Well, maybe a little."

"This job I have, I just fell into it. Came out of college, wore a short skirt to my first interview, got a job, and I've had it ever since. Never really had to think about what it was I wanted to do. What would really make me happy. I'm good at this job. *Really fucking* good. That's why they let me work from home. That's why I could come all the way up here, away from the office in Chicago. That's why I'm on the telephone all the time, why I fly so much. Because they don't want to let me go. And I used to like my job, quite a bit, actually. But you know what? I started to think, *This is a distraction.* This is a trap. Because what I really wanted, if I was being honest with myself, what I've always wanted, was to be a mother. And I'd walk down Main Street"—she pointed out the door without looking in that direction—"and I'd see these girls. These fucking *girls,* pushing strollers with babies. Or at the grocery market, pushing carts with babies, and I would just lose it. You know? Why *in the hell* do they get families and *I* don't? What am I even doing? When is my life going to start?"

"I'm so sorry," I said. "I just—I didn't know."

She exhaled deeply. "Look, it's not your fault, sweetie. It's his. I'm sorry for dumping all this on you."

I reached out for her hand, and she took mine.

"I'm so sorry," I said.

"It's just—I'm running out of time, you know?"

"I understand."

She took another deep sip of her beer. "God. All we've been talking about is me. I invite you to the bar and you get to hear me bitch all afternoon. Ugh. What about you? How are you guys? How are the kids?"

I looked down at my hands.

"Everybody's great," I said, looking up, nodding. "We're great. You know, same old same old."

For their part, our kids didn't seem to take any notice, which is, I guess, a credit to Henry. He might have hated me then, might *still* hate me, but he kept it under his hat. In fact, he was better with the kids than I'd ever seen him before. Weekend mornings, he'd wake up early, make pancakes or waffles, and then get the kids organized. Almost before I knew what was happening, he'd have them out the door—the three of them—and I'd say, wiping the sleep from my eyes, in pajamas, bedraggled, "Where are *you* guys going?" And he'd say, "We're going to Eau Claire. I thought maybe we'd go to the logging museum. We haven't done that in a while. Maybe have lunch at Chicken Unlimited. Go see a movie."

"Um, can I come?" I'd ask.

"Naw," he'd say. "Relax. Stay here. Sleep in. Read. We'll be back this afternoon." And then he'd close the door and they'd be gone. Gone without a wave, a kiss good-bye, anything. Suddenly just a big, empty house and a pile of dishes in the sink, soaking.

It only happened two, three times, but I began to realize that I was losing him, losing control of my family. So one morning, the week before Christmas, I woke up as soon as I felt him leaving our bed. "Hey," I said, "come back here."

"No," he said, "I'm awake. I was just about to go downstairs. Put some coffee on. Maybe make some omelettes."

I got out of bed, went to him, kissed him, pushed him down on the mattress, kissed his shoulders, his ears, ran my fingers through the hair of his chest, down past his belly button, all the way to his cock. Made love to him, said things into his ear I could not, don't want to repeat again, ordered him to do things to me and then, when we were done, and lay panting in bed, morning light beginning to pale the bedroom, I just said it, I took a chance and just said it:

"Baby, I'm sorry. I'm really, really sorry. I should have told you. I should have told you ten years ago. Five years ago."

"You're damn right," he said, pushing himself up on one elbow. "How do you—"

"Shut up," I said. "All right? Shut up. You've been sulking around here for months, and I understand that, but I'm trying to apologize. Okay? So shut the fuck up and let me apologize." I gathered a breath, sat up, looked at him. "We weren't married, Henry. It happened one time. *One time.*"

"Must have been some night."

"I don't love him. I love *you.* You're my husband and I love you."

He shook his head. "The only reason why I haven't and why I *won't* file for divorce, *Beth,* is because this *did* happen before we were married, okay? And I get that." He sucked in a breath. "But it's still a pretty big goddamn ugly secret. Christ! He's my best friend. Was my best friend. Okay? Of all the people. Goddamn it."

"I made a mistake. You know?"

The fact was, before that moment when I saw Henry alone, out in his truck, out in the dark in our driveway, I don't know that I would have thought about that night with Leland as being a mistake, but I did now. How could I not? Would I forfeit Henry for him, forfeit my children, what they've come to think about me, and will yet come to think of me? My house, my life? All because I was lonely, because I was curious.

"Looking back, I totally regret what I did," I said. "I'm sorry. Sorry for doing—sorry for keeping it a secret."

"I mean, *do* you love him? Do you want to *be* with him? Because frankly, Beth, I don't want to be married to you if you're not in love with me anymore. I mean *fully in love.* Do you understand me?"

I punched him, and not just lightly, I mean *hard,* right in the meat of his arm. And then I smiled. I don't know why—I couldn't help it. First with my lips, then with my teeth. Then I said, "I love you." I punched him again, in the arm, except this time even harder. "I've *always* loved you, Henry fucking Brown." I wound up and tried to punch him again but this time he caught my fist and rolled on top of me, his body heavy on top of mine, his body between my coiling legs, and now my legs wrapping around him, tight. I bit his lower lip.

"I love you so much," he said. "Don't you understand that?"

And then he fucked me and it felt like we were trying to make another baby.

Felicia had just returned from the bathroom and was settling back down in the booth.

"Sure would be nice if this town had, you know, like a normal café, where, you know, normal people could go to talk about how their lives were so fucked up," she said. "Is that asking too much?"

"Make a mistake," I said.

"What?"

"Make a mistake. Are you on the pill?"

"Not for a little while. *He* doesn't know that though."

"Good. Get back together. Go on a vacation. Someplace hot. Someplace near a beach. Drink too much. Enjoy yourselves. Relax and don't think about it. You wouldn't be the first couple to accidentally let a puck through the goalie's legs."

"But you're asking me to pull the goalie, right?"

I shrugged, sipped my beer.

"You're serious?" Her eyes were wide. She finished her beer.

"Are you still in love with him?"

Felicia shrugged, nodded. "Yeah. Sure. Of course I am."

"He ever cheat on you, use drugs, gamble too much, beat you?"

"No."

"So the only thing that you want, that you can't have, is children?"

"I mean, I don't want to trick him into having a baby if he's just going to freak out and leave us. That's not exactly the foundation I want for parenthood. Trickery. I don't know, Beth. Really? Just make a baby and talk about it later? Like I'm buying a new Lexus without his permission or something? I mean, I'm a feminist. I minored in women's studies."

"So, what's your other plan?"

Felicia looked at me, arms crossed.

"I mean really—what? Get on the Internet, start dating that way? Move back to Chicago and try out a few guys from the office? I don't know how these things work. And who's even left these days? We're in our thirties. And you think that new guy is going to want to jump right in to things? Start a family on the fly? Maybe. *Or* maybe you just try harder. Maybe you move out of *here*. Go back to Chicago. Have a kid. Forget this whole thing ever happened. Maybe it was, just, like, a bad holiday. You know? You meant to stay here a week and somehow ended up staying a few years. Don't worry about the mill. Come to think of it, maybe the best thing's just to blow the whole thing up. Start all over." My voice trembled, my hands shook just slightly. I sipped, then gulped my beer. I had just told my only friend to leave, and the advice I was dispensing almost sounded like I was talking to myself.

"I don't know," Felicia said. "I'll have to think about it." She lowered her gaze.

We sat in silence. Old men were beginning to enter the bar. A Monday night football game. Packers versus Vikings. The place would be wild, a frenzy of green and gold.

"Let's go," I said.

Felicia slid off her bench seat, stood, swayed. "I don't think I can drive," she said.

"I'll call Henry," I said.

"What time is it?"

My watch was hard to see in the dark but it seemed to say four or five.

"Every time I see you," Felicia said, "we seem to drink too much."

You can almost see the curvature of the earth from up here. It's beautiful. The world laid out forever. Sometimes, back when I lived in Chicago, I'd take the Mustang out on a Saturday morning. I'd wake up before the city started stirring, and just head west, just drive, the rising sun in my rearview, like I was racing the day, trying to get back into the night. Open that big engine up and rush across Illinois, across that flatland, those black earth fields, those strange, lost canals, and lazy rivers. Past greasy truck stops and junkyards, past towns with nothing to show for their efforts. Stop for gas and let the ragtop down, the blue sky so big above me.

Once, at a gas station in western Illinois, not far from the Mississippi, an old farmer approached me, complimented me on the car.

"How far you headed?" he asked.

I remember shrugging, saying coolly, "Oh, I just try to get as far as I can before Monday morning." Before I had to get back. I was a bachelor then, as I am now perhaps. My condo in the Hancock building spartanly furnished, cold-feeling, like the cell in some cement-and-steel hive.

"Where you from?" he asked.

"Chicago," I said, aiming my thumb behind me. Though I wasn't *from* Chicago. I was from Little Wing, Wisconsin. A no-nothing town like the one I then stood in, a dot on the map, not yet known as the home of Corvus, America's most famous flannel-wearing indie troubadour. Back then, it was just a down-on-its-luck Midwestern village with a falling-apart mill near a set of rusty railroad tracks.

"Must be nice," he said, "to be free, not to be chained down. Go anywhere you want. Anytime you want."

A plastic shopping bag blew between us, toward a barbed-wire fence where I knew it would become entangled. I nodded, ready to push on. But the gas pumped out slowly, as if the tank buried beneath our feet was dry. "You a farmer?" I asked.

He nodded. "Soy." Adjusted his seed cap, spat at the space of asphalt and gravel between his boots.

I handed him my business card. It was my practice. I had a whole box in my glove compartment, and another in the back-seat. I handed out cards at cocktail parties, baseball games, bar mitzvahs. I hear colleagues, other brokers, say that they never hand people their cards, that the secret is getting someone inter-ested in you and your spiel right up to that point where the thing they want most in the world is *your card*. But that's never been my m.o. I'm proud of who I am, proud of what I do; proud that I've made it to a point in my life where I actually have a business card.

He peered at it, so clean and white in his dry, dirty hands. "A broker," he said. He flicked a thick forefinger at the card. It made a noise like a baseball card flapping in a bicycle spoke.

"Yes, sir." The numbers on the gas pump were barely moving, moving slower than time on a wristwatch.

"Why don't you work on getting me some higher prices?" he said. Then, "Naw. I'm just fooling with you."

He stared at me with blue eyes so pale they might have dripped out of his face, onto the dry ground beneath him.

"Well, come on out sometime," I said, looking at his left hand, only four fingers there, but yet a ring finger and a golden wedding band so dirty it looked like he wore buried treasure. "Bring your wife," I said, taking a chance that he was no widower.

And then we were quiet a moment. The sound of gasoline pumping into the filling tank, the wind rattling some loose vinyl siding, a tin sign swaying on its noisy rusted chains. On the highway: eighteen-wheelers rushing by like runaway trains and a pair of crows picking at a blackened deer carcass, their feathers stirred crazily by the constant traffic, though the birds hardly seemed to notice.

"Well," said the farmer, holding my card in the air. "Maybe we'll do that. We'll have to give you a call sometime."

"What's your name?" I asked. "You got my card, but I never got your name."

"Harvey," he said. "Harvey Bunyan." He rummaged around in his pocket for a pen and a little wire-bound notebook. He jotted down his name and telephone number in a neat cursive. "There. Now you got my card, too."

He wiped the palms of his hands on his overalls, fumbled to slide my card into the breast pocket of his bibs, and we shook.

"Safe travels to you," he said.

"You, too," I said, though I immediately regretted it. The man had never traveled anywhere, and it showed. Back in Little Wing I'd seen that farmer's face hundreds of times on men my father's age, men older than him, too. Their eyes so used to squinting out at the sun that you'd swear they were near-sighted as voles. Their world always *right there* before them. In their bedroom, the kitchen, their televisions. Out in the fields, out just ahead and more importantly, behind their tractors.

Over the Mississippi and into Iowa. Eighty, ninety, a hundred miles an hour. Off the highway and onto gravel roads, racing clouds, racing horses in their fields. If I kept driving west, there was the sense that I could beat the sun, drive forever against the revolutions of the planet, slow time itself down. I probably lost Harvey's "business card" before I even entered Nebraska. Probably had stopped for fast food in Iowa City or Des Moines and somewhere along the line, threw his name and telephone number into the garbage along with the other junk in my pockets: gum wrappers, dirty pennies, gas-station receipts.

I made it into Nebraska. Pulled off the highway before a storm filled the ditches with water. Watched the night sky crack itself like a broken window. In the motel room, eating gas-station snacks, drinking lukewarm beer, listening to televisions in neighboring rooms, lovers, arguments, reconciliations.

In the morning, I drove back east, seven hours straight into the rising sun, my face burning so badly, you might have thought I watched an atomic bomb detonate at Las Cruces.

But that morning, that morning in Nebraska, that was about as happy as I've ever been. Because I'd gone over the known horizon, that flatland I well knew from Chicago skyscrapers with their top-floor martini lounges; the planes I'd flown in. In that Mustang I was my own explorer. It didn't matter that a million, million people had trampled every inch of America for hundreds, hell, tens of thousands of years. *I* hadn't. Doing it by myself. Not listening to music, not talking to someone else, no maps, no agendas.

If I could do it all over again, I wouldn't have come back here. I wouldn't have brought Felicia here. And if I'm being totally honest, I'm not sure that getting married was the right thing either. Nothing wrong with Felicia. It's me.

I don't think I'm a good man. I'm not good to people. I know that. What I'm good at, what I *understand* and what I *intuit,* is how to make money. Or, at least, that's what I used to be good at. How do I explain it? That all I needed were two things, a world weather report and the nightly news, and I could tell you where to stick your money the next day in such a way that I was rarely ever wrong. I made millions, *millions.* Sticking money that most people would put into IRAs or bonds or Coke stock into corn futures, coffee, hog bellies.

But throw me into a dinner party, invite me over for your kid's birthday party, and suddenly I'm helpless. Worse than helpless, because I can never seem to say the right thing, never do the right thing. So instead of being just plain awkward, it looks like I'm being cruel. Because I should be smart enough to navigate these things, but I can't. Some nights Felicia would just tell me to be quiet, not to embarrass her.

I thought this mill, this building, would be the catalyst to change things for me. I thought it would give me something concrete, something real to deal with. I thought that if I came back here, resurrected this thing, that the town would pull me in, embrace me, maybe even set myself up for a run at being mayor, or a run in the state legislature. Go around the county, glad-handing farmers, kissing babies, Felicia right there at my side, looking the part, guiding me with a strategic whisper in my ear. I know that she's smarter than me. I don't have a problem admitting it. It's one of the big reasons why I fell in love with her.

And now the mill is done. The basement is dry for the first time in *decades*. The general store is busy. The parking lot is full of trucks. Trains are not just coming through, they're stopping. I've got a tenant lined up to take one of the converted spaces beside the general store—a Mexican restaurant. This town *needs* it, needs some spice, some flavor. The towers are all painted. All the broken windows of our teenage years and our early twenties, they've been replaced. When the painters asked if I wanted something, a name or a logo painted at the top of the towers, I gave it some thought, then told them that what I wanted them to paint up there was *Welcome to Little Wing* in nice, old-fashioned, slanted, cursive red paint. I could have had them paint my name up there, but I'm really trying. I'm trying to do the right thing.

Sometimes I come up here and I don't even know why. To get away, I guess. To look out at the world. To see what's coming next. To smoke a cigarette.

Felicia left me. She wanted children and I—I just couldn't do it. I could never muster the excitement, the love. I loved her, I really did. I still love her. But I couldn't see being a dad, being that kind of upright, decent man. I look at a guy like Henry—how easy he makes it look, how his kids adore him, how Beth adores him—how this town adores him—and I just think, *I can't compete.* I can't do that. I know who I am and I'm not Henry Brown.

She left yesterday, moved into a motel between here and Eau Claire. I told her she should have gone all the way into Eau Claire, should have gone to a nice place, a proper hotel. Even Minneapolis or St. Paul. But the wedding is on Saturday and she wanted to put her best foot forward, wanted to be there for Lucy and Ronny, stringing streamers and whatnot. Passing out wedding cake. Ushering in guests. I don't know, helpful things, thoughtful things.

"I hope," she told me, "that you can change your mind. Because I love you. I just can't keep waiting. We're not getting younger."

"You should go," I said. "Go, before you lose any more time. I'm sorry."

We'd dated for seven years. She wanted to get married right away, and I wouldn't. I wanted everything to be perfect. I wanted the money, the house, the job—everything lined up just right. Our life arranged like a vase of flowers. Beautiful and controlled. She didn't care about any of that, she said she wanted to have kids right away, but, I don't know—I guess I just never took it seriously. Never took *her* seriously. When we first fell in love, sleeping in my apartment on the sixtieth floor of the John Hancock building, feeling the sway of that building against the constant winds off Lake Michigan, she told me, "I want three kids before I'm thirty. I know that much. I want a house *full* of kids. I want a loud house."

I loved her, so I kissed her head, listened to her dreams. But to me, that life she was describing seemed like living in a riot. The mess and noise and crumbs and the diapers and spilled milk and crying. What about *our lives*? What about traveling? What about nice clothing and nice hotels, what about collecting art and building up a good wine cellar?

With children, with babies, you can wait too long. My dad used to say, *He who hesitates is lost*. With men, it doesn't matter. You can be king of the land at eighty years old, drooling on your throne, barely able to keep a crown on your head and still, you can make a baby with a beautiful young woman. But with women, it's different. All that business about clocks—it's true. Think about it. Once a month an egg drifts down from above, as if a little parachute, and lands in a valley of good blood. But you have to know when the egg is there, you have to hope that conditions are perfect, that, in fact, the egg has dropped, that there *are* eggs. And that the parachute opened at precisely the right time. All of that sounds very much like clockwork to me, like the machinations of a very complex, delicate system. And nights lying in bed beside Felicia, I could hear that tick-tick-tocking, too, and it scared the shit out of me.

So. She's gone.

And I have no idea what's next. The mill is finally finished. We're—no, *I'm*—buried in debt. The only thing holding us afloat before was Felicia's job. So if I now find myself up shit creek, I can hardly blame her. The only reason she agreed to move here, to Little Wing, was that she loved me. And more to the point, that she agreed it would be a good place to raise children. After that, time just got away from me. I kept thinking we had time, more time.

I'd jump. I've thought about it. In my line of work, in commodities and stocks, jumping is our seppuku—I know some guys who think it's the only honorable thing to do. If not jumping, then a nickel-plated Colt. I've come up on three different occasions, actually, with the intention of ending it. But I couldn't do it. I just couldn't. And I can't tonight. Saturday is Ronny's wedding. Hardly the week to make a mess on the sidewalk, as it were. Saturday is also the grand reopening of this mill, and the whole town is invited to tour the building. Saturday, I'm going to put on a nice suit (no tie, though) and I'm going to give a short speech, hand out free plastic glasses of beer, and lead a bunch of tours. Then, that evening, in one of the unrented spaces, a space with great natural sunlight, with in-floor heating, and nice, ample bathroom facilities, Ronny is going to marry Lucy. I didn't charge them a dime. The whole town is invited. Guests are encouraged to bring a gift and a nonperishable food item. I figure, if you're going to go bankrupt, you may as well throw a party to mark the occasion.

As I told you, I'm *trying.*

———

Lucy is six months pregnant, but you'd never guess. She looks great. Felicia threw her a baby shower a few weeks ago out at our place. It was nice. Henry and Beth came. The Giroux—sans dates. Eddy Moffitt and his wife, their kids. Lee was there, though obviously no Chloe. The town really doesn't know what to think. In the tabloids for sale down at the IGA, Chloe is shown in low-quality, grainy photographs with rappers, guitar gods, bonzo drummers. And they're not even divorced yet, apparently.

The women formed a circle in our living room, the stack of presents in front of Lucy four feet high. We'd hired a caterer, and the kitchen was full of cold cuts, fresh fruit, pasta salads, wine, beer. It was cold out, but the guys huddled outside around a campfire, away from the frou-frou wrapping paper, ribbons, sub-dued manners, and finger sandwiches. It was oddly quiet around the fire. I don't think Lee and Henry exchanged a single word. Normally those two are thick as thieves. We formed teams and threw horseshoes, broke out the bocce balls and smoked cigars.

"What's the deal with Lee?" I asked Eddy. "He seems pretty sullen."

"If my wife was banging the Billboard Top Forty, I'd be pretty friggin' sullen too."

So, I let it go. I'm trying to just *let things go*.

After everyone left, after the caterers took their wares away, the house was quiet. Felicia crawled into bed early that night and I found her in there, a little later on, crying.

"What's wrong?" I asked.

"Go away," she said. "All right? Just leave me alone."

I sat on the edge of the bed, looked out the windows at our big dark lawn and the fields beyond, the stars winking down on them, a set of headlights crawling over the countryside. I sighed.

"They're pregnant and we're not," I said.

"*Ronny Taylor* is going to be a dad, and you're not! Does that *sound* right to you? Ronny and a stripper are having a baby and you won't do the same for me. Goddamn it, Kip. It's like that board game I used to play as a little girl. You know? The one with the little cars and the colored pegs and you go around the track and you either go to school or not. You become a doctor or not. You fill your car with kids."

"Life," I said. "The game of Life."

"I always wanted a full car, Kip, and I was always pretty fuck-ing clear about that. So *fuck* you, all right? *Fuck* you. But you have to decide, *buddy*. You need to decide if you want to be a man or not, here. You need to *grow up*. Because right now, I come home, I crawl into bed. All I see is a coward. Some guy with a bat-shit crazy fantasy for an old mill in the middle of fucking nowhere. So let me be perfectly clear, in case you weren't listening before: Ei-ther we make a baby together, or I'm out of here."

Weeks passed. Nothing changed. When we made love, I wore a rubber. Her pills in the bathroom cupboard beside a box of tampons. Good nights and good mornings. Dozens of meals together sprinkled with polite conversation. Occasionally a bottle of wine, but not with enough frequency to necessitate a cellar.

So, she finally left. I came back from the mill one night, and she was sitting slumped over the granite countertop in the kitchen, her head resting on her arms. She looked up at me and her eyes were more tired than sad. The keys already in her hand. She stood up, walked over to me, kissed me on the lips, hard, and said, "I'm checking into a motel. I'll come back on Friday to get ready for the wedding."

One day, in my office in Chicago, my secretary knocked on the door, came in with a puzzled look on her face. She was a nice woman, Denise, reminded me of my aunt Carol. Denise still calls me once a month or so, actually checks up on me. Asks me whether or not I might want to reconsider and come back to Chicago.

"There's a man on the telephone," she said that day. "Says he knows you. Says it isn't business-related, but that you'll remember him. *Harvey Bunyan?*" She held up her hands in mystery.

Initially, the name did not resonate. "Harvey? Bunyan? And he's not a client?"

Denise shook her head. "I already told him he had the wrong number, but he called right back. Claims he's looking right at your business card. That he and his wife were in town for a wedding and that he thought he'd give you a call because, you *invited* him here?"

"Look," I said sharply, "Denise, I really can't be . . ." *Harvey Bunyan.* The farmer. Jesus, how long ago was that. . . . "I'll take the call," I said firmly. "Thanks, Denise."

I collected myself, picked up the telephone.

"Hello," I said. "Mr. Bunyan? What can I do for you, sir?" My intention was to brush him off. To file through my imaginary date book, claiming any and all manner of appointment. Everyone ranging from Warren Buffett to the secretary of the Department of Agriculture. The Jolly Green Giant. Tony the Tiger. Juan Valdez. *A man I'd met one time? At a gas station? In a town I couldn't even remember the name of?* I could hear the sound of wind from his end of the connection; a woman's voice, very faint, politely urging something.

"Yeah," he said at last, the sound of gruff relief in his voice. "Harvey Bunyan. Uh. We met about a year or two ago. Talked over at the Kum & Go, and you had that fancy car. That red Mustang."

"Absolutely. How can I help you, Mr. Bunyan?" I tried to remain formal, busy-sounding. I shuffled papers loudly, typed nonsense on my keyboard.

"Well, the thing is. Edith and I are in town for a niece's wedding up to Evanston and I told her about you and, you know, I've had your business card in my wallet. Well." He paused, coughed. "We were downtown, and I just wondered if maybe you had time for lunch."

I looked out the window. The view was forever.

"Mr. Bunyan," I began. "I—"

I could hear the receiver rubbing against dry hands, or maybe clothing, then murmuring, polite arguing.

"Mr. Bunyan?"

"Hello," a voice suddenly said. "This is Edith Bunyan. Is this Mr. Cunningham?"

"Ah, yes. Hello there, Mrs. Bunyan. How can I help you, ma'am?"

"Well, it might be imprudent of me, but I'm just going to lay Harv's cards out on the table, because you must be a little confused, and I think I can save you some time. So here goes. Harvey swears you look just like our boy, Thomas. Swears by it. Says you could be brothers."

"Ma'am?"

"Thomas was killed in Iraq. Fallujah. IED. Our boy was. Thomas. The one you look like."

"Ma'am, I got calls stacking up, and you know how it goes, the market doesn't stop, I can't just, I can't just take the afternoon off, I'm sorry but, but I don't even really *know* your husband—"

"Harvey."

"Right, Harvey. Obviously I'm sorry about your loss and all but, I mean, we met just that one time, and he seemed, you know, like a very nice man and all. . . ."

"Harvey Bunyan. You gave him your card."

"Well, right, but . . ."

"Look." She lowered her voice. "Thomas was our only boy. He worked in Chicago. Commodities, same as you. Went to Northwestern. Smart boy. Put himself through school on the GI Bill and then one day he gets called up, and next thing we know he's gone. And Harvey, well, he just won't accept it." She paused. "I'm asking you, could you please just meet us for lunch. Forty-five minutes. We'll buy. I think he's lonely. Like I said, you remind him of Thomas. You must be a very nice man."

Denise stood in my office doorway, a look of concern on her face.

"Where exactly are you guys?"

We met at Giordano's, a famous pizzeria stuffed with tourists. They were standing by the door, Harvey and Edith, two people older than my own parents, looking stiff in their Rockport walking shoes, pressed pants, and windbreakers. Harvey looking older and more frail than what I'd remembered, constantly parting his thinning hair with thick fingers, his wet eyes darting all over me, the restaurant's frenetically decorated walls, the crowd of patrons, and the young servers. Edith: plump, with thick, wobbly forearms, thin lips, and a gigantic purse dangling off her meaty elbow. I decided just to relax, to while away the hour, to humor them—two harmless old people and me, some ghostly reminder of their poor son.

We ate pizza, sipped Coca-Cola. They asked about my work, where my office was, nodded appreciatively, Harvey squinting up at me, looking all around the buzzing room. "Sure is busy here," he said. Edith talked about their little farm, about wanting to sell, about buying an Airstream and driving the highways of the American Southwest. I imagined her arms growing pink with sunburn, a streak of zinc oxide down her nose, her eyes hidden behind gigantic drugstore sunglasses. And Harvey: forever distracted by the memory of their farm, complaining about the cost of gasoline, traveling everywhere with a frown and arms crossed over his chest.

"You *do* look like Thomas," Edith said. "At first I didn't see it. But now. You rub your hands together the same way he did, you know, when you get impatient. And your ears are the same." She patted Harvey on the arm. "Sonuvagun."

"Well," I said, "I'd like to pick up the check, if you don't mind. It's my pleasure. Really. And you're my guests." I *had* invited them.

"Oh," Edith said, rummaging through the cavern-land of her purse for her billfold. "We won't hear of it. Now."

"No, no, no," I said, deftly handing my credit card to the passing waitress, who scooped it up like a baton in a relay. The hour had passed more quickly than I would have expected. "Really, this has been a nice surprise. A nice break for me."

When we stood outside the restaurant about to part ways, I was surprised to find Edith giving me a long hug, her body pressed firmly against mine, the sweetness of her cheap perfume almost overwhelming. And then Harvey, never really making eye contact, presenting his dry, old hand, shaking mine, saying, "I'm sure that if you could have, you and my boy'd have been good friends. He was just like you. Strong. Smart. Polite." He settled one hand on my left bicep, and I felt his grip there. He could not look at me and I heard his voice failing, the traffic sounds suddenly too loud, too frenetic. I wanted to shut the city off, to pause every action. Then Harvey stepped away from me and Edith took his hand in hers. They looked lost in the city, cowering almost, their shoulders slumped yet somehow proud, grave smiles etched on their faces. I peered down at my cell phone, unsure what to do with my own eyes.

"So, when's the wedding?" I asked.

"Tonight," Harvey said. "My sister's daughter."

"And when do you guys head back home?"

Pedestrians pushed between us. Suitcases and rolling luggage, cell phone squawkers and joggers.

"Tomorrow," they said in unison. Then Harvey: "Tomorrow morning. We'll try to hit the road early."

I nodded.

"Well, look," I said, not even thinking about what I was going to say, to offer. "Maybe you might like to come on over to my place tomorrow morning before you go. I'll make you breakfast. That way you won't have to spend money on some expensive big-city brunch. I live in the John Hancock. Come on over. I've got a great view. You can tell me more about Thomas." It felt good, felt right. Those two lost geezers. I'd never done anything like that before, or since, really, maybe until now.

Their smiles slowly grew radiant. I wrote my address down on a scrap of paper, and waved them good-bye before Edith could cover my cheeks in any more lipstick, or my clothes in the scent of her perfume.

They *did* come to breakfast the next morning, stayed on until just past noon. We drank two pots of coffee and Harvey paced around my condo, staying a cautious distance from the floor-to-ceiling windows. Edith, sitting at my dining-room table, showing me photographs of Thomas from a small album she kept in her purse. He *did* look like me. It was unsettling. The same hair, eyes, face, build. In the photographs, he even seemed to favor the same brands of clothing I wore, clutched the same bottle of beer I would drink. In many of the photographs he stood in the very same Chicago bars and restaurants I often visited.

"Did you have other children?" I asked, not looking at Edith, already aware of what the answer would be.

"No," Harvey said from across the room.

She closed the album and placed it carefully back inside her purse, then seemed to settle very deeply into her chair and for a count of three seconds or so, closed her eyes tightly, pursed her lips, and then exhaled.

You pour everything into a child, all your love, all your attention, all your hopes, all the promises of those kinfolk who preceded you, and *you just don't know*. It isn't like anything else in the world. Except faith, I suppose, and I'm not a very religious person. But when you invest in stocks or commodities, you can hedge your bet, you can put your money in a dozen different places, or a thousand. You can diversify your hopes and fears, and in the end, sure it's a crapshoot, sure it's a gamble, but I've always known that I could get a return. That I could get *something* out of it.

Twice a year I got a greeting card in the mail from Harvey and Edith. Once at Christmas, and once on Thomas's birthday, which happens to be only five days away from my own. The greeting cards are inscribed with Harvey's bold, neat cursive. They never say much. The same farmer-gripes I might hear from Henry or the Giroux twins—not enough rain, *too much* rain, crop loss, diesel prices, an expensive hip replacement, et cetera. Sometimes, Harvey sent me pictures of their farm, the photographs clearly taken on a disposable camera and the quality of the film vague and overexposed. I'd see a field of seedlings, rows and rows of tender green, or a purple sunset over a field of pale, dry corn. Snow up to the windowsills of their house or a cardinal at their birdfeeder. There was never any explanation for the pictures he sent me, no pattern or theme. Just his life. The same pictures he would have sent Thomas perhaps, when the young man was stationed in Iraq, or even back in the States, at some fort in the humid American South.

"Remind me who these people are again?" Felicia would ask, examining their address on the outside of the card's envelope. "How do you know them again?"

How would I even begin to explain it? That I met an old man one time, at a gas station in the middle of nowhere, that I gave him my business card and then months, years later, he and his wife came to visit me one time in Chicago? That I look like their dead son?

"Oh," I'd say, "they're just old family friends."

"Well, should we invite them to the wedding?" she asked me on more than one occasion.

"No. They're all the way down in Illinois, near the Iowa border. Harvey's a farmer and he doesn't like to travel. I wouldn't want to bother them. We're not that close, not really."

"Are you sure? They seem to really care about you. I mean— they send more cards than your parents do."

"No, trust me. It's okay."

And then, a few months ago, there's a note. But it isn't written in Harvey's cursive. This is a softer script, more elegant, more curvaceous, the indentation of the pen less severe. And walking back from the mailbox I read the news that Harvey had died. That he'd had a bad accident with a piece of farm machinery. That Edith had found him out there, in one of his fields, that there was nothing for her to do, no more time, that he was gone too.

And I've thought, as I'm thinking now, why *hadn't* I invited them to the wedding? Of all people—why *not* them? Who would have been more proud? Who had given of their time and faith more unwaveringly? Who had actually loved me, like a son? And what had I done? Telephoned them? Not once. Written? Maybe once a year. Visited? Never.

How proud would they have been of me? Of Felicia?

How can I be a father? How can I be trusted? What have I ever done but fail? Fail with Felicia, fail Leland, fail poor old Harvey. And now, this business. God. Who am I?

The sun is rising. Soon, the day's first customers will begin to trickle in. Lee used to hear music in sunsets—jazz. I don't know about that. And the sunrise? I don't think sunrise has a musical sound. To me, it's like a beautiful woman yawning as she first wakes up, or maybe, I don't know, a baby. A baby opening her eyes. Maybe both. Either way, I feel less and less that I deserve another day, another dawn like this one.

WE WATCHED THE BLIZZARD come creeping across the Doppler radar on the teevee like some kind of alien invasion: a huge blob of white stretching from Oklahoma all the way to Ontario, but the brunt of the storm aimed square at us, right at Wisconsin. On the teevee there were pictures of what lay behind in the blizzard's path: streets buried in Iowa City, Iowa, and telephone lines down in Lincoln, Nebraska. Cattle frozen to the fucking ground in Pierre, South Dakota, and a forty-car pileup outside of St. Louis, Missouri. The weather woman wore a very yellow blouse as she told us the storm was set to strike on Saturday, January 5—the day of my wedding to Miss Lucinda Barnes.

The Friday afternoon before the wedding, Lee drove me into Eau Claire, to the men's clothing store inside a little strip mall off Hastings Way, near the Army Navy store and a closed-down Chinese restaurant shaped like a red pagoda. We went there to pick up our tuxedos, to make sure everything fit just right. Lucy wanted me and Lee to wear tuxedos that matched, but I insisted on choosing my own wedding suit. For one thing, I planned on wearing a new pair of cowboy boots and a turquoise bolo my dad had bought on a family trip to Albuquerque. I smiled into the mirror, checked myself out.

We ate lunch together at Lee's favorite fried chicken restaurant right down the road—Chicken Unlimited—the last business left alive alongside an old highway that got bypassed a long time ago. We sat on red stools and ate French fries, fried chicken sandwiches, and cheese curds. We sipped root beer, and he read me articles out of some old copies of *Sports Illustrated*.

After lunch Lee drove us to the bowling alley. Lee is a straight-up *shitty* bowler—he really is. He scored a 101 and I got a 215. But it was fun. The bowling alley was sort of abandoned, and we supposed that was because the blizzard was coming, and people were at the grocery stores stocking up on food and whatnot.

"Christ," Lee said, "you'd think a hurricane was brewing the way people are acting. This is *Wisconsin*."

"Lucy's worried about the wedding," I said. "She's worried people won't be able to drive out to Little Wing, or their planes'll get delayed over Minnesota."

"Ah, well," Lee said, "the important thing is, you're getting married. Right, buddy? I'll be there. And Kip and Felicia. Eddy. The Girouxs. Beth and the kids."

"And Henry."

Lee nodded, spun a bowling ball in his hands. "Yep. Henry, too."

"Maybe we ought to head back," I said. "We don't need to bowl two games. Let's get home." Outside, the sky was going gray.

Lee drove slow back to Little Wing, taking back roads and glancing up at the sky through the windshield.

"Gettin' dark out there," he said.

I wondered what Lucy was doing just then, wondered if her hands were resting on top of her stomach, if the baby was kicking her. I remembered my own parents, wished they were still alive, wished I could see them on my wedding day.

"Well," Lee said. "Your last hours of bachelorhood." He looked across the bench seat at me. "Any last requests?"

There was already a fresh layer of snow covering everything. The sun had turned in for the day. Lee turned on the headlights, though it was barely four in the afternoon. He was a good driver, slow and deliberate.

"You know what I wish?" I asked.

"No."

"I wish I knew why you and Henry ain't talkin'."

Lee looked away from the road for a second, toward his driver's-side mirror; not a car or snowplow or salt truck in sight, I knew. It was just us out there on those roads.

"Because, Lee, it just don't feel right. Something's wrong. You two are never 'round each other no more."

It was true. I couldn't figure it out, but something had come between them like a wedge, and when we all got together, them two seemed to push each other to opposite sides of the room. They didn't joke anymore. They didn't get together like they always used to, so close they might be horses in a stall, their shoulders rubbing, talking to each other behind cupped hands, laughing in a way that made you wish they'd include you.

"Is it money?" I asked.

"No," Lee said sternly. "We never talk money." He looked at me to let me know he was pissed, and not just at Henry either. "You know that."

"Well, are you moving again?"

"No. I'm here for good now. I ain't going anywhere," Lee said.

I hadn't found a way to tell him yet, but Lucy and I *were* going. Come spring, we'd be moving to Chicago, to a neighborhood called Bucktown, which I guess isn't too far from Wrigley Field. Lucy'd been keeping in touch with Lee's old wife, Chloe, and turned out Chloe really liked Lucy. Got her a job working for a dance company down there. She'd be starting off in the office, like answering phones or something, but it'd be something. A foot in the door. I didn't want her stripping anymore, and with the baby, neither did she. It was our time to be a family, to be normal people, like everyone else.

Lucy knew about how I'd tried to get away. She thought maybe this was our chance, to *do it,* and move on with our lives. To try something different. She'd been saving up for years. She said I could stay home with the baby while she was working. She said that with a baby, if we don't try to go now, it'll be too easy to stay here forever, and she knew that I felt trapped.

"All's that I want is for everyone to be friends again."

"Ronny, it isn't always that easy."

"Did you do something wrong, or did he?"

Lee looked ahead. "I guess I did."

"Then apologize. Say you're sorry."

"Well, we're not really talking that much right now, me and Henry."

I thought for a second.

"I don't know if you already got me a wedding gift or not, but if you didn't, you could do one thing for me."

Lee was silent, his knuckles white and flexing on the wheel. It looked like he was trying to snap it in half.

"You could apologize. That's your present to me."

"That's all you want?"

"Well, I mean, you want to fly me and Luce to Hawaii or somethin', I ain't going to fight you."

He laughed. I love making him laugh. And I had the feeling he didn't laugh much when he's away from Wisconsin. I've never had much of an idea what his life's like, but I think it must be pretty tough, pretty lonely. He travels more than anyone I've ever known, and I know from my days on the circuit that travel ain't all it's cracked up to be. You just get tired of *moving*. Right when you find a spot that interests you, right when you find a bed that's pretty comfortable or a restaurant that isn't too greasy, you got to keep moving on.

"Well," Lee said, "I guess I'll go ahead and keep those tickets to Aruba then."

I laughed. "Where's Aruba?"

"You know, I really couldn't tell you. The Caribbean, I guess? I don't know. I'm a musician, not a geographer."

We watched the snow gather. It was coming down harder, but ahead, I saw Kip's mill, the yellow of the towers against the gray sky.

"He did a good job with all that, Kip did," I said, pointing.

Lee nodded. "Yeah. You're right about that."

"You want to come over to my place?" I asked. "We could watch teevee. Lucy's with her sister and family, I think. Guess I'm not supposed to see her tonight. Or maybe I ain't allowed to see her dress? I get confused. Either way . . ." What I wanted to say was that I didn't want to be alone, that I didn't like my apartment very much anymore. It didn't smell like Lucy, didn't remind me of her. It was no place for a baby, that was for sure, no place to grow a family. I had exactly: one frying pan, two pots, a micro-wave, a hot plate, three bowls, two plates, and a handful of silver-ware. And some of my silverware was plastic, from McDonald's. The teevee was new, but my bed was so used up it looked like a taco, all bent into a tired old U shape. My pillows were yellow and the sheets were old as hell, covered in Green Bay Packers logos—which I liked, but Lucy said we wouldn't be taking them with us to Chicago. I supposed she was right. Sometimes I'd look at them and think, *Goddamn it Ronny, you ain't a little boy anymore.*

"Naw," Lee said, "why don't we just stop off at the VFW? Isn't there a basketball game on tonight? The Badgers . . . I can't remember for the life of me who they're playing . . ."

"Sure. Sounds good," I said. Already I was thinking about pork rinds or a frozen pizza, potato chips or warm cashews.

Lee parked the truck in front of the bar and the neon lights weren't on, which was strange, especially considering how dark it was. Normally, you could count on them to glow the sidewalks, to attract moths and beetles in summertime. I pressed my face up against the glass: inside, the bar looked closed, not a soul along the rail, everything dark as can be.

"You sure they're open?"

Lee held the door open for me, said, "Pretty sure. The door's unlocked."

"SURPRISE!!!"

Inflated condoms and balloons fell from the ceiling where someone had kept them waiting for us, in a bedsheet that had been tacked up there. People started to bat around beach balls and the old Wurlitzer suddenly kicked on like a time machine and played one of my favorite Garth Brooks songs from back when I was nothing more than a horny, zitty teenager.

You could've about knocked me over with a feather. 'Cause I thought no one had organized a party for me and I didn't know how to ask for one. I ain't sayin' that I wanted to go to Vegas and behave like a shitheel or nothin', but I *did* want to do *somethin'*, some kind of bachelor party, and I'd begun to think no one remembered, or that no one cared. I even told Lucy, "Luce, we may as well get the hell out of here. All my friends have about lost their minds."

It seemed like just about all of Little Wing was at the bar, stacked up on top of one another right out to the alley behind, where the overflow was packing snowballs and flinging them at the broadside of a purple Dumpster. The snow was really beginning to come down by then. And many of the folks there had kazoos in their mouths, or noisemakers. Others had brought their elementary school recorders and tambourines, cowbells and triangles. So the bar was about as loud as a hometown rodeo crowd, and everyone was slapping my back and giving me hugs and there was Lucy too! My girl! And she came right up to me and wrapped her sweet arms around my neck and gave me a big sexy kiss and when the bar saw that, you'd have thought the damn roof was about to come unstuck.

Then Lee got up on the bar and he called for silence and he took up a glass of beer and said, "To Lucy and Ronny and their little baby, too. If you can hear us in there, give your mom a little kick. But hold on first." And then he got down from the bar and he waded through the folks that separated me and Luce from the bar and he put my hand on her stomach, and then he said, "All right now everybody, let's give Lucy and Ronny a big hip-hip-hooray!" And the bar went wild with people blowing their noisemakers and people pounding the bar with their fists and people stomping and singing and sure enough just below my hand, the tiniest flutter, like a kitten trying to escape a paper bag.

Lee hugged me, said, "I love you, buddy. Congratulations."

I couldn't believe it. Couldn't believe that everyone was there, everyone that I knew, that I loved. They all came up to us, hugged us both. Henry, Beth, their kids—Alex and Eleanore—kissed me on the lips like I was their uncle, squeezed me just as I tight as I squeezed them. Kip and Felicia. Felicia saying something into Luce's ear that I couldn't hear, but it must have been something sweet, 'cause Luce got to bawlin' and they were hugging like two long-lost sisters such that you'd swear they'd never see each other again. Eddy and his family. The Girouxs—those twins—like two big bears. A few old teachers of mine, of ours. Old classmates, old girlfriends, cousins and second cousins, guys from the rodeo circuit I hadn't seen in *years*. Got to be that my hand got tired from shaking so many hands.

And somewhere along the line, somebody—probably one of my rodeo buddies who didn't know no better—handed me a shot of tequila, and I tossed it down the hatch like cough medicine before I even realized what I'd done. I guess no one noticed either, everybody else already in their cups and livin' it up, for sure, Lucy waylaid by some women over at the bar, them touching at her belly, Henry and Beth sitting at a booth with their kids in their laps, Lee playing shuffleboard with Eddy, both of 'em sweating like crazy, their forearms covered in the shuffleboard table's sawdust. So when the next shot came, and the next, there wasn't anybody there to knock it out of my hands. And so it went, down my throat.

Before the night was through, I think I may have shotgunned three or four more shots. Five maybe. More alcohol than I'd tasted in almost a decade and yet, not even enough to fill a coffee mug. And after that fourth or fifth shot, I don't remember much at all, except knowing that I wasn't in the bar anymore and that it was real goddamn cold, and I was real goddamn lost. I don't remember Lucy leaving, don't remember saying good-bye, don't remember kissing her. Don't remember Lee offering to walk me home, or Henry and Beth offering to drive me. Don't remember whether Eddy offered me a job or not. Whether Kip said that he could use a hand around the mill.

Truth is, I blacked out. I blew out my own candle, good night.

By the time I came to, I must have been some distance from the bar, 'cause I couldn't see them neons. Couldn't even make out the streetlights that glow over Main Street. Everything just real quiet and white and cold. No headlights. No screams of midnight snowmobiles or the low, dull roar of plows out clearing the roads. Nothing. Just snow. Big, heavy snow. A little bit of wind and the snow sizzling against my skin. You don't have to be a bright person, a rocket scientist, as my dad used to say, to know that you're lost, and that's what I knew—that I was lost. And drunk. It got to be that I was dizzy, that up and down didn't make sense and I got afraid, too. But I think I might've been laughing as I went, 'cause I remember feeling, *How the hell do you get lost in Little Wing?* I know I had my hands out, because they got so damn cold and I didn't have no gloves. I just kept reaching out ahead of me, hopin' to touch something: a wall, a car, hell, even a tombstone, which would have meant I was north of town. But no. I didn't touch nothing. And so, I just kept on. Kept on saying Lucy's name, kept saying it with each footstep I took, like a way to count my paces. And thinking, *This is real stupid. Tomorrow you're going to be a groom, a husband, a daddy-to-be. Moving to Chicago. And, then too . . . you're going to have to put together a crib. Paint some walls . . .*

I kept thinking that if I could just find a car, a building—a window to smash, a door to kick down—any old way inside, to warmth, away from that snow. It piled on my shoulders, fell down into my shirts, melted against my chest. And where the hell was everyone anyway? Where was Lee? Where was Henry? Eddy? Kip? Where were my friends? I think I must have begun to sober up a bit because I got colder.

Inches, feet, yards. They felt like miles. Long cold miles. My thighs ached with the cold through the denim of my Wranglers.

My kneecaps felt like ice cubes. I began to sing a song, one of Lee's real early songs that I still knew by heart, thinking that maybe someone'd hear me, would hear my terrible singing voice and come lookin' for me. It also kept me warm for a while, like being a kid at summer camp and walking in the rain singing some camp song with your buddies just so you weren't focused so damn much on how wet and muddy you were. All the time I tried to have my hands out there in front of me, reachin' for a touch, but never, not once running into anything and then, just about when I'd lost all feeling, I stuffed them into my pants pockets and kept on moving.

Maybe, I thought, *you should just sit down, stay in one spot. Call for help.* So I laid down, and the snow was thick and soft enough that it sort of felt like a bed, and anyway, it was better than my old cowboy boots, better than fighting a damn Wisconsin blizzard. *Just don't fall asleep. Maybe rest your eyes a little bit, rest them legs, but don't fall asleep. Just keep singing. Everyone will know that song. Just keep singing. It will keep you warm. Sing loud. Don't ever be afraid to sing loud. Just keep singing, it'll keep you awake.*

That's all I remember. Just feeling very, very cold and wondering where the hell everyone was.

THE TELEPHONE ON MY BEDSIDE table rang in the middle of the night, and I grabbed it before the second ring, my heart suddenly pounding; no good news comes at that hour—never. I was terrified one of my parents might have passed away. But it was Lucy. I couldn't understand a thing she was saying. She was sobbing into the telephone, screaming almost, and the odd thing about it is, the moment I heard her voice I sort of relaxed enough to almost fall back asleep; I know that must sound strange, even monstrous, but I was just so relieved that it wasn't my mother or father calling, telling me to hurry to some hospital, that there wasn't much time left. I handed Henry the phone, and he took it, and began trying to calm her down. He sat on the edge of his side of the bed and I touched his backbone, his spine. The drapes were open on one of our windows and outside, though it was night, the darkness was brighter for all the snow.

"All right, I'll be right there," Henry said. "Just hang on."

He handed me the receiver to place back in the cradle. "What's wrong?" I asked, sitting up. "Where're you going?"

"It's Ronny. They can't find him."

"What do you mean they can't find him. We just *saw* him."

"Well they can't fucking find him, Beth, all right? I'm going out. I've got my phone."

"Let me come with you."

Henry was pulling on two pair of socks, long underwear, his thickest pair of Carhartts, flannel shirts, and a wool sweater.

"No, don't. Listen, I don't even know if I'll be able to get out the driveway. You just stay with the kids. We'll find him."

He was already almost out of our bedroom, and I had the feeling that I wouldn't see him again, ever, that this must be what it was like to be married to a fireman, or a policeman, that this was what a soldier's wife must feel. No time for good-byes or kisses, and everything left up in the air—life—just suspended, so that the person you love most in the world can go charging out into a fire, into a gunfight, into a blizzard, their mind utterly focused on helping other people, their comrades or friends.

I stood up, followed him down the stairs and into the kitchen, where he swung on his jacket and seized his keys off the table. He turned toward the garage and I grabbed his arm.

"I love you," I said, and then I kissed him.

"I love you, too."

"Wait."

"What," he said, exasperated. "Christ, Beth, *what?*"

"Here." I handed him a wool cap and some gloves, a scarf and a granola bar. I reached into the refrigerator and handed him a Coke, a candy bar, and an apple. His hands were full.

"I gotta go," he said.

"Just in case."

"All right."

"I love you."

He slammed the door, fired up the truck, and I watched as he pulled out into the blizzard, down our driveway and out onto the road, the red taillights of our truck disappearing. I sat down at the kitchen table. The clock on the microwave read 3:09. The kids wouldn't be up for another four or five hours, but I was wide awake. I walked into the living room, slumped onto our couch, began leafing through some magazines Felicia had dropped off earlier in the week.

She subscribed to some of the trashier magazines that I occasionally flipped through at the IGA, while waiting to pay for my groceries. All photographs, no articles or stories or poems. Just pictures of celebrities, and so many these days I don't even recognize them all. Courtships and weddings and divorces. Planned or real—who even knew? Couples that you thought were perfect, breaking up after a month, a year, two years. Couples that you might see on television and say, "God they're beautiful. And so happy. I bet she's good for him." Or vice versa.

And then, you're reading about their divorce, and it's always the same things: . . . *irreconcilable differences, we grew apart, it was no one's fault, I just wasn't "in love" anymore* . . . Sitting there on my couch, squinting at those glossy pages, I saw a picture of Chloe and Lee walking down a New York City street. They're holding hands, but neither one is smiling, both of them hiding behind expensive sunglasses, both wearing a lot of black. Were it not for their trendy sneakers and skinny jeans, they might as well be going to a funeral. I turned the page, began working a crossword puzzle, anything to relax my mind.

After that night with Lee so many years ago, I spent a listless few months at my waitressing job and at the salon, and it's fair to say that, inasmuch as my life's ever come off the rails, it did during that period of time. I never slept with Lee again, but for weeks we called each other at night, almost breathlessly, lying on our backs in our separate beds, like lovestruck teenagers, except that neither of us would admit that we were in love, or not in love.

And it's true: in that mixed-up time of my life, I slept with three other men, though none of them were especially memorable. I don't know what I was doing, or what boundaries I might have been trying to test within myself. Maybe I was hoping I could just forget about Henry once and for all, and move on. That if I had sex with enough people, that if I betrayed his longest friendship, I could push him away forever and just be free.

But it took me a long time to stop thinking about him.

It was about three months after I slept with Lee that I got a call from Ronny on a Friday morning. He called me at the salon.

"Ronny, how in the *hell* did you find me here?" I asked.

"Ronny Taylor's got his contacts. How are you, girl? You have any plans for Saturday night or Sunday morning?"

I don't know why, but my first thought was that now Ronny wanted to get into my pants, that all of Henry's friends had waited *just this long* until they came out of the woodwork to court me. I have to admit that for that moment, I was as flattered as I was offended.

"Look, Ronny, I don't know. I mean, Henry and I, we *just* broke up not that long ago. I mean . . ."

My words trickled out into silence as I heard him laughing at the other end of the line. Real Ronny belly laughter. I could feel myself blushing, covered the earpiece of the receiver as I glanced around the salon to confirm that none of the girls had witnessed my humiliation.

"What in the hell are you laughing at?" I asked. "Ronny! Cut it out! Ronny?"

He caught his breath, finally said, "I'm in Minneapolis for a rodeo on Saturday night. I was *wondering* if you might like to come. I have tickets for you, if you want 'em, right down by the action."

The word prompted him to snicker. "That's what I was laughing about, if you need to know."

"Oh," I said.

I had seen Ronny compete in local and regional events, little rodeos and competitions around the Little Wing area, but that was years before, toward the end of high school and not long after Ronny swore off football, wrestling, and softball. We'd all drive out to see him ride these tired-looking horses and overfed bulls in ramshackle arenas where the grandstands were broken in places, paint chipping off the fences in big, ugly swaths.

But this was different. There were thousands of people in attendance, maybe tens of thousands, and there was Ronny's face up on the Jumbotron at the Hubert H. Humphrey Metrodome, waving goofily, and some girls, seated behind me pointing at him. They kept saying, "He's so goddamn *cute*." Ronny, my friend.

That night in Minneapolis he rode one bull in particular, Jax, and I remember holding a hand over my mouth as I watched Ronny in the corral, as I watched that great creature surge and rile beneath him, and then the chute was opened and off he flew out into that arena, swinging around like the bravest ragdoll I'd ever seen: one hand high in the air, his spurs two perfect silver stars in a perpetual blur, his jeans a deep navy blue, and above his upper lip, the faintest wisp of a mustache.

He didn't last long—3.2 seconds—but I cheered him as he ran out of the arena, jumped the fence, and waved his hat at the crowd. You could see that he had fans, people who knew his name. He rode one more time that day, but did not qualify for the finals. After his last ride and after the bull was safely sequestered again, he removed his black Stetson, bowed deeply for his admirers, and then dusted off his Wranglers and chaps.

I met him outside the Metrodome in downtown Minneapolis, the huge unsightly building's cloth ceiling aglow. He was smoking a cigarette with some other guys, and one of his friends whistled as I approached. Ronny jokingly knocked that man's cigarette out of his mouth and then flipped his hat off and frisbeed it twenty yards behind him. Everyone laughed.

Then, he produced an elbow for me to hold on to, the perfect gentleman. We walked for a while, though it was windy and cold, an early April evening in Minnesota, and I was in heels, my feet freezing. I was constantly wiping hair out of my eyes, and he had to clutch on to his hat. We might have been a couple from a hundred years before, walking through the streets of that river town, though in truth, we were just friends.

"Let's get a cab," Ronny said at last, pushing me into a yellow automobile and signaling the driver to head to his hotel. "Don't worry. I won't put the moves on you."

"I'm sorry. That was shitty of me. I don't—I don't know what's *wrong* with me lately." I felt like crying, covered my face, took a deep breath. "You were great out there, by the way."

"The hell I was. That was a terrible showing. Good thing you were the only one here to see it."

"Um, I wouldn't say that. I noticed quite a few Ronny Taylor fans out there in the audience tonight. Pretty young for a guy like you, but they were definitely fans."

"Oh, don't you worry," Ronny said, "every now and then I'll make a friend who's a little more *mature*." He grinned at me, some of his false teeth showing, and knocked his knuckles against the window just to make a noise. "Hey. You okay?" he said, when I didn't respond. "What's wrong?"

"Nothing's wrong. But I really hope your hotel has a bar."

We both gulped two overpriced drinks in the first-level fern bar of the hotel, an oddly lighted room with too many mirrors and not nearly enough patrons. We sat in a booth and Ronny told me about his travels, about how he and a buddy had split gas money and drove all around America, hitting various county and state fairs, winning little purses here and there, and just barely eking out a living.

In New Mexico their wallets had run dry, and his friend's truck had needed a new radiator, so they slept on the floor of a girlfriend's apartment and Ronny babysat her two-year-old son, while his friend, Clint, washed dishes at a country club until they could patch together enough money to move on. In Oklahoma, they beat up a bucktoothed oilman who had tried to molest a teenage girl in a public bathroom. They had stumbled on the scene just before a rodeo, and Ronny told the girl to go find her parents. Then Ronny and Clint carried the man out to a parking lot and beat his ribs into mush, stole his wallet, his hat, and his boots.

"See," Ronny said to me, pointing at his feet, "they don't look as good as they did when I first got 'em, but still, nicest pair of boots I ever owned."

We touched glasses. Outside, it began to snow big, wet flakes the size of doilies. We ate a plate of chicken wings and a plate of onion rings, our fingers, lips, and chins greasy.

"I'm happy to see you," Ronny said, not looking at me, just working on a chicken bone.

"Me, too."

We went up to his room, not quite drunk, but getting there. Those were the days when Ronny drank *a lot*, and when we entered the room, there were empty cans of beer everywhere, and a little table in the corner covered with cheap bottles of whiskey, vodka, and rum. A note attached to the outside of the door reading:

> *Ronny,*
> *Don't wait for me. Met a girl who*
> *looks like Shania Twain. See*
> *you in the morning.*
> *Clint*

We sat on separate beds, under the covers, drinking rum and Cokes, growing drunker and drunker, talking about Little Wing, Henry and Lee, Kip and Eddy.

"None of my business," said Ronny, "but you ought to get back with Hank. He loves you. You know that? He really, really loves you."

I nodded into my cup, took a big sip.

"I mean, I don't know what you've got going on right now, but I gotta tell you. Hank's my friend, and he's a good guy, and he's fucking *crazy* for you. Always has been." Ronny set his cup down. "I know we're all supposed to be out there, sowing our wild oats and whatnot, but the thing is, I think all that stuff is a big crock of *shit*. Everybody's just holding out for that *one person* anyway." He held out one finger at me, to further his point, but he was drunk, and so the finger waved a bit, as if he were reprimanding me. "And trust me, *I know*. I get around. I've had my fair share." He was shirtless, a little stand of chest hair sprouting over his breastbone, and a smaller line of hair linking his flat little belly button to his Wranglers. He tipped his Stetson over his eyes, sipped at his drink. "I'm telling you. You'll regret it. Marry Hankie, Beth. He's a *good* man." He nodded. "A good man."

"Ronny, you ever coming back to Little Wing or what?"

"I hope not," he said. "I like Wyoming. You know? I really like it out there."

"I'd miss you if you never came back."

"So come on out and visit me. We could ride horses. Climb mountains. Look at the stars."

He was falling asleep, small snores gurgling in his throat and nose. I drained my cup.

"Little Wing really where you're gonna end up?" he asked drowsily.

"Probably."

"There are worse places, for sure."

"Ronny?"

"Huh?"

"Don't fall asleep."

He tipped his hat up, peered over at me. "And I thought you didn't want any funny business." He winked, slowly.

"I don't. Maybe we can just watch some television. Here"—I held up my cup—"give us a refill."

"Well, all right. Now we're talking. You think they got any nudie channels?"

A week after I saw Ronny, I called Henry. Within a year we were married. Within four years we had our first child, Eleanore. There are people in your life who are angels. Who pick up the telephone at the right time and call, because they're worried about you, because they want to hear your voice. People who tell you it is all right to cry, or that it's time to stop crying and get up, move on. People who tell you that you're beautiful, that you're enough, that they love you. It sounds strange maybe, but when people ask me about Ronny Taylor, I tell them he's an angel.

Outside our living-room window, the snow was still falling, and I could no longer see the tire marks where Henry's truck pulled out of the driveway, not so long before.

IN THE DREAM I am a golden retriever, and the sun is shining the kind of white, overexposed color you only see in photographs and movies from the 1970s. I'm running through the tall grass of my fields and someone is throwing me an old baseball. I can feel it between my teeth. I don't know who it is, but I suppose it's my master. We go for a walk. I feel *so* happy. I am thrilled to have so much hair, such thick, beautiful hair. My tongue feels like a hot, undercooked piece of bacon. We are walking up my driveway and the gravel is cool beneath my paws. I lick from puddles, I chase a pheasant from his hiding spot. My master stops at the mailbox, but it is empty, only a newspaper, which he throws back down the driveway like a toy. I chase it. I become aware, suddenly, that I am dreaming, that my bedsheets are wildly tangled and that I feel exasperated, as if running a marathon in my sleep.

The telephone was ringing beside my bed, the alarm clock-radio to its left reading 3:01. *Chloe wants to try again,* I thought for a moment. *It's got to be Chloe.* But it wasn't. It was Lucy, and I could tell immediately that something was wrong.

"It's Ronny. I keep calling and calling, he doesn't answer. I've tried a hundred times and it just keeps ringing. I called Eddy and he went down to Ronny's apartment and banged on the door and Ronny didn't answer so Eddy broke the door down, and *he wasn't there. He wasn't there!* What the fuck, Lee? Where's my baby? *Where's Ronny?*"

"Call the police," I said as calmly as I could. "Call the highway patrol. Call everyone you know. Get 'em down to the mill. I'll be right there."

The snow was nearly up to the running boards of my truck, but I dropped it into four-wheel low and just kept in the center of the road. I'd stowed about a cord of wood in the bed of my truck for traction, and that helped, though I did fishtail a half-dozen times before I finally saw the faint glow of other headlights and then the looming towers of Kip's mill. Already, about ten cars and trucks were gathered in the parking lot of the mill, with a few snowmobiles pulling up, too.

Kip was there, and he took charge, partnering people together and handing them lengths of new rope, new flashlights already equipped with new batteries, signal flares—items he must have just commandeered from the inventory of his general store inside.

I headed out into the night on foot with Eddy, a length of rope uniting us, tied to our belt loops. We called out Ronny's name, kicked at the snow, prodded at snowbanks with ski poles and walking sticks. The northern wind was like the teeth of a rusty old saw and still the snow kept falling as we moved farther and farther away from the mill and what little light that building and the vehicles around it could offer. I thought about Ronny, about losing my friend, and it seemed suddenly very *real*, very *possible*. We trudged on, shouting his name.

———

Not long after Chloe and I were married, Ronny called me, catching us at dinner. At first, I didn't want to take the call. This was only the first month of our marriage, but already things were in decline. That evening we were actually having fun—talking, holding hands, drinking wine. It was the kind of evening that gave me hope. So when my phone rang and I saw that familiar 715 number, I let it ring five times before finally standing up and tossing my napkin onto the seat of the chair. I held a finger out, mouthed *Back in a minute* to Chloe, and then stepped out onto the street.

"Hey, *Lee*, it's Ronny. How are you, buddy? How's Chloe?"

A nearby bar was pumping out dance music onto the sidewalk, and so his voice was hard to hear. I plugged a finger in my ear. "We're good buddy, real good. Look, I don't want to cut this short, but we're actually out at dinner. Can I call you back?"

There was a pause on the other end of the line, and I knew that I had deflated him. Ronny's like me, goddamn it—he's never liked telephones; always likes to talk face-to-face, likes to look at people's eyes, says he can get a better read on people that way.

"Well, I have some good news," he began again. "Do you have a minute for some real good news?"

I exhaled. "Sure I do, Ronny. I'd like to hear some good news. Tell me some good news."

"I'm getting married. I'm getting *married*, buddy. You believe that? I'm getting fucking *married*!"

He was laughing, and I could hear Lucy's voice in the background, and I thought about how I'd announced my own engagement to Ronny, to Henry—to the most important people in my life. I stuffed an envelope full of plane tickets and a little note. And later, Chloe's personal assistant had sent out a bunch of formal invitations. I never called them; we were too busy, or something, I don't remember. *But Christ, this was how you were supposed to do it.* I could picture Ronny in his apartment, Lucy beside him, maybe their limbs intertwined, smiles on their faces broad as a prairie rainbow. I leaned up against the building behind me, but it was a window, and the patron on the other side rapped their knuckles angrily at me. I stepped away, gravitated toward the nearest parking meter, and leaned against that.

"Ronny," I said, stammering, not half as happy as I ought to have been, caught up in the simple disbelief that he had found someone, "that's *great,* man. That's just—Jesus, that's the best news!" And only then did the joy of it really hit me. Straightening myself up, I felt a building excitement, the volume of my voice rising, suddenly and truly I wanted to hug my friend, to lift him off the ground. "Jesus, Ronny! That's the best *goddamn* news I've heard in fucking forever. Good for you, buddy. Good for *you.*" I nodded to myself.

"You remember Lucy, right," he asked. "From your wedding? First time I met her was at Kip's bachelor party. Remember that?"

"Sure I do, buddy. Sure I do. Of course. Beautiful Lucy."

I heard them kissing, heard her say in the background, "Hey, Lee."

And then Ronny again: "Well, I really want to talk some more, but I know you're busy out there. I just wanted to say . . ." And here he paused. I could hear him, thinking, collecting his words, as if they were spare change spilled across the sidewalk— his entire fortune. "I just wanted to *ask you,* if you would be my best man. Would you? Would you be my best man?"

A car horn honked angrily, a long low note that seemed to fill my world.

"Lee?"

"I'm here, Ronny. Of course. Of *course* I'll be your best man. It would be my honor."

"All right, then! All righty, man. I'll let you get back to whatever you were doing. I just wanted to tell you first, man. You're the first person to know. Shit, I'm so excited! I can't hardly wait. Bye, Lee. Thanks. Bye."

He hung up before I had a chance to tell him I loved him. Must have hung up because he thought he was inconveniencing me, his so-called best man.

I walked back into the restaurant. Chloe was staring intently at her iPhone, the bill already paid. I sat down, drank all the wine in my glass. Refilled my glass, drank again.

"I'm ready to go," she said.

"Ronny's getting married."

"Who?"

"Ronny. Ronny is getting married. Ronny is getting fucking married." I laughed, drank, swallowed.

"Really?" she said, still looking at the phone. "That's amazing. How fabulous."

"I want some more wine," I said.

"All right. Do you mind if I make a dash, though, sweetie? I have a brunch tomorrow. That Czech director."

"Chloe, my *friend* is getting married."

"You know what? I'm just really tired. Okay?" She bent down and kissed my forehead. Her lips felt very cool. "I'll grab a cab."

All I could think of, plodding blindly through that blizzard in hopes of finding my friend, was that evening in New York City, and how I had not wanted to take his call. How I had wanted to avoid hearing his voice.

"Let's head back," Eddy hollered over the wind. "It's been almost an hour. We should check in with everybody else. Someone must've found him."

"Christ, Eddy. They'll start blaring car horns if they find him. We've got to keep going."

He leaned in close to my ear so I could hear him, even if I couldn't make out his face. "There's too much snow, Lee. I don't know how we'd ever even see him." He put a hand on my shoulder. I shrugged it off. "Look, Lee. There comes a time—" he began.

"No, damn it, Eddy—we keep looking. We ain't splitting up and we *ain't* quitting. We'll just keep moving. We've got to keep looking."

The snow was crotch high in places and where drifts had collected, we waded through snow past my belly button. If he was buried under a drift like that, we'd never find him. We called his name, shone our flashlights through the gloom. I could not even remember what he had been wearing, though I remembered that after he tried on his tuxedo, he had switched into his old pair of cowboy boots, and I thought of the number of times I had studied how worn the heels of those boots were, how it affected his gait down Main Street, rolled his feet and knees inward. How I had offered to buy him new boots—any pair he wanted—but how he always declined, how he defended those boots. And then I thought of Lucy, pregnant, and terrified of losing him.

"He *can't* have gone too far," I said. "We'll find him. Somebody's got to find him."

"Sure we will," Eddy said, relenting, panting out his exhaustion. "We'll find him. Hey, Ronny! Ron-ny!"

We kicked through the snow with our boots, groped through the night with our hands, screamed out his name, shone our flashlights in vain. I couldn't remember any storm as tenacious as this one.

We found him not far from Main Street. He was lying down in the school playground, close enough that we could hear the swings blowing in the gusting wind. He was singing—that's how I heard him. Eddy and I walked toward the sound. We could hardly believe it. We crouched beside him.

"You found me," he mumbled. "Shit, I think I must be drunk."

"Come on, buddy. We're going to carry you back."

"Did you hear me singing? That was one of your songs. I always liked that one."

I wiped the snow from his face. We lifted him off the ground, Eddy taking one arm while I took the other, and Ronny bowed over between us, head hung low.

"I can't move my feet," he said.

"Well," said Eddy, "the least you could do's sing for us then."

"Everybody left me," he mumbled. "Why'd everybody leave me like that?"

"We're here now, Ronny," I said. "We got you."

We carried him a hundred yards or more before the Girouxs heard our calls and came running. Cameron Giroux, all six foot three, two hundred and fifty pounds of him, swept Ronny up and placed him on his shoulders the way you might transport a lamb, and then disappeared toward the headlights of our parked cars and the new lights of an ambulance that had arrived to the accompaniment of police sirens. Soon, we heard the horns of cars and trucks and the night was no longer so quiet.

We marched back in Cameron's size-sixteen footsteps.

AFTER THEY FOUND RONNY, I went back inside the mill, brewed some coffee, and sat in my office, looking out the window. My watch read 4:44. He was supposed to be getting married in all of twelve hours. The morning of my own wedding, I had a hot-stone massage, a latte heavy on the cinnamon, and a two-egg omelette. I shook my head.

Ever since the day of our wedding, I'd wished I could have done things over, done things differently. For one thing, Felicia and I would have talked about everything we needed to talk about, everything that had been bubbling up, right underneath the surface the whole time. Kids, Little Wing, the mill, money, everything. Also, I wish I hadn't called the paparazzi. What good did that do me? Sure, I was able to pay a few bills, but in the meantime, every friend I had in the world decided that they'd effectively boycott my business—boycott me—for the next eight months, probably costing me about the same amount of revenue I got from selling my friend out to a bunch of gossip rags.

I got up from my desk and began walking around the mill. It is a huge building, the biggest building in Little Wing, by far. You could probably fit three or four small-town Lutheran churches in here, especially if you accounted for all the space in those grain towers and all the space in the basement. It's a strange thing, to walk around inside the mill at night, alone, in all that space.

The building was first owned by the Little Wing Farmers' Co-operative, which organized in about 1885, best I can tell from some old records in the library. Just a group of like-minded Norwegian farmers looking to consolidate their buying and selling power. And they hung together until the 1980s, when small farmers really were getting their asses handed to them. The co-op dissolved, and some guy named Aintry bought the building as a warehouse. His idea was pretty good, in theory: he wanted to subdivide the place into self-storage units, get about forty dollars a month, and just sit back and collect his retirement. The trouble was, the building was falling apart, the basement was filling with water, he had mice and bats everywhere, and, in a small farming community where everybody lives on one-acre lots, there really isn't a great demand for more storage room. People just store their stuff in barns, or pole-buildings, or their front yards. After that, the mill sat vacant, waiting patiently for a wrecking ball. Or a fool like me.

I walked into the old warehouse, where once pallets of powdered milk might have sat, or bags of grain. Everything was set for Ronny's wedding. The folding chairs were set out in rows, perfectly spaced, all facing a central podium and a little stage. I walked up there and looked back at the chairs, thinking of my own wedding, thinking of Felicia.

I decided to drive out to where she was, to that old motel between Little Wing and Eau Claire. I went outside, climbed into my Escalade, let the engine warm up. I took the roads slowly. Forty-five minutes to go only a few miles.

I knocked on the door, gently at first, hoping not to scare her,

236

and then a little louder. She opened the door an inch, and I could see the chain pulled to its farthest extent. She looked tired.

"Hello," I said.

She closed the door, causing a momentary lump in my throat, and then opened it.

"Take off those wet clothes," she said.

I slid into bed beside her and she wrapped herself around me. I looked at the bedside table. Pulled open the door and felt for the Gideon Bible. Someone must have stolen it. My fingers only touched a cold glass ashtray; I ran my fingers around its smooth, square concave shape.

"Let's leave this place," I said. "Little Wing."

"I want a baby," she said. "Someone told me I should trick you. But I don't want to do that. You give me a baby and then let's go."

I looked at the motel's old curtains. They were printed with a hunting scene: ducks flying away from three men armed with shotguns, spent shells ejecting jauntily from the smoking chambers. And below the arc of their flight, cattails and what looked to be a very peaceful slough. The walls were smoke-stained, the carpet old and worn. Above the bed: a nautical scene of a schooner crashing through angry seas. I sighed, thought, *Chicago wasn't so bad.*

"In the morning," I said, closing my eyes. "Tomorrow morning, let's make a baby."

But Felicia would not wait that long.

THE WHOLE TOWN CAME OUT and there were not enough folding chairs, not enough room for the bystanders and gawkers to stand in. Many stood outside the mill, in the cold, peering in through windows already fogging with heat. Others gathered in the mill's basement, which Kip had stunningly transformed into a dance hall of rustic elegance: where once dead mice and rats had floated in six inches of tepid water, now the huge stone space glowed a golden yellow beneath white Christmas lights and candles. You would have thought it was some kind of royal wedding, two houses of the American Middlewestern aristocracy merging. As big as Kip's wedding was, Ronny's surpassed it by far. And perhaps due in part to the prior evening's excitement. Because despite frostbitten fingers and a bright red nose, Ronny insisted on getting married on schedule.

I had been among those urging him to lie in bed and recuperate. "Ronny," I said, "Lucy will understand, I promise. You can get married next week, next month, next year. This is crazy. You're lucky to be alive."

For her part, Lucy sat so close to his hospital bed that she may as well have crawled into Ronny's lap. She nodded her head. "Lee's right, baby. I ain't gonna leave you. Never ever."

"Just get me out of here around noon," Ronny said seriously. "I'll stay here 'til noon. I'll rest that long. But that's it." He pointed a finger at me, at Henry, at Eddy, Kip, and the Girouxs. "I'll sign the goddamn paperwork myself if I have to. I ain't no invalid."

At noon, he was taken by wheelchair to the vestibule of the Sacred Heart Hospital, where Lucy's aged Dodge Neon sat idling. His hands and feet were heavily bandaged, and when he rose wobbly out of the chair, we raced to support him.

"Gimme a break," he said, "I ain't dead. I been worse off than this. Just get me back to my place. Just get me the hell into my tuxedo."

I rode in the backseat of the Neon while Lucy drove, her protruding belly rubbing the steering wheel, nervously glancing over at Ronny from time to time, holding his hand in hers, asking if the heat was too much. He waved her off, pretended to inspect the world outside his window.

"Baby," she said softly, "baby, what *were* you doing out there last night?"

"I don't know . . . ," he began, his voice trailing off.

"Baby."

From the backseat, I watched them, their faces, her fingers in his hair, the road before us.

"I just got lost is all."

"But what were you even doing out there? Why weren't you home?"

"I don't know. Lost track of time, I guess, and then I went out to take a leak, and when I turned around the bar had moved or something." Ronny laughed, turned around to me. "Shit, maybe the bar got lost, too."

I smiled at him.

"Baby," Lucy said. "You're going to be a dad now. You know that. You're going to be somebody's *dad*. There ain't any more getting lost, all right?" She'd begun crying now, and pulled the car to the shoulder of the road. "You stick by me, you hear? We stick together now."

He looked at her. "I wanted to be with you," he said. "But I thought we wasn't supposed to be together the night before. Tradition, or whatnot."

She rubbed his face, his cheeks, with her hands. "After tonight, you don't never have to worry about that no more."

They kissed each other, straining against their seat belts. "You know, I could drive us the rest of the way back," I said. And without saying a word they both unbuckled their seat belts, stepped out of the car, let me move into the driver's seat, and then hurried into the backseat, where they spent the final miles holding each other as tightly as possible. I watched in the rearview for a few seconds before aiming my eyes away.

The ceremony itself was held in what would have been the main warehouse of the old mill, a cavernous room that still smelled vaguely of malt. There was no church organ, obviously, but Kip had spared no expense with the sound system, with a professional deejay to handle the soundtrack.

I stood at the front of the room, beside Ronny, holding the wedding bands that had come to him through his grandmother . . .

His grandfather's old ring, the one Ronny has been wearing for weeks, almost like the string a forgetful person ties around his finger as a reminder, and hers, this ring I rubbed between my thumb and index finger within the confines of my pocket, felt the softness of the gold, imagined all the places the ring had gone, all the fingers and objects it had touched. I felt the little diamond—this was the wedding ring of poor people, of middle-class America, it was a promise of things to come, not some gaudy galleria ring, some designer monstrosity like the one I bought for Chloe.

Waiting up front as well was Lucy's younger sister, the maid of honor, a girl not yet twenty-one years of age. Her makeup already ruined with tears, she clutched a bouquet of flowers so severely that from several feet away I could hear individual stems breaking, could smell something that I imagined to be chlorophyll— the smell of freshly cut grass or shrubs. I imagined green stains on her palms, and possibly the puncture marks of thorns.

It was a nice, traditional Lutheran wedding. The same worn-out Bible verses you always hear at Midwestern weddings. The pastor spoke about time and patience and forgiveness, his voice warm and tired-sounding. Lucy's sister pulled herself together long enough to sing a shaky rendition of "I Will Always Love You," a selection that few of my own friends at the highest echelons of American popular music would have attempted on their best days. But thankfully she veered toward a more subdued Dolly Parton rendering, rather than going for a full-throated imitation of Whitney Houston.

Ronny and Lucy listened to the pastor's words with rapt attention. Their voices hushed, serious when it came time to exchange vows, spoken with the right amount of thought and emotion. Ronny looked away from his bride just once, in order to reach back toward me for the ring.

After their kiss, a cheer rose up in the mill that was the loudest sound I'd ever heard in Little Wing, and from the little Lutheran Church off Main Street, you could hear the peals of bells tolling. Even with his bandages, Ronny joined Lucy in shaking everyone's hand, *everyone's* hand. And then the hors d'oeuvres, dinner, and finally: the party.

Most of the women had lost their heels and the men were sweaty as hockey players, with neckties knotted around their foreheads and plastic cups full of water and ice cubes. It was a dry wedding—no booze allowed—but no one seemed to care. The whole damn town was out on the dance floor it seemed, and they were *giving it,* leaving it all out there, letting it all hang out. Eddy on the floor doing the worm and Henry, displaying an especially prominent white man's overbite, clapping his hands to music you damn well knew he'd never heard before. *But it's got a beat! You can move to it!* And the groom: Ronny Taylor, looking like an original king of disco, with the kind of lithe body that might have given John Travolta pause. He was out there, cowboy hat on his head, hands perched snug on that belt buckle, kicking and strutting in new alligator cowboy boots and dancing with his pregnant bride, a woman who came equipped with her *own* set of moves. And even pregnant as she was, she moved *well,* showing her husband moves that promised much more than what was appropriate for public consumption.

And then the whole town was surrounding them, forming a kind of huge circle and everyone clapping, everyone cheering. Cheering for those two unlikely newlyweds, cheering with the kind of unrestraint that builds in a community buried by snow and kept mostly without sunlight from Thanksgiving to Easter. Children were there, up way past their bedtimes, out on the dance floor and moving exactly how the music told them to, moving without a care or inhibition in the world. Children, making sorties to the tables where the sheet cakes waited, melting. Running sugary fingers through thick frosting. Children, guzzling soda. Rubbing their sleepy eyes and going back for more, dancing in circles, dancing with their parents. Teenagers, sulking in the corners, checking their phones, looking up, wanting to join the action, but embarrassed to. *Look*: there are their parents, dancing, even grinding in ways that make the teenagers blush, moving in ways that made the teenagers say, *Oh my god.* Teenagers, sneaking off for cigarettes stolen from mothers' purses, from fathers' jacket pockets, smoking in the bathrooms or out by the train tracks. Kissing in the quiet spaces of the old mill, eyes big, eyes full of love and wonder and new ancient sensations. And the old people, sitting in chairs, watching, clapping, and in some cases, sitting almost catatonic motionless, only the smallest of smiles cracked on their wrinkled faces. Some of the old women rising to join the dance floor fun, but the old men, shaking their heads *no, no, no,* crossing their arms and crossing their legs, doing everything but sitting on the floor and locking arms together in solidarity. *Didn't dance back then, and I sure as hell ain't going to start now.*

And there was Kip, leaning against a wall, making a plastic cup of ice cubes sound like a half-dozen dice, a strange look on his face, a happy look. A look of accomplishment. He didn't see me, but I saw him, saw him from where I was out dancing with our friends. I stepped away from the wild ruckus of it all and went over to him, wiping the sweat away from my face. What I needed was a roll of paper towels, a cold shower. But I was having too much fun, everyone was. Somehow, the sonuvabitch had pulled it off, had brought everyone together.

He saw me coming and stood up straight, as if I were a teacher coming to correct his posture. I saw his jaws crush an ice cube. He nodded, extended his hand, almost sternly. "Leland," he said. I noticed he employed my full name, Leland. Not *Lee*, not *buddy*. That's where we were at, he and I.

"Come on outside," I said. "Let's take a walk. I'll buy you a beer."

He shook his head. "No, I really ought to stay here."

"Aw, come on," I said. I put a hand on his shoulder, felt his body tense up. "Shit, man, let me say that I'm sorry. All right?"

He looked at me for a second without saying a word and then moved away from the dance floor. We went out into the cold together, like two men emerging from a sauna, plumes of steam rising off our heads like columns of smoke. There were others out in the winter night too, standing outside the mill, smoking cigarettes, looking at the stars, catching their breath. They nodded their heads in our direction, though I'll say this, when they nodded, it was clear to me that they were nodding at Kip and not so much at me. What he had done was a rare thing, a good thing. The kind of thing that I suspect has been lost in America. Whole towns, whole communities getting together to celebrate, to have fun. No politics, no business, no Robert's Rules.

Once, a long time ago, when I was first starting out, I was invited to a square dance up on Lake Superior in one of those small towns that seem to have lost their reason to persist. No downtown, no businesses, no working port or railroad tracks. And yet, at seven o'clock on a Friday night, a hundred people came out of the hills and forests and down to the old town hall, and I was the opening act for a bluegrass band and a contradance caller. There was a potluck and bowls of punch and Kool-Aid and coolers of soda and someone turned the lights down low and I played my guitar for an hour or so, played some Springsteen covers too, and they were polite and clapped, and no one's cell phone went off and no one was distracted or talking. I was the only thing in town at that very moment.

After the set was finished, the bluegrass band took to the stage. The fiddle players rosined their bows, and the piano player lightly touched the keys, and the bass player made his big fat strings talk in a deep, low voice, and then they exploded—and the music they played was like a giant bucket of water poured over a great tree, fully leaved, the notes dividing and dispersing themselves down, gradually growing smaller and smaller, joyously running, bouncing, flowing down, down, down from leaf to leaf, as if racing one another. A one-child family suddenly multiplied a thousand, a million times over, each rivulet, each bead, each tear, a drop of sunlight and glee. And everyone started dancing, and soon the town hall was pungent with body odor, deafening with laughter, dense with the smell of wet wool and feet, and the whole town embraced me—*literally embraced me*—swung me into their square dances, and taught me their promenades and their steps and their claps and their calls. And I have to say, that was the first time I ever understood what America was, or could be. And the second night was the night of Ronny Taylor's wedding, in Kip Cunningham's lovingly restored mill.

America, I think, is about poor people playing music and poor people sharing food and poor people dancing, even when everything else in their lives is so desperate, and so dismal that it doesn't seem that there should be any room for any music, any extra food, or any extra energy for dancing. And people can say that I'm wrong, that we're a puritanical people, an evangelical people, a selfish people, but I don't believe that. I don't *want* to believe that.

———

Clearly, whoever wasn't at the mill was at the VFW. The place was packed. Kip and I elbowed into the bar and no sooner had we got through the door than someone pressed cold glasses of tap beer into our hands and we stood close together, the door ajar, very cold air coming in, but feeling delicious all the same. Waylon Jennings on the old Wurlitzer.

"You did good tonight," I hollered into Kip's right ear. "That's a hell of a party back there."

Kip nodded his thank-you, but said nothing, sipped his beer. He had changed, I saw. Or maybe it was just my perception of him that had changed. *Something* was different. The Kip I'd always known, or thought I had known, would have made some self-aggrandizing speech, would have made everyone feel obliged to patronize his business, would have even passed the hat. But he had done none of those things.

"Hey," I screamed, "I want us to be good. You know? I want us to be . . ." I stopped, glanced at my wedding shoes. "I want us to be friends."

He leaned in to my ear. "Come on," he said, "finish that beer. Let's get back to the party." He slugged his back, set the tap glass down beside the frosted windowpane where the warmth of the neon lights seemed to soften the ice there. I followed him back out into the cold.

The night sky was perfect, the sound of music drifting through Main Street, car horns honking at they drifted away, out into the countryside, laughter.

"I figure that I can keep this thing afloat about another year before it sinks," Kip said. He walked with his hands in his pockets. He looked at me, not sadly, but firmly, and I understood. "Turns out I bit off a little more than I could chew." He blew out a cloud of steam, shrugged his shoulders. "I'm not asking for your help. This damn mill has failed before, and it'll probably fail again."

I walked along beside him, my sweat growing cold in the chill. The music back at the party was slowing, and I pictured couples moving in close, holding hands, women resting their heads on their partners' shoulders. I thought of Beth, and then shook that thought away. Funny, that I'd think of Beth just then, and not Chloe.

"How much do you need?" I asked.

He shrugged again. "Christ, Lee. I'm up to my ass. Even if business picks up, I don't think I can keep up with the payments. You understand? Renovating everything was one thing, revenue is another." He kicked at a chunk of ice, waved his hand. "Forget I said anything. You probably got enough people looking for handouts. Let's just have some fucking fun." He picked up his pace, moved ahead of me, shook the hands of the Giroux brothers, out leaning against the side of the mills, smoking cigarettes. They nodded at me.

Back in the basement of the mill, everyone was slow dancing. And there were Ronny and Lucy, orbiting together, turning slow circles, her big, hard belly pressed against his very lean, narrow one. I watched them, watched Henry and Beth dancing, watched Felicia find Kip and drag him out to the floor, watched other wallflowers peeled away to join the rest of Little Wing, but no one came for me, and there was no bar there to retreat to and no fancy phone to hide my face in. Nothing but the lights of the disco ball, Louis Armstrong's sweet growl, and the desire not to be alone.

"Hey," a voice said, "you want to dance?"

I looked over to find a woman standing beside me. Her face was covered in freckles and I could see that she had long red hair. Her dress was pink, her shoulders very pale.

"Hi," I said, "I'm Lee."

"Rachel," she said, shaking my hand. "I'm Lucy's cousin. From Milwaukee."

I pointed to Ronny's Lucy. "Cousins?"

She bit her lip, nodded. "So you want to dance?"

"Yeah, sure."

She led me out toward my friends, and we danced and for a while I wasn't alone at all anymore and I stared at Rachel's shoulders and sometimes the light of the disco ball sprinkled a confetti kind of light on her skin, and the only thing I wanted to do was to touch those freckles, each and every one, the rest of my life.

I slept at her motel that night, but in the morning, when I invited her back to my place for pancakes and coffee, she just smiled in a winsome sort of way, kissed me on the forehead, and said, "I'm going to take a shower."

And so I drove home, through Little Wing, where the Sunday morning streets were quiet, a few cars already in the parking lot of the Lutheran Church, and a few more parked out in front of the Coffee Cup Café.

When I got home, I called about buying two tickets to Hawaii. Then I fell asleep on the couch, holding a pillow against my chest. By the time I woke up, it was already dark again, and spring a long time coming.

A GIANT JAR of pickled eggs. Dozens, maybe hundreds, of eggs, suspended in an amniotic green murk as if a great reptile had laid a clutch there, in that vessel, for some later hatching that might well never come at all. Two feet tall and one foot wide at the base, it sat behind the bar, against the same wall where an expansive mirror reflected the tableau of the long, narrow room. Just outside, the hot neons blinked on and off in the window, attracting fireflies, mosquitoes, moths. Inside, the jukebox cast a milky light in its corner, and the two felt rectangles of the pool tables bathed green under their own separate cones of light, players circling round with purpose, indicating their shots with long cue sticks, stubby fingers, toothpicks. At the bar, old men shook leather cups of dice, old men playing cribbage, singing: "Fifteen two, fifteen four, fifteen six, a pair for eight, and knobs for nine." And outside on the street, the newly exiled cigarette smokers, standing in the spring mist, nodding their heads in conversation, kissing yellow filters, blowing blue-gray smoke at the night.

A Monday night, the door flung open to Main Street. Lee and I sat at the bar, looking at each other in the mirror, behind all those bottles of liquor. We drank our beers quickly, not sure how to talk to each other anymore, not sure whose *turn* it was anymore. A heavy rain had come earlier in the day, and the sparse traffic on Main made a pleasant vernal noise as the wet tires passed—*swwwwoosssssh*. My planting done, I was happy for the rain.

We cracked peanuts, the shells collecting beneath our stools. Both of us sullen, our hearts heavy in our chests, both of us wanting somewhere inside to be friends again, but unsure what was even possible anymore, what we might or might not be able to forget or undo. I think it's fair to say that we both felt, without saying so to each other, that after thirty-plus years, our childhoods had finally come to an end. That the steady easy friendships of our youth were at last coming undone. We had gone a half-hour without exchanging so much as a hundred words. We didn't even make small talk about the weather. There was a desperation to the gulps we took. We drank to get drunk, to get loose.

"I'm going to steal that jar," Leland said.

I peered over at him. "Oh yeah?" I popped a peanut into my mouth. "How many eggs're even in that jar do you think?" I brushed some peanut debris out of my arm hair, considered the jar.

It had been months since I'd taken anything he said seriously. I no longer had the patience. There had been a time when I'd not only been his friend, but his *fan* too. Now all that seemed so long ago, so childish. It was embarrassing to think how much I'd adored Lee, the way my young son Alex adores Green Bay Packers players, the way he unabashedly wears their jerseys, hangs posters of them from his walls. All day I'd been dreading this—meeting him at the bar, having to make conversation. Earlier in the day I had stood behind a cow marked #104, attaching milking equipment to its teats, when it took a huge shit not a foot and a half from my nose. And yet— that didn't bother me. *This* bothered me. You'd have thought I'd be eager to get away from my cows and crops, to have a few hours with an old friend, drinking some cold beers, but really, all I wanted to do was take my boots off, ease back in my chair, and close my eyes while blue television light washed over my face, numbing me off to sleep.

"I don't care," Lee said. "But I'll tell you, I'm going to steal that jar tonight."

"I bet there has to be a thousand eggs in that jar," I said. "You think you can even carry that thing? You're looking a little skinny these days."

The eggs floated on, the pickle juice a brackish pond water.

He pointed a finger at the jar. "And you're going to help me steal that jar."

What he meant to say was, *We're going to do this together.*

"Fuck *that*, man. I don't have to help you with anything. It's gonna take a lot more than a few beers to get me in a thieving kind of mood. *And*," I went on, sticking my rigid index finger into the scant meat of his right bicep, "I figure I damn near have the right to kick your ass right out of the bar right now, as much of a friend as *you've* been to me." I hadn't meant to snap at Lee, but I also frankly didn't much care anymore. What could he do to me that hadn't been done already?

"Well, keep drinking."

"I am."

Craaack! A rack of billiards balls broke. On the television: a fast break slam dunk. And outside, a '79 Impala wheezed by without an excuse for a muffler, though the wet street seemed to do something to mellow the hoarse sound of that decrepit automobile.

Lee slugged back his beer. He looked away from me, wiped some foam away from his lips.

"I owe you an apology," he said.

"I'd say so."

"I shouldn't have done what I did, and I'm sorry."

"Listen, I really don't want to talk about it. You know? Don't really want to dwell on how you slept with my wife."

"You weren't married—I mean—*Christ,* Hank! *Goddamn it. Ten years ago.* What was I supposed to tell you?"

"That you were a fucking asshole? For starters. That I sure as hell couldn't trust you. Want me to keep going?"

We each took a long swallow of beer.

"I mean, you want to fight?" he said. "Is that it? 'Cause shit, I'll let you just beat the crap outta me, if it means we can be friends again. I don't really care."

"Well, that wouldn't really be much of a fight then, would it?"

"No. I suppose not. So what do we do?"

I didn't know what we were supposed to do, and somewhere, in my gut, I had decided months before that there was nothing *to* do, that we were done. Every time I got even close to something like forgiveness, I'd conjure some image of him and Beth together in bed, and it drove me crazy. I would get so livid, my only tonic was going to the four-lane bowling alley in Whitehall, where I could throw a sixteen-pound ball as hard as I could at ten pins, bent on shattering something into smithereens. I'd drive as fast I could there and back, over a hundred miles per hour and then, approaching a four-way country intersection, slam on the brakes just to feel the seat belt dig hard into my chest and lap, just to hear my Firestones scream in protest. Just to feel something other than jealousy and rage.

I ran a hand through my hair. Finished my glass of beer and ordered another pitcher. "I don't know, Lee. I don't have any idea."

"Well, somehow I got this notion that stealin' those eggs is the key."

The pitcher came and the barkeep moved away again, tallied our damage. I refilled our beers, and, I have to say, something in me softened for a moment, just adding beer to Lee's glass, doing something familiar and kind for him. Because it was true, we had passed many hours, days even, doing just the thing we were now doing: drinking and talking. And yet.

"So you'll do it, then? Steal that jar of eggs with me?" he asked.

"No."

"Will you, sir? Will you please just steal that jar of eggs with me?" He was being playful now, and I may have even smiled, wondering what his grand plan was exactly, leaving the bar encumbered by a giant glass jar full of pickled eggs.

"Nope, I ain't quite there yet."

"But you're at least *considering* the heist, right?"

"Possibly. Possibly I am a little intrigued. And, possibly I think you're, ah, totally full of shit."

"Because you're an accomplice now. You have no choice in the matter, except to report me to the proper channels." I could see he was getting drunk now, guzzling that cheap pale beer. "The proper authorities, so to speak."

"You're serious."

"I'm drunk—I don't know. Maybe I don't know what I'm saying. *Yes*, I'm serious. Those eggs are taunting us, right now. Look at them. Also, I'm desperate. All right? I don't see how else you and I can get right without some sort of juvenile act of, you know, mutual solidarity. And sitting here beside you, gazing over at those disgusting fucking pickled eggs, I suddenly had the notion that, you know, maybe we could just steal the fuckers."

"You're a complete moron."

"So, how many eggs you suppose are in there?" He began

pointing at the jar with his index finger, his eyes squinty with mock concentration, his brow almost comically furrowed.

"Look—no!" I snapped, slapping his finger, suddenly angry again. "This is fucking infantile." I stopped, lowered my voice a little. "You, you fucked up my marriage! You fucked up my family. And now we're sitting here counting eggs? Sitting here counting fucking eggs, talking about stealing some goddamn jar of pickled eggs, as if *somehow* that's how you're going to make everything okay again? Like that's gonna make everything go away?"

Lee looked at me now, directly in the eyes, and I could see they were misty, that he had nothing more to say, that he was indeed sorry. That there was nothing left to do.

"Christ," I said. "So this is the real world." I clenched my fist, wanted so desperately just to pound him.

"I'm sorry," Lee said. "I really am. I thought I'd found my wife in Chloe, and well, things just didn't work out. I don't know what's wrong with me. But I hope that you can find it, you know, find it in yourself, to trust me again. And honestly, I guess I'd understand if you never did. But you're my best friend in the whole world, all right? And I love you. I just don't know what the hell else to say."

Then Lee stood up from his bar stool, drank an entire glass of beer, and moved toward the back of the bar where the bathrooms were.

I sat there, examining the wood pattern of the ancient mahogany bar and then outside to Main Street, where the streetlights cast a pleasant glow on the slick, wet asphalt. I sighed. Because there was nothing left to do, and sometimes that is what forgiveness is anyway—a deep sigh. I loved my father very much, but was never as strong as he was, and I couldn't imagine my life without Leland or Ronny, for that matter, or even Kip or Eddy or the Girouxs. I *wanted* Lee back inside our house, *wanted* him to come over for bonfires and dinners, *wanted* to hear about his life and travels and the music he was making. So what was I supposed to do? Go through life harnessed to some yoke of anger? And what would *that* do to my marriage, to Beth, to the kids?

I sighed again, heard his weight compress the black cushion top of his bar stool, heard him pour himself another drink. Out on Main Street, a wet dog trotted by, its tail between his legs, head held down low.

"So, how are we going to get that jar out of here?" Lee said. "Undetected-like." He surveyed the bar for witnesses, of which there were perhaps a dozen. It was a slow night.

"Look," I said, "I don't know how to say this to you."

"I won't be deterred," he said, pointing at the jar of eggs.

"I'm serious. I've got something to tell you, and I just need to get it out and I don't want you fucking interrupting me with this goddamn pickled egg talk." I took a breath. "I'm so goddamned angry at you that I could kill you. I really could. You understand? I've *never* doubted Beth until last year. Always trusted her. Always felt *in love*. And now what? *Huh?* She's all I got, man. The kids, they're all I got. And it just feels like—" I paused.

"Like I took it from you."

"Shut. The. Fuck. Up."

He held up his hands.

"Yes. Like you fucking took it from me."

We sipped again at our beers.

"And, look, I almost understand it. It was years ago," I continued. "We weren't married. But do *you* understand? I'm not rich, Lee. I'm not famous. She is all that I have. My family is all that I have. And if I could, I'd beat you until there wasn't anything left."

I drank my beer until it leaked out of the corners of my mouth, wiped it away with my forearm. "*Goddamn it*," I said, slapping the bar with my palm hard enough to make our glasses jump, hard enough to still the whole barroom, the other patrons glancing up from their booths and their billiards games.

"I'm so sorry, Hank. I really am."

I shook my head.

"I apologize. I'm so sorry. I'm just so sorry, man. It's all I can say."

"Fine, you're sorry. Great. So, look—here's a start, be the big famous fucking rich guy and order us another round. How 'bout that?"

I walked away, to the jukebox, punched in some Credence and a few Crosby, Stills, Nash, & Young tunes. Returned to the bar to find my glass full, Lee gorging on a bag of potato chips and offering me some. I took the bag, shook some into my mouth, and chewed, looking at everything in the bar but Lee.

"Those chips were like crumb dust," I said.

"I know. It's like someone stepped on the bag or something."

"Still," I said, "better than nothing."

"No one's gonna miss them goddamn eggs, I'm tellin' you," he said to me quietly. "When was the last time you actually even saw someone buy one? Probably the same eggs that been in there since Dad was a kid coming in here. Those eggs could be twenty, thirty years old. They *deserve* to be stolen. They *want* to be stolen. That's what I'm telling you. And I won't be deterred." He spoke conspiratorially, took a sip of his beer. "No, sir."

I could not keep well enough alone. "How many times did it happen?" I asked.

Lee stopped his drinking and stared at me, the foam of his beer clinging to five days' worth of stubble. He ran his thin, veiny fingers over his face, adjusted his baseball cap, and looked at me without blinking. I stared right back.

"Once."

"Once?"

"Once." He held up his index finger, then quickly put it away. Shrugged his shoulders apologetically, a gesture that I didn't care for too much.

"Once?"

"I'm sorry."

"Can I trust you?"

"Yes." He nodded.

"Did you want it to happen more than that?"

He shook his head. "Look—no. It was just a mistake."

He's lying. Sonuvabitch is lying. "Yeah? I don't believe you. See, that's what I'm talking about. Even if I *do* forgive you, how the hell am I supposed to *trust* you again? You're a fucking liar."

"Okay. Yes, all right? Yes, I wanted it to happen more. I was lonely. Fuck, I was stuck out at that farmhouse in the middle of nowhere with three Mexicans and an old lady, and I was pretty well convinced I was a failure. Of course I wanted to sleep with someone."

"Could it have been anyone?"

He seemed to consider my question. I watched his face, drank my beer.

"Yes. Yeah, I suppose so."

"Do you think Beth wanted more?"

"No, man! Look, she loves you. Everybody knows that. She's *always* loved you."

"Did you love her?"

"No. Well. Shit." He rapped his knuckles on the bar. "A little. Yes. Not anymore. But back then—a little. Of course I did. How could I help it? Yes."

I looked away from Lee, back toward the jar.

"Revelations," I said. "Sobering revelations coming left and right."

I held two fingers in the air toward the heavily perspiring

barkeep, Joyce, who by and by came down the rail toward us, an unlit cigarette clenched between her wrinkled lips.

"Boys," she said flatly, "what'll it be?"

"Two shots of something cheap and a pitcher," I said.

"What're you two aiming to do? Drink me out of beer?"

"We're gonna give it a shot," I said.

"Gonna give it the ole college try," Lee reiterated.

She began to move away, toward the line of beer taps, when Lee stood quickly on his stool. "Wait! Joyce, come here quick. Hey, how many eggs in that jar, anyway?"

She looked at us. "How the fuck would I know? You want one? Fifty cents."

"No," he said, "I don't want one. They look totally fucking disgusting. What I want is to know how many are in there."

She sighed deeply, as if in defeat. She knew us, had worked in the elementary school cafeteria, had slopped food onto our molded plastic trays when we were not much taller than her waist. Her husband was a farmer and had dealings with me and the Giroux boys. She looked at the jar, and then back at Lee and said, "Two hundred and twelve." She started to move away.

"No! No! No!" Lee yelled. "Come back! That can't be right!"

"Lee!" she yelled. "You're *drunk*. And Hank's drunk, too. I'm going to get your beer and shots and then I'm coming back here to get your money. And then, after that, you're outta here. I don't care if you got a *hundred* Grammys. You can wipe your ass with 'em. And that's that." She went away.

"Nice work, asshole," I said. "I never been eighty-sixed before."

"Well," Lee said, "where are we? We okay?"

"I don't know," I said. "I don't think that's how these things work. I think it's just going to take time, you know? If it can happen at all. I have to trust you again. I have to trust you again around my wife. I mean . . ."

A slow song came over the jukebox, and there was a moment then, between us, I think, when time congealed, when the fabric of things was as it had always been and continued to be for those others in attendance, but between us, a kind of fault separated itself noiselessly like a small mass of land breaking away and going into the ocean. And I was sadder than I had ever been before, and more alone, too. Because I *knew* that we could remain friends, but I also knew that I could *never* trust him again in my house, or around my wife. Life had happened. Decisions had been made.

Joyce came toward us, arms wobbling with effort, a pitcher of golden beer in one hand and in the other, three shots of maple-syrup-colored fluid. She set these things down on the bar, and passed out the shots: to Lee, to me, and then one in her own hand.

"Mud in your eye," she said, tossing hers down the hatch.

"Salut," we barked in unison. We drank quickly and hammered our shot glasses down on the wood of the bar.

"Huzzah," said Lee.

"Ten bucks," said Joyce.

I handed her the money and she leaned over the bar toward us. "Seriously, drink up and get out. You two are spookin' the other patrons. All right? So, get your shit on outta here."

We drank down the pitcher fast, clanking our glasses together angrily, as if intent on breaking them, or each others' fists, sad and loose and unmoored, the noise of the bar rising about us.

"What we *need*," Lee said, "is a goddamn diversion. A smoke-screen, so to speak."

"I have no idea how we're going to accomplish that."

"You could start a fight."

"No. This is ridiculous. I want to go home. What time is it, anyway?" I looked at my watch—11:39.

"Wait a minute."

"What?"

"I got an idea."

He stood up from the bar, crept toward the Wurlitzer, and searched around in the pockets of his blue jeans for what I could only assume were a few hot quarters. Then he punched in a letter and a number, and from the first few notes of music that came on the old jukebox, I knew it was A1, the very first track on that album that had been a soundtrack for us on so many summer nights of our teens. I shook my head. In a small town, it's so hard to get away from anyone.

Lee now stood on a stool near the back of the bar and in his deep baritone, called out, "Hey! Hey! Listen up, my friends! Anyone care to sing along with me? Anyone? 'Cause if this ain't the best goddamned song ever, and I would like to sing this song right here, right now."

A group of perhaps four or five women, all in their fifties and sixties, gathered around him as those first piano notes started to be bucked up with the drums and the electric bass, as that classic piece of Americana slid under way. . . . And then he winked at me, motioned toward the jar, and sure as shit, Joyce was watching him from the far side of the bar, her back turned to me.

And there I was, back behind the bar, on tiptoes for no good reason, smiling the faintest hint of a smile that I couldn't nearly help, closer and closer to that absurd, gigantic jar of pickled eggs. Thinking, *This is really stupid. What in the hell are you doing?*

And all the while, the jukebox choir sang along:

> *I was a lonely, teenage broncin' buck*
> *With a pink carnation and a pickup truck*
> *But I knew I was out of luck*
> *The day the music died*

Then Lee pointing at me, as he nodded to the beat mouthing: "Now! Now! Now! Get that jar!" And Lee, really putting on a show, really distracting them by knocking over glasses of beer, pushing over pool cues, squeezing the asses of a few over-the-hill barflies.

And me, my arms around the jar as if tackling a giant, my knees bent wide so as not to blow out my back, and *lifting it*! Lifting that goddamned thing like it was an Olympic event . . . Off the bar . . . And there, in the space where it sat, *look*: the wood there a completely different shade of mahogany and with a great thick halo of dust to mark its old resting spot. And now, Leland, smiling broadly at me, clapping his hands, and the eggs obscenely sloshing in their jar, and Lee breaking ranks, still singing, stumbling to the door, and out into the night we went, two egg thieves, giggling crazily, stupidly—heartbroken, heartbroken, heartbroken. Going, going, *gone*, into the misty Wisconsin night, with nowhere to go and a giant jar of pickled eggs between us.

"What now?" I asked, out of breath and stumbling, the jar slipping, Lee there to steady it, to help me regain my grip. We walked quickly down Main, away from the VFW and toward Little Wing's hundreds of houses, all mostly darkened, a few windows glowing blue with midnight televisions, and sleeping viewers, their feet propped up on battered recliners.

"I don't know," Lee said. "But I don't want to think too much about it, right now."

We crossed Main and trotted down Elm Street, where there had been no elms for many years, save for a few persistent stumps that had yet to rot fully, all those decades since their disease had wiped out Little Wing's elm-tunneled streets. Lee stopped a second and pried off the lid of the jar, threw it into the front yard we were standing beside.

"Here," he ordered, "grab an egg."

"Hold on now, just hold on. This's our chance to *count* them," I slurred, still carrying the jar, and suddenly very drunk. Then, "Shit. Um. You mind if I set this thing down for a sec?"

"You're in no condition to count," Lee said.

"I'm a better counter than you."

"Just grab an egg like I told you, all right? Grab an egg while they're still hot."

"This is stupid."

He laughed, pointed a finger at me. "But it ain't *sad*, is it?"

I set the jar down and reached my arm into the juicy sea of pickled eggs and grabbed four, but not before my arm hair was drenched in pickle juice.

"Is it?" he insisted.

I removed my hand from the jar, and it shone slick in the night as if shellacked.

"This was a bad idea," I said. "We shouldn't have stolen these stinking eggs."

"Throw an egg at that car over there."

"That's Eddy's car," I said. "I can't throw it at his car. He's our friend."

"Yeah? But if *anyone* has good insurance, he does. Least nowadays."

Lee stopped, reached out for one of my eggs, tested its weight in his own palm, felt the pickled, clammy, gray skin of the egg, and then reared back and fired it hard, an oval fastball, right at Eddy's Ford Taurus.

The egg did not splatter, not quite. It collided loudly with the American steel of the automobile's driver's-side door, dimpling the metal there. Lee laughed. The egg must have been easy to throw, its weight facile, its shape perfect for the middle and index fingers to hold with the thumb before flipping the thing out into the night. Just then, from down the street, a set of headlights illuminated the wet pavement, announcing the approach of a midnight motorist.

"Get behind a tree," Lee hissed, hefting the jar up on his hip now, his pants thoroughly soaked with pickle juice and the two of us suddenly noxious smelling. Hiding behind young maples hardly thick enough to conceal us, we listened as the car approached, and then let it pass before Lee moved away from the tree and drew back his arm to throw. An egg went out, end over end, wobbling in its trajectory before hitting the bumper of the advancing Toyota Camry. We leapt back into the shadows, watched as the car jerked to a stop, then sat idling, then drove off.

"Can we go home now?" I asked. "Are you *done*? I mean, I've got kids, for Christ's sake. I can't get caught doing this shit."

"Oh, come on! Live a little." He picked up the jar and began walking farther down Elm, away from Main. "Come on, *trust* me."

"Where the hell are you going?" I yelled, refusing simply to follow him. But when he did not respond, I went along, trailing him at a distance of twenty feet, watching my friend stumble as he went, tripping on the broken sidewalk or on the persistent roots of trees that pushed up past the concrete. "Hey, all right, wait up. Let me carry that thing. I'm stronger than you anyway."

He yielded the jar and then took up eight eggs, enough to fill both his hands. "I want to sit on that railroad bridge. The one over the county highway," he said.

"All right," I said, and so we went that way, very drunkenly.

———

The steel of the bridge had worn into a long series of rusty scabs over which generations of high-schoolers had graffitied their names and sacred pronouncements of love and contempt in gaudy spray paint. Boots dangling off the bridge, we sat over the county road, the jar between us, the eggs almost glowing in the night.

"It's just us now," Lee said.

"What do you mean?"

"Everybody else is gone. Ronny and Lucy. Kip and Felicia. It's just us. The last of the Mohicans."

I shrugged, dropped an egg off the bridge, where it exploded on the pavement beneath us. Not a wet explosion, more like dropping a Jell-O mold—the particles of the egg simply surrendering and slightly scattering. I dropped another, and another and another again, and still the jar was not nearly depleted.

"I'm the only one tied to the land," I said. "The rest of you—I can't blame you. Even you," I said, "you'll leave again. You'll find somebody else, and she won't want to live here either. She'll drag you to Los Angeles or Paris or New York. You'll see. People like you," I said, throwing another egg out into the night, sobering up a little, getting meaner, "you don't belong here. You don't fit in anymore. Not properly. You've got too much."

Lee looked at the wet road, peeled a great flake of paint off the bridge. I could see that what I had said had hurt him.

"You're wrong about that," he said. "I'm here for good, old buddy. I bought the mill. Bought it from Kip. So, I'm *all in,* as they say. Might be a goddamned boondoggle, but I'm in for a little over a million, and there's no way I'm quitting. Gonna start a recording studio in there, set up a little theater, and this old town's gonna have live music if it likes it or not. I don't care if ten farmers show up for a goddamned show. We're going to draw people in from the Twin Cities and Eau Claire and La Crosse and goddamned Milwaukee, and they're going to come because it's *my mill* in that quaint tiny town of Little Wing. And I might never find a girl, but I tell you what, I ain't going to be looking in New York City either."

Absentmindedly, he took a bite from an egg, then spit it out, wiped at his tongue with a corner of his shirt. "Shit."

I sat, speechless. "You bought the mill?"

He shrugged. "It was the right thing to do. What else was I going to do? Let Kip hang out to dry? I'd do the same thing for you, bud, you ever *let* me. We could be partners."

"Yeah, don't hold your breath."

He looked out at a set of headlights, far off, coming toward us. The car was moving fast, swerving on the slick road—we could both see that, hear the tires shrieking on each turn. It was the sloppy too-fast driving of a country-road drunk, compensating late on the turns for dimmed-down reflexes and beery vision.

Lee took an egg in his hand nimbly, his fingers making fine indentations in the slick gray skin. Arm poised, he waited until the car was within forty feet before rearing back and chucking that egg—hard and straight and true. Even in those milliseconds of egg flight, the vehicle came into finer and finer detail: a souped-up little Mazda neither of us recognized, rims flashing, the undercarriage glowing an ethereal purple, loud music dopplering toward us, the windshield darkly tinted and then—*smack!*—the egg detonated like a little, white stink bomb over all that smoked black glass, the tearing shriek of tires skidding and all but the grinding out of sparks as the alien vehicle's brakes ground in resistance, and the vehicle jerked to a halt.

"*Shit,*" I said. "You fuckin' *nailed* 'em, buddy. Bull's-eye."

The countryside went quiet and we stood up from our spots, glancing below, where the vehicle sat unmoving. Then a door opened, and a skinny young man disembarked—more of a kid, really—dressed in oversized clothing, several lengths of gold chain about his neck, and loose silky shorts that terminated not much higher than his fragile ankles. And gripped in his right hand, an impressively chromed Beretta pistol. He didn't see us at first, the Mazda's headlights directing his attention underneath the bridge and out onto the road beyond. "Hey, who's out there? Who broke my muthafuckin' windshield?" he shouted into the night. The boy sounded unsure, and I saw that he was doing his best to posture for us, trying to make his voice sound deeper against the immensity and darkness of the night, and though I knew he was just a kid, a teenager, I was also afraid of him, afraid of his pistol.

"Well, what now, wise guy?" I whispered to Lee.

"Shit," Lee said, suddenly sounding sober. "Shit. Wasn't supposed to have a *gun*."

"You recognize him?"

"Hell no. He looks lost to me."

The boy stood not far in front of us, in a flowing plain-white tee, his arms out in challenge, the gun glinting. He wore a baseball hat cocked heavily askew, the brim flat as a book cover, and we noticed he was trembling slightly. A faint blond goatee adorned his weak, quivering chin, long blond hair braided back behind his head.

Then Lee spoke up. "I'm up here," he said, putting his hands up in surrender.

The boy glanced up, aimed the pistol, and fired. The jar of pickled eggs exploded and down they cascaded, riding an awful wave of pickle juice and egg alluvium. The eggs and brine did not shower the boy exactly, but they detonated violently off the pavement, soaking his basketball shoes, shorts, and white tee.

We held our breaths, Lee's arms still up in the air. I crouched down in the shadows, felt the cool, wet railroad tracks with my hand.

"What the *fuck*?" the kid said in horror.

We watched as he stood stock-still, his arms out, his mouth agape as he studied himself. The air suddenly smelling like egg salad sandwiches.

The boy looked up at us, sneered, and fired his pistol.

Lee fell over, a bullet in his leg, and he was not then screaming, but gasping for breath. Satisfied, the boy sheathed his pistol against the elastic band of his underwear and retreated into the idling import before roaring off into the night. We were returned to darkness, and I went to Lee, to my friend, bent down over him.

"It hurts," he moaned out. "I'm telling you, Hank—it's hot as hell."

"I'm going to get the truck, buddy," I said. "I'm going right now. We'll get you to a hospital."

"Get the truck."

"You bet, Lee. I'm going to get the truck and we'll get you to the hospital."

His hand shot out in the dark and seized me. "No," he said. "Can't do that."

"Why not?"

He sucked air loudly through his teeth and coming back out it made a whistling sound. "Because for one thing, that's some fuckin' bad press." He drew another pained breath. "And for two, somebody like me, the cops are going to want to look into that. And for three, shit, we started this whole thing off by stealing anyway."

"So, what do you want me to do?"

"Just get the truck and come back for me."

"All right then, you hold tight, buddy. I'm going to get the truck and come get you."

"I'll get down to the road."

"No—fuck, don't move," I said, and then I went off running toward Main Street.

By the time I returned to the bridge with my truck, he hadn't gone very far, inching down the slope of the hill leading to the road. Already, his pale forehead was lathered in sweat.

"We gotta get you to a hospital," I said. "This is ridiculous." I took his arm over my shoulder and we moved unsteadily down the hill.

"No! No hospitals. It ain't even bleeding that bad. We can get it." He peered down at his leg. "I don't think it came out the backside, so we just, eh, get a tweezers or something and dig that musketball out of there, you know, and wrap me up. No problem. Look, it'll be a good story, maybe a new song. Something for those fucking journalists to write about, uh? When all the dust settles." He attempted a chuckle, but then sucked in for more air, seized at his leg with both hands, and closed his eyes tightly.

"This is what you get for stealing."

"Damn," Lee said. "I never thought. Never thought it would be hot." His breathing was all hisses and sharp pants, the pain such that occasionally, he screamed out a string of f-bombs, or even laughed at himself, anything to breathe deeply, to expel the air inside him and to take in new air. His pant leg was soaked a dark, dark burgundy, almost black. We took off his shirts and knotted them about the meat of his leg. Then he sat beside the road, examining the stars to distract himself, and marking the progress of a passing satellite. I gave him a minute before helping him up and loading him into my truck, and then I ran around the hood and slid into the vehicle.

"Where to?" I asked.

"Fuck. I'm not bleeding on your truck, am I?"

"No, I threw down some garbage bags on the seat. Come on—where to?"

"My place," he wheezed. "I got pills, liquor. I can bleed anywhere I want to. The place could use some new carpeting anyhow." Then, after a moment of grimacing, "Fuck. Fuck, fuck, fuck! Okay, go."

"All right," I said. "Your funeral." And then I gave his wounded leg one good squeeze, which elicited a hearty scream as he stared at me, disbelieving and irate, before softening just a bit and resting his head against the cool, foggy window.

"Fuck," he said. "I suppose I deserved that."

I nodded and stepped on the gas.

I WAS STAYING IN WATERLOO, Iowa, with my uncle Delmar, who had just then got himself out of jail after doing about two years for stealing an ex-girlfriend's dirt bike. He was living in a trailer near a river I can't remember the name of, and the trailer was actually pretty clean, but he had no furniture, and the prior tenants had taken all theirs except for a coffee table, a lamp, and a shitty old mattress which they'd set fire to and which was nothing more now than a pile of melted, rusty coils in Del's firepit.

We weren't close, me and Del, but I was passin' through Waterloo at that time on the circuit, and my mom told me to look him up and I did. He was happy to hear from me, said I could help him scavenge up some furniture. I said sure, long as he'd put me up for a few nights' lodging.

So the next two days we rode around Waterloo, drivin' slow in an El Camino he swore was his own. We drove through neighborhoods starin' out at the boulevards and lookin' for thrown-away furniture we could take. And we did find some stuff, actually. A kitchen table, some chairs, a twin mattress, a couch. We loaded it all into the bed of the Camino and drove back to his place, set about making his trailer a little more comfortable. When we were done, he lit a cigarette, let out a ragged cough, and said, "Shit. I suppose I haven't fed you all day. Want some hot dogs?" He reached into an empty refrigerator and threw me a package of Oscar Mayers after taking one himself and biting into it, cold.

I shook my head at him. "Uncle Del, I'm gonna need to *roast* this thing 'fore I can eat it, if it's all the same to you."

"Suit yourself," he said. "Let's get a little bonfire together. Sit by the river. Shoot the shit. I ain't got much for food, but I do got about a case of beers."

So we got drunk and Del talked about prison, asked me about the rodeo, things in Little Wing. My memory is terrible since the accident, but I remember that conversation pretty clear, because that was the night when I got *CORVUS* tattooed on my chest, right next to a little crow, which is what "corvus" actually means, I guess.

Del had learned tattooing in prison, and as we sat around the campfire he showed me all of his ink; see, he'd used his own body for practice, let other inmates practice on him, too. Most of the tattoos weren't so good, but some were, including his rendering of Moby-Dick, which he claimed he'd read all of while behind bars.

"I'll ink you up, if you'd like," he told me. "Gratis."

"But, I mean, we could just go into town and get one done too," I said.

"Sure, sure thing, nephew. The only thing is, you'd have to pay."

———

Del sat me down at his new kitchen table and shaved what few hairs there were on my chest, just above my heart. He used a yellow Bic shaver, I remember that, and then he disinfected the area with some vodka and a handkerchief.

"Well, what do you want?"

"Corvus."

"Who's that? A girl?"

"No, he's my friend."

"You want a man's name tattooed on your chest? What happened? He die?"

"He's my friend. And he's going to be famous. You watch—soon enough, I won't be the only one."

"Here, write it down for me. Big block letters. An' make sure you spell it out just right. You can't wash this away."

He used a sewing needle and the ink from some pens inside the Camino's glove box. When he finished carving the letters, he asked, "What's it mean, anyway?" His face was as close to my own as I could ever remember another man's being, and he blew his cigarette smoke out and across my own face. I looked at the wrinkles around his eyes and mouth. At the yellowed teeth inside his mouth, the dark gums.

"I think it means crow. At least, that's what all his T-shirts show, crows."

"You want a crow to go along with it? I could probably do a pretty decent crow."

"You ever done one before?"

He looked at me.

"All right," I said. "Maybe I'll have me another beer though, first."

"Good idea. Grab me one, too."

———

I like Chicago just fine. Sometimes, I ride the El with our girl, Christina, just to get out of the apartment. She's an angel. I think she likes the train. People come over, peek into her little bassinet. We can ride all day if we want to, and sometimes we do. I stare out at the big buildings, and already I can pick out the Sears Tower or whatever the hell they call it now. And the John Hancock, where I guess Kip used to live. We ride past Wrigley Field and go up all the way to Evanston, then all the way back down, way south, past Comiskey and Chinatown, to where the city begins to level off.

And nobody looks twice at me. And nobody tells me what to do, or what not to do. And when I get lost, I just ask for help, and having a little baby in my arms always seems to help too.

WHEN WE WERE JUST TEENAGERS, Henry brought me to the top of the feed mill. It was a summer night without any breeze and I snuck out of the house after my parents had gone to sleep. We walked downtown, holding hands, and anyone might have seen us, except that no one was out, no one was watching, just one old widower, sitting on his front porch swing, swinging, and he waved at us through the darkness.

Up on top of those silos, there *was* a breeze, and far off over the countryside, lightning connecting heaven to earth. We took our shoes off, let our feet dangle. We kissed, and I was aware that my upper lip was sweaty, but Henry didn't seem to care. He touched my ears, my neck. He told me he loved me. An eighteen-year-old Henry.

It's all been worth it. Every fight, all those years of childish experimentation, the occasional heartbreak, the paltry checking account, the used, old trucks. To have lived with another human being, another person, this man, as long as I have, and to see him change and grow. To see him become more decent and more pa-tient, stronger and more competent—to see how he loves our children—how he wrestles with them on the floor and kisses them unabashedly in public. To hear his voice in the evening, reading books to them, or explaining to them what his father was like while he was alive, or what I was like as a girl, a teenager, a young woman. To hear him explain why our part of the world is so special. To hear him pray for trees and for dirt and for rain and for those people in the world less fortunate than us. To hear his voice in church, singing. To hear him urge our children to protect those kids at their school who others bully. To see him stop our truck in the middle of the road to carry a snapping turtle off the asphalt and into a nearby pond. To watch him on our tractors, in the last orange light of day.

When Eleanore was born, I ruptured my uterus. The amount of blood was horrific, but the doctor said that everything was normal, that it was just a tear. But Henry was adamant that something was wrong, and that if the doctor didn't do something *right that fucking second* Henry was going to break the man's jaw. Two male nurses were called in to subdue him, and even I said, "Henry, it's *fine,* as long as the baby is healthy, *please* don't worry. Just go on into the hallway and get yourself a glass of water."

I remember the doctor, clear as day, saying, "Listen to your wife, mister. Listen to your wife before I have to call the police."

Most men, most *people,* in that situation, would have backed off, would have submitted to the doctor's authority, to the two nurses clutching his biceps, to the calmness of my voice. Henry didn't.

He said in a tone of voice I can still recall, "Doctor, something is wrong with my wife, and if you don't fix it right now, I won't *sue* you, I will break every *bone* in your body."

It was a nurse, an old woman, who took a closer look, who noticed the extent of the bleed, saw my face going sallow, took charge of the room, called the doctor back to work. They stopped the bleed, and maybe they would have found it without Henry, but what I know is that I would have lost much more blood if he hadn't spoken up, that the situation would only have become more difficult, and that he was right all along.

Days later, back at home, lying in bed nursing Eleanore, I asked him, "How'd you know something was wrong? I didn't even really know. Just thought I'd torn some stomach muscles or ripped something down there. How did *you* know?"

He was there, too, right beside us, and said, "I don't know. I guess I just *knew*. It didn't seem right."

What he could have said is, *I know you better than you know yourself.*

And this, I think, is what marriage is all about.

THE DAY BETH AND HENRY were married was like this:

Low-slung clouds to scrape the yielding earth, the streams and rivers swollen and dirty, green and yellow tractors in the fields doing their discing. Vs of wild geese in the gray woolen sky, flying their ancient and yearly sorties, red-tailed hawks on telephone poles scoping voles and field mice, cows lazing in the mud, and a tire fire miles off, smudging a spot of sky.

A Lutheran church alone on its parcel of prairie, a humble parking lot newly asphalted and partitioned in yellow paint. A line of arborvitae to break the wind, another line of white pine for shade. The cemetery: one hundred and ninety-nine headstones, one dating back to 1877. BJORN ERICKSON still legible though the engraving had been softened by acid rain, by lichen, by western winds, by ice and snow. A swing set, the chains rusty in places and protesting loudly even against gentle breezes. The bell tower—taller than anything for miles but two or three corn silos and one cottonwood tree down by the irrigation ditch.

Inside the church those in attendance sat in their oak pews: fingering the paper programs, thumbing the Bible, playing tic-tac-toe, loosening their ties already, adjusting pantyhose, blowing noses, murmuring gossip, adjusting hearing aids, repeating gossip. . . . In the balcony, a widow began playing the church's gassy old organ, and everyone rose loudly. The processional music was meant of course to be a march, but the widow played it like a dirge.

We were badly hungover, our nerve endings frayed, our skin jumpy, our pores leaking the day-after poison of too many shots and beers. Our mothers scowled at us through tears they had no intentions of shedding, our fathers groggy and oblivious. Even for springtime, the church felt overly warm, everyone fanning themselves with the programs. I glanced across the aisle at one of the bridesmaids, who sported a unicorn tattoo on her right shoulder. The bridesmaid just next to her, for her part, a giant black butterfly of a breastplate tattoo. Both creatures seemed to me to be genuinely *in motion,* enough so that I began to feel nauseous and above my shoes I know that I must have been swaying back and forth ever so gently, like a very green fern in the wind. We waited for Beth to appear.

Maybe it's telling that Henry never chose me as his best man, opting instead for his younger brother Simon, who at the time of Henry's wedding had not yet graduated from high school. Simon was the right choice of course; family comes first, and had Henry known some of the thoughts fluttering around my brain, or the emotions percolating in my heart as I stood up there with him at the front of Trinity Lutheran Church, he wouldn't have invited me at all, and he certainly wouldn't have chosen me as a groomsman.

We had misbehaved the night before—no tomfoolery, just *serious* drinking at the VFW following which at two A.M., we lugged two cases of warm beer up to the top of the feed mill and sat there, drinking and laughing.

Melancholy is such a dramatic sounding word, but sometimes it's the right one. When you're feeling both a little happy and a little sad; it's the feeling that most people experience at a high school graduation I suppose, or watching their child board a school bus for the first time. The night before Henry and Beth's wedding, that's exactly what I felt—*melancholy*. Every time I allowed myself to loosen up at all, have some fun, I'd come back to thoughts of Beth and that night we had together—about how she was the only one I'd reached out to, and why was that? Why her? Why her, and not Ronny or Henry, or even Eddy? Did she think about me as well, and had she ever loved me?

A freight train came roaring through the night and I sat watching it, wondering where it was going. That first album, *Shotgun Lovesongs*, had just been released by a small record company, and it was beginning to sell better than anyone had expected (a few hundred copies every week). I wasn't really getting paid yet, but reporters were calling. Those were the days I welcomed interviews, welcomed any chance to talk about that album, about the chicken coop and Wisconsin, winter and being lovesick.

Ronny threw our empty bottles down at the train as he danced around. He had just come back from the road with a black eye and a tooth missing, souvenirs of a particularly nasty bull in Cody, Wyoming.

"You nervous?" I asked Henry, raising my voice to carry over the train.

He shrugged, leaned in close to my ear. "I don't know, a little bit, maybe," he said. "And at the same time, it feels like a long time coming, you know? I guess I'm just a little nervous about the ceremony, about saying the wrong thing or fainting up there or something stupid."

"You'll do fine," Ronny said, waving Henry's worries away like so many horseflies.

"You're a lucky man," I said.

"I know."

"Beth is . . . she's incredible. I'm just so happy for you two." I sipped at my beer, was glad for the darkness, that Henry could not see my face.

"Thanks." Then, "You okay, Lee? You seem a little, I don't know, out of it tonight."

The train finally passed, *Ca-clink-ca-clink, ca-clink-ca-clink*, then its whistle, that sweet midnight jazz, all horns and rhythm . . . *ca-clink-ca-clink, ca-clink-ca-clink* . . .

"No—listen—I'm fine, buddy, I'm fine."

"Well." Henry patted me on the back, drank the dregs of his beer, then stood, said, "I think I have to call it a night. Big day tomorrow." He held out his hand for me to shake, and after I transferred my bottle into my left hand, I did.

"Really? You're packing it in? It's *early*."

"Lee, it's three o'clock in the fuckin' morning. You should go to bed too."

"Whatever, Dad. Dawn's in, like, two hours. Come on. Let's catch the sunrise here, like old times."

Henry just chuckled, gave a friendly wave, and then climbed down the rebar stairs of the mill, disappearing down the side of the building, followed soon after by Eddy, the Girouxs, and then Kip, until at last it was just me and Ronny, the way it always was, and we sat, facing east, drinking the remaining beers, each one warming up, taking our turns to stand and pee off the side of those towers—*a cheap thrill*—until the horizon began to soften into blurry shapes and a progressively lighter shade of blue.

"It's coming," I said.

"I don't think so," said Ronny. "Blasé. Gonna be lackluster, I can tell. I predict rain."

"Did you just say *blasé*?"

He nodded. "French for *not much to see*. I know a few things, asshole."

We waited for the morning colors to blossom, but they never really did. Finally, we gave up and climbed down, exhausted and drunk, and slunk toward Ronny's parents' house, where Ronny collapsed into his childhood bed and I fell onto the floor. Later, Mrs. Taylor must have covered me with a blanket and, at noon, she carried two coffee cups into the room, opened the curtains, and said crossly, "You two are too old for this, you know. You're grown men. Christ, Lee, get ready. The wedding's in a few hours." She kicked at me, lightly, with the pink toe of her plush slippers.

The organ suddenly quieted and everyone who had been staring at us in the front of the church now turned to look behind them, where Beth now stood next to her father. She was beautiful. More beautiful than I could ever remember, and I had known her as long as anyone, since back when we were in kindergarten and Beth wanted to be a veterinarian. I swallowed so hard my throat ached.

And then the organ resumed, louder than ever, the old widow really *giving it* now, and Beth came forward, slowly, languidly, as if skating. The whole church must have been marveling at her just as I was: the muscles of her arms, the moles on her shoulders, the veins and sinew of her throat, her white teeth, damp eyes, the helixes of brown hair, Revlon red lips. Never, not in the whole history of Little Wing, Wisconsin, could a woman have looked as beautiful as Beth did at that moment. Just watching her march toward us was enough to sober me up, cause me to stand up a little straighter. I watched the men in the church attendance as she walked past them, watched some of them lower their faces to examine the slate paving and smoothed-out old grout of the church's floor; she was almost too pretty to look at. The last thing I remember in much detail was the bald Lutheran minister saying some words that relaxed the parishioners back into their pews and directed those of us at the front of the church to alter our positions and face the groom, bride, and pastor. I swiveled carefully on drunken heels.

I didn't register much of the ceremony. The soloists were ho-hum, the readers read familiar passages, the pastor moved into a monologue about the importance of family, the gift of children, the bounty of the land. I shifted my weight from foot to foot, imagined Beth laying on top of me in bed, her lips, her long hair shrouding me, all fragrant, her bright eyes hidden behind mascaraed eyelids. *Shit*, I thought, *you have to stop.*

At last, Henry lifted her veil delicately, deftly, and then he kissed her, his jawline like the blade of a scythe, her eyes closed sweetly, his hands on her face. They kissed well, confidently, like a pair of people well practiced.

The kiss concluded, the church erupted in whistles and applause, and the new couple paraded down the aisle, hand in hand, away from where I stood, their smiles impossibly happy and Beth seeming near about light enough to levitate right over the center aisle. I could see Ronny's mother in the pews, a mess by now, ruining Kleenex after Kleenex and clutching his father Cecil's sleeve, saying, "Never a more beautiful bride. Never ever."

In the narthex the bride and groom received well wishes beside a pyramid of Mexican wedding cookies balanced precariously on a table, and thanked in turn every great-aunt and -uncle, every second cousin and cousin, every high school friend, neighbor, and teacher. I followed Ronny out into the parking lot, near a side entrance to the church, where a few old farmers smoked unfiltered cigarettes and the younger ones spat tobacco into the gravel. Ronny bummed two smokes and we stood off to the side, rubbing our pounding foreheads. The bells of the tower began to boom out over the flatland and from the arborvitae three dozen starlings suddenly erupted out into the sky. I suddenly remembered our fifth grade teacher, Mr. Smith, telling us: a group of starlings is called a *murmuration*.

And then, someone, one of Beth's aunts maybe, came rushing around the side of the church and told us to make cups of our hands and into our awaiting palms came mounds of rose petals, the softest, reddest things I've ever seen or felt. They felt about as fragile as my feelings, those petals, something that could be blown away by the smallest gust of wind, and I stood that way, beside Ronny, hungover and a little mournful, considering the minute weight in my hands, until a mighty cheer rose up and we moved toward the front of the church where the air was already filled with not-flowers—thousands of those petals tumbling low in the air and into women's hair.

And then they were gone . . . ducking into the Lincoln, an older model to be sure, but a limousine and no doubt furnished with champagne and chocolate, and there she was, popping up and out of the moonroof, so happy, so beautiful, so shining. And I don't know that she ever looked at me, ever even saw me, as she blew kisses at her friends and relatives and then disappeared back inside the limousine. But I saw her, and I'll never forget that moment, that pile of petals still in my palms, then my fists, waiting to be thrown.

As the crowd dispersed, Ronny and I sat on the sandstone steps of the little church, the bells above still resonating, rose petals beneath our shoes. We looked out over the countryside where a single tractor plowed the black earth, a small flock of birds hovering just above it, searching for tilled-up worms.

"I'm so hungover," Ronny said.

"Yeah."

"You don't seem too happy, buddy. Kinda bringing me down a little."

"Just the weather, I think. So gloomy."

"Well, soon it'll all be green."

"Should we go?"

"I can get my mom to drop us off."

"All right."

Long after Ronny and his parents had gone into the Palladium Ballroom and Supper Club, I paced the parking lot, too nervous to be late, too proud to be early, there, in my tragic rented tuxedo, the cummerbund suffocating across my stomach and enough to make me think of a corset. I watched mostly Beth's people go into the hall, then five cars of Henry's farming kin, all big-looking people, fit people, their faces and necks sun-tanned, though no doubt their barrel chests and flat bellies white as a fish's. They came from all around Little Wing, all the little farming towns, each one a variation on the same sad theme of decline: a boarded-up movie theater, a vacant Woolworth's or Sears Roebuck, and a used car lot that never seemed to sell any cars. I waved to a few of Henry's cousins and uncles, men I knew vaguely. The clouds had been steadily burning off, the sky by now the color of sherbet, all American pastels swirled against the fertile horizon.

"Well," I actually said aloud to myself finally, "can't stand out here all night long." Then I dragged my sad-sack ass into the reception, where small groups collected here and there, pulling at canned beer and sipping on cocktails in opaque red plastic cups. I was grateful when Ronny approached me, with two cans of beer in his hands.

"Hair of the dog," he said, knocking his can against my own.

"Probably too late for that remedy."

"Cheer up, asshole, and drink your beer."

A deejay was situated on a stage at one end of the rectangular space, a slightly overweight man in a tuxedo and red suspenders. I watched him as he peered down at a laptop and adjusted a wall of oversized speakers. The pastor was there too, reclined in a metal folding chair, a bottle of Grain Belt in his thick fingers. He'd once been a pig farmer, I knew, and his sermons were often predicated on farming, on harvests, on the earth. A bank of windows along one wall showed some of our high school friends outside, throwing horseshoes barefoot in the uncut spring grass and smoking cigarettes behind Ray-Ban sunglasses; everyone out there, warming back up to one another, jocular and friendly— none of the feelings I could possibly feel right then. The sound of the horseshoes clanking against a steel stake buried into the ground. The *ooohhs* and *ahhhhs*.

The room steadily filled, older people taking their seats at round tables, younger people at the bar, the wedding party now arriving to scattered applause and catcalls. And then, Beth and Henry, entering the Palladium to the accompaniment of Queen's "We Are the Champions," arms raised victoriously, new rings glinting on their fingers, hugging everybody in their path to the stage, where a long dinner table crowned the space.

"Please give a warm and hearty welcome to Mr. and Mrs. Henry and Bethany Brown!" cried the deejay.

The crowd went bonkers as Beth and Henry took their spaces at the front of the room, and suddenly there was that good, old cacophony of cutlery against glass, as every uncle, every nephew, every best friend, urged in a sea of voices soon coalescing into a single chant: *"Kiss her! Kiss her! Kiss her! Kiss her!"* And then Henry bending Beth as if a single reed, a single blade of grass, her body now nearly parallel to the floor, his arms so strong holding her there, her body so weightless and elegant.

Before dinner, the pastor stood from his chair, no notes in his hands, no Bible—he'd done it all before a thousand times or more—saying, "Please join me in prayer. . . . Dear lord, please bless this beautiful couple—Beth and Henry. . . . Fill their hearts every day with love, with reverence, with patience, and kindness. . . . And lord, bless this brand-new couple as they grow closer and closer together each day, growing their own family and love. In your name we pray."

And the room said, "Amen." And I said "Amen" as well.

I watched everything from the bar: the first dance, the father-of-the-bride dance, the chicken dance, the mambo line, the electric slide. I didn't feel like dancing. Ronny's parents, who had known me since childhood, came over to me from another table where they had been sitting with other pairs of parents.

"Doesn't she look beautiful?" Ronny's mother, Marilyn, said, kissing me on the cheek.

"Hey, Mrs. Taylor," I said.

"Nice party," said Ronny's dad, Cecil. "*Real* nice party." A can of Pabst in his hands looking small. He was a construction worker, always sunburnt, always smelling of a combination of fresh air and asphalt. But he *loved* music, had seen Lynyrd Sky-nyrd in concert. Cream, MC5, The Stones, and Led Zeppelin. He was the first person I ever smoked up with, down in Ronny's basement around their wet bar. "How's the music coming along,

Lee?" His voice was all cigarette smoke, gravelly as the roads he worked.

"It's coming," I said.

"The dollar dance's coming up," Marilyn said, the tone of her voice rising with excitement. Then, "Cecil, do you have five dollars?"

"Five dollars!" He laughed. "That's Beth! We've known Beth for years!"

"It's so they can have a nice honeymoon!" she insisted. "And besides, I want to dance with Henry. He's looking good. He taken over his daddy's farm yet?"

Cecil held out a five-dollar bill and Marilyn took it, then walked over to stand in line for a dance with Henry, dozens of women ahead of her.

"Well, boys," Cecil said, "there they go. Two of your best friends marrying each other. You ask me, that's how you do it. Marry your best friend. Let me tell you, the sex will eventually run dry, it *will*, and then you're stuck looking at each other. May as well find someone who can hold a conversation. Who seems to genuinely care about you. "

Ronny and I stared at his father.

"Look, I know how you feel," he said, sipping his beer, pulling up a chair. "I know how it is." He nodded, drummed his fingers against the beer can. "You don't know that your dad's watching you, but he is." He stroked his mustache, hitched up his belt and pants. "Everyone's getting married but you two. And now, look at that. Either of you probably could have married her. Shit, you're her friends too. Henry's just brighter than you two. More determined."

"Dad—" Ronny said.

"I remember coming to one of your school talent shows. She sang a song . . . I think it was 'California Dreaming.' And I just,

I remember sitting there, thinking, *That girl is special.* That was her, wasn't it?"

I'd actually forgotten that Beth was a wonderful singer, because she didn't sing that much, she kept it to herself, wasn't even in the choir, but sometimes you'd catch her, at a party, or riding in the car, and she'd forget herself and let loose and out came this voice, this beautiful, sweet, self-assured voice. Had I been a smarter man, I would have asked her to record a duet with me, but maybe, for Henry's sake, it was a good thing I never did.

Cecil rose, touching his mustache and brushing back his hair. We watched him stand and gather himself. He straightened his tie and smoothed his lapels, brushed dust off the fabric of his sleeves and shoulders. He took a final drink of his beer and looked toward the dance floor, where Beth and Henry were busy dancing with all comers, the best man and maid of honor holding hats already brimming with cash.

"I don't know what your problem is, Lee," he said, more sternly now. "But you've been pouting all afternoon long. Hell of a way for the groom's best buddy to be acting, and now, *Jesus,* you got Ronny back here sulking with you. I ain't your daddy, but I know if he was here, he'd say quit being a bunch of assholes and get out there and dance with your friends before they go join the real world." Then he went without waiting to hear our rebuttal, though in truth, we had nothing to refute. We hung our heads like little boys, took a last few sips from our beers before following Cecil to the line of men. Ronny first, me following behind, forming the tail end of the dollar-dance line.

We inched forward over the next twenty minutes, the playlist shuffling between love ballads across various decades of American popular music. I saw that Ronny had a few wrinkly singles in his hand and I reached into my pocket, found a fiver. It was all I had after almost two days of straight drinking. Then it was Cecil's turn and he handed the maid of honor some money and went out to dance with Beth, who swept some hair away from her face and then began clapping delightedly when she saw it was Cecil Taylor come to dance with her in his black polished cowboy boots.

We watched as Cecil paused before he reached her out on the dance floor. Then, he bowed deeply to her, a thing I've never seen duplicated at any wedding, and such a regal gesture you'd never have expected it from Cecil, the construction worker and Skynyrd fanatic. Beth placed a hand on her chest, then went to him, helped him up off his knee the way a good queen might help an old knight. And as they embraced and moved into the dance I noticed for the first time the look of love on his face. I watched him dance with Beth, and it was enough to break my heart all over again, into a million little pieces. A grown man who perhaps had always wanted a daughter, dancing with a grown woman—one of his son's good friends.

I looked at my hands, remembered the weight and feel of those rose petals.

I don't remember Cecil's dance with Beth ending, or Ronny's dance with Beth beginning. I just remember standing in line, waiting, so lovesick and sad. When my turn came I handed my five-dollar bill to the maid of honor and then moved out onto the scuffed parquet in a kind of trance. I took Beth's hand in mine, and she placed her other hand on my shoulder and my right hand found her hip, and we slowly began to circle each other the way you do when you slow dance, the way you do at a prom or homecoming. I hadn't felt her touch in a year or more, and we moved a little haltingly at first, before at last slipping into a slow-circling groove, our hands damp with perspiration, my eyes on her face, her eyes here and there, not *unhappy* but not happy either, and finally, if only out of exhaustion, her head very lightly on my shoulder.

"You all right?" she asked. "You don't seem yourself. . . ."

"It's okay, I mean. I don't know what it is. The important thing's that you look just so beautiful tonight."

"Hey."

"Yeah."

"Don't get weird on us, all right? Henry and I have always been together. You know that."

"I know that."

"You're part of our family, all right, Lee? Come on now. Look happy."

"I know it, I get it."

I wanted to kiss her, to stop the music, the dancing, the champagne flow. I wanted to tell everyone, everyone in attendance, that Beth and I had shared something—something special and real—and that maybe, *maybe,* I was still in love with her, and she with me. But I couldn't of course, and wouldn't. I held her tight to my body, looked her straight in the eyes. I was aware of some people watching us as we orbited the floor, our abdomens touching, faces like Cecil's and Ronny's staring at us, no doubt thinking, *My word is he holding her close.*

Her hand fit so perfectly in mine and I allowed myself the briefest reverie: lying together in a white bed, our limbs entangled, her chestnut hair, morning sunlight and the joy of making a baby together. I saw her hair growing white in intervals: first a few fibers, then waves, and finally her whole head of hair, until finally it became fragile, brittle, flyaway. I saw her face now, and then imagined it far off, inscribed by the sun, the cold, the prairie winds, her squinting and laughter. God it made me sad, to pull away from that reverie only to see my own future as it lay ahead, decades without this woman, decades watching her with my best friend. But there it was.

"Maybe what I should say is, 'I'm sorry.'"

She looked at me. "Sorry about what, Lee?" We had stopped.

"No," I said, "please, don't stop dancing with me. I just mean, look. I don't even know how to say it. I just . . . I'm sorry about that night. I'm sorry about what happened."

She had returned her head to my shoulder and I could no longer see her eyes. "Lee, I don't know what to say," she said. "I haven't even thought about that night in months now. We've been so happy. Everybody's been, you know, just so happy."

"I haven't been happy."

"Well I don't ever want to talk about it again, okay? I don't even want to think about it."

"Okay."

"I don't want *you* to ever think about it again. Okay? Lee? It's done," she said, "and now here we are."

"Beth?"

She looked up at me.

I wanted to say, *I love you.* "Nothing," I said. "Don't worry about it."

And then we were quiet, just the steady shifting of our weight, foot to foot, our tiniest movements: the traffic of blood in our veins circulating, pumping, our lungs at work and the lightning of our brains, the smallest currents of air and breath pushing strands of our hair and our sad eyes blinking, taking in light, taking in darkness. The parquet flooring of the rundown Palladium Ballroom below us sinking and rebounding ever so slightly. I thought of a night, many, many years ago, when Henry, Beth, and I were just kids, and we'd erected a canvas pup tent beside Lake Wing. I thought of that night now, the dance of our flashlights and the sound of midnight laughter.

The song ended, and an elderly man much wrinkled and leaning on a cane was suddenly beside me, tapping a finger against my shoulder and smiling broadly. "I apologize," the old man said, "but you'll forgive me for cutting in. I don't get too many chances to dance with young women these days." And then he handed me his cane, as if I were a coatrack, a hat tree. Beth kissed me fleetingly on the cheek before curtsying politely at the old man. They began to dance, and I returned to the bar, where I ordered a beer and stood beside Ronny and Eddy.

"Got to watch those geezers," said Eddy. "They're cold-blooded."

I stayed until the end, until the lights came on and everyone groaned for more: more music, more beer, more dancing and fun. Beth and Henry waved at us as they left the building and climbed back into their limousine, bound for a hotel in Eau Claire. I waved good-bye along with everyone else, waved at them until I could no longer see the red of their taillights.

And then I went home with Ronny and his parents and lay on their couch, gazing at the ceiling fan as it turned, not even the slightest bit sleepy.

Four o'clock in the morning, and my right hand was in the air, my knuckles poised millimeters away from the door of the hotel room where Beth and Henry slept, newly wedded and without a care in the world. The hallways of the hotel were abandoned, the night auditor watching a little six-inch television screen behind the front desk. The only sound was the ice machine.

But I couldn't do it. I couldn't knock. Because time had passed, because we were all adults, and there are boundaries that adults don't cross, and this was one—two people fairly married, and what reason, what possible reason did I have now to ruin it? And why? Why at that moment? Why not a year ago? Or two? Or five? Cecil was right: she had lived within five miles of me my whole life, and now, here I stood, in a stale hallway, a peephole staring blankly back at my sorry face, my fist raised in announcement of what? Of love? Of friendship?

I thought about the future, *my* future, my life, and I could see it now spreading out before me as surely as I knew every line of topography around Little Wing, the hills, valleys, sloughs, coulees, ridges, country roads and cornfields, railroad tracks and game trails. I could see it all: that I would keep writing and playing music and touring and soon, things would take off. The magazines would begin to print reviews, and then stories. I'd be commissioned to write songs for television shows and movie soundtracks, until one day, I'd be standing up on a stage, holding a little golden gramophone and talking to an auditorium of my heroes. I could see it, because I believed in the music, believed in my own voice, in what music I heard the world make. I could see that Henry and I would slowly grow apart, at first by increments of weeks and months, and then by years, until when I called him, he would no longer even recognize my voice. My friends would have families, children, and comfortable homes—homes with tired, comfortable furniture. While I would date and marry women who loved and then loathed me, who didn't understand the first thing about me, who were bored by me, who detested my hometown and no more than tolerated my friends. And then, one day, there would be nothing to come home to. No more friends, no family, no smiling faces and no hellos or good nights. I saw myself buying a big penthouse, maybe a beach house, a place along a coast, a place with a massive selfish view, and I saw myself roaming that floor plan, restless as an old dog.

I lowered my fist to my hip and exhaled years of love. I walked down the hallway, out into the early morning, and climbed in Ronny's parents' car, and drove all the way back to Little Wing.

WE THREW NO DUST as we rocketed toward Lee's schoolhouse over those dewy midnight gravel roads. Fireflies rose up in the ditches and fields like tiny lanterns. Moths to dust the windshield.

"Hope you're not bleeding too much on that bench seat," I said.

"Just on your damn garbage bag. *For shit's sake,* Jesus, it hurts."

"We're close now," I said. And we were, Lee's mailbox coming into the cones of the truck's headlights, and beside it, the taxidermied bull, its red glass eyes reflecting our arrival, and now the bumpy driveway, the potholes with their miniature ponds of water and the night frogs leaping for safety, Lee hanging on for all he was worth, hanging on to that seat belt, grimacing, muttering something about a new asphalt driveway and then there—his pasture, a dozen deer or more turning their doleful muzzles to stare at our approach and the lights of his house and garage and outbuildings. I drove us as close to Lee's front door as we could get, shut off the engine, and came around the truck. Already he was stepping down gingerly, draped an arm around my shoulder, and together we stumbled inside.

"Just get me to the bathroom, okay?" he said. "Put me in the shower. Less mess to clean up."

"Good thinking," I said, though I couldn't have cared less about any blood trail. This mess was Lee's, all Lee's.

We peeled his pants off, then his underwear, and socks. Untied the shirts that were acting as a tourniquet.

"Christ you're pale."

"I'm throwing it all away," he said, "burning it. Worst night of my life." He lowered himself into the bathtub, and I began to draw him a bath, testing the water with my hand until my fingers went pink, then red.

"You want it hot?"

"Sure, burn me all to hell. Stupid fuckin' pickled eggs."

Soon the bathroom was filled with steam. I sat on the toilet and listened as the water filled the tub, holding my head in my hands, Lee making small childish noises with every little readjustment of his body.

"Henry?" he asked.

My drunkenness was receding, even the pounding within my head was beginning to diminish. But I was tired, God was I tired. Ready to fall into my own bed. Ready to cuddle Beth. Ready to push Leland's boat clear away from my shore, ready to push him far out into the foggy surf. "Yes," I said.

"Mind checkin' my medicine cabinet? See if I got any of those Vicodins left? Or codeine? I need something."

"Sure," I said, "hold on for a sec."

I went through his medicine cabinet, rattling empty orange pill canisters, spinning them around to read the prescription notes. And there it was—Vicodin, recently expired, twelve pills left. I handed two to Lee, then turned on the bathroom sink and filled a palm with cold water, swallowed two myself for good measure.

"Think that'll do you?" I asked.

"Maybe some whiskey too," he said. "Something hard and quick. Something to help me swallow. I feel all dried out."

In the bathtub, the water was turning pink now, and I stared at the wound in Lee's thigh, the hole there wisping out a feathery stream of blood, the slug of a bullet still somewhere inside him. I went into the kitchen, found the whiskey, took a sip from the bottle, and then poured out a shot for him. Walking back toward the bathroom, I passed through Lee's dining room, and nearly ignored the new painting hanging above his sideboard. It was mine—the missing St. Vincent's painting. I just stood there.

"Henry!" he called out in irritation, desperation really.

"Yeah!"

"I'm dying here!"

"Shut up. I'm comin', I'm comin'."

He was writhing in the tub when I walked back into the bathroom, eyes pinched shut with pain. He pounded at the wall with his fists.

"Here you go," I said, holding out his shot.

"Thanks," he said, and tossed it back in a gulp. Closed his eyes and clenched his fists.

We sat together a long time, lulling off into intermittent sleep, Lee in the bathtub bleeding, and me on the toilet. I stood to shut the tap off at some point and looked down upon my friend, stretched out as best he could, bleeding, in the bathtub, his arms and neck tanned a deep brown and the rest of him white as the porcelain that held him. I saw Lee's thousands and thousands of hairs blowing gently in the tub, as if seaweed.

"You got a new painting," I said casually.

"Yeah. Got it at the St. Vinnie's of all places." He opened one eye and peered at me. "Why?"

"It's ugly as sin."

"I like it."

"Why?"

He shrugged, closed his eyes again. Then we were quiet again for a while.

"Henry, I have to tell you something about me and Beth."

I shut my eyes, wincing against whatever he might say.

"It wasn't like you think it was, Hank. Or, hell, I don't even know what you think it was like. But it wasn't like that. And what I have to tell you, it's not an easy thing, but it's the *truth*, okay? And so I'm going to tell you, and then you'll know and we can be done if you want to." He was clearly in great pain, his teeth bared as he looked up at me sitting on the toilet, the shower curtain pulled far off to one side, the air between us gauzy with a condensing steam that must have held molecules of his blood.

"Look, we're well past wherever we used to be, buddy. I don't know as anything you could say now's going to make it better or worse. So I'm going to just close my eyes again, but I'm listening."

"I'm sorry, man," he said. "I'm so sorry. You're like my brother. You're *better* than any goddamned brother, and I'm sorry."

"I don't want to hear it."

"I have to tell you."

"I told you I don't need to know any more," I said, squinting at him, my eyes tired and probably bloodshot, my body so weary.

"I've always been jealous of what you have. But I only *used* to love her. But I don't feel that way anymore. And look, I'm sorry for what I've done to you. But I did what I did and said what I said only really because I've always basically wanted what *you* had. She's the best. You know? Beth is the best."

He took a deep breath now, and allowed his body to sink beneath the water, little bubbles rising from his nostrils.

I counted the seconds he was submerged until I lost track and then replaced my head in my hands, *so exhausted,* and said, "I forgive you," though I'm sure he could not hear me. But maybe that didn't even matter. With Lee, the important thing was always that he heard himself.

I stood, went into the kitchen, and called Beth from Lee's landline, having left my cell at home. It was nearly two o'clock in the morning, and now I rubbed my face, yawned, and waited for her to pick up. I'd probably scared her to death—I'd told her I would be home before midnight. She answered after the second ring, I could hear her fumbling with the receiver beside our bed.

"Lee?" she said—the caller ID.

"It's me, baby. Henry. Sorry I didn't call earlier. I'm over at Lee's."

"Why? Where were you? You left your phone here, I tried calling, I don't know, a dozen times before I found your phone in Alex's room. Are you okay? What happened?"

"No, I'm fine. We're both fine. Look, I'm going to spend the night here, okay? For one thing, I'm too drunk to make it home." I decided to leave out Lee's bullet wound.

"Are you okay?"

"Yeah, Beth, we're fine, both of us. Really, I'm fine."

"You're fine?"

"Hey. I love you."

"Okay, but just—can you call me tomorrow morning?"

"Will do. I love you."

I hung up and walked back into the bathroom to make sure

Lee hadn't drowned. He was standing, a trickle of blood emanating from his thigh where he seemed to be poking at the wound with his index finger.

"Maybe we should have gone to the hospital," he said weakly.

"I told you so."

"I think I might pass out."

"Sit down, okay? Let's get you bandaged up. I'll get you some orange juice. You'll make it."

"Fucker shot me."

"Yeah, you threw an egg at his car."

"And then he fucking shot me."

I awoke on Sunday morning to the sound of Lee's screaming, the sun just then rising in the east. I went to his bedroom, where he laid in his bed, feverish, the sheets soaked with perspiration, the room feeling terribly hot and stuffy. I looked out his bedroom window and watched a crow glide over the pasture, then land on an old fencepost where the barbed wire had been bundled into a tight crown of rusty thorns. In the sky, a cloud the shape of an angel blowing a trumpet. And at the very rear edge of the pasture: a coyote, trotting along the tree line, sniffing the spring air. Lee raked at his legs, scratching. I opened the window.

"We're taking this thing out ourselves," he said to me, his voice cracked and raw.

"Yeah?"

"Get some water boiling."

"All right."

Feet on the floorboards, one hand on the bed, Lee sat up, itching the half-scabbed wound until it oozed fresh blood.

"You need a hand?" I asked.

He shook his head. "Nope. Just get some water boiling. We'll make some breakfast. And then get this thing outta my damn leg. We're going to play us some Operation, old buddy. You and me."

If only out of curiosity, I followed as he hobbled into the bathroom. I certainly didn't want him to pass out, crack his head open against the porcelain. Standing in the spray of the shower, he lathered the hair of his chest and then his head, his armpits, drank the spray of the showerhead, lifted his feet to wash them with his hands. Finally, he attended to his wound, carefully scrubbing and washing it before taking a razor and shaving the entire area clean. He shook the razor at intervals, knocking off used cream and removing the long brown hairs with his fingernails. The first razor dulled quickly and he retrieved another from the medicine cabinet without ever noticing me. He also hurriedly tamped two more pills from the orange Vicodin bottle. He opened his mouth wide to the shower spray and swallowed.

"*Goddamn,*" he swore, spitting shower water. "*Goddamn.*"

When he was finished shaving, he collected the shorn hair in a ball and tossed it into the toilet. It looked like a wet little bird's nest. He began to towel off, and that is when I crept downstairs, put on some water to boil, started cooking breakfast.

"What's there to eat?" he asked, limping into the kitchen, pulling on a shirt. "I'm famished."

"I'm making us eggs, a package of bacon, some toast, and some sausages. Coffee's on. Orange juice on the counter," I said, shaking my head. Lee poured a cup of coffee, blew into it, muttered something, peered out the window. I stood at the stove, scrambling the eggs and flipping the sizzling strips of bacon.

"Buying that mill might've been a bad idea," he said. "You think?"

"Oh, I don't know, Lee. You seem full of good ideas lately."

"Maybe I should just move out to Los Angeles, sit by a fuckin' pool all day, visit the Playboy mansion."

"You could use some sun. Or maybe, I don't know, just a little more *well-distributed* sun." The sleeves of his T-shirt were just short enough to display an inch of very white flesh before the sleeve of tanned and tattooed arm.

Lee nodded his head, then shuffled over to the basement door and hopped lightly down the stairs. I could hear him down there, rattling coffee cans full of old nails or screws, glass jars full of tools, and a few minutes later, he pulled himself up the stairs, returned to the kitchen, and threw a pair of pliers into the pot of water. He looked out the kitchen window again, to the creek below where once we had sat and talked, back when everything was normal and copacetic. Then he looked over at me, to the stove, where the water was beginning to show tiny bubbles at the bottom of the pot. The bacon was growing black and smoking. The eggs were beyond ruination. We stared at each other, neither of us certain about how to proceed.

I stood outside the old schoolhouse waiting for him, the pliers hot in my hands, the sun still rising. I hoped that Beth had already begun to milk our herd, or called the neighbors for help. I couldn't remember the last time I had missed a morning milking, though I suspected it was our weekend in New York City for Lee's wedding.

He was still inside, readying himself; he had already swallowed two more Vicodin and several shots of whiskey. I could see him, through the window, pacing, and suddenly I thought of one of the formative stories of my youth—a story involving a nearby farmer who had lost both arms to a hungry combine. The man, a friend of my father's, had calmly walked the distance back to his home, climbed into the bathtub, and then dialed nine-eleven using a pencil that he'd clamped down on with his teeth. He sat in cold water until the paramedics finally found him, shivering, bleeding profusely, but alive. He spat the pencil out and hissed to the paramedics, "I left them out by the tractor." *His arms*, he meant. Later, they were reattached and he resumed farming. My father used to like telling that story, saying every time in summary, "That about pretty much nails it, don't you think?"

Lee finally came out of the schoolhouse in just his white boxers, a dowel that normally held paper towels in his right hand, a scary sort of determination powering him awkwardly forward. He got down on the ground, motioned for me to come brace him down with my knee. And then he clenched his eyes shut, motioned at the pliers in my hand, bit down on the dowel, and I did like he wanted.

And now he was beneath me, fighting me: rolling on the ground in his newly dusty underwear, teeth clamped down on that dowel, his legs painted in blood. And me: my knee pinning him to the dirt and gravel and blowaway grass, those needle-nose pliers half-buried in the gore of his leg and somewhere deep down inside all that tissue: the fragment of bullet fired almost a day prior. Dirt caked to our sweaty bodies, blood on our hands, tears in our wild, sad eyes, our hearts still raw—but *maybe* then mending. . . .

How we startled grasshoppers, butterflies, bees . . . rolling through patches of nettles and the small thorns of raspberry bushes. And through the dowel and its coming splinters, through the smithereen shrapnel of our undone lives, through bared teeth, through the waves of infinite pain and past the medication of whiskey and Vicodin—

"I'm so fuckin' sorry, man! I'm so goddamn sorry!"

And me: through gritted teeth, my muscles an unbound circuitry of red-blue wires, my eyes two searchers, my body nearly trembling apart, like delivering a calf, but worse, so much worse, and me saying—

"Hold still, buddy. Just hold still. I feel something in there. Hold on now."

The mouser-tomcats on Lee's wraparound porch stared, the black eyes of sneaking raccoons, a terrified skunk scampering away from it all. . . . And in the blue-blue early afternoon American sky, unsuspecting airplanes flying over us, leaving behind their white contrails and the planes' passengers flipping through glossy magazines or thumbing expensive telephones as the flight attendants pushed beverage carts up aisles in the skies and a single turkey vulture wheeling high overhead, inspecting the carnage.

"Hold on, buddy, okay? Hold on. Take a deep breath for me, now. Hold on. . . ."

Long after Ronny's departure south to Chicago, long after the mill was sold to Lee, who rejuvenated the building and turned it into an unlikely music venue and recording studio, long after Kip and Felicia bought a brownstone in Lincoln Park and a five-hundred-dollar stroller for their new baby girl—on any given night down at the VFW, folks were still laughing about that new space on the bar where the giant jar of pickled eggs once sat, and sometimes, on hot summer nights, I would tell the story of my famous friend Leland Sutton, passed out on the edge of his own pasture, a pair of pliers bristling straight out of his leg.

And people would buy me beers, and ask me to recite the same unlikely details: my friend's sallow face mumbling dumb nothings, the jog back into the kitchen for ice water in the coffee pot, splashing him back awake, coaching him, saying, "All right, goddamn it! You want to do this thing then let's do it—let's do it together! I love you, all right? But this is going to hurt like a fuckin' bitch." And what the old farmers and seed salesmen and implement dealers and teachers and real-estate brokers and tourists all laugh at, wonder at, was us: two grown men, friends, covered in gore, saying things like, "I love you, buddy," or "Breathe deeply, buddy."

And now: a new jar behind the bar there, just a little Mason jar this time, suitable for chutney or jam or a few dozen string beans, mostly holding just air, except for one thing, heavy and loud at the bottom: Lee's bullet, pickled in nothing, and shot from the pistol of a stranger passing through town.

ACKNOWLEDGMENTS

To my teachers: St. James Alan McPherson, Sam Chang, Dean Bakopoulos, Ethan Canin, James Galvin, Rebecca Walkowitz, Rob Nixon, David Dowling, Bridget Draxler, Bill Cronin, Joel Raney, Mary Mickel, Steve Umnus, Fred Poss, and Doug Smith. To the Iowa Writers' Workshop, where this novel began. For the helping hands: Connie Brothers, Deb West, Jan Lacina Zenisk, Nicole Neymeyer, Ben Percy, Marysa LaRowe, Mathew Rothschild, Jen Woods, DeWitt Henry, Rick Bass, *Ploughshares*, *Narrative Magazine*, *The Kenyon Review Online*, *The Lumberyard*.

For much guidance, patience, and tenacity: my agent, Rob McQuilkin, who worked with me for months to smooth this rough-hewn thing into something more than I ever thought it could be. I'm a fortunate man to have such a talented advocate and thoughtful consigliore. For spotting me: Christina Shideler.

To my editor, Katie Gilligan, who fought for this book and galvanized an army behind it: I am forever grateful.

For my friends: Josh and Charmaine Swan, Nik Novak, Nicholas Gulig, Mike and Hilary Walters, Sara and Chris Meeks, Chuck and Shannon Stewart, Sheridan and Betsy Johnson, Virginia Evangelist, Tony and Kate Trapp, Tim and Gail Kohl,

Tara Mathison, Tracy Hruska, Doug Milek, Mark Horton, Jeff Moore. For my Iowa People, who braved blizzards: my main man Marcus Burke and the camaraderie and smoke of his Starlight, my *very civilized* shooting partner Scott Smith, Kannan Mahadevan, Christina Kaminski, Chanda Grubbs, Adam Soto, Jessica Dwelle, Amy Parker, Lori Baker Martin, Ted Kehoe, Don Waters, Henry Finch, my office mate Stephanie Goehring. To Star Liquor: for keeping me afloat. To Erin Celello, Aaron Olver, Carrie Kilman, Chris Bittler, (and Marysa LaRowe, again): thanks for early encouragement. To Round River Conservation Studies, for changing my life and opening my eyes.

To my father, Raymond F. Butler, Jr., who handed me a typewriter one Christmas and said, *I believe in you.* To my brother, Alex, and to his wife, Cynthia, the biggest hearts in the world. To my mom, who holds the weight of the world on her shoulders and never shrugs or asks for help. I love you so much. To Jim and Lynn Gullicksrud—the best in-laws a guy could ask for. To Reidar—my sometimes roommate and always brother-in-law. To my relatives, I love you: all the Butlers, the Langs, the Gullicksruds, the Heitmans, the Gumzses, the Petersons, the Wigmores, the Ferrises. To my grandparents—all of you, for what you've done. To Eleanore Butler—I miss you very much.

To the city of Eau Claire, Wisconsin. To the city of Madison, Wisconsin, and East Mifflin Street in particular.

But most importantly, to Regina.

And to Henry and Nora, forever.

306

ABOUT THE AUTHOR

Nickolas Butler was born in Allentown, Pennsylvania, and raised in Eau Claire, Wisconsin. He holds degrees from the University of Wisconsin and the University of Iowa Writers' Workshop. He has worked as a Burger King maintenance man, a hot dog vendor, a telemarketer, an innkeeper (twice), an office manager, an author escort, a meatpacker, a coffee roaster, and a liquor store clerk. His writing has appeared in *Narrative Magazine, Ploughshares, The Kenyon Review Online, The Christian Science Monitor, The Progressive,* and elsewhere. He lives in Wisconsin with his wife and their two children.